*Please Re
ME*

THE
SCARLET
CROSS

THE SCARLET CROSS

LYN McFARLANE

PANTERA
PRESS

PANTERA PRESS

This is a work of fiction. Names, characters, organisations, dialogue and incidents are either products of the author's imagination or are used fictitiously. Any resemblance to actual people, living or dead, organisations, events or locales is coincidental.

First published in 2022 by Pantera Press Pty Limited
www.PanteraPress.com

Text copyright © Lyn McFarlane, 2022
Lyn McFarlane has asserted her moral rights to be identified as the author of this work.

Design and typography copyright © Pantera Press Pty Limited, 2022
® Pantera Press, three-slashes colophon device, and *sparking imagination, conversation & change* are registered trademarks of Pantera Press Pty Limited. Lost the Plot is a trademark of Pantera Press Pty Limited.

This work is copyright, and all rights are reserved. Apart from any use permitted under copyright legislation, no part may be reproduced or transmitted in any form or by any means, nor may any other exclusive right be exercised, without the publisher's prior permission in writing. We welcome your support of the author's rights, so please only buy authorised editions.

Please send all permission queries to:
Pantera Press, P.O. Box 1989, Neutral Bay, NSW, Australia 2089 or info@PanteraPress.com

A Cataloguing-in-Publication entry for this work is available from the
National Library of Australia.

ISBN 978-0-6487951-9-3 (Paperback)
ISBN 978-0-6487952-0-9 (eBook)

Cover Design: Christa Moffitt
Cover Images: Phant/Shutterstock, Mark Winfrey/Shutterstock, Buslik/Shutterstock, melissamn/Shutterstock
Publisher: Lex Hirst
Copyeditor: Sarina Rowell
Typesetting: Kirby Jones
Author Photo: Alan Richardson
Printed and bound in Australia by McPherson's Printing Group

MIX
Paper from responsible sources
FSC® C001695

The paper this book is printed on is certified against the Forest Stewardship Council® Standards. McPherson's Printing Group holds FSC® chain of custody certification SA-COC-005379. FSC® promotes environmentally responsible, socially beneficial and economically viable management of the world's forests.

*To the people in our communities
who deliver care to the vulnerable*

PROLOGUE

FRIDAY 4 SEPTEMBER 2015
10.05 pm
DARLEY'S BEACH

It was just meant to be a short walk by the sea.

At the paint-peeled sign for Darley's Beach, Meredith drove towards the coast and took the high road that cut along the granite cliffs. The way was fringed with cedars on her left and sheer drops to the ocean on her right, and she followed it to the abandoned lookout on Grasmere Point, where the broken boards of picnic tables stake the ground like fallen crucifixes.

When her tyres hit gravel, she stopped. That was where they always stopped – she, Charlie and Evelyn – for one last look at the sea.

The wooden steps to the beach were hidden by an overgrown hemlock, but she found them – cracked and wind worn and still solid. So she took them down to the shore and walked to the steady pulse of the surf.

As daylight faded, images of an open casket punctured her thoughts. The funeral director had followed every instruction: an Hermès scarf around her neck, lips painted a rich Chanel red. With an anguish that sucked the air out of her, Meredith pushed away those images and tried to think of earlier days, when the three of them walked along Darley's Beach together, watching the autumn storms roll in.

She passed the rock where they sat on the afternoon of her father's memorial service. The search team never recovered his body and that fact – the lack of a body – made becoming an orphan even worse.

Now, Meredith is orphaned all over again.

She looks up, her face wet, but sees only darkness.

Night has fallen.

The moon rakes the beach like a searchlight, seeking out the bleached bones of driftwood.

Then the clouds shift again and drape the shore in black.

She peers into the darkness pooling around the cedars that edge the beach, their lacy leaves twitching in the shadows. She scans the beach for landmarks, but the shifting moonlight disorients.

She doesn't know this place. She's wandered too far. The car is miles away.

Her throat constricts and she thrusts a hand into her pocket. It's a reflex still deeply coded into her: the unrelenting need for a quick high. She doesn't find pills, but her fingers touch cool metal. Her phone. It's been off since the funeral.

She presses the power button, facing down the cedar forest – just in case, she thinks, as the waves crash on the sand behind her. Just in case she isn't actually alone.

Her phone jumps to life with its harsh blue light. As texts pop up, fear floods through her.

At what point did her body become auto-set to panic? She can't remember. Was it in the hospital morgue, when she saw the first dead woman sliced open? Or when the body count kept rising?

She squints at the bright screen. Ten texts. Seven in the last two hours. All from Leo.

Call me at 8.20 pm. Then at 8.45 pm – *Need to talk.*

She keeps scrolling.

At 9.10 pm – *Where the fuck are you?*

The wind is rising and waves pummel the beach. She can smell another storm rolling in but there's something else in the air: a hint of sweet rot. The light from her phone finds the remains of a gull at her feet. Its eye is a black hollow. Seaweed circles its neck.

The cedars creak in the wind and her hands shake as she scrolls through more texts.

When she sees the last one, there's a pivot. Deep down. Like the bottom of her belly has twisted around her spine. Cold liquid trickles down her back.

It's there, in Leo's last text.

The name of the next victim.

A twig snaps and her head shoots up.

She turns to run, but the sand is deep and sucks at her feet. There's a pounding in her ears – it's the surf and the sound of her own blood pumping. She tries to run faster but the wind throws its whole weight against her. It whips at the top of the waves, sprays salt water in her face and then rounds back for another go, wrapping her coat around her legs. She tastes blood. There's the taste of blood in her mouth. The sound of blood in her ears.

She trips on driftwood and just before she falls, sees a bloody cross, cut deep into soft flesh.

JUNE 2015

Chapter 1

Dawn is breaking but a heavy gauze of rain keeps the city asleep. At this early hour, the road is hers. As she drives towards the harbour, fog creeps up from the sea and bleeds onto the streets.

Her car crests the high arch of the Georgia Bridge and the dark outline of St Jude Hospital reveals itself on the other side, rising like a fortress against a sky of fractured clouds, backlit by the weak dawn light.

June has seen the heaviest rain on record, flooding the entire west coast of North America, and this morning it's torrential. She drives under the thick granite arch that guards the entrance of St Jude, parks, and runs from the deluge, shouldering her way through the heavy staff doors.

If someone had told Meredith Griffin when she began nursing that after a while the smell of hospital would put her at ease, she would have thought them mad. But after thirteen years at St Jude, it does. It's the organising principles of the place that settle her – to receive the injured, to do no harm – and the faint smell of disinfectant always reminds her of them.

She walks silently in her soft-soled nursing shoes towards Emergency, skirting the statue of St Jude in the hospital's main atrium. The saint appears in different ways around the building, but the statue at the front is the most tragic. He kneels in supplication, his gaunt face cast down, tattered robes hanging from his outstretched arms. The words of Matthew 25:40 are engraved in the hard granite underneath him: *Whatsoever you do for the least of my brothers, the same you have done for me.*

Peeking into the storeroom on the way to her office, Meredith grimaces at the mess and makes a mental note to talk to her staff. But before closing the door, she freezes. Perched on the edge of a shelf is an open box of Ativan single-dose packets. 'Fuck!' she mouths. Ativan – a benzodiazepine and highly addictive – had to be ordered from Central Pharmacy and locked in a meds cart or an automatic dispensing cabinet, accessible only with a double swipe. To leave a box here, open, in an unlocked storeroom? She can't believe the breach of protocol.

She exhales and stares at the drugs, hand squeezing the door handle, vision tunnelling into the box. There are just a few strips of pills left inside. Their foil packaging sparkles in the light.

Prickles under her skin grow into a compulsion to scratch. She tries to deny the urge, but her desire is an animal, straining at the leash. She moves quickly, and with a nervous glance up and down the corridor, reaches for the box, stuffs it deep into her bag and pads silently away.

In her office, routine takes over – coat on hook, umbrella in corner, bag under desk, long, unruly red hair pulled and pushed into a tight topknot. She flips open a cosmetic mirror, wipes the smudged mascara from under her eyes, pulls on a lab coat, and crams a strip of pills into her pocket.

As if on cue, the intercom sounds, reverberating through the corridor. Two nurses run past her office door, barrelling a gurney towards the trauma room. 'Blue! We have a Blue,' they say in low, harsh voices. The nurses speak in code, mindful of what patients may hear.

She runs after them and catches sight of a thin arm hanging over the edge of the stretcher, swinging back and forth. It's long and delicate – scoured with a thick mesh of scars. Each mark's hue signifies its vintage: old white scars crisscrossed with healing plum-coloured lines, and then the most recent slashes, bright crimson and vicious.

The nurse running beside her speaks urgently under his breath: 'Young woman, found down at Victor Allen Park, bleeding out.'

The woman's clothes are soaked in blood. A heavy-duty pressure bandage is wrapped tightly around her upper thigh. Meredith scans the woman's colour and sucks in her breath – she knows that face.

'Katherine!' she whispers, leaning down.

Sensing awareness in the patient, her voice gets sharper. 'Katherine! It's me, Meredith Griffin.' The patient's eyes flutter open and Meredith whispers more gently, 'I need you to hold on.'

She puts her hand in the woman's open palm, and Katherine's fingers curl up and hold on.

A voice yells to her. It's Rosalyn, Meredith's lead clinical nurse, motioning urgently. 'The bat phone just rang – we need all hands!' The intercom crackles: 'Code Orange, South Door.'

Orange means multiple casualties – likely a multi-vehicle accident. Meredith turns back to the patient and shoots a desperate look at the nurse. As she leans over the bleeding woman, the strip of Ativan springs out of her pocket like a silver snake.

'Go,' the nurse says, eyeing the drugs. Then he points his head at Ros, who's rounding up hospitalists. 'Go help Ros with what's coming in. We'll take care of her.'

The patient's eyes are closed again and Meredith doesn't want to leave her, but she can hear the sirens of ambulances bringing in the injured.

She turns towards the noise, hollering for porters and care aides. As she shoves the drugs back into her pocket, Katherine's hand slips away.

* * *

Later, back at her desk, Meredith checks her voicemail. 'Hey, Mere. It's me – winning the battle these days. Call me when you can.' Her sister Bella's voice is clear, her tone strong. It's a sign her new meds are working, letting her spirit bubble to the surface.

She's about to call Bella back when a text pops up from Leo: *Trivia night for cancer fundraiser on Sat – be my date?* Nice, she thinks. *Yes but I suck,* she texts back. After pressing send, she realises what she's written and cringes. *I mean at trivia,* she texts again. *I mean I'm really bad at trivia,* she texts, a third time. Fuck, she thinks, throwing her phone on the desk. With everything you can do with a smartphone, why can't you 'undo' a text?

'Knock, knock.' Ros is at the door, rugged up against the cold, her face popping out of a mountain of wool like a rosy button. Her voice is steady – and steadiness is the quality most treasured by Meredith in her lead clinical nurse. Trauma, psychosis, violence – whatever onslaught the Emergency ward unleashes simply runs like water down the granite of Rosalyn McLean.

'Quite an end to your shift,' Meredith says.

'And quite a start to yours,' Ros replies in her wry Scottish brogue. Ros has three young boys at home and is taking night shifts as a favour to Meredith – normally, she's racing to leave, but now she stays put.

'People are raving about your talk at the RN conference,' Ros says, leaning against the open door. She's five foot eleven and her thick-soled nursing shoes make her even taller.

'Oh yeah?' Meredith says, distracted by a code report on her computer screen.

'Yeah, especially how you skewered that journalist who tried to corner you on healthcare costs.'

Meredith flashes Ros a conspiratorial smile. 'I just did what any of us would do – took him through a normal day on the ward – saving lives, treating pain, resources stretched thin. You know,' she shrugs, 'same old, same old.'

'Well, it must have felt good seeing him wither on the vine.'

'Yeah, I hate public stoushes, but they're fun when you win,' she says, winking at Ros and turning back to the report on her computer.

'Mere ...' Ros says, at which Meredith looks up sharply – only Ros and Bella call her that. 'The girl ... Katherine Richardson.'

Their eyes lock and Meredith's teeth clench. She knows Ros's tone.

A conversation between doctors in the corridor floats into the room and then floats out, as the two nurses acknowledge what's passing between them. It's a moment of darkness, losing a patient. Like being rudderless in the night, watching the last light on land go out.

Ros shifts her weight, clears her throat. 'We saw Katherine so many times. She was so funny and smart, and the injury, you know ... the amount of blood loss. Some patients feel like family—'

Meredith's hand shoots up to stop Ros and she squeezes her eyes shut. 'What was the cause of death?'

'Cardiac arrest. I can—'

'Which doctor signed the death certificate?' Meredith asks, getting up so fast she knocks over her chair.

'Dr Jackson. He's still on shift if you want to—'

'Is she in the morgue?' Meredith asks, walking past her.

'I assume so,' Ros says, following her out of the office.

Meredith speaks over her shoulder as she runs down the hallway, heading to the morgue. 'I want to see the patient file, Ros. Pull it, please.'

* * *

Riding the elevator down to the morgue, Meredith recalls another early morning, about eight months earlier, when she first saw Katherine Richardson. The girl had been cutting herself in the public bathroom in Victor Allen Park and recognised she had gone too far. She stumbled into St Jude Emergency dazed, slipping in a puddle of her own blood, dark hair pasted on her sweaty forehead. Her eyes were glassy and her arms, sliced open and bloody, hung limp at her sides. As Meredith hollered for a wheelchair, the girl looked her up and down and said, 'Those are really ugly shoes,' before collapsing.

After the shoe incident, Katherine Richardson had come to Emergency more times than Meredith could count. She was a frequent flyer – and each visit had its highlights. There was the time she popped the nurse for trying to restrain her. 'Go to hell!' she yelled, before winding up and clocking him in the jaw.

The next time Katherine came in, Meredith referred her to Psych – but not without a fight. 'I've already had a Psych eval, why should I get another?' she demanded, shaking her head, her dark hair moving in angry waves across her face. 'What'll it be this time, Nurse?' she spat. 'Marginal OCD? Bipolar tendencies?' Her voice cracked and then returned with contempt. 'Psych isn't science.' And then the final sting: 'I'm a med student. I know more about it than you do.'

The last time Meredith saw Katherine conscious was in the recovery room, sitting with her bandaged wrists folded in her lap. 'Katherine?' she asked, leaning over to look the girl in the face and sitting beside her. 'You remember me? I'm the nurse with the bad shoes.' Katherine looked down at Meredith's practical orthopaedics and a smirk flashed across her face.

'I just noticed you were here,' Meredith said, eyeing the bandages on her wrists. 'Do you have someone coming to get you?'

'My mom.'

'Okay. Okay, that's good,' Meredith replied, searching for a way through her hard shell. 'You know, Katherine, you can always call that number I gave you. They're there to help.'

They sat quietly for a while and then Meredith made to leave. But when she stood up, a hand shot out and pulled her back down on the chair. Katherine's dark hair hung across her face like a curtain. 'Thank you,' she whispered.

It was just the bare outline of a phrase, perched on the edge of her breath. So quiet, it could have been imagined.

* * *

The slow descent of the elevator rankles and Meredith jabs roughly at the lit basement button, tormenting herself with questions ... Why didn't we refer Katherine to Psych earlier? How many others are going to slip through our hands? The thought of losing more young patients turns her stomach.

The elevator convulses as it opens onto a dim and quiet basement hallway. There is no bustle of nursing staff on this level – just the sporadic, faint whistle of air vents and silence.

Her shoes make no sound against the polished concrete floor as she walks slowly to the morgue.

Knowing the pathologist's schedule, she's pretty sure he won't be in the morgue so she swipes herself in. Seeing no one, she heads to the fridges, slowly adjusting to the bright lights, the stinging scent of chemicals and the cold. It takes her a few seconds to scan the names on the fridge doors before she sees *K. Richardson* scribbled on the whiteboard fixed to the third fridge.

After pleading with her old friend Ben to let her have one quick look at Katherine, Meredith hangs back and watches the grey-haired, ruddy-faced morgue technician snap on a pair of sterilised gloves. He trudges past her, slides Katherine's corpse onto a gurney and wheels her shrouded body to the post-mortem table. Ben's nearing sixty-five, but his stocky wrestler's body is as powerful as ever, his arms still sculpted with muscle and vein.

'There you go, Meredith,' he grunts and checks his watch. 'I'll be back in five minutes – that's all the time you get.' He snaps off his gloves, wincing slightly as he rolls his shoulder, and raises an eyebrow. 'Going for coffee, want one?'

'No thanks, I'm fine,' she says, smiling at his sing-song Yorkshire accent. 'What's up with your shoulder? That ski injury still troubling you?'

'Oh, I don't know, Meredith,' he says with resignation. 'I can't tell anymore, the aches and pains are all merging into one.'

'Go get some coffee. It'll help.'

'Opioids will work better ...' he says with a sly grin.

'I didn't hear that and no, they won't.'

'Oh, I know, I know,' he sighs, waving her away and trudging out the door. 'I'll be dead by the time you young folk find the cure for old age. It's bloody unfair.'

As Ben leaves, she feels the silence of the dead creep back into the room. She quickly unzips the body bag, then gently peels it away from the young woman's stiff upper limbs.

Sweeping her eyes across Katherine's arms and chest, Meredith gets the full picture of the damage she's done to herself. Young women present with scars like this every day – on the conveyor belt that moves countless self-harmers between Emergency and Psych. Bending over Katherine, she traces the angry marks carved into the woman's body, the intricate red slashes on white skin, the places where scar tissue has built up.

'Oh, you – you poor thing,' she whispers, recognising the scars from cuts that she herself has bandaged during the many times Katherine was in her care.

Utterly absorbed, she jumps at a sound behind her.

'Meredith, what's up?'

The voice is familiar and sends her mood due south.

'Mark,' she says, with feigned brightness, suddenly wishing she'd said yes to Ben's offer of coffee. A lean blond man walks past her to the head of the gurney, stands over Katherine's body and crosses his arms in front of his broad chest. A badge is pinned to his lab coat: Mark Roth, Deputy Head of Psychiatry.

'Katherine was a regular in Emergency, Mark. I heard she passed and I want to know how she died.'

The man's face remains still but his pale blue eyes drill into Meredith, as if searching for weak spots. She meets his gaze and then slides her eyes slowly up to his forehead, where a dark red scar blights his fair complexion.

'Should you be in here?' he asks.

She feels her face get hot – she knows permission's required for her to access the morgue, but the same applies to him. 'Should you?' she shoots back.

Mark lifts his chin at her. 'Katherine was a long-term patient of mine. I spent months helping her. More than you would've been able to in Emergency.'

The comment is signature Mark and makes Meredith's face twitch. It's no secret she had qualified as a psychiatric nurse after becoming a specialist in emergency care. Mark never misses an opportunity to point out she's not a doctor, but everyone on the ward knows that when the psychiatrists aren't around, the nurses rely on her for preliminary psych assessments. If life hadn't taken Meredith in a different direction, she'd be where Mark is – the second-in-command of Psychiatry at St Jude. He knows that. His path first crossed hers years back when they were competing for first place in their pre-med courses. Since he was hired at St Jude two years ago – him well down the road to a stellar career in psychiatry, and Meredith battling away at the nursing frontlines – he's relished every chance to stir.

Meredith ignores his feint, as well as the hackles he's raised in her. 'We all know Katherine was a cutter but her suicide risk was low. Her presentation was always non-suicidal self-injury.'

Mark runs his fingers through his short hair and breathes out slowly, with an air of disappointment. 'Those who didn't know her as well as I did might agree with you. But Katherine definitely suicided.' He glances at his watch. 'Is there something in particular you want to know?'

'No, Mark, just give me a minute to take a look on my own. She was my patient too; her wounds will tell me.'

He laughs out loud at this. 'Oh, right – so now you're a pathologist, are you?'

Meredith slowly exhales. 'Mark, you counselled Katherine for a while. I get that. But I brought her back from semi-consciousness, carried her through Emergency and stitched her up, countless times. My whole team knows Katherine.' She fixes Mark with a cold stare. 'I've asked for a minute.'

'Okay, Griffin,' he says, holding up his hands in surrender, using her surname like he does with the junior nurses. He takes an exaggerated step back. 'This is me giving you a minute.'

Another slow exhale. More than anything, she wants him out of the room – second best would be a drop of respect. She ignores him and tries to focus on Katherine, but he's moved to where she can't see him.

'You know,' she says, walking to the other side of the gurney, trying to get the conversation back on a professional footing, 'young female self-harmers come through Emergency all the time. We should set up some training, so everyone can identify these cries for help.'

'I hardly think this was a cry for help.'

'Why do you say that?'

'The nature of her injuries, of course,' he says, reaching over to open the bag all the way to reveal the lower half of Katherine's body. 'You're looking in the wrong place.'

Katherine's legs are untouched up to the delicate crease between her pelvis and upper thigh, but there, on the soft plane of her inner hip, is a brutal injury – two deep gashes, driven deep into her skin, in the form of a cross. Katherine's flesh is butchered.

'She exsanguinated, just as they were identifying her blood type. Assured cardiac shutdown,' Mark says. 'This wasn't a cry for attention, Griffin. Katherine was a med student – she knew her anatomy. She vivisected herself and, in the process, nicked her femoral.'

Meredith stands, paralysed, recalling the pressure bandage Katherine had around her leg in Emergency. She only regains her senses as Mark is rearranging the bag over Katherine's body.

It's crude, the way he assembles Katherine's limbs and covers her corpse – out of character for a senior professional who's just lost a patient.

But, more than that, it's Mark's fingers, curling around Katherine's limbs, that flick the switch in her. She remembers those hands and the strength of their grip – even now, after all this time. They're long and thin and perfectly manicured, and the sight of them here, on a woman's body, rips away any trace of professional restraint.

'Wait! Just … just wait,' she stutters, grabbing his wrist to stop him. 'Just a minute, Mark. You call this self-harm?' She says, pointing to the ripped tissue on Katherine's upper thigh. 'You really think Katherine did this to herself?'

Mark roughly shakes off her hand. Colour rises to his face but his eyes remain cool. 'Meredith, I know it's shocking, but you're not a psychiatrist. And you clearly haven't read the file. Your own team found a medical scalpel in her pocket this morning. You wouldn't know this, but that's what she often used to cut herself.'

Meredith feels this news like a blow to her solar plexus. She did, in fact, know Katherine used a scalpel to self-harm – she had told Meredith herself, during their many chats in Emergency. Meredith's hands start to shake and she rushes to put them behind her back, but not before he notices.

'Quite a tremor you've got there, Griffin,' he says, his face breaking into a cruel smile. 'Big night last night?' When he sees her sharp look, he starts to laugh. 'Just joking. Nothing that a bit of Ativan can't cure, right?' He shakes his head at her, as he stands over the body bag. 'You know, Meredith, I worry about you sometimes.'

She looks at him coldly, priming herself for another offensive remark.

'You might want to think about how much you let work get to you.'

His words drop heavily into the silence between them and their eyes lock for a moment too long.

Meredith briefly senses actual concern from Mark, but then his face snaps shut and he checks his watch. 'I have to go speak to the parents,' he sniffs haughtily and turns to leave. 'Take care, Griffin.'

Mark's clipped footsteps echo against the tiled walls of the morgue, leaving Meredith alone again with Katherine. Underneath the body bag, she can see the delicate dish of her pelvis. She zips the bag up tight, smoothing out its last wrinkles, unable to stop her hands from shaking.

I must call Bella, she thinks, recalling her sister's voicemail. She sounded fine, but still, I must, I must call her.

Meredith turns towards the exit, but her heart is going like a jungle drum and her legs are weak. A surge of vertigo makes her stumble and the floor tilts up at her. She catches herself against the tiled wall, leans her moist forehead on its icy, smooth surface. Her fingers reach hungrily into her lab coat pocket for the small packets of Ativan. She rips one open and swallows the pill down dry.

It's not the freezing temperature that's making her shake.

Nor the drugs – despite what Mark might suspect.

It's the deep gash in the shape of a cross on Katherine's upper thigh.

It's the fact that she's seen that cut before – on another woman.

* * *

St Jude sits on the tip of Dorset Point, a granite promontory named after Alexander Dorset, the English navigator who founded the town of New Westdale. The land was gifted to the Catholic Church by an early colonial government dominated by Protestants – a barren crag of granite, jutting into the Pacific Ocean like chipped driftwood.

Everyone said nothing could grow on Dorset Point. But over time, a chapel grew out of the rock, stone by stone, roughly cut and laid by hand. At the western foot of the chapel, a walled courtyard was built and, within it, a quiet garden was planted. Firs and cedars took root and flourished in the acidic soil, and when the sun broke through and heated the chapel's stone walls, the smell of cedar, azalea and phlox drifted towards the town.

When the Chapel of St Jude became part of St Jude Hospital, the courtyard was converted to a garden for patients and that's where Meredith sits now, relishing the cradle of trees and shrubs around her, eating a cheese sandwich from the staff canteen. As sea mists roll over the garden's stone walls, she pulls her coat collar tight against her neck.

The coat was her mother's – cashmere and stylish – and it fits like a second skin. Meredith had inherited her mom's light bones and small size. There was something of the bird about both of them, her father always said. Quick and precise, small boned and tiny, two neat little packages. But the other things – Meredith's thick red hair and sharp cheekbones, her green eyes in a heart-shaped face – they're all from her father: the Griffin side of the family. No, Meredith thinks, it's her sister Bella who is most like her mother. With her black hair and impossibly violet eyes, and her psychosis, which follows Bella around like a crooked tail.

Thinking about her sister, she pulls out her phone.

'Hey,' Meredith says. 'You called. All good?'

'All good,' Bella says. 'Are you at work?'

'Yeah, how's things?'

'Really good, actually. I called to tell you they've asked me back to present for In Our Shoes.' Over a year ago, Bella had started volunteering for a city-wide program that brought people with mental health illnesses into classrooms to talk to kids about mental health and stigma reduction. Bella assisted with the program and presented when she wasn't symptomatic – she played piano for the students and spoke about living with schizophrenia.

'They're running the program again?'

'Yup, they got funding, and they're extending it from grades nine to twelve.'

'That's fantastic, Belle!'

'Yeah, I know. I can't wait! They might even film it this year. I need your help picking the pieces I'm going to play.'

'Of course, this weekend?' Meredith asks, her spirits lifting.

During the whole of the previous year, Bella's volunteer work had made her happy. It allowed her to contribute, to teach, to be with kids. When Bella hangs up, Meredith searches for classical music on her phone – until a drop of rain lands on the screen. Around her, the wind picks up and the temperature drops. She shivers as the rain gets heavier, and sprints back to Emergency as a dark thunderhead splits open above.

* * *

Throughout the week since Katherine's death Meredith has tried to remember the other woman she saw die from the same brutal wound. In the moments when she wasn't presenting at board meetings, recruiting staff or supporting frontline trauma care, she tried searching Emergency records but couldn't pin down the patient's name. The only detail Meredith can remember is that the patient was admitted by Psych.

'But you ... you're the Google of St Jude, Barb,' she says to the woman at the Psych admissions desk. 'You know everything. You must remember her.'

'I know, I'm awesome. But I'm also tired, I want to go home and I need more than what you're giving me to find a patient file.'

Barb Finnegan has headed up administration in Psychiatry for twenty-five years. She's her usual surly self as she shuts down her computer and locks up her cabinets, the corners of her mouth turned southward with grim purpose. But Meredith's unfazed by her rough edges. The number of presentations in Emergency that feature mental health issues and then lead to Psych admissions is high, making Barb and Meredith close colleagues. So Meredith just hangs back, watching Barb pack up for the day, both women lost in their own thoughts, comfortable in the silence between them.

Nowhere closer to identifying the patient's name, Meredith starts to ruminate. She tries to recall who the attending physician was, whether Ros worked that day, what time the patient came in, who else was on shift, what the weather was like – anything that might trigger details that will help Barb locate the patient's name and file. Lost in the struggle to remember, she hears Barb as if through fog, speaking to her in the soft voice she uses for Psych inpatients.

'Meredith – all okay?'

Barb is hovering, her manner having softened from militant to maternal, and Meredith realises she's been there for several minutes, sitting on the edge of Barb's desk, shuffling papers, lining up their edges, ordering and reordering the pages.

'Yeah. All okay, thanks, Barb,' she says, standing up and composing herself. As she walks back through the underground tunnels that connect Psych to Emergency, the image of

Katherine's strange fatal cut invades her mind in a steady, repeating loop. The tunnel's light gets dimmer and the walls creep closer. Water, running through pipes overhead, whistles and screeches, tightening the nerves between the base of her neck to her forehead. She starts to run and is out of breath when she gets to the elevator. Once inside, with the doors closed, she feels the pull of the hungry ghost inside her and pops an Ativan. She leans against the wall, waiting for the drug to quiet the ringing in her ears, as the elevator shakes her up to the ground floor.

Back in her office, she finally brings herself to review Katherine Richardson's file – Ros had left it on her desk days before. But halfway through Katherine's admission documents, treatment plans and referral notes, she's struck by how remarkably un-tragic her life appears. Her home address is in Westport, an exclusive suburb to the southwest of the city, not unlike Shaughnessy Heights, the wealthy neighbourhood where Meredith grew up, until things fell apart at home.

Katherine attended the University of New Westdale, a top-tier university for high achievers – in medicine, as she had told Meredith often. Her anxiety and depression began at sixteen, along with panic attacks and cutting. After Meredith referred her to Psych, Mark Roth conducted the initial psychiatric assessment.

There's an autopsy objection note in the file indicating her parents had not consented to a post-mortem, which suggests they shared Mark Roth's view that the cause of death was suicide. But from Meredith's quick review of the patient file, Katherine looked like an accomplished young woman with immense opportunities, whose family was helping her manage her mental health. It's baffling how she could have ended up cutting herself in such a brutal way.

The last page of the file, signed with Mark Roth's angular writing, is a referral to the St Jude Psychiatric Outpatient Clinic, where Katherine was to see him for regular counselling.

After this – there's nothing.

Meredith frowns and sits back in her chair.

What did Mark say to her in the morgue? He said he *spent months* helping Katherine Richardson.

If that were true, there would be plenty of records.

But the file just stops, as if Katherine's life ended as soon as her therapy began.

Chapter 2

A steady pounding of rain seeps into Meredith's consciousness. The daylight through the crack in the blind is dim and grey – its hue suggests late morning.

Her entire head aches – like its support beams have collapsed. Piercing through the rubble of her hangover is a throbbing lump of pain two inches behind her right eye, like a hot bullet to the brain.

Burning pins and needles spike up her calf. She rolls out from under Leo's heavy limbs, and stumbles through the dark to the bathroom as nausea churns her belly. She's unsure what's causing her stomach to turn – her hangover, or the bloody cut on Katherine's upper thigh that she can't shake from her mind.

When she emerges from the bathroom, her hair in a towel, Leo is sitting up in bed, sipping coffee, bare chested and musclebound, dark hair crushed from sleep into a half-hearted mohawk, his long legs akimbo.

'Making yourself at home, I see,' she says, noticing how relaxed he is and trying to keep the tetchiness out of her voice. A part of her likes him at her place, comfortable and in her bed, but still. It's early days.

She feels his eyes on her as she walks naked across the room. Leo Donnelly is senior homicide – very little escapes him –

even when he's half asleep and in need of caffeine. 'I made you a cup,' he says sheepishly, aiming to please.

She takes a sip from the cup by her side of the bed and grimaces. 'God, Leo, that's wretched.'

In response, he takes a long, slow sip, swallows and then says with feigned patience, 'Meredith. Like the rest of the world, I haven't used a moka pot since university. I could make you a killer espresso if you owned a coffee maker from this century.'

'You dropped out of university – remember?' she says over her shoulder while opening her closet to find underwear. She's still slurring her words, a fact that makes her even more irritable.

'Right, but I'm smarter than most who stayed the course,' he says, with a wide grin of self-satisfaction. 'That's why you like me.'

She bats her long eyelashes at him with exaggerated affection, and then leans against the open closet door to steady herself as she climbs into a pair of woollen leggings suitable for the unseasonably cold June day. 'You're actually a bully, Leo. You *goaded* me into that last whisky series.'

'Yup,' he says, taking another long pull at his coffee. 'That was my fault, especially when you stood on your chair and challenged the *whole homicide department* to a drinking contest.' He laughs at the memory as she turns her back on him, scanning her closet for something to wear on top.

'You're a lightweight, Red. It's time you faced it.'

Leo names her in colours – sometimes Red for her hair; sometimes Silver, when he wants to tease her for growing up in a 'fancy' neighbourhood. 'If you grew up on my side of the tracks, you wouldn't last a sec—' he stops short and she turns around to find out why.

Leo is looking over her shoulder with horror. 'What the fuck?'

She follows his gaze to her closet to see what the drama is.

'You can't be serious,' he says. He takes another slug of his coffee as if to right himself with caffeine and shakes his head. 'Colour coding? Really?'

Meredith scowls and shuts her closet. She's still smarting from his moka pot comment. That was her special coffee maker, which she bought from the Italian market in her second year of pre-med, before she decided to go into nursing. Is nothing sacred? And then his comment about the other stuff – her obsessive need to colour-code her clothes, to organise her shoes according to colour, then style – she couldn't go there with Leo. Not yet. And certainly not with a hangover.

Ignoring him, she pulls on a sweater, firmly closes her closet and pads barefoot to the kitchen.

She can hear his slow, even steps down the hallway as she drowns her cereal in milk.

'Who was the guy at the bar who called us a cliché?' she asks when he sits down beside her, noticing he's in jeans and nothing else, her eyes sliding over the smooth planes of muscle in his chest.

'Cliché? Oh – that guy. That was Dex. And he didn't call us a cliché – that prick's English doesn't extend to French. All he said was there were five guys in his department dating nurses and in homicide the rate was higher.'

Meredith makes a sound that's somewhere between a grunt and a snort, and Leo sidles up closer, putting his arm around her shoulders. 'Red, it's Sunday. Neither one of us has to work. Why are we not still in bed?'

She looks hard at him and frowns. 'It's past noon, Leo. And my head is too sore to talk.' If she can keep the cereal down, she'll be one step further along the road to recovery. 'Do you understand? Talking requires thinking, and thinking *hurts*.'

He squeezes her closer. 'What's wrong, darling, did I disappoint you last night?' he says, smiling and kissing her lightly on the forehead. His heavy forearm moves from her shoulders to the small of her back, pulling her closer.

She turns to him, concentrating hard on chewing and swallowing. Leo's gentle eyes are a deep brown with gold flecks, in a lean, muscular face. His olive skin is smooth and clear but for a livid white scar that runs across his left brow, eye and cheekbone. Whatever caused it must have been painful. After a few months of dating she hasn't asked him about it and he hasn't offered, but his contempt for bullies and the odd remark about gangs in his old neighbourhood provides a bit of colour – all the signs point to a violent childhood. The skin around the scar has healed unevenly and tightened, leaving a slight squint in his left eye and a subtle curl in his upper lip. The effect is faint, but combined with his sinewy bulk it gives him the look of a thug and, when he's angry, a touch of the demented. Both, she thinks, must come in handy in his profession.

'Come on,' he says eventually, taking a thirsty swallow of coffee. 'Talk to me. Tell me what's on your mind.'

She shakes her head dismissively. 'It's just a patient we lost at work. A self-harmer. Young.' She says all this while eating large mouthfuls of cereal, giving him the bare bones, skimming the surface of what's raging in her head.

As Meredith starts talking about the self-harmers coming through Emergency, she can see Leo file away the facts. He watches her closely as she talks but his face reveals nothing – he's a careful listener: taciturn, non-judgemental, his settled attention focusing on her every word. When she explains Katherine's death, her voice gets tight. Bound by confidentiality, she's careful not to mention names, and also doesn't reveal the specific nature of the injury – the deep perpendicular cuts to the thigh, the femoral bleed.

'Cause of death was cardiac arrest, due to excessive bleeding. She had deep gashes – brutal ones – so unlike the other cuts she had made to herself. It was almost ritualistic.'

Leo just looks at her calmly, slowly sipping his coffee, but then he squints, as if slightly confused. 'You see this stuff all the time, Red. Why so troubled by this one?'

Meredith doesn't know, but she rambles on anyway. 'This woman. She had issues but she was strong. She had spirit.'

Leo remains quiet, swirling the remaining coffee in his cup, assessing what she's saying. 'Does she remind you of Bella?'

Meredith pushes her bowl away, letting the question sink in. She hasn't told Leo much about her sister, but he knows enough to get to the core of it. Katherine had a similar upbringing to Meredith and Bella. She was Bella's age when she was finally diagnosed with schizophrenia. Katherine was beautiful, like Bella, and they both had a searing intelligence that could burn if you weren't careful.

She thinks back to when Ros came to her office to tell her about Katherine – how she cut Ros off, mid-sentence. 'Perhaps,' she says, filling a long pause. 'Perhaps she did.'

She pushes the cereal away, preferring to look at Leo than feed her stomach. As if on cue, he helps her off her chair. He stands a full foot higher than her, with legs that stretch up like the poker-straight cedars of the coast. Straight is how Leo is. The way he talks. The way he goes at a case. The way he is with her – deliberate and incapable of half-truths. Above all, that's what Meredith needs from the man in her bed.

When he moves closer, she can feel a heat rise from him and breathes in the faint smell of salt. Fresh out of the shower or after a long day, Leo always smells like the air that rolls in with the sea – fresh and salty at the same time. His fingers move along her neck, probing deep into the tissue between the bones of her back, relaxing her head. His hands are firm and confident, just the way she likes them. She closes her eyes, letting her head fall back, pulling his hips against hers.

* * *

A couple of hours later, Meredith wakes to see Leo sleeping beside her. She reaches for her phone to check the time and scrolls through texts to see if her sister has made contact. There's nothing from Bella, but there's a text from Barb Finnegan: *I think the patient you're looking for is T Norsman. Medical Records should have her complete file. All the best, Google.*

The message propels her out of bed. Careful not to wake Leo, she dresses silently. She writes a note: *Shopping, gym and then to St Jude to do some work. Please lock the door on your way out.* Meredith leaves it on the neat pile of clothes he's made in the corner and closes the bedroom door.

Sleep isn't possible. There are now two women scratching at the walls of her mind, driving her to find out why they've both ended up dead in her emergency room.

* * *

As she pulls into the St Jude parking lot, her phone buzzes with a missed call from her girlfriend Charlie. 'I *resent* having to stalk you, Meredith Griffin,' her voicemail says. 'How can I do the seating plan for Evelyn's birthday party without a confirmed guest list? Call me, or I'll bump you from the Saturday night dinner and banish you to the Sunday tea.'

Her old friend's rebuke is delivered in an Australian accent, which even now, after all these years, still sounds English to Meredith's untrained ear. Smiling, she deletes Charlie's voicemail and punches in a quick text: *We both know you can't party without me – of course I'm coming for dinner!*

The message from Charlie lifts her spirits as she rides the elevator down to Medical Records in St Jude's basement. But when the elevator lurches to a stop and the doors open, she can't help the shudder that runs through her. It's Sunday afternoon and she's alone, but she never really feels alone in the hospital tunnels. There is always a lingering presence of the old and forgotten, of discarded medical devices, of the dead.

St Jude began its days as a hospice for soldiers returning from World War I. Between the wars, it took on the patients that no other institution wanted and a wing was built for the mentally ill. In 1932, the Palliative Care Unit and Psychiatry were connected by a tunnel that formed the northern perimeter of the complex. That same year, St Jude was licensed as a hospital.

St Jude was set up to serve vulnerable populations, and its Psychiatry department was the most established in the region. That was why Meredith went to St Jude, why she gained her Psych qualification there, why Bella was so often admitted there. Of all the hospital specialities, Psych rarely has high status, but that wasn't the case at St Jude. Having recently recruited world-renowned psychiatric researchers, it was on a clear trajectory to lead the country.

Like all the other tunnels that connect the wings and pavilions of St Jude, the northern tunnel is dark and clean, industrial and dead quiet. On either side are unlit storage rooms – gaping eyes that leak obsolete supplies into the corridor. Old IV stands are shoved into corners, next to cabinets, broken gurneys, splintered tables and chairs. On their own and set apart from the bustle of staff or the pulse of care, the medical devices look suspicious, even deadly.

In the northern tunnel these obsolete instruments feel particularly sinister. Among the discarded furniture lie the macabre artefacts of early psychiatry – wheelchairs with restraining belts, straitjackets and muzzles. As Meredith hurries past, these dark objects exude a sense of watchfulness.

The sound of footsteps rises up behind her. They are heavy steps: a man's. It feels like they're right behind her but when she looks, there's no one there. It's hard to know what's behind you in the tunnels – or what's in front. The way isn't straight and there are few signposts.

The sign for Central Pharmacy appears overhead, along with a twenty-four-hour camera trained on the door. What the camera doesn't record is the automatic drug cabinet located around the corner, so Meredith calculates quickly, glancing up and down the tunnel. The Ativan she found in the storeroom will help for the time being, but she needs more Clonazepam for when she really needs to sleep deeply. Maybe a bit of Ritalin, for when she needs a pick-me-up? It's a huge risk to divert drugs this way and she wouldn't do it if her street source had not become unreliable of late. Normally, she'll only pocket drugs when the opportunity presents itself – when the drugs appear out of nowhere, like they did in the storeroom the morning Katherine died, or when a patient declines their meds, or leaves their pills beside their bed after being discharged. But she's running low and it only takes a few swipes of the special access card arranged for her by her friend, Jacob de Rhiz, the manager of IT and Facilities, to effect a critical override and dispense what she needs. In a few minutes, it's done. She takes a guilty swallow and continues on to Medical Records, feeling the stolen stash heavy in her pocket.

A second later, the footsteps come back. She speeds up, but so do they. With another quick glance behind, she sees the heavyset figure of Lachlan Murphy, St Jude's general counsel. He's a large burl of a man, more wide than tall, and he's moving fast. Before she can acknowledge him, he turns abruptly and punches through a set of doors leading to Surgery, disappearing from sight. Meredith has little to do with Lachlan, but he's known to barrel around the place, particularly late at night and on weekends, sharing a punishing schedule with senior medical staff.

A quick glance above her indicates the sign to Medical Records, so Meredith swipes herself in. The attendant at the desk is leaning on the counter, his sleeves pushed up high over toned forearms. He's scrolling through his newsfeed as his other hand plays with the crucifix around his neck.

She asks the young man to retrieve T Norsman's file and thinks about the diversity survey the hospital ran earlier that year. Meredith's atheism is unremarkable in the stew of religious beliefs at St Jude. Catholic, Muslim, Jewish, atheist – practitioners of all stripes work alongside each other in the heat and hustle of acute care. It's only when an issue bubbles up, like a female patient asking about abortion, or a discussion of a patient's suicide risk, that the implacable influence of the Catholic health directives – strict rules for healthcare infused with Church dogma – roll down from on high, quashing any debate.

When the young man leans over to put the file in a cart, the crucifix tumbles out of his shirt collar and swings back and forth like a heavy pendulum. 'Thanks, Daniel,' she says, noticing his name badge. He gives her an angelic smile back.

Sitting in a far cubicle along the wall, she opens the file and finally sees the woman's first name – Tabitha. She scribbles key details in her notebook: Resuscitation failed. Time of death –

7.20 am, 21 February 2015, declared by Dr Olivia Lu. Classed as suicide. Coroner concurred. As she reads further, the details of the day crash into her memory. Tabitha had arrived as a Code Blue. Meredith was doing chest compressions, shouting for ventilation, as Ros ran to get extra blood. By the time Dr Lu took over as code doctor, they had lost her. It was only when Meredith was preparing the body for the morgue that she saw the woman's fatal cuts – the deep gashes in the shape of a cross in the soft crease of her upper thigh. Like everyone else, Meredith had been quick to consider it a suicide: there were thick scars all over Tabitha's legs and arms – the self-harm was clear.

A handwritten scrawl in Tabitha's file states the cause of her death was 'exsanguination' by way of 'penetrating perpendicular cuts to the skin over the femoral artery'. There are no photos of the injury and no autopsy results. Just Meredith's memory and the notation on the file.

The rest of Tabitha's file is just as hard going as the recollection of the day she died – a testament of abuse and neglect from start to finish. There are multiple visits involving high-powered IVs to treat sepsis, and numerous presentations for abscesses and fungal infections – all signs of an immune system crippled by intravenous drug use. There are two near-fatal ODs, several broken bones, and a swath of repeat visits to treat violent injuries and personal neglect: a fractured cheekbone, detached retina, broken teeth, urinary tract infections that progressed to the kidney, infected domestic burns ... the list is endless. She's surprised she wasn't more aware of Tabitha, given the number of times she'd been in Emergency. But Meredith's speed read of the first few pages of the file leads to a clear conclusion: Tabitha lived on the street, and sold sex to support a drug addiction – she was most often wheeled in at night, when Meredith wasn't on shift.

After a violent outburst in Emergency when she presented with a fractured tibia, Tabitha was referred to Psych for evaluation. The psych assessment is impossible to read – it's a bad scan of an original document that seems to have gotten jammed in the photocopier. Whole sections of the assessment are obscured and it's not clear who the admitting physician is. What is clear is that Tabitha was referred to the St Jude Psychiatric Outpatient Clinic for counselling sessions. Her first session was scheduled to start almost ten months ago. And then – there's nothing. Just like with Katherine, her file ends there.

Frustrated by the state of the patient file and surprised, given Barb Finnegan's usual fastidiousness, she thumbs a text: *Thanks so much Barb – hey, the patient's psych assessment must have got jammed in the scanner. Can you re-scan it?*

A voice distracts Meredith and she peeks above the cubicle to see Mark Roth leaning over the reception counter with his boss, Stuart Chester. Mark's wearing spandex and looks like he's just finished a hard bike ride but Stuart's in his usual white lab coat, appearing crisp and professional. Recruited to transform and modernise the St Jude Psych department two years ago, Stuart almost lives at St Jude, working through weekends and late into the evenings. By all accounts he gets by on four hours of sleep a night, but you'd never know it from his clear complexion, the calm set of his face and his effortless ways with staff and patients alike. Meredith is starting to like Stuart, especially given her nursing staff like him. Not to mention the money his research brings to the hospital, which has benefited everyone, including her trauma rooms.

Both Mark and Stuart are leaning on the reception desk, laughing and chatting with Daniel, who smiles eagerly back at them, his expression marking their every word. The three men seem relaxed together, like they go way back. But that's the way Mark Roth always is with men, Meredith thinks caustically. The men at St Jude are his inner circle – at every level – from the clerks all the way up to the CEO. They are the little insurance policies that he plants around the entire institution to insulate him from the rumours that surround him like a fume.

The most recent one centred on him and a junior Psych resident – Valeska Stein. Rumour had it Mark was sweet on her – the fact that he was, and still is, married was seemingly irrelevant. They were a stunning item – both tall, fit and blond – until his eye wandered and the tide turned. Then Valeska stopped getting a full caseload and was disinvited from departmental meetings. Meredith heard she filed a complaint of sexual harassment against him, but the substance of it was vigorously denied and the dispute fell into a black hole of bureaucracy. Meredith observed it all from afar: how Mark spotted, favoured and courted Valeska, then embarrassed and sidelined her – all with no consequences. She had wanted to get involved, or at least reach out to Valeska as a colleague. But they didn't have a close relationship, and Valeska left St Jude before Meredith found the right moment. The last she heard, Valeska had transferred to Psychiatry at New Westdale General and was kicking field goals in the profession. Good on her.

Noting the time and hearing Mark and Stuart leave in a trail of laughter, Meredith tries to refocus on the patient file. Tabitha's world, described in the rough scrawl of assessments, diagnoses, treatment plans and prescriptions, was one of bare survival. And there were so many patients like Tabitha, living on the edge, rushed into St Jude Emergency. On that very day, within the hour, a member of her staff would save someone and fail to save someone, watch a patient pull through and another give up, nurse a victim then a perpetrator, sometimes right next to each other. Everything her team did – each task, procedure, spoken word, movement – each and every moment, was funnelled towards helping someone. No matter how subtle the gesture or delicate the touch, these small unhistoric acts of care formed a beat for Meredith, a deep rhythm that she could set her own clock to. It's why, over the years, through everything that had happened to her family and to Bella, St Jude was home.

* * *

On her way out, she stops at Emergency to check on things, and just as she arrives one of the weekend shift nurses, Tamara, hails her down. 'Meredith! Glad to see you. We have a new joiner on staff, Laura Stone.' She motions to a fresh-faced nurse with a blond ponytail. 'She wants to talk to you about a self-injury we had in this morning.'

After they say their hellos, Meredith moves the conversation to a computer station that's set aside from the bustle in the corridor.

'Welcome to St Jude, Laura. What can I do for you?'

'Ros told me when I started that we're to report self-harming and that makes sense – we did it at New Westdale General, where I trained. I just had a really young girl in this morning, with cuts on her forearms and thighs.'

'How young?'

'Thirteen.'

'Is she okay?'

'Yeah,' Laura nods, her pigtail bobbing. 'She was discharged a few hours ago.'

'With a family member?'

'Yeah – after we bandaged her up she seemed okay,' Laura says. 'It's just that she was on her phone in the recovery room and I caught a glimpse of the website she was on. It was called "Ritual Cuts", and when I asked her about it, she acted really strange. She shoved the phone into the pocket of her coat and got pretty snarky.'

'What did she say?'

'She told me to mind my own business, like any thirteen year old would, and then tried to look cool and said that when tattoos don't cut it, scarification's a great mod.'

Meredith nods. 'Right. Not surprised you got some attitude! Did she look like she was into body mods and piercing and all of that?'

'Not at all. That's what was so strange. She looked like me,' the junior says, motioning to herself. 'Super straight.'

'Do you think she made the cuts herself?'

'I doubt it – unless she's ambidextrous. They were the same design on both forearms and thighs, very straight and clean, so I suspect someone else did the cutting. And they were deeper than any scarification I've seen before.'

'What did they look like?'

'They were crosses.'

Meredith leans against the wall as her guts start to churn. 'Right,' she says, a bit harshly, her thoughts speeding up. 'Like what kind? Catholic?'

'Yeah.'

'A Latin cross?'

'What's that?'

'Long vertical, short horizontal.'

'Yup.'

'You said the thigh,' Meredith says quickly. 'Crosses there too?'

'Yup.'
'Where?'
'Top.'
'Inner?'
'No, front.'
'You're sure?'

'Yes. Definitely anterior,' Laura says, nodding, her ponytail bobbing faster with the speed of Meredith's questions.

'Anywhere near an artery?'
'No.'
'Blood loss?'
'Not more than we could manage.'

'Right, okay, thanks, Laura,' Meredith says, her pulse racing. 'I appreciate you raising this – please ensure you put full notes in your chart narrative and send me the patient's name so I can keep an eye out for her.'

'Sure thing,' the junior says. 'Absolutely.'

Meredith assumes a calm smile for the young nurse's benefit. 'Let me know if I can help you settle in, Laura. Glad to have you on board.' Then she turns to summon the elevator, feeling sweat running down her back. Time to start ramping up reporting on self-injury, she thinks. Once the elevator doors close, she punches an email to Ros: *Ros, we need a staff huddle on self-injury. I want to increase record keeping on any relevant presentations with full written details in the chart – ALL locations of cutting must be noted clearly in the narratives.*

She presses send and then starts googling 'ritualistic cuts'.

Chapter 3

It's the night of the birthday party for her old friend Evelyn McCrae, and Meredith is late, cold and wet. In the settling dusk and the steady rain, she power walks past the lavish estates that line the wide streets of Shaughnessy Heights. Tall cedar hedges loom over the sidewalk and swallow the light, but through the rare spaces between the thick branches she catches fleeting glimpses of luxury – wide expanses of green grass, tennis courts, heavy stone water features.

Where the cedar gives way, cast-iron fences hold the perimeters, armouring each estate with elaborate designs. Meredith remembers these iron borders from her childhood. The mazes of floral patterns always drew her gaze upwards towards the pointed arrows that stand at attention at the top – a sharp finish to the enticing swirls beneath. Shaughnessy Heights is the British heart of New Westdale, where the original English establishment staked its claim – at scale, with defensive walls of metal and stone.

Meredith knows these streets well. She knows the houses behind the hedges and the rooms behind the walls. She knows the families and their stories. She can even guess who might be peering out of any dark window at any given moment. She can hear the clink of ice in crystal glasses, the sound of whisky being poured, the laughter of the women and the prejudiced arguments of the men. It's where she was raised – three estates down from her best friend Charlie, who grew up at Arden, the house of her great-aunt, Evelyn McCrae.

As a child walking to Arden, Meredith would have lingered over the sound of the wind in the trees, the bounce of tennis balls, or the simple luxury of silence that money provides. But it's unusually cold tonight, she's late and, for so many good reasons, she's entirely indifferent to the grandeur of the neighbourhood. Sometimes, being back in Shaughnessy is only possible under the influence of a strong barbiturate. But the Ritalin she took before leaving home is giving her enough of a buzz. That's all she'll allow herself, knowing full well that Charlie will have her swimming in a vat of alcohol by the time the cheese course is served.

When she gets to Arden, Meredith punches in the pass code and hears the gate click open. Closing it behind her, she runs up to the large oak doors where Evelyn's housekeeper, Josie, grabs her, pulls her in, takes her coat silently, and pushes her through to the dining room, sternly treating her like the misbehaving tomboy Meredith was when she was ten.

As her shoes clip down the marble-tiled hallway, she can hear Charlie holding court. 'Of course lawyers are universally reviled, Auntie Ev, but at least they're not investment bankers!' The guests are laughing as Meredith enters the room.

'Finally!' Charlie says, standing up at the far end of a dining room table lavishly set for thirty. Her cherry-red off-the-shoulder jumper sets off her black pixie cut, and she's sporting her two-carat diamond studs – the ones reserved for very special occasions. 'I thought you'd never get here!' she exclaims, waving Meredith over to sit in the empty seat next to her. 'I need you here by my side. Aunt Evelyn is making swift sport of me.'

Meredith laughs and moves towards Charlie, but stops first at the head of the table to give Evelyn McCrae a kiss on each cheek. 'Evelyn. Lovely to see you and happy birthday. I apologise for being late.'

'That's quite all right, dear.' Evelyn is physically frail but still indomitable, and her haughty voice softens to greet Meredith. 'Now that you're here, we're complete.' She pulls Meredith down and whispers in her ear. 'I've been thinking about you for weeks, dear. I want to know how you and your sister are doing. Charlie told me Bella's faring better? I want to know *all* about it. We *must* talk after dinner.'

Releasing Meredith, Evelyn's voice amplifies across the table and all thirty heads turn in her direction. 'Some of you know this young woman, but for those of you who don't, this is Meredith Griffin. She's like a daughter to me.' Nodding in Charlie's direction, she says, 'Meredith, you can take your place next to Charlie, who was just giving us a summation of her venerable profession.'

As conversation around the table resumes and Meredith sits down, her phone vibrates in her handbag. She takes an anxious look and is relieved it's not Bella. Instead it's a text from Leo: *Call me*. The words are uncharacteristically sharp. *At Evelyn's birthday dinner*, she texts back, and throws the phone in her bag with mild annoyance.

Seeing they're serving one of Charlie's favourite Crémants, Meredith quickly motions to the catering staff for a flute. The bubbles go down in a fruity, creamy wave and she closes her eyes to savour it, thanking her good fortune for having a best friend with spectacular taste in wine.

Charlie was a late arrival in Shaughnessy Heights, having moved into Evelyn's house when she was nearly ten. Her parents were eminent professors in Australia, so no one in the neighbourhood understood why she was shipped across the Pacific Ocean to New Westdale to stay with her great-aunt.

But Evelyn McCrae felt no need to offer reasons for the arrival of her family member. Supremely confident of her place in social circles, she was deaf to the murmurings around her and simply pushed Charlie on society with the unquestionable sense of entitlement with which she had been bred. Her great-niece was there because she was family. Accept it or be ousted.

Evelyn had no children of her own, and her loyalty to Charlie was as tough as obsidian – but it came at a price. She was Charlie's biggest fan and harshest critic, and the two of them often crossed swords. From the time Meredith met Charlie, when they were both ten, her friend was in continual dread under Evelyn's tough love. 'I live in constant fear of disappointing her!' Charlie said of her great-aunt, her big blue eyes wide with terror. 'But if I ever let her know how much she terrifies me, she'll crate me up and ship me back across the ocean! Dancing on a knife edge, that's my life at Arden!'

Even as a child Charlie soaked up drama and unleashed it on the world. But the fury of her passions and sting of her strong opinions were always soothed by deep, unwavering friendship. 'I'm *freternal*,' she pledged to Meredith, after they had known each other for a few months. 'That means I'm maternal for my friends,' Charlie explained with a determined set to her jaw, deploying her self-made vocabulary with the burning certainty of a ten-year-old.

Sitting around the dinner table with Charlie and Evelyn holding court, Meredith starts to forget about Katherine and Tabitha. And after dinner, when they all move into the games room and the Château Margaux starts coursing through her blood, she forgets about everything.

That's when her mobile rings.

'Hey,' Leo says, his voice distant and tight. 'Are you busy?'

'A bit. I'm still in Shaughnessy, at Evelyn's.'

'Oh sorry, Red. I'll let you go.'

She's about to say goodbye but something in his voice makes her think twice.

'It's okay, Leo. What's up?' she asks, moving off the sofa and into the hallway.

'I can't really describe it over the phone. I need to *show* you something.'

Meredith hears Charlie laughing and looks longingly back at the games room. 'Seriously? Like, right now?'

'Yup. Right now.'

'Well, can you give me a hint?' she pleads. 'I'm kind of … It's a bit hard to leave right now. Eating and running …'

The tension in Leo's voice springs up again. 'Red, I need your professional opinion and it's urgent.'

'Okay,' she says, realising he is in homicide-detective mode. 'You need to give me some time to make a graceful exit here. These people are like family, you know. It's like leaving your mother's birthday—'

'Meredith.' Leo's words drop like stones on the other end of the phone. 'It's about the patient you lost. The self-harmer.'

Suddenly there's a chill on the back of her neck, like someone's just opened a window. She turns to see one of the catering staff walking by with a tray of affogatos, but she doesn't feel like partying anymore.

'Okay,' she says, heading back to the party. 'I'm coming.' She enters the games room just as a new hand of poker is being dealt, and places her hand on Evelyn's shoulder.

* * *

Meredith takes a cab to Leo's neighbourhood, the wide streets and broad estates of Shaughnessy giving way to middle-class neighbourhoods, and then finally to the original port of New Westdale, and Portside, the small community that grew up around it. Its narrow streets are lined with interconnected terrace housing, originally built for the men and women who worked the shipyards and canneries on the old wharf. Now, these practical, simple houses are selling by the dozens to young professionals. Cafes line the streets and many of the old shipping warehouses have been converted to condominiums, catering to those who can afford the hefty mortgages. Born and raised there, Leo got in early. His mother worked in one of the canneries, and when she died, he managed to buy the family home from the landlord – on a junior officer's salary – well before the neighbourhood changed from the rough little ghetto it once was.

A police car is parked in front of Leo's house, so her cab pulls into the driveway, behind his motorbike. It's a low, heavy machine with a jet-black petrol tank. Under the cover of the carport, it's safe from the rain, rubbed and polished. When she passes it, she imagines Leo's hands firmly polishing the chrome and a warm flush courses through her.

She knocks on his front door and hears the low growl of Juno, Leo's German shepherd, on the other side. Juno is a retired police dog – too long in the tooth for work and deserving of a comfortable retirement. When the growl turns into a whine, Meredith knows the dog recognises her.

'Door's open!' she hears Leo say.

She lets herself in and hangs her jacket on his antique coat stand, which is bare but for a heavy raincoat and Juno's leash. Simplicity is the credo at Leo's place. It's a small house and he's a big man – there's no room for clutter. One pair of boots, one coat, one bike – Leo has just one of what he needs. Except for well-chosen antiques and retired police dogs, both of which he tends to collect.

His other treasured canine is Jezebel, a Staffordshire terrier with three legs. Jez is ex-search and rescue, and lost her leg to a piece of torn metal fuselage while sniffing for the injured in a plane wreck. The brindled terrier is curled up by a heater in the front hallway, and when she sees Meredith, tries to get up, her stumpy tail thumping loudly on the wooden floor. 'You stay put, old girl,' Meredith says, leaning over to give Jez a tummy rub. 'Rest your aching bones.'

When she walks into the lounge room, Leo is sitting with his long legs squeezed between the coffee table and the sofa, his back forming a slow curve as he leans over a set of photos strewn across the table in front of him. There's a whisky bottle on it and a tumbler full of the amber liquid in his hand.

'Meredith Griffin – at your service,' she announces with a drunken flourish. She's right on the edge of having had one too many and can't hide her disappointment at being taken away from a great party. Just as Leo called, Charlie was dipping into Evelyn's collection of vintage Armagnac.

'Sorry, Red,' he says, giving her a sharp glance. His eyes are fierce and it's a look she's seen before, when he's come into Emergency with questions for her staff. 'Didn't mean to pull you away from the soiree.'

Seeing the whisky bottle almost empty, Meredith refrains from any playful banter. Even the dogs seem subdued, not wanting to upset him. 'You look tired,' she says. 'How can I help?'

'I need to talk to you about the self-harmers you've seen at St Jude.' The tension in his voice gives her a pang of anxiety. A quick glance at the photographs tells her he's studying a crime scene, and her guts tighten as she starts to expect the worst.

'Okay,' she says, slowly moving towards him. It's only been a week since she's seen him but he looks like he's aged years. She bends down to look at his face more closely. 'Leo, I'm serious – when was the last time you slept?'

'Just have a seat and take a look at these.'

Inching between the coffee table and the sofa, she sits beside him and notices a photo of a tub in the middle of a chic bathroom. The walls are marble and the fixtures look expensive.

'Wait,' he says, quickly turning the photos face down. 'Before we go any further, I need to set some parameters.' He holds up one finger. 'First, this is confidential. I am not going to give you any identifying information. Agreed?'

Meredith nods. 'Agreed.'

'Two,' he says, holding up a second finger. 'All I need from you is some advice. I want you to tell me if the injuries strike you as self-inflicted.'

She nods again. 'Okay.'

'Three, are you drunk?' he asks, looking at her intently.

The Ritalin has made her buzzy and the liquor has made her tipsy, but tipsy and buzzy do not equal drunk. 'No,' she says firmly, with a hint of self-righteousness.

'Okay,' he says, looking only slightly sceptical. 'I just need a quick opinion and I'm in a hurry.'

'Okay – sure.' Leo is all business and it flips a switch in Meredith. Her back straightens and her mind snaps into Emergency-room mode. As she looks through the photos, Leo provides the background.

'The victim is seventeen years old and has been known to injure herself – she's a cutter. She was having a house party last night. Her guests left and she ended up in the bathtub, bleeding. A straight razor was sitting on the bottom of the tub. Her parents found her this morning – dead.'

Meredith holds up her hand. 'Wait – you've spoken to her parents – where were they?'

'They have a place in the country. Usually the whole family goes together, but the parents had to go for one night to take care of some maintenance. Their daughter stayed at home. As far as I can tell, that wasn't too unusual.'

'Was she at risk of suicide? Do you know?'

'She experienced a traumatic event about a year ago – a family friend was hit by a drunk driver. She was meant to be meeting this friend for dinner. She was sitting in the window of a restaurant on Queen Street, literally waving at her friend who was crossing the street, when the driver ploughed into her. The accident happened right in front of her. She saw it all.'

'Wow.'

'Yeah. We interviewed her friends today. They say she suffered from pretty dramatic mood swings and anxiety from that point on. Her parents said she was getting counselling for PTSD. They confirmed she self-harmed but said the counselling was helping. Her friends said she never mentioned suicide. They said the family was close-knit and the parents would never have left her alone if they'd known she was in danger. But one of her closest friends said that after the accident, she was becoming more and more difficult to be with. She was devastated, but not surprised at what's happened. Of course, the parents – well, they're destroyed, and convinced it's foul play.'

Leo pushes some other photos in front of Meredith. 'We've scoured the house but evidence gathering is hard – there were too many people at the party to isolate DNA. She was with a young man and we questioned him this afternoon. He left the party with friends and several people confirm they were with him, dancing at a club, until well past the time of her death. His alibi is solid. He said she was acting more and more unstable during the party and her friends corroborate this. He tried to stay with her, but they had a fight and she told him to leave. Her girlfriend offered to stay the night, but she was also told to leave.'

Leo looks at Meredith, eyebrows raised. 'So – suicide? Or a vicious attack?'

'What does the autopsy say?'

'I don't have the report yet, but the thing I can't get over is this,' Leo says, picking up a photo and giving it to Meredith. 'It seems really odd, and reminds me of that patient you were telling me about the other week – the one who self-harmed and died from the cuts.'

The photo shows a young woman's body, her limbs fully visible but her face obscured with a towel. Seeing a body labelled for forensic photography is not what Meredith's used to. It's not like a trauma patient arriving in Emergency or even a corpse in the hospital morgue. It's raw and sinister. The girl's skin has the grey–blue tone of a body immersed in water for several hours. It looks like stone.

'God, please tell me the parents haven't seen these photos,' she says, picking up Leo's glass and taking a nervous drink. Then she looks at him self-consciously. 'Sorry,' she says, stealing another gulp. 'You must be used to seeing stuff like this.'

'Nope,' he says, reclaiming his whiskey glass from her, 'you never get used to seeing stuff like this.'

The slashing on the girl's arms is clearly systematic – they're cut, scarred over, then re-cut – clear evidence of self-harm. But on her upper leg, in the soft skin beside the pelvis, there are two perpendicular gashes – a long vertical cut, crossed with a short horizontal one, deliberate, brutal, and unmistakably the same scarlet cross Meredith's seen twice before.

She studies the photo closely. An involuntary tic runs down her face. 'That's deep,' she says in a whisper.

'I know. Definitely ritualistic. Do the cuts look like ones you've seen?'

Her breathing speeds up and she can feel sweat on her forehead. She shakes her head weakly. 'Hmm, I'm not … I can't be certain, not really,' she says, not sure why she's hesitating.

'What do you mean – "not really"?'

Meredith's mind starts to swim and nausea nearly overwhelms her. Why is she not telling him the truth? What is the truth? The moment she saw the cuts, she was sure it was the same cross. Now, a second later, she's drowning in doubt.

Hoping to clear her head, she grabs the glass of whisky out of Leo's hand and takes a large swallow. Speak, you idiot, she tells herself. Say something.

'Self-harmers are not necessarily suicidal,' she blurts out, as if reciting from a psychology textbook. The medical facts are the stones she plants her feet on, to ground herself, as the image of yet another woman slashed the same way makes her vision blur. 'They *can* be suicidal. But quite often, the cutting is a method of releasing intense emotional pain – a *substitute* for suicide. A better option than doing something more drastic.'

She swallows hard, thinking of Tabitha, and wondering how many times she's mistaken the injuries on her Emergency patients for something else. 'I think all of us – nurses, doctors, police – anyone in a helping profession, can draw incorrect conclusions. We can wrongly assume a particular self-harmer is not at risk of suicide. Or we can conclude a self-harmer suicided and, as a result,' she hesitates and inhales, 'wrongly rule out foul play.'

She looks directly at Leo. As the thought of Katherine and Tabitha bubbles in the back of her mind, there's a pressure around her heart, like it's beating in a steel box too small for it.

'I'm not perfect in this area, Leo. I've made mistakes. Some that I'm probably not even aware of.' She waits for his response, steeling herself for the slightest hint of judgement. But Leo just looks at her gently – like a comrade, traversing the same territory she's trying to describe: that lonely place you find yourself, when you aim to do the right thing and miss.

Feeling the relief of confessing, Meredith takes another deep breath and straightens her back. This latest victim proves she misread Tabitha's injury as a suicide and that the similarity between Katherine's and Tabitha's injury is not a coincidence. The least she can do is motivate the police to dig into it. 'You've asked for my professional opinion and here it is: I think it's a mistake to call this suicide.'

'What exactly makes you think so?' Leo asks, his voice even.

Back on the facts, her thinking becomes forensic again. 'This cut is clearly different from the cuts this woman did to herself. To get to the femoral, you need to either cut deeply through thick, fatty tissue and muscle in the leg, or know precisely where the artery lies close to the skin. The former method takes force and the latter takes skill. I suspect the forensic pathologist will agree: these are not cuts that could be made easily or without medical knowledge. They're surgical.'

She thinks back to the self-harmer with the Latin crosses on her limbs, reported to her by the new junior nurse. 'I'm sure you've thought of this, but have you checked this young woman's mobile? Do you know what platforms she's on? Internet sites she's visited? We see young women who are influenced by some pretty dark internet content – platforms, Facebook groups, chat rooms. All of it can lead to ritualistic self-injury or put them in the crosshairs of a predator.'

'Yeah,' Leo says, nodding slowly, 'I have computer forensics looking into that.' Seeing his whisky glass is back in Meredith's hand, he grabs the bottle, stands up and walks to the antique wooden drinks trolley in the corner of his lounge. 'I need to see that girl's file,' he says, pouring a new drink for himself. 'The girl you told me about, the one who came in and died from the cuts.'

Meredith nods her head firmly. 'I know you do, Leo – but I can't just give it to you. There are protocols, you know that. You'll need a warrant.'

Leo turns around quickly. 'I know,' he says crisply.

'St Jude management won't allow you to go on a fishing expedition.'

His face hardens. 'Yeah, I *know*,' he says, putting his glass down hard. 'Listen, I don't want you to speak to anyone about this. Don't mention it to St Jude senior management.'

Meredith looks at him, dumbfounded. Seeing her confusion, he explains, 'I trust you, Red, but I don't trust anyone else. I've seen investigations get thrown off the rails and thrown out of court because people didn't exercise discretion.'

She puts up her hands and shakes her head. 'Don't worry, Leo, I won't say anything. But you know, I *am* St Jude senior management.'

Leo leans against the drinks trolley staring at her darkly, and she's just about to counter his attitude with a lecture on patient confidentiality when her phone vibrates. When she answers, Bella's voice peals through it. 'Mere?' her sister asks, her tone high-pitched and tight. 'I'm at your place. Where are you? Can you talk?' Meredith checks the time – it's almost midnight.

'I'm at a friend's, Belle. Stay there. I'm coming home.' She ends the call and looks plaintively at Leo. 'I gotta go, Leo. Bella's in trouble.'

'Shit,' he says. 'Sorry to hear that, Red.' He quickly gathers the photos from the coffee table and shoves them under his arm. 'I've gotta get back to the station.' He makes his way to the door, then stops in the middle of the lounge room and turns. 'I'm sorry, Red. Do you need my help? Do you want me to give you a lift? I could take you ...' His voice trails off.

Meredith gets up quickly. 'No, that's cool. I'll call a cab.'

'Okay,' he says, walking over and putting his arms around her. 'Can you lock up?'

'Of course,' she says, returning his hug, but then, smelling the whisky on his breath, she pulls away. 'Are you okay to drive? I can get my cab to take you to the station first?'

Leo shakes his head. 'No, really, I'm fine. I've only had a couple.'

She searches his face for clues. 'Leo – you yourself referred to this girl as a victim. What do you think happened to her?' she asks softly.

In the low light of the lounge, Leo's face is partly shrouded in darkness and she can only see the side with the scar. It makes him look sad and defeated. 'In this job, you get a sense of things,' he says hoarsely. Then he kisses her forehead, turns and walks out, leaving her wondering what he isn't telling her.

Meredith punches a number for a taxi into her phone and sits down heavily by Jezebel, who is now curled up on the sofa. Juno sits at her feet and leans against her leg with a deep, satisfied whine, using her as a substitute for Leo, as she usually does when he's not around.

She leans back into the sofa, struck silent by what she now knows: three women have bled out from their femoral artery, slashed in the form of a cross – two of them in her Emergency room. And with what might be on the internet, that number could grow fast.

As she waits for her ride, she thinks about the photos Leo showed her. One in particular stands out. It's a photo of a plastic bag with a woman's slipper in it. Either he was too rushed to realise the plastic bag was labelled or, more likely, knowing Leo doesn't make careless mistakes, he purposefully let her see the identifying details, knowing she would file them away for future reference and perhaps look into things herself. In the rough scrawl of the crime scene officer, the plastic bag listed the date, time, place, case number – and one more thing, which she punches into a note on her phone, so she doesn't forget.

It's the name of the third victim: *Patrice Ladouceur*.

* * *

Come on, Belle, keep it together, Meredith thinks in the cab ride home.

Mere and Belle is what their mother called them, until she was close to her death, when she used their full names, Meredith Georgina Josephine and Isobel Loretta Lucinda. In the final days of her mother's cancer, Meredith would often wake to find her mom staring out the window at the garden, sounding out the syllables of her daughters' names, over and over like a mantra.

When Meredith heads up the steps of her townhouse she hears Bella playing the piano and recognises the music immediately. It's the Bach Partita in G major and it's a sure sign her sister is trying to stay on-piste. Bach is what Bella always plays to bring calm to the chaos of her inner world. Music is real – the crisp chromatic harmonies allow her a pathway to logical thought and drown out the voices in her head. The connection between the sounds of the instrument and the feel of its keys brings chronology and causation to Bella's sensory world as her mind threatens to shear it apart.

Knowing not to interrupt her, Meredith closes the front door softly and tiptoes silently past, removing her coat and shoes in the kitchen. As she stands by the kettle, waiting for it to boil, Bach's rippling harmonies wash over the knots of her mind like a bubbling creek over stones. For a moment, it feels like it did before her dad left and her mom died, and Bella's psychosis set in for good. Meredith's nerves begin to settle.

But then the piano playing stops – abruptly, mid-melody. Silence follows and Meredith freezes, tuned to the silence, listening for movement.

She hears steps, a door slamming, a toilet flushing. She waits. It's quiet – the usual hum of traffic outside her place, even at that late hour, seems dull and far away, as if the entire neighbourhood is waiting for Bella to emerge.

With still no sound from the bathroom, Meredith moves to the laptop in the kitchen and starts to surf the web, trying to look casual but keeping track of time. When the bathroom door finally opens, Bella walks heavily into the kitchen and sits down opposite Meredith.

She's wearing one of Meredith's old tracksuits and the look on her face is harrowing. Her thin, translucent skin is stretched over the bones of her skull, her cheeks as hollow as a spectre's. Bella never recovered from the severe weight loss that accompanied the onset of her schizophrenic symptoms and now even a brief lapse in eating makes her look skeletal. Blue veins circle her eyes and run down her neck like a spider's web. She stares at Meredith, her violet eyes wide.

'What's up, Belle?' Meredith recognises the expression on her sister's face – as if she's trapped behind glass, her eyes imploring Meredith to help her. Bella's fingers start to smooth her hair, which is tied tightly into a topknot. Bella's hair rituals are another way she tries to control things – brushing it, braiding it, wearing it tightly wrapped on top of her head, washing it, over and over again.

'Did something happen?'

Silence. Bella's fingertips keep raking her hair up towards her topknot.

'I really like that Partita, Belle. I think you should play it for the program,' she says.

Meredith gives her time to respond. She lets her eyes casually drift down to the computer screen, but stays on guard for an eruption.

'I lost my job,' Bella finally says.

Meredith pauses. This is bad. Or not. Bella has said similar things before.

'Can you tell me what happened?' she asks calmly and clearly, hoping to keep her sister feeling safe.

Bella's response is a jumble of words. 'I left my clothes off at work. I took them and then left them there after leaving. I think they're dangerous. Looks can kill. It's hard.'

The statements could just be random associations, a sign of Bella's slipping perception of reality. But they could also be true. Bella could have taken her clothes off in public, at work. Meredith had rescued her from a misguided stint as a stripper only a few months earlier. The job was unpredictable, high stress and a colossal misstep, but one Meredith felt incapable of preventing. Bella had become convinced that sex work was the only industry in which women controlled the means of production and was dead set on making it her profession. After that, she had taken a part-time job at a local library, helping with music programming for after-school care. It was the perfect role – flexible enough for her to take time off when she was symptomatic. If what Bella said was true and she'd had an episode at work, Meredith hoped she could convince the library to keep her sister on.

'Did this happen today?'

'No, no,' Bella says, shaking her head. 'Yesterday.' Her headshaking becomes more violent, as if she's arguing with herself. 'No, it was the day before!' A sound like an injured animal rises from deep in her throat and she brings her hands to her face.

'Okay, Belle,' Meredith says. 'It's okay – we'll call the library tomorrow and talk it through. They love you there, you know that. Come on. You're here with me now, and you're safe. Are you tired?'

Bella nods once, as though it's all she can do. Her breath is faint and fast and catches in her throat as she chokes down sobs.

Meredith goes to Bella's side, putting her arms around her. 'I'm tired too. Let's go to bed and we'll work it out tomorrow. We'll get your things. You can move in here.'

It doesn't matter if Bella lost her job, Meredith thinks as she fetches water and Bella's meds. But this is the thing with her sister – there can be cognitive interference at the point of entry, storage or recall. Bella's recollections of an event can be either precisely correct, or they can be a precisely recalled hallucination, or she can be recalling real events incorrectly, like people often do.

It's what caused their parents such despair. Of the two sisters, Bella was the more intelligent, the more musical, the more intrepid. In her teens, even when her mind started to slip and psychosis crept into the gaps, her episodes were spotted with moments of pure lucidity. There were times in the middle of a hallucination when Bella would stop and look at Meredith and give a penetrating insight – about their mother, about her, about the world. Times when she would run into the bathroom and start brushing her hair, over and over, as if to connect what she was feeling with what she was doing, to stitch her reality back together. Times when she would run to the piano to play scales and arpeggios in rapid succession, to collect her mind.

In these moments of awareness, her brilliant mind ripped through the chaos and asserted itself. No matter how ambiguous her world or how much her perceptions slipped, Bella was always present. And no matter how far her mind wandered, she always managed to reach out and bring it back.

* * *

'These pills are the right ones for me, Mere,' Bella says, getting under the covers on Meredith's bed.

'Do you think so?'

'I know so – they don't tire me out. The meds are working – they're not perfect but they're better than before.'

'Do you think you need to increase the dose?'

'No, I just got a bit forgetful with them.'

It always relaxed Bella to talk about her medicine; just as it was a comfort to her to finally be diagnosed. She often referred to herself as a schizophrenic – or a schizo, for short – sometimes in jest but also in all seriousness. No mental health advocate would do it, but it was Bella's way to reclaim the label. Sure, the category led to a host of stereotypes, but it gave Bella certainty and with certainty came agency. Living as a schizophrenic was hard, but living in undefined chaos was much worse.

Meredith crawls under the covers and Bella curls up against her.

'How was Evelyn's party?'

'It was fabulous. Totally excessive. Charlie's fingerprints were all over it,' Meredith says.

'Typical,' Bella laughs and Meredith joins in.

'Yup, Charlie was true to form.' She squeezes Bella closer. 'You were missed. You can still go to Arden tomorrow to see Evelyn. We can go together.'

'That'd be good. How's St Jude?'

'Oh, you know. It's work. Every day has a different shape. These last few weeks have been … intense.'

'Lots of Code Blues? And Oranges?' Bella likes hearing about Meredith's hospital experiences – she knows so many of the staff there, having been a patient numerous times herself.

'Not more than normal.'

Meredith can feel Bella relax. They lie there like they did when they were young. When Bella was little and prone to fits, she would come to Meredith first for consolation before she would let anyone else touch her. It was as though her parents were too large, like she needed comfort from the one person in the family who was as small as she was. They would rock back and forth, their whispers turning into giggles, until Bella fell asleep, finally safe from the monsters in her young mind.

'Thanks for leaving the party early to come home,' Bella says.

'No problem,' Meredith replies, thinking about Leo and the photos on his coffee table. 'You saved me from a vicious hangover.'

'I'm like a big storm in your life,' Bella says.

'Well, you do whip me around, but … you also keep my feet on the ground.'

'You're a liar.'

Hearing Bella's breathing become regular, Meredith eases herself out from under her arm and gets up. As she prepares for bed and turns off the lights, she passes her hallway table covered in photos, stopping to pick up one in particular.

When their father, Geoffrey Griffin, left them all, it was to move in with his other family. An extramarital affair had produced a child and then two more – all kept hidden. When their mother – Elizabeth Cavendish Griffin, a proud woman with deep, recurring depression – finally found out, a speedy divorce followed, and the financial aftermath meant much of what the family owned was lost to an auction.

Meredith remembers rushing through the house, secreting things, before the auctioneers arrived: her mother's cashmere coat, a few antique lamps, and photos, including this one, taken at a holiday house in the Florida Keys. Meredith and Bella are sitting on a wide wooden terrace, surrounded by palm trees. Bella's long, tanned legs sprawl into the foreground of the photo and her arms are wrapped possessively around her big sister's narrow shoulders. They are both smiling widely, caught mid-laughter, but it's Bella's confidence that dominates the photo. Her eyes are clear and mischievous, and her black hair is wildly blowing in the wind, partly hiding Meredith's heart-shaped face.

A soft moan from the bedroom pulls Meredith back to the present. She puts the photo back and creeps quietly back into bed with Bella, stopping only to pop a Clonazepam, just to help her get through the night.

* * *

At 3 am Meredith wakes with a thick, dry throat and a tremor in her gut. The sheets are damp with sweat. Rain sheets down against the bedroom window, like waves of rubble against the glass. Her mind is hot with thoughts that loop round and round, always taking the same track, leaving a deeper rut each time.

It's the women – Katherine, Tabitha and Patrice – who haunt her. Just as she feels herself slipping into sleep, images of injuries tear through her mind, pulling her back up to consciousness: a thin arm swinging on the edge of a gurney, scarred in furious red and cold white. A bloody cross sliced deep into tender skin.

By 4.30 am, hearing Bella's raspy breathing by her side, she rolls out of bed, giving up on sleep. She shuffles soundlessly to the kitchen and puts the moka pot on to boil, remembering Leo's playful teasing about her kitchen technology and wishing it were him keeping her awake.

She scans the sky and sees the rain has stopped, so with some caffeine in her system she sets out for a morning walk. A solid block of cloud bruises the western horizon, hanging over the Pacific Ocean like an iron anvil, while grey storm clouds roll in from the south, as if mustering their forces for war. Below, New Westdale lies helpless and swollen, trying its best to absorb the collateral damage.

Her street is razed by the night's storms. Massacred branches hang limply off trees, like fractured, contorted limbs. Leaves and garbage bob in the gutters. As she walks, her insides feel like the damaged trees – torn and tender. In her dreams Meredith was tossed amid elemental forces, thrown by the rushing of water, but now, surrounded by tall trees and languid ferns that droop alongside the sidewalks, she is strengthened by the air that smells cleansed by living things. In the early dawn light, the confident chorus of sparrows and cormorants brings order to the world – like a royal house reasserting itself after rebellion.

Back at home, she's about to turn on the shower when a mark on the glass distracts her. She pulls out a spray cleaner from under the sink and starts to scrub. Then she moves on to the sink, the tub, the vanity. Then the walls and the lights. Then she stacks the towels according to size and straightens them; then restacks them according to colour, then restraightens them. She gets on her knees and scrubs the floors.

Sitting back on her heels, calm descends as she looks around at her work, but a glance at her phone indicates she's been at it for two hours. She can get annoyed at her compulsions, but the peace they bring is worth it.

Order for Meredith is what Bach is for Bella.

She looks in on her sister and the hallway light spills across Bella's white shoulders. She's on her stomach, the way she always sleeps – ever since she was a little girl – spread-eagled on her tummy, free-falling into her dreams, her shoulder blades poking up like two delicate wings. Even emaciated, Bella is luminous. Just like Katherine was. Like both women were ablaze on the inside.

Chapter 4

The pattern of three similar deaths takes root in Meredith's mind. What else do these three women share? Katherine and Tabitha were both patients at St Jude. Was Patrice?

It takes Meredith a week of stealing moments, between budget meetings and management presentations, resuscitations and code reports, to see if St Jude has records of a Patrice Ladouceur. There's no record of a patient by that name in Emergency so, following the trail of Katherine and Patrice, her next port of call is Barb Finnegan.

Hey, Barb, do you have that re-scan for T Norsman?

Barb responds quickly: *Even better, the original is now in the file. Had a new starter that day. Thanks for pointing out the issue.*

Np, can I check on another admission? Do you have a P Ladouceur?

Sure enough, a Patrice Ladouceur was admitted to Psych almost a year earlier. The records are scant, but they indicate self-injury, and after an initial consultation, she was referred to St Jude's Psychiatric Outpatient Clinic for further evaluation.

That nugget of information burns a hole in Meredith's stomach – each victim, at some point, was a patient of St Jude's Psych department. Leo has said not to mention it to senior management, but she *is* senior management. How can she not say something?

On Friday afternoon, after a long week and much ruminating, she clocks off a bit early. On the way home, she pulls up beside her boss's cottage. It's a tiny house, dwarfed by the grander homes nearby, with an abundant vegetable and flower garden out front. Both garden and house are well-tended and simple – a legacy of Camilla Santos's upbringing in the Philippines by an order of nuns called the Daughters of Mercy.

Meredith knew she would find Camilla at home – Friday afternoons were reserved for thinking and planning. Since Meredith's promotion to Lead Operations Manager, managing nursing in Emergency, she had spent many a Friday afternoon at Camilla's – setting budgets, reviewing construction plans, designing training exchanges with other hospitals. As she walks up the front path, she checks on the status of Camilla's herb garden, which she helped plant in May, on one of those Fridays where thinking and planning were mixed with physical work – another principle from her convent upbringing that Camilla swore by. Seeing the thyme and lavender thriving puts a smile on Meredith's face – despite having no interest in gardening, she got a surprising amount of pleasure out of those few hours.

'Did you miss me at work?' Camilla asks with an ironic smile as she welcomes Meredith at the front door. She's in her usual costume – a dark, long-sleeved shirt dress and a golden crucifix around her neck. Her salt-and-pepper hair is parted in the middle and pulled into a bun at the nape of her neck, forming a perfect frame for her symmetrical features and high black brows.

No matter how many times Meredith's been there, she's always a bit nervous at her boss's home. Rushing to explain her surprise visit, she stumbles over her words. 'I know we could have talked at the office, but I don't think this can wait until Monday ...'

Camilla waves away her apology, leads her into the lounge room and waits in silence as Meredith gathers her thoughts. Patience is one of Camilla's top talents. That, and ferocity. Before she became director of nursing at St Jude, she oversaw the construction of new Catholic hospitals in Rwanda, and new clinics in the Philippines and El Salvador. And now that she's been given the added role of deputy CEO, the St Jude gossip places Camilla as the real powerbroker at the hospital. She's been there longer than almost anyone and has outlasted countless management teams.

'Do you remember Katherine Richardson, the young woman who died of a self-inflicted cut to the femoral artery? She was the one I told you about.'

Camilla nods, her eyes softening momentarily, acknowledging the loss of life. 'That must have been very difficult, Meredith. To treat a young woman through such intimate, vulnerable moments, over and over, and then to lose her. I know it's part of the job, but you must give yourself time to grieve these things.'

'I do.'

'Good. Patient losses always hit us hard and I know it goes deep,' Camilla says, giving Meredith the gentle, winning smile that she's come to expect. The way her boss makes her feel in a crisis is what Meredith values most and it compels her forward.

'Katherine wasn't the only patient with cuts like that.'

'I know – we see more and more cutters and they're getting younger every day. We've talked about this. I blame social media.'

'No, I don't mean the cuts on her arms and limbs. I mean the fatal injury. Katherine exsanguinated due to lacerations to her upper thigh, near the pelvis – two slashes in the form of a cross that sliced open her femoral.'

'And you—'

'I've seen that injury before. On a different girl. A girl named Tabitha Norsman.'

'Did Tabitha pass?' Camilla asks quietly.

'Yes – there were lots of drugs on board, but the cause of death was exsanguination from the femoral. Again, two slashes in the form of a cross.'

Camilla takes a moment to compute the information. 'So, you think there's a connection? Like what, some sort of ritual behaviour?'

Meredith shifts in her chair at Camilla's suggestion, thinking again about the young self-harmer who had cuts on her arms and legs in the form of a cross. 'It definitely could be, I don't know, but we're certainly bumping up our records and reporting on presentations that involve self-injury, particularly anything that looks ritualistic or out of the ordinary.'

'Good.'

'Yeah, but there's another reason we need to be on high alert – the police have asked me for some confidential advice on another death. That woman may have suicided, but died of exactly the same wound.'

'When did you speak to the police?'

Sharing information with the police without approval would be a serious breach of protocol, so Meredith jumps to her own defence. 'It was about a week ago. A detective I know asked me for some advice on an apparent suicide,' she says firmly. 'It was clear that the victim was cutting herself, so he asked me about the habits of self-harmers. I'm sure he didn't mean it to happen, but I got the name of the deceased woman from the photos. She was a seventeen year old named Patrice Ladouceur.'

'Okay, so it was just a regular conversation with a detective in the ward?' Camilla asks, looking concerned.

'Yes. In a way. Not entirely,' she says, trying to back-pedal and shift Camilla's attention from the police. Her nerves start to twitch with panic as she thinks about Leo warning her not to tell anyone – how it could compromise his investigation.

Camilla just looks at her – confusion, as well as worry, starting to creep onto her face.

Having broken her promise to Leo, Meredith holds forth, baring all, as if she's in the confessional. 'I've started seeing a detective named Leo Donnelly and I told him weeks back about Katherine Richardson.'

Seeing Camilla look even more concerned, Meredith again races to explain. 'I didn't tell him Katherine's name or anything about the cause of death. I only told him that we lost a patient who was a self-harmer and that I was worried about how many self-harmers we see in Emergency.' She repeats herself for emphasis. 'He doesn't know her name or anything personal. Nothing. He also doesn't know about Tabitha. I held that back too. I really don't know why – I just feel—'

'No,' Camilla says quickly, clearly relieved, 'you were right to be discreet, Meredith. Obviously to protect patients, but for your sake as well. You must keep strictly to protocol in your position – confidentiality is absolutely key.'

Feeling that Camilla is on her side, Meredith presses on. 'I know. I held a lot back. When Leo showed me the images of how this third girl died, it was clear – her cuts were exactly like Katherine's and Tabitha's. But I wasn't ready to tell him.'

'Okay, so what's your next move?'

Meredith just breathes as Camilla tilts her head to one side, waiting to hear more.

'Well, it feels really close to home.'

'I'm sure it does. You're on the frontline and see constant trauma – it's mostly the vulnerable you're treating, isn't it? I know how much it affects you.'

'No, I mean – that's not it,' Meredith says urgently. 'All three of these young women – they were patients at St Jude.'

Camilla frowns. 'Well, is that so unusual? We serve an extremely wide population – many people in this city have been St Jude patients at one time or another.'

'Yeah, I guess so,' Meredith says. 'But all three women were admitted to our Psych department at some point in the last year.'

Camilla's face changes. 'What?' she asks. 'What, so you think the problem's in our own hospital?'

'No, I don't think anything yet.'

Camilla straightens her back and slowly stands up. She walks to the front window and is silhouetted against the dusk light outside, her back turned to Meredith. Sounding as though she's picking her words carefully, she speaks. 'I understand that you spoke to Leo about Katherine, and that he spoke to you about Patrice. You may see a pattern emerging, but you need to tread carefully. Don't jump to conclusions. Don't pretend you have investigative expertise.'

She turns to face Meredith, her features still in darkness. 'But, of course, you also need to make sure this is not more than a terrible coincidence. Pull all the files we have, review them and let's talk in a few days.'

'Of course, Camilla,' Meredith says, nodding. 'Of course.'

Camilla makes a move towards the hallway, signalling their chat is over. As they walk to the front door, her voice softens. 'It probably feels like you're in treacherous territory, but you're not alone. But please keep this to yourself – no more police – until we talk again.'

Saying her goodbyes and walking to her car, Meredith pushes away the guilt that grinds in her belly. Leo had told her not to say anything, but she can't hide this pattern from her mentor. Telling Camilla gives her the security of having an ally, and a sense of lightness, like confession without the sin. She has a few days to dig, to see if the answer lies somewhere in St Jude.

The weather has softened from rain to mist, and she can smell the faint perfume of rosemary and lavender from the garden. As she looks back to the house, she sees Camilla standing at the window. Meredith waves to her, but realises that her boss is staring off into the distance, lost in thought, not looking at her at all.

* * *

Heading home from Camilla's, Meredith takes the old coastal road, plunging down through thickly forested gullies, and then up, to the tops of the granite cliffs with their wide views of the sea. When the road crests, she has a clear view north where the coastline crumbles into a string of islands carpeted in spruce, fir and cedar – the emerald chain, as her father used to call it.

They spent hours scouring those tree-filled cliffs and shores together, just the three of them – Meredith walking behind her dad, and Bella walking behind her. She remembers struggling to keep up with him on the trails, losing him around corners, keeping an eye out for his bright yellow backpack that hung heavy with the implements of a geologist: his rope, rock pick and telescope hooked on the back of it, swinging with his stride. As they walked, he spoke of the deep history of the coast, telling them stories of inland seas and underwater volcanos and shifting tectonic plates.

As she drives, Scots Harbour lies to her right and beyond it, the dim light of early evening flickers along the horizon of the Pacific Ocean. The rain has let up for a moment and the air is rich with the smell of a rainforest, swollen with water. She opens her window wide as she drives and lets the scent of cedar and fir course through her like a tonic.

When Meredith turns down her street, dusk is inching out the day, but all the lights are on in her townhouse and it's glowing like a burning beacon. Parking, she senses something is up and her mood turns tense when she sees Jeremy, the man who rents her small basement suite, marching down the front steps, his round paunch shaking with every step. When he sees Meredith, he heads straight at her and she has to resist the urge to turn the ignition back on and drive off at high speed. Instead, she gets out and walks around the car to him, bracing herself.

'We've got a real mess here and it's going to be *on you* to sort it out,' Jeremy says, pointing in her face for emphasis.

'Jeremy ...' Meredith backs away, trying to dodge the spit spraying from his lips. 'What's happened?'

'My bathroom ceiling is starting to cave in, thanks to your psycho sister,' he says. 'She's a freakin' maniac. She left the damn bath going, didn't she?'

A sinking feeling comes over Meredith and she pushes past Jeremy through the front door.

She can't see Bella, but there is evidence of her everywhere. The hallway floor is covered in mud, a glass is shattered in the kitchen, red wine is splattered over the tile floor. A quick look in the bathroom proves Jeremy's case. Water is everywhere. Jars of medication have been thrown against the wall, spilling onto the floor and dissolving, leaving blue sludge and plastic clogged around the drain. She has about five seconds to catch her breath before she hears Jeremy's voice behind her demanding that she sort out the mess.

It's more than she can bear. A reasonable person might understand that Bella was more a danger to herself than to anyone else, but Jeremy is not a reasonable person. After a few minutes of mollifying him with talk of her insurance cover, she closes her front door with him on the other side and takes stock. She actually has no idea if her insurance will cover this, and as she moves from room to room, doing calculations in her head, she tries not to panic about the cost.

As she assesses the damage in the lounge room, a faint sound comes from a small mound in the corner. In all the fracas with Jeremy, Meredith had assumed Bella was out somewhere, but her sister is there, crouching in the corner, murmuring to herself, hunched over a fallen lamp. It's still lit, but lying on its side, with the shade bent and the base cracked. It was another of the few things Meredith had rescued from the auction. Their mother had brought it home from a visit to China, back when their father was running geological surveys around the Three Gorges Dam. The traditional ink painting on its porcelain base is a rendering of the Summer Palace in Beijing.

Bella is curled over the broken porcelain, sobbing quietly. Her bony spine sits proud under her thin white T-shirt, like a long pearl necklace running the length of her back.

At the sound of Meredith's approach, Bella looks up, her eyes red and swollen. She chokes in a breath. 'I'm sorry, Mere. I know it was Mom's favourite—'

'Don't be sorry.' Meredith's voice is tight, but then she softens. 'Belle, please, don't worry about it. You know it doesn't matter.'

'You liked that lamp,' Bella says, slurring her words – whether from medication or alcohol, Meredith can't tell.

'Not really,' she says, bending down and lifting Bella to standing. 'It was OTT – like most of mom's things.' She grunts as she adjusts Bella against her hip and helps her down the dark hallway to the bedroom. 'We always had too much stuff in our family. Too much stuff to take care of.'

'Too much stuff,' Bella mumbles as Meredith lays her down on the bed.

'Yup – too much stuff,' she says back.

'Too much stuff, like me,' Bella says, sitting up and grabbing each of Meredith's hands. 'You always have to take care of me.' She sighs and her breath sounds like it will break into a sob, but then becomes even again. She looks up at Meredith, her eyes soft and clear. 'I'm sorry, Mere.'

'You don't have anything to be sorry for, Belle,' Meredith says. 'We're all that's left. We look after each other. It's what we do.'

'No, I am,' Bella says, clearly and insistently. 'I'm really sorry. Mom always said a mother is as happy as her saddest child. I think she died of sadness because of me.'

Meredith takes a long look at her sister. 'Don't think that way. I'm sure I made her just as sad.'

'But I'm crazier.'

Meredith laughs despite herself and puts her arms around her sister. 'Oh, Belle,' she whispers in her ear. 'You're smarter. You're more musical. You're more everything than me except crazy.'

'No, no, you're not crazy, Mere,' Bella murmurs back, 'you're just OCD. You're obsessed someone's going to die, so you always try to save people.'

Pretending she didn't hear the comment, Meredith coaxes her sister to lie down and take a sedative. Amazing, she thinks, watching Bella quickly fall asleep, that she can diagnose me – correctly – right after a psychotic episode.

Back in the lounge room, Meredith resurveys the damage. Having walked into rooms like this many times, she can work out how things had gone. Bella had missed a med. There were storms that afternoon, and the wind and trees would have hit the lounge room's large windows. Her sister would have started hearing things, losing control of the vagaries and eruptions in her mind. The wind and the rain would have become the fulcrum for a hallucination. It was nature, the one thing that they had enjoyed so much with their father, that became the trigger for Bella's psychotic episodes. At the age of fourteen, she stopped abiding the smell of the trees, the sounds of the birds overhead, the feel of leaves against her skin. It was all too unordered, too random. Their dad would have to restrain Bella, turn back and carry her to the car. They'd race home, and take her to her room or to her piano, to play the calming chromatic melodies of Bach. After Bella's psychosis settled in for good, the long coastal walks with their father came to an end.

As Meredith circles the apartment, righting things and making a note of what can be fixed, her hands start to shake. Waiting for Bella to get better was like waiting for a moment that never comes.

A low pull in her gut starts to connect with a throbbing behind her eyes. She runs into the guest bathroom and retches. All Meredith can see when she opens her eyes is the unbroken road of her sister's illness, stretching to the horizon. The thought makes her retch more.

She tries calling Charlie but it goes through to voicemail, so she sends a text: *Can you call. At home. It's B.*

Then she calls Leo, who picks up on the first ring. 'Hey, Red. What's happening?'

'Not much,' she lies. 'You?'

'Yeah – I'm just cooking. Fancy some stew?'

She hears chopping in the background and imagines him standing at the butcher's block in his tiny kitchen, balancing his phone under his ear, wielding his favourite knife. She exhales slowly, realising she's been holding her breath. For Leo, food is life. When she hears Juno bark in the background, something warm starts to creep back into her. 'That sounds perfect.'

'You sound tired.'

'I'm exhausted.'

'Dinner'll be ready in an hour. Why don't you come over?'

'I'm not really able to … Bella's with me. I can't really leave her alone.'

Juno barks again in the background, as if she knows Meredith is in need. 'No problem, I'll bring it over. You can introduce me to your sister and we can eat together.'

She closes her eyes and chokes back a silent sob of gratitude. He has no idea what it means to her – the comfort of his simple boyish enthusiasm. And the offer to meet her sister, to bring them dinner – it was precisely the move she wanted him to make. Just not tonight.

'I would love that, Leo, but my place is in no shape for a dinner party. Give me an hour. I'll call you back, I promise.'

Ringing off, she lays her head back down on the cool floor of the bathroom.

The next thing she sees is Charlie's short black pixie cut bobbing over her, as she gently wakes her up. 'Usually, I'm the one who's passed out on the bathroom floor,' her friend says, smiling. 'Why are you lying here?'

Meredith peers into Charlie's blue eyes and tries to sit up slowly, propping her back against the wall. 'I don't know, actually. Felt a bit ill.'

Charlie simply nods and smiles, sitting back on her heels. She nods towards the lounge. 'Looks like a storm hit your place.'

Meredith nods too, explaining what she came home to.

'Don't worry. We'll sort it out.'

She's right. Over the years, Charlie's often stepped in to help with Bella. After both her parents died, Meredith was the last woman standing. She knew she wasn't going to be able to do it alone. She had filed the court documents herself – to give *both* her and Charlie power of attorney over Bella's affairs.

'You really don't have to, Charlie,' she says. She shakes her head, but can't seem to move much else. 'I can totally handle this. I'm going to … I'll call … I'll make an insurance claim tomorrow and it'll be fine.'

'Meredith.' Charlie tries to catch her friend's gaze. 'Why do we have to have this conversation each time I try to help you? Look around. Your place is a mess and you've been sleeping on the bathroom floor.'

She puts both hands on Meredith's shoulders and looks at her straight on. 'You know what I love? About us? I love that we don't judge each other and we don't lie to each other. I'm telling you the truth when I say there are moments you need help and this is one of them.'

'Okay, okay, okay.' Meredith leans her head back against the wall and tries to push herself up. 'I hear you. But first, can you just help me stand up?'

Charlie gets Meredith on her feet but doesn't let her go. 'Can you balance?'

'Yeah, thanks. Give me a minute?' Meredith asks, looking at her in the mirror.

'Sure,' Charlie says cautiously, taking a few steps back, her eyes locked to Meredith's.

With her friend out of the room, Meredith reaches for a bottle of pills in a drawer and slips a few Ativan in her mouth. She catches Charlie watching her in the hallway mirror, but sees her quickly avert her eyes. It's been like that since her parents died and she was left alone with her sister – Meredith taking pills and Charlie discreetly looking away.

As if to change the subject, Charlie starts to issue instructions. Pack a bag for Bella. Charlie's office will arrange a cleaner to deal with the mess and she'll speak to Meredith's insurance company herself. She then calls Evelyn to let her know she's bringing Bella to stay at Arden.

When Charlie gets off the phone, Meredith comes up beside her in the hallway. 'You can be really bossy, you know,' she says.

'And you can be a total control freak.' Charlie gives Meredith a sympathetic look and tilts her head to the bathroom, as if pointing to the drugs. 'I can let you off the hook for lots of things, but I'm not going to stand back and watch you drown. Evelyn's got money and I've got brains.' When Meredith stares at her defensively, Charlie gets more adamant. 'You know what I mean. Stacks of people out there have to deal with things like this on their own. You have us.'

Meredith wraps her arms around Charlie, her limbs starting to relax from the drug. 'I'll come to Arden with you. Let me get my coat,' she mutters into her friend's ear.

'No,' Charlie says, giving her a squeeze and then gently pushing her away, 'that's not letting us help.' She holds Meredith's face in her hands and looks straight at her. 'This is your cue to relax. Why don't you call that good-looking cop you've told me about and let him take care of you this weekend?'

Chapter 5

The following Monday, Meredith wakes with a start. Panic presses on her chest, constricting her lungs like a leaden vest. She climbs out of bed feeling breathless, as if she's still running beside Katherine's gurney.

The rain turns nasty on the drive to work, hurling water against her windshield. With each passing day, its sheer force transforms the landscape. Puddles metastasise into ponds. Rushing water leaves muddy ruts in lawns, like a mad beast clawing its way through the terrain. When she looks up through her windshield, the heavy clouds sag overhead, caging them all in a padded cell.

On the ramp up the Georgia Bridge, her car smashes through a deep pool of water and starts to hydroplane. As the rear wheels lose traction, slipping to the right and then the left, adrenalin washes through her. Her hands tighten on the steering wheel. She spins it in one direction, then the other, but it's futile – her front wheels stay fixed on a deadly course. Sweat breaks out on her back as the car veers towards the side rails of the bridge. An image of herself going over the edge flashes in her mind – the car hitting the concrete barrier, turning over in mid-air, plunging down into the river – the angry currents of the Richmond Delta surging up to meet her. She grips the wheel even harder and closes her eyes, body stiff as a board, waiting for impact – but, just then, her back wheels gain traction with the road. 'Fuck', she whispers, exhaling as she opens her eyes.

Back in control, Meredith gulps down some air and focuses on the horizon, where she can see St Jude, lying like a metal anchor at the bottom of a purple sea.

* * *

Walking slowly through the hospital to Emergency, she takes in the signs of the early morning. The hour before morning changeover is a rare quiet moment, like the slow movements of an animal waking from slumber. By then, most of the night's damage is done. If someone's going to beat up their girlfriend or crack their head open in a drunken brawl, it's happened already. This is the time to breathe – and Meredith does – knowing the calm won't last.

The nurses huddle at the rapid assessment zone – the main station for Emergency triage. At the RAZ, they operate in tandem, like one organism, cooperating without speaking, quickly assessing acuity, directing traffic, chatting up and charming paramedics and police alike. She greets them and feels a rush of emotion. The gratitude she feels for her team wells up in her at unexpected moments.

Her phone vibrates with a morning update from Arden. Charlie had promised to send Meredith a 'Bella update' every morning and night. Over the weekend, the updates came in like clockwork. This morning, it's a photo of Bella, Evelyn and Charlie. *All good here. Sunday roast dinner with B and E and then Netflix. B's in good form – remembering her meds.*

Meredith scans the roster and sees Ros's name. The thought of her unflappable lieutenant immediately puts her at ease. With Ros on board, Meredith seizes the opportunity to investigate Katherine's, Tabitha's and Patrice's files, as Camilla had asked.

'I'm going to be swimming in paper today,' she says as she passes Ros in the corridor. 'I have to do a complete chart audit on some patients, so I'll be spending a few hours in Medical Records.'

Ros turns to walk beside her. 'Wow – lucky you,' she says drily. 'I'll take a double gunshot victim any day over a few hours in Medical Records.'

Ros gives Meredith a summary of the night's events – two overdoses, both patients stabilised and admitted into the hospital, several domestic burns, nothing else that was serious. Generally, a quiet night.

They pass the fast track room, where a bearded man is propped up on a gurney with an IV in his arm, gesticulating at the wall. 'What's Gary's story today?' Meredith asks quietly.

'The paras picked him up at Super Valu last night. He was in the vegetable section, throwing peppers at the shoppers.' Ros's expression becomes soft. 'He just fell off his meds,' she says, with quiet acceptance. 'Nothing serious. We're giving him some hydration. Psych is sending down a resident, and his wife will be here soon.'

They turn the corner and head towards the elevators. 'Hey,' Ros says, 'Sarah Sampson's devised a system to report and record self-injury cases. It's pretty elegant, tied to triage, shouldn't put too much more work on the staff. It's still in draft, but do you want to see it?'

'Yes, definitely, let's do that later today.'

When they reach the elevators, Ros bids Meredith goodbye but catches herself. 'Oh, by the way, did you look at the plans for the nursing station redesign?'

'Yes, I did,' Meredith says, annoyance rising in her voice. 'It's crap. It doesn't give us visibility of the patients, there are no circulation paths and no room for social interaction. It puts the new triage station a mile away from the bays. It's totally flawed. Our nurses are stressed, overworked flight risks – the redesign will send them round the bend. I'm telling the consultant to bin it and start over.'

She jabs at the elevator button and Ros smiles at her. 'I knew you'd have a strong POV and I happen to agree. I'll leave you to your admin,' she says as she strides down the hallway.

Meredith jabs at the button a few more times. New elevators wouldn't hurt either, she thinks.

* * *

On her way down to Medical Records, she reflects on the people with body mods and scarification they see in Emergency. These features rarely sounded alarm bells, unless they couldn't be linked to alternative lifestyles or came with other suspicious presentations. But four women with cuts in the form of a cross, and three dying as a result, is too much of a coincidence.

She recalls Olivia Lu was the code doctor when Tabitha passed. When the elevator opens at the basement, she rings her but the call goes through to her office assistant.

'Sandy, Meredith Griffin here.'

'Hey Meredith, what can I do for you?'

'I know Olivia is heading off on sabbatical – have I missed her?'

Finding out the doctor's gone on leave prior to a three-month sabbatical, she hangs up. She recalls another note in the file, indicating Tabitha had attended a methadone clinic in

Portside called Safe Stop. She knows a few of the public health nurses who staff the clinic.

Turning down the long corridor that heads to Medical Records, she tries Safe Stop and, luckily, one of her friends is on shift.

'Meredith, how're you going? You good?'

She can hear the activity of the clinic in the background. 'Hi Rafi, yeah, I'm okay. Listen, I don't want to take too much of your time, so I'll be quick. We had a really tragic situation with a patient here and I'm trying to make some sense of it. I know she spent time at Safe Stop.'

'Do you have a name?'

'Tabitha. Tabitha Norsman.'

Meredith can hear Rafi sucking his teeth. 'Tabitha,' he says. 'Yeah, I knew Tabitha.'

'I was with her in Emergency when she died.'

'That must have been tough,' he says, his voice getting slower and sadder. 'It was certainly tough for us. When we heard she was gone, it was terrible, really terrible.'

'So, you knew her well?'

'Yeah, she came in a lot. She really tried to kick the junk. She really, really tried. You know the cause of death?'

'Yes. And I know she was doing it really rough, Rafi, but from what I understand, it didn't seem like she was courting suicide.'

'Not at all,' Rafi says. There's a pause and Meredith can hear him close a door. 'Like I said, she was really trying to kick it. I mean, she had it tough, really tough. And she was fiery. She didn't have a lot of filters – but she was good, you know? She had a real sweet side. She was older than a lot of the kids. She'd take care of them, you know? Like a big sister.' He starts to chuckle sadly. 'Despite everything, she really liked people, you know. She was really social.'

'Hmm,' Meredith says. 'Speaking of which, was she on social media?'

'Are you kidding? Always. Her phone was her lifeline. She didn't have much money, but she always had enough for her data packs!' Rafi chuckles sadly. 'But I always worried about it. She spent a lot of time on Facebook groups — got all her news there — and she was on lots of strange sites. I tried to talk to her about it, told her to be careful, you know, but she was pretty stubborn.'

'Do you think that drove her to the cutting?'

He pauses. 'I don't know, Meredith, I mean, how do you ever really know? All I can say is that suicide didn't square for me. She hated life, but she loved it too, you know? We all knew she did damage to herself once in a while, but we never saw that coming.'

Meredith can hear a door opening and someone beginning to talk to Rafi. 'Meredith, I gotta go. Happy to talk again, but we have a situation here.'

'Go,' she says, thanking him. Then she sends herself a note to tell Ros to add social media activity to the reporting process for patients with self-harming presentations.

When she swipes herself into Medical Records, she sighs deeply, staring at the stacks of files on each desk, bookshelf and file cabinet. If she had time, she'd spend a week reorganising the department, lining thing up and finding a place for everything.

She stops her obsessive-compulsive thoughts as she approaches the reception desk. The attendant is a young girl this time, too deeply involved in her newsfeed to notice Meredith at first. Waiting for the paperwork, Meredith plans her method of attack for the chart audit. She's already looked at Tabitha's file and reviewed part of Katherine's, but she knows each woman was admitted several times and wants to compare all three histories at once. She also needs to see Tabitha's complete file, now that Barb has provided the original psych assessment. When the records attendant brings her the files in a cart, she opens them all.

The content in each follows a normal pattern – an admission note from the attending Emergency physician, vital signs, cardiac status, lab work results, standard toxicology screen. Seeing the physical health signs for Katherine and Patrice were normal, she turns her attention to the psychiatric files of all three patients.

In the psych assessments, the women are identified by surname and first initials – Richardson KA, Norsman TC, Ladouceur PD. It's Psych department protocol – introduced by Stuart Chester when he rebuilt the team.

Patrice's assessment was completed by Mark Roth and it reads like Katherine Richardson's: an intelligent and articulate young woman from a wealthy family, with much to offer and a life of endless opportunities. The suicide risk assessment was done only a few weeks before Patrice was found dead in her parents' bathtub. It referenced past self-harming activities but indicated a complete absence of suicidal thoughts, a plan for suicide or ruminative thoughts of suicide. The young woman, while clearly distressed, was not hallucinating, delusional or psychotic. Meredith sits back in her chair, as stumped by Patrice as she was by Katherine: here was a young woman who was unhappy and struggling with a recent trauma but clearly capable of living a normal life. Why would she cut herself so viciously?

Reading sections of the report over and over, she gets a feel for Mark Roth's method. His notes were what you'd expect – clinical and objective. What you'd hope for, in fact. The empathy that the psychiatrist feels for their subject often has to be dialled down. The professional must cut through the emotion to see the patterns and identify the signals that will lead to an accurate diagnosis – to find the one weed in a forest of generalising characteristics that, when tugged, will lead to the root of the problem.

But there was a tone in Mark's files – a keen emphasis on deficiencies and deficits, a tendency to score the patient, to categorise. It must be his system – his way of cutting through the underbrush – she thinks. Meredith couldn't judge him for it, but it leaves her uneasy nonetheless. She recalls how many doctors had done the same to Bella over the course of her life. It took years for Bella finally to be diagnosed as schizophrenic. The thought of the number of hospital files on her made Meredith swell with guilt. Every attempt to diagnose required a penetrating assessment, as if every act of compassion was rimmed with betrayal.

When Meredith scans Mark's follow-up plan, she sees his recommendation that Patrice attend regular psychotherapy sessions at the St Jude Psychiatric Outpatient Clinic. But when she reaches for Patrice's outpatient file, she finds only one piece of paper – a list of proposed appointments. Meredith stops stone-still. It's just like with Katherine and Tabitha: a comprehensive psych assessment, a recommendation for counselling sessions and then nothing. She wraps her arms around herself, feeling the chill of the air conditioning. The fact that the files end where they should begin makes no sense. Why are there no notes? Did the women end up not attending the counselling sessions?

No, that can't be right, she thinks. In the morgue, the day she died, Mark admitted to knowing Katherine extremely well. The thought drives her back to the psych assessments and outpatient files for each patient. Her eye tracks down the pages.

Then she sits upright. Now that she has a properly scanned psych assessment for Tabitha, it's clear as day. Lining up the three files, she can see it on all of them.

Meredith's mind races as she returns the files to the cart, and the cart to the attendant. She runs through the tunnels to the elevator. Seeing it's now closed for maintenance, she takes the stairs two at a time to Camilla's office on Level 5 West.

Racing down the main corridor, she careens into the empty anteroom in front of Camilla's office where her assistant, Jessica, usually sits. Seeing Jessica not there she starts to pace and hears Camilla talking on the phone through the half-open door.

'You have the data in front of you, Senator. People like Stuart Chester in Psychiatry, Tom Landor in Surgery, Meredith Griffin in Emergency – I can't keep this talent without more funding … Case in point is Emergency. You and I both know how things looked before Meredith became Operations Lead – the department was a nightmare. She's transformed it—'

Meredith knocks hard and fast on the door, and when Camilla notices, she puts up a hand to stop her coming in.

'Senator, can you please give me a moment?' Camilla says, getting up from behind her desk and walking towards the door. She shakes her head, looking apologetic. 'Sorry, Meredith, I can't talk right now,' she whispers, softly closing the door.

Shut out of the office, she turns to see Jessica walking into the anteroom and runs up to her. 'Any chance of a meeting with Camilla today?'

'Impossible,' Jessica says, sitting behind her desk. 'She's presenting at the Senate Inquiry into the Funding of Catholic Hospitals.' Seeing Meredith's look of frustration, she adds, 'I know, it's a total punish, but she'll be out for most of the week.'

Meredith's face is damp with sweat as she makes her way back to Emergency. She nods to Ros, who looks at her quizzically from down the hallway. 'Audit's over,' she mouths as she closes the door to her office.

What the files have shown gnaws at her like a hungry rat, and she has to tell Camilla. She reaches for the stash of single-dose Ativan packets in her lab coat pocket and feels the smooth foil between her fingers. There's a rush of blood, a prickling of her skin. It's irresistible – like an itch she can't stop scratching. Keeping her eyes on the closed office door, she grabs one, rips it open with her teeth and swallows the pill. Fuck it, she thinks, and grabs two more.

JULY 2015

Chapter 6

Delicate beads of sweat line Camilla's forehead. Despite her composure and the cool way she shuffles the pages of the report, Meredith can sense her anxiety in a musky, salty wave.

She was ready to give Camilla her full chart audit of Tabitha, Katherine and Patrice the Tuesday after she spoke to her. But getting time with her boss has been strangely difficult. Since the day Meredith went to Camilla's house and asked for permission to investigate the young women's deaths, she's been unavailable. Always too busy. Always off-site.

Meredith has known Camilla long enough to know something's off – since their talk about the three dead women, the gears of communication have gummed up. When she manages to catch Camilla – in a busy hospital corridor or outside her office – a faint shadow crosses her boss's face, like she's trapped and wants to run the other way. And when they finally talk, she can sense Camilla's circumspection – as if Meredith is no longer trusted; as if *she* were the dangerous one. Her own transgressions loom in the back of her mind. Has there been yet another report from Central Pharmacy of 'unexplained losses' from the hospital's drug supplies?

Now, after much wrangling with Jessica, Meredith has managed to pin Camilla down and they're sitting in a small meeting room, with her chart audit on the table between them. As Camilla turns the pages, the air in the room starts to thicken.

Meredith is just about to excuse herself to go to the bathroom so she can swallow a couple of Ativan, when Camilla clears her throat. 'So,' she says, sitting back in her chair, pushing the report away. 'What do you think?'

Meredith's ready to dive in – Camilla never has time to dance around a subject. 'Based on the information available, each woman,' she puts up a finger for each point, 'was a chronic self-harmer; experienced some form of psychological issue; died of blood loss due to two deep cuts to the femoral artery and ...'

She pauses. Camilla raises her eyebrows, waiting.

Meredith continues: '... was a patient of Mark Roth.'

Camilla's eyebrows lift further.

'After each woman was referred to Psych, they began regular counselling sessions *with him* at the Outpatient Clinic.'

Camilla leans in and asks impatiently, 'Right, so, what do the outpatient files say?'

Meredith shrugs her shoulders. 'I don't know, Camilla. There *are* no outpatient files. Each woman was referred to the clinic and assigned to Mark Roth, and then, poof,' she mimes an explosion, 'they fall into a black hole. The Psychiatric Outpatient Clinic has four consulting psychiatrists, any one of whom could have helped these women, but Mark was appointed to be the ongoing consulting psychiatrist for each one and his session records don't exist.'

Meredith stops there, waiting for a sign of indignation, but Camilla remains motionless in her chair, arms crossed firmly over her chest, face inscrutable. 'Well,' she says, 'I'm not happy the Psych department's filing is poor – that's one of the things we hired Stuart Chester to fix. But I'm also not surprised that Psych is all over this. Do you know how many patients in Stuart's clinic suicide every year?'

'Two per cent,' Meredith says confidently.

'Two per cent was the number from two years ago, Meredith,' Camilla says curtly. 'The entire machine of the Psychiatry department is alert to suicide prevention, and since Stuart's been here, he's brought that down to point five per cent. I know you have issues with Mark,' she says, putting up a hand as Meredith rolls her eyes, 'but that stat is the lowest in the nation, and it's a credit to Stuart and his team, including Mark. You know St Jude's mission is to understand and treat vulnerable populations. Stuart's helped us achieve so much towards that aim. He's been immeasurably helpful with funders and donors, in a very short space of time.'

Meredith can feel where this is going. She and Camilla have spoken before about the competition between her and Mark. To date, Meredith has failed every opportunity for diplomacy. 'Look,' she says, 'I'm not judging Stuart or Mark or Psych. I'm just setting out the common factors between each patient, and Mark Roth was the psychiatrist for all three—'

'No, Meredith,' Camilla cuts in. 'That's not what you're doing. If you're looking for common factors, where are the names of the other doctors, nurses, pathologists, porters, record keepers, these girls share?' She doesn't wait for an answer. 'If Mark is a suspicious common factor because he treated each of these girls, then we're all suspects. What about you, Meredith? Surely your name should appear on each of these girl's files?'

Meredith understands the logic but her mind races through the facts. She actually *can't* confirm if there are any other hospital professionals common to the women. *She* never saw

Patrice. It may very well be that Mark *is*, indeed, the only common factor – but she knows she hasn't asked herself this. With Camilla calling her on it, she sees that her antipathy for Mark led to a short cut that she took with reckless pleasure. When she found Mark's name in each of these women's files, she was satisfied and stopped hunting.

Meredith pauses, grappling for a means to continue to press her point, trying to keep a shrill tone out of her voice. 'I take your point, Camilla, and I'm not here to accuse Mark. But he's a common thread, and the gaps in the records don't make me feel sympathetic to him.'

'Well, I agree with you on that point,' Camilla says quietly, staring at the wall like she wants to put her fist through it. Then she looks at Meredith. More forcefully, she says, 'It's against hospital policy for doctors to keep separate files on patients. We don't have time for prima donnas who set up independent filing systems. I'll take it up with Stuart Chester. It's his business to fix it. But, please, Meredith, ask yourself what's driving you to link this to Mark.'

Meredith pauses again. There are so many things she could say, where should she start?

'You haven't liked Mark since Stuart brought him on board. Why?'

Meredith looks away, feeling her throat tighten. The meeting room walls seem closer and, for a moment, she is somewhere else. She tastes whisky on her tongue, smells hot breath on her face, feels a man's hand around her neck. The sound of university students, partying on the other side of a closed door, rumbles away in a far corner of her mind. Her hand goes up in defence and claws at a man's face.

'You and Mark were in first-year pre-med together at New Westdale University,' she hears Camilla saying. 'He told me so.'

It takes Meredith a second to collect herself. 'Yes, we were,' she says, brushing away the topic like it's nothing. 'And that was a lifetime ago.'

Intent on steering the conversation elsewhere, Meredith launches down another track: 'Camilla, we know that three girls have died of a very similar injury. The police know about Patrice, but they don't know about Katherine or Tabitha. We're withholding information that could be critical to an investigation. This needs to be shared with the police.'

Camilla shakes her head and looks at Meredith as if she's lost her mind. 'For goodness sake, you're my best senior manager – you know the protocol.' She shoves the report back in the file. 'There won't be any discussion with the police until I speak to Lachlan Murphy.' Handing the file back to Meredith, she says crisply, 'No further steps until we get legal advice.'

Thinking of St Jude's general counsel makes Meredith's guts twist. 'Right,' she says, trying not to sound sarcastic. Lachlan Murphy is a man Camilla usually works hard to avoid – he's the official liaison between St Jude and the Vatican, and a strident Catholic. Putting the lives of these young women under his gaze? Meredith imagines Lachlan locking the report away, never to be seen again.

Camilla stands up to signal the meeting is over and, for a brief moment, her face becomes more open. 'As always, Meredith, you must act in accordance with your conscience.' For a second, Meredith sees the compassion that she relies on so deeply from Camilla, but the moment passes. 'You yourself have suggested these women could be involved in some strange community of self-harmers, or could be following internet sites that promote self-injury. To jump so quickly to the conclusion that this is a problem in our Psych department feels really premature. This is a legal matter with serious implications,

Meredith – not just for Mark, or for the clinic, but for the hospital too. It's Lachlan's job to tell us what to do.'

Camilla looks at her watch and pushes the report back to Meredith. 'Email a copy of the report to me and I'll let you know how I go with him.' Her tone gives nothing away and her face is expressionless. 'I'm sorry, but I have to attend the budget session at the board meeting. It's due to start in ten. Are we good here?'

Before Meredith can respond, Jessica runs into the room, holding a folded piece of paper. 'Another note,' she says, giving it to Camilla.

'What do you mean?' she asks, not looking up as she arranges her papers and prepares to leave.

'Another note from Lachlan.'

Camilla's head shoots up. 'Oh, for god's sake,' she mutters under her breath. 'Can't the man pick up a phone?'

She catches herself when she sees Jessica and Meredith watching her, says a quick goodbye and leaves. When Camilla's out of hearing range, Meredith sidles up to her assistant and asks softly, 'What's with the notes?'

Jessica rolls her eyes and throws up her hands. 'It's how Lachlan Murphy does things,' she says. 'It's his way of summoning people,' she adds in a whisper, putting air quotes around the word 'summoning'.

Meredith laughs. 'Handwritten notes? Seriously? That's just old school and weird.'

Jessica shrugs her shoulders. 'He's a Catholic school boy. Old school and weird doesn't explain the half of it.'

Meredith says her goodbyes and walks back to Emergency imagining her report growing dust on Lachlan's desk and thinking she may take a few days before she sends it to Camilla.

As she heads back to her office, her anxiety grows. Camilla's resistance is too unusual to pass off as her merely being busy.

She thrusts a hand in her lab coat pocket, feeling for a packet of Ativan. But then she makes a different decision – and reaches for her phone.

* * *

The envelope is tucked under Meredith's coat and its thick corners chafe at her skin. It's not until she's ushered to Leo's office that she realises how silly she's being. She may be at a police station but it's not like someone's going to stop her and conduct a search. She pulls the envelope out and waits.

There's no sign of Leo, so she stands just outside his door, trying to look natural, avoiding eye contact with people passing in the hallway.

She peers into his office, seeing typical public service fare – no windows, fluorescent light, bad air. Clean but cluttered. And not with the normal stuff of messy offices – there are no piles of papers or bowls of paperclips. The clutter is knick-knacks. They're organised along the front edge of Leo's desk like a line of toy soldiers, except each one is different: a stress ball covered in layers of coloured elastics, a small statue of a collie, a ceramic fish, a polished stone.

She walks to the desk and picks up the stone. It's glossy and dark green, almost black, and fits neatly in her hand. Hearing Leo in the hallway, she puts it back and walks out to meet him.

'Hey, Red. How's things?' he says, moving fast, as if between meetings. He goes past her into the office, motioning that she follow him. He sits behind his desk – all business – and gives her a sideways look. 'What's so urgent?'

First things first, she thinks, as she nods at the desk. 'Nice collection.'

Leo looks at the figurines. 'They help me think,' he says and then adds, eyeing her shyly, 'I have an affinity for small things.' Meredith registers the compliment and blushes, picking up the stone again. It has a white seam sandwiched between its dark green sides, shaped like a slanted eye.

'That's a beauty,' Leo says, watching her touch the glossy rock. 'It's serpentine stone. I found it up north, on the side of the Dempster Highway in the Yukon.'

As Meredith grips it, she feels its weight. It's small but feels substantial all the same. In her sweaty palm, the stone forms a cool circle.

'Looks like it was made for you. Keep it.'

Her eyes dart up at him. 'It's lovely, Leo. But I couldn't—'

'It's yours,' he says quickly. When their eyes meet, he looks at her gently. 'It may help,' he says, and when her forehead creases in confusion, he continues slowly, 'you know, when you're feeling anxious.'

Meredith just stares at him, not comprehending. He doesn't know about the Ativan, she thinks. How could he know? She never takes pills when he's around.

Leo runs his hands through his hair, his eyes searching the room. He motions to the figurines, 'I started collecting these little things back when I was at the police academy,' he says, reaching across the desk and picking up the miniature fish. 'I was recovering from a motorbike accident and started liking the painkillers too much. Before I knew it, I was addicted.'

Meredith watches him roll the fish between his fingers and thinks about her first taste of Ativan, back when her father died.

'Addiction is probably putting it too strong,' Leo says. 'Dependence may be a better description. Opioids became a part of my life – they calmed me down and made me feel less dissatisfied.'

She stays quiet and still, as if any movement might give her away.

Leo clears his throat. 'But let's say I *was* addicted. If I were talking to you about addiction, I'd talk about how widespread it is. I'd talk about how we group things into bad addictions – drugs, alcohol, gambling, illicit sex, sugar – you name it. We have countless ways to judge people with addictive tendencies.'

Then Leo gets up from his chair, walks around his desk and starts to pace. Meredith just turns around and watches. 'But we rarely talk about addictions to money, power, achievement, despite the fact that these addictions trigger the same brain chemicals and are just as anti-social.'

At this point he places his hands on the arms of Meredith's chair and leans over her. 'The human brain's a complex chemical soup, Meredith. Some brains crave altered states. Of course addictions need to be regulated, but they're part of being human, and regulating them starts with acceptance.'

He gives her a smile and she gives him a weak one back.

'Anyways. Lots of things helped me deal with my dependence. Dogs helped. Exercise and counselling helped. But so did these little things. They kept my hands busy. I could take them anywhere.'

Meredith knows it's her turn to speak – to acknowledge what he's saying and connect with him somehow.

'I didn't know that about you,' she says weakly.

'Well,' Leo says, sitting back behind his desk, 'now you do.' He pauses. 'And I want you to have the serpentine,' he says, looking her straight in the eye.

She returns his gaze and nods once.

'Right,' he says, rolling the chair back from the desk and slapping his thighs. 'Let's get to it – let me guess – you're here about the women.'

With the pressure off, Meredith relaxes a bit but then does a double take at the question. 'What do you mean *women*?'

'Sorry, I meant you're here about the young woman – the photos I showed you back at my place.'

Meredith pauses. Leo doesn't make mistakes like that. When they first met, he was lurking around Emergency, asking questions about a recent gunshot victim. Usually Ros handled the homicide detectives, but Leo had come with a warrant so, as the person in charge, Meredith got involved. She saw how his humour and humble politeness charmed the nurses, but for her, the attraction started when she overheard the forensic precision of his questions – 'Did the perpetrator ask for his friend before you applied the sedative or after? At what point in the procedure was blood taken? Is that a professional tourniquet? Can you show me why not?'

That day, Leo left Meredith his business card. And it wasn't until the next day that she turned it over and noticed his scribble on the back: *Dinner?* She didn't know it then, but for Leo Donnelly, that was a love letter. It took Meredith a week to get the nerve to call him, and one date for him to get her into bed. Her face gets hot when she thinks back to that night.

'I really didn't mean to bug you at work, but you're right, I'm here about the women,' she says.

'No problem, Red. You helped me. Now it's my turn.'

She stands up, shuts the door and waves the envelope containing the full hospital report meant for Camilla. 'I have information that you'll find interesting. But before I hand it over, there's a catch.'

Chapter 7

In handing Leo the confidential report on all three victims, Meredith had breached umpteen hospital rules and policies – it was definitely a sackable offence. But her cynicism about St Jude's bureaucracy rode her like a demon: *Camilla isn't going to do anything without Lachlan. He won't take it seriously.*

The bargain she made was a simple one. Leo got the report on two conditions: no one could know who gave it to him, and he had to keep the press out of it. Her reasons for secrecy weren't just self-preservation. She knew the police would crawl all over the personal lives of the three women and she didn't want the general public doing the same.

Now, a week later, she's at Leo's place, lying on his grey settee with Jezebel next to her, kicking herself for not negotiating a third condition.

'It's tit for tat, Leo. It's only fair,' she says. When he doesn't answer, she sits up and nudges Jezebel off the settee. 'Off, Jez, you have terrible breath.'

Leo looks at her coldly and she feels a sharp pang of guilt for being so harsh with the search-and-rescue dog. Jezebel whines and limps over to Leo's side of the room with her tail between her legs as Meredith considers her next move.

'Leo, I've done my bit. I've sat in Medical Records for hours on end. I've audited the files, I've found the gaps, I've broken hospital protocols and put my job on the line. I've given you everything we have. You *owe* me this.'

'Meredith.' Leo rarely calls her that and it makes her uncomfortable. It also suggests that she's made a tactical error. 'You're an anonymous source – nothing more, nothing less. You came into my office and provided me with information. I thank you for that, but let's just get one thing straight. We made a deal and I've held up my end. No one knows how I got my information about these cases and the media has been silent so far. I don't owe you more than that. Anyways – everything you've provided would have been delivered to me if I'd served St Jude a warrant.'

'But you wouldn't have *known* to serve a warrant if it weren't for me,' she says, hearing the whine in her voice. She decides to take a different tack. 'If you bring me into the tent and tell me what you've found, I can help you find patterns that you'll never find yourself. Like Tabitha Norsman.'

'I knew about Tabitha. I could have told you about Tabitha.'

'What do you mean you knew about Tabitha?'

'The night you told me about Katherine's injuries, I started looking into it. A couple of conversations at the coroner's office about suicides by females who self-harm led me to Tabitha Norsman.'

Leo stops, looking satisfied with himself, but Meredith refuses to concede. 'It would have taken you ages to connect the dots if I hadn't given you my report, Leo. And you wouldn't have even started to look if I hadn't told you about Katherine.' He had to grant her that much.

'True.'

Gaining ground, she presses on. 'And what if a new Tabitha turns up in Emergency?'

'Then you really are required by law to tell me.'

'By what law? What am I supposed to tell you?' Careful not to lose her footing, she keeps the melodrama out of her voice. The best strategy, she thinks, is to hold fast to her role as the aggrieved party — the one excluded from the investigation, undeservedly so. 'How am I to identify any other patterns if you don't tell me what I'm meant to be looking for?'

'Okay, Red,' Leo says, standing up. When Meredith makes to follow him, he shakes his head. 'Stay put. I'll be right back.' Juno, who's been watching the conversation like it's a tennis match, follows him out of the room.

Meredith slouches back into the settee and looks at Jezebel, who hasn't taken her eyes off her the whole time. The staffie's tail starts to thump. She struggles up and limps back to Meredith to sit on her feet.

'At least someone's on my side,' Meredith whispers, giving Jezebel a scratch behind the ears.

A couple of minutes later Leo's back with a bottle of pinot noir in one hand and the other behind his back. He plants the pinot on the table and holds out his hand, palm up. 'Give me your phone,' he demands.

'Why?'

'Protocol.'

She looks at him askance as she reaches into her handbag and gingerly gives him the phone. He isn't being that pleasant. She takes it as a sign that she's won the argument, but keeps her feelings to herself.

Leo pulls his hand from behind his back and shows her three files. He slaps one down on the coffee table, hard. 'Katherine Richardson,' he says. The second one comes down beside the first. 'Tabitha Norsman.' The last one comes down the hardest. 'Patrice Ladouceur.

'These are copies of police files,' he says. His tone is official and she feels like she's being read her rights. 'For the record, it is the eighth of July 2015, and the time,' he checks his watch, 'is 5.05 pm. Meredith Griffin, this is confidential and I am seeking your advice, as a senior nurse practitioner familiar with Psychiatry and Emergency medical protocols, on any patterns that you see from the information so contained.'

'I can't be an expert in this case, Leo,' Meredith says, taking a big gulp of wine and coughing when it goes down the wrong way. 'You and I ... our relationship ... they would tear my objectivity apart.'

'Don't worry, Red, I know that. You'd never make it as an expert witness in this case.' He holds his hand up in response to the stink eye she gives him. 'You know what I mean. It's not about your skills or your intellect or your expertise – you're just too close to it. You're an adviser here. No more. No less.'

She nods, and looks up at him with her eyebrows raised. 'Okay,' she says, 'I can live with that.'

'You should. You've graduated from whistleblower, to anonymous source, to adviser in only a few weeks,' he says and turns to leave. 'You're going to be here for a few hours, so I'm going to go braise some lamb shanks,' he continues, walking out of the lounge room.

'Do you want any of this wine?' she says sheepishly to his back, hoping he'll accept the peace offering.

He turns and says coolly, 'I'll drink from my own bottle.' Then he adds over his shoulder as he disappears down the hallway, 'and, just to be clear, Meredith, now *you* owe *me*.'

Hearing the distant sounds of Leo in the kitchen, she stares at the files. The room darkens with the dusk and a cool breeze comes in from the open window behind her. Pouring the wine, she considers which police file to start with, but then decides to open all three.

That the cases are related is abundantly clear from the files. Each attack followed a similar pattern and they all happened in private, isolated places. Katherine was found in a secluded washroom in a park in the dead of night, Tabitha in her friend's abandoned apartment, Patrice in her parents' ensuite while they were away. They're intimate places. To find each woman there alone, at a particular time, implied knowledge of their habits and calculated planning.

Katherine's parents had objected to an autopsy for religious reasons and the coroner didn't insist on one for Tabitha, given her death wasn't noted as suspicious. Patrice was the only victim who received an autopsy and her residence was the only place that received complete forensic review, immediately after her body was discovered. Significant traces of chloroform were found along her entire jawline, indicating that the killer's hand was large enough to press the chemical deep into the skin over a large surface area. It was likely, therefore, that the perpetrator was a long-limbed male.

The only indication of force was a slight bruise at the back of Patrice's neck. A note in Leo's handwriting on the autopsy report suggests that her head was held down against the lip of the bathtub, as the perpetrator pressed the chloroform over her nose and mouth. There was no other evidence of assault – and no evidence of self-defence. Nothing under Patrice's nails – no fibres, no skin.

Similarly with Katherine and Tabitha, the hospital reports showed no evidence of bruising, abrasions or scratches. The suggestion posed by Leo in the files is that, like Patrice, Katherine and Tabitha were chloroformed. Without autopsy evidence it can't be proven, but it's a reasonable supposition given the lack of other injuries. It was an indication of stealth – a sign that the women had been observed and monitored, and that the perpetrator waited until he knew he could find them alone and easily overtaken. Meredith shudders and takes a deep swallow of wine.

The police had searched all the crime scenes for the instrument used to make the cuts and in all cases, it was found nearby. The medical scalpel that Mark Roth had mentioned was in Katherine's pocket when she was brought in had been returned to her parents with her personal effects. A razor blade was found near Tabitha's body, with her fingerprints on it. A straight razor was found on the bottom of the bathtub where Patrice had died. Statements from Patrice's friends confirmed she had told them that this was often the instrument she used to cut herself.

In all three cases, there was no attempt to remove clothing, no signs of attempted sexual penetration, no indications of sexual predation or violence. An interview with the paramedics who attended Katherine at Victor Allen Park suggested her body looked 'peaceful'. Her skirt was pulled down respectfully over her legs. Her underwear, while soaked with blood from the femoral cut, had not been removed. There were no indications of her being hit, falling or being dragged. Her skin was untouched and there were no marks indicating impact.

Jason Scott, the senior paramedic who found Katherine, insisted in his statement to police that the placement of her body was deliberate. He'd had the foresight to take a photo as his attendant checked her vitals and, looking at it, Meredith can't argue with him. Katherine's body looks 'arranged' – this is the word Jason uses in his statement. She's wedged into the small space between the wall and the toilet, her legs tightly curled around its ceramic stem. Her arms are bent and her hands are placed under her head, as if she's sleeping. Jason's statement indicates that the particular placement of the body would enable the blood from the wound in her upper thigh to drain into the grate at the centre of the stall, masking the quantity of blood and making it look as though Katherine was simply sleeping. Jason said it was the strangest scene he had ever come across.

As Meredith thinks about it more, she realises that the placement of her body was the reason Katherine still had vital signs when the paramedics found her. It was so tightly pressed into the space, so curled in on itself, that the pressure on the cut slowed down the bleed.

The person who found Katherine's body corroborated Jason's description. The call to emergency services had come from a young man who was taking a short cut through the park. He'd used the women's public bathroom because the men's was closed for repairs. As he stood at the mirror, he saw the reflection of the sole of a shoe under the farthest stall, near the wall. When he opened the stall door, he saw Katherine's body and thought she was sleeping, but when he tried to rouse her, he saw the blood. A printout of the call report from Emergency Services was of a bleeding woman that looked like she might have had a miscarriage.

The clear lack of violence is corroborated by the forensic psychologist's report in the file. Its author, Dr. Rachel Gelfand, prefaces her conclusions with an overarching caveat: 'If these are murders, and the theories of suicide and ritualistic or fetishistic self-harming are ruled out ...' She goes on to say the perpetrator appeared to have handled the victims gently, with an apparent desire to keep their bodies otherwise unharmed. Specifically, Dr. Gelfand stated that it 'appears that the perpetrator went to great lengths to ensure Katherine was not hurt, bruised or scratched. She was carried into the stall, laid down carefully, her hands were placed under her head as if to protect it. This perpetrator took care not to inflict any injury other than the fatal cut.' Dr Gelfand's report stated that this was fundamental to the pattern of the murders to date – they appeared not to be violent crimes of passion, nor were they sexual. There was something else at work.

There's a significant amount of information in the files about each young woman's internet activity, but Tabitha's was the only one that showed any search activity for ritualistic cutting. A report from a forensic computer analyst in Leo's team, D Santander, suggested that she had spent time on dark websites that were information centres for ritualistic scarification. The three women's social media histories didn't indicate there was any connection between them or that they, other than Tabitha, frequented sites or groups concerned with suicide, self-harming, cutting or scarification.

All the places the women were found had been frequented by many people, making DNA isolation almost impossible. After Leo took charge of the investigation for all three women, he'd ordered the crime scene office to return to each location for retrospective forensic reviews. This turned up frustratingly little – as of the date of the reports, no similar DNA had been isolated from all three locations.

Photographs of the area surrounding the bathroom at Victor Allen Park revealed nothing amiss. There were no CCTV cameras: despite the public demand for them, they hadn't yet been installed in the park.

The apartment where Tabitha died was a shooting gallery. Her friend had called an ambulance and a member of Jason Scott's team had arrived and photos were taken. The police came later. The pictures show a small, sparsely furnished garden apartment, with garbage and dirty dishes strewn on the floor. The bedroom where Tabitha's friend found her had a single mattress on which Tabitha was found at the centre of a dark bloom of blood. She too was wearing a skirt and, like Katherine, no clothing had been removed. She too was lying on her side, as if to stem the flow of blood, her arms draped protectively around her chest.

The perpetrator had entered and exited through a window. There was a CCTV camera in the street but it had been broken for weeks.

Police walk-and-knocks turned up nothing. No one reported any strange activity on the night Tabitha was found – in that neighbourhood, people minded their own business.

Patrice's neighbourhood could not have been more different. Her parents' house is perched on Church Point – a lavish peninsula jutting out into Scots Harbour, on the northern edge of New Westdale. She was a popular seventeen year old, and many came to her party that night.

The Ladouceur residence has several entrances and exits, but the security system records showed that everything had been locked all night, save for the front entrance, which was how partygoers came and went. In that neighbourhood, every house has a CCTV system and the Ladouceurs' was functioning. But at around 2 am, approximately the time Patrice would have been in the bath, the CCTV powered down. The video recording simply turned to black at 2.02 am.

The police report indicated no damaged or cut wires in the CCTV system. Instead, it appears the system was actually turned off. It seemed that someone, who knew how to shut it off and didn't want a record of what happened the rest of the night, did it themselves – via the control panel inside the house.

Patrice Ladouceur's time of death was estimated to be 2 am to 4 am. The CCTV allowed the police to track who went into the house, and who went out, until 2 am. Whoever wasn't recorded leaving the party could be identified, which narrowed the suspects significantly. Of these, one person in particular stood out. There was a screenshot of him entering the house at approximately 11.30 pm: a slightly taller than average man, in trainers, dark Gore-Tex running pants and a hooded navy sweatshirt. His head was covered by the hood, so all that could be clearly discerned was his build. He looked between five foot ten and six feet tall, lean and broad shouldered.

The police had interviewed several of Patrice's friends, confiscated their phones and downloaded photographs from the party. Several photos were in the file but only one showed a man in a hoodie, standing at the back of a semicircle of people. The photo looked off kilter, as if the person taking it was dancing, and the man's face was cut off. All that could be made out was his jawline. His skin was fair and he was wearing a crucifix around his neck.

Meredith reaches to grab her wineglass, but just as she does, a crow caws loudly through the open window, making her jump and the glass topple. Red liquid sprays over the file and she races to wipe it off with her sweater sleeve.

She stands and moves away from the window, eyeing the crow perched in the tree, barely visible in the gathering dark. The small pitch-black bird looks at her with its head cocked. It must be young, Meredith thinks – it doesn't know enough to be afraid of her and its eyes are still pale blue, not yet darkened with age.

Standing in the centre of the room, Meredith looks down at the paper spread out on the coffee table, stained red. Blood, pain, trauma – that's her terra firma. She knows the world of broken people and she's trained to deal with death. But what's in these files turns her entire body cold.

Leo announces from the kitchen that dinner will be ready in ten, but she has no appetite. She gets back on the sofa and curls into a ball, letting it all soak in. 'Coming,' she says, trying to keep the exhaustion out of her voice.

Chapter 8

From down the hospital corridor, sharp conversation slices the air. As it grows louder, a narrow strip of muscle tightens like a vice around Meredith's skull.

For weeks, since Charlie took Bella to stay at Arden, her nights have been vexed. Sleep is fleeting and confused, tainted by a recurring dream – one that she can never remember but leaves her mind bruised. Sleep deprivation is turning her into putty. Her body feels submerged, her thoughts impossibly muddled. Daily Bella updates keep arriving from Charlie reporting that all is fine – so it's not her sister keeping her up at night.

The voices intensify, their harsh edges echoing off the hard tiles of the hospital walls. She starts to run when shouting erupts. Rounding the corner, she bumps into a young orderly, hollers an apology and keeps going. Around the second corner she sees the source of the fracas. Mark Roth's long neck is red with rage, tendons straining, as he bends over Sarah Sampson, a junior nurse, yelling in her face.

Ros has her hand on Mark's arm but he's oblivious, jabbing a long finger at the young woman. His bared teeth are white and sharp. 'There are protocols – the difference between life or death – learn them,' he snarls, shrugging off Ros's hand and turning in Meredith's direction.

For an instant, she wants to dash into an adjacent room to avoid him, but stands her ground as he bears down on her like a despot. 'What's up, Mark?' she asks quietly, letting her gaze slide up to his forehead, where his dark red scar is shining like an angry burn.

'Fix your fucking staff,' he snaps in her ear, as he walks past.

Meredith approaches Sarah but a look from Ros tells her to keep walking.

She can hear the conversation as she passes them. 'But I didn't *do* anything,' the nurse sobs. 'He's *lying*.'

'Why would he *lie*, Sarah?' she hears Ros say in a reasonable voice.

Her desperate tone turns angry. 'Because he's a *fucking prick*?'

It's the last thing Meredith hears as she closes her office door and she can't help but smile.

* * *

She's packing to leave for the day when Ros comes in and sits down heavily, legs sprawled in front of her.

'What was that about?' Meredith asks.

'Mark Roth targeted Sarah Sampson today.'

'Oh yeah?' Meredith says tightly. She slams her bag on the desk and throws some files into it. 'Since when does Mark lower himself to come into Emergency?'

'One of his bipolar patients came in off the street and was having a manic episode,' Ros replies, through a wide yawn. 'Oh god, excuse me,' she says, covering her mouth, 'I'm exhausted.' Finishing her yawn, she continues, 'We called Psych, and usually they send a resident but this time Mark came.'

Meredith tilts her head at the hallway. 'So what happened with Miss because-he's-a-fucking-prick Sampson?'

Ros smirks. 'Mark lost it on her. He said she moved the restraints and heightened the risk of injury to the patient.'

Meredith looks at Ros sharply and her bag sags, sending the files spilling to the floor. Ros stoops to help pick up the paper as Meredith's anger erupts. 'Since when is Mark Roth ever concerned about protocols in Emergency, Ros? I was here when he told the nursing staff to store the restraints in the closet. *Against* my recommendation. We had a big debate about it, in front of everyone – just the way he likes it. I said they had to be on hand, for quick access.'

Ros gives Meredith a knowing look. 'Well, the patient wasn't restrained fast enough and fell against an IV stand and some other equipment. He got some cuts and scrapes when Sarah couldn't hold him down. Nothing serious.' Gathering the last of the papers from the floor, Ros sits back down with a sigh. 'If the restraints had been where they normally are, it never would have happened.'

'So, Mark blamed her.'

Ros nods and looks at Meredith, annoyed. 'It's not the first time I've seen him do it, Mere. Give him half a chance and he'll bait anyone who looks like an easy target.'

'Fuck him,' Meredith says, thrusting her arms through her raincoat sleeves. When Ros raises an eyebrow, she barrels on, wrapping a scarf around her neck. 'I mean it, Ros. Thanks to the flu, we're short-staffed, the ambulances were five deep in the bay all day, we have level twos sitting in the waiting room for lack of beds. And he decides *today's* the day to bully one of *our* nurses? About his own fucking mistake?'

Ros starts to clap. 'That's the fighting spirit!' she says, giving her a big smile. 'Couldn't agree with you more.'

'I hope you told Sarah not to worry about it.'

'I did indeed,' Ros says, standing up and making to leave. 'She'll be fine. Sarah's like you,' she continues, smiling down at Meredith, 'tiny and tough. She can handle this. We'll put the restraints back where they ought to be. And,' she says over her shoulder as she leaves the office, 'make sure the bastard knows you won the argument.'

Meredith's skin prickles at the thought of Mark messing with her team. The man is like a stone in her shoe – this wasn't the first time he had targeted one of her junior nurses. Only six months earlier, a young Irish nurse on a temporary visa was caught in his crosshairs. Maddie O'Connor was her name, and Mark took too strong a liking to her. She happened upon them in the storeroom during a night shift – he had clearly cornered the young woman and, as Meredith walked in, saw her struggling to get out of his grip. They both acted like nothing had happened, but when Meredith tried to talk to her about it the next day, she burst into tears and ran away. Meredith was unable to convince Maddie to report Mark, and within a few weeks she was on a plane back to Dublin.

As ropes tighten around her head, she reaches for the lab coat hanging on the back of the door, her hand searching its pockets for a single-dose Ativan – but her fingers come up empty. She feels a sharp pang in her stomach, a piercing yearning for something to take the edge off, that feeling of lamb's wool around her brain, numbing her senses.

In the other pocket, there's only Leo's serpentine stone. She'd brought it to work after seeing him and it's been there ever since. She grips it hard as she starts to pace the room.

When Stuart brought Mark Roth to the hospital as his deputy, her life telescoped to the night she'd found herself alone in a room with him, at the first-year pre-med Christmas party. And from Mark's first day at St Jude onwards, they've acted towards each other like they did the day after that party – every interaction laced with anger and confusion, fear and shame.

At first Mark just put a little jag into Meredith's already chaotic days. But now his influence trickles through Emergency like a toxin. At St Jude, the Emergency nurses are in charge. The doctors follow their rules, falling easily into routines that have an inner logic and make their lives easier. But not Mark. He leaves his charts at reception, rather than in the filing cart, where she's asked the doctors to store them. Or puts his personal effects in places where they'll be convenient for him but in the way of delivering care. She's talked to him about this on several occasions but things don't change. He just laughs off her 'funny little rules' – particularly when the male nurses are around, all of them looking in her direction, chuckling when they think she can't hear.

She stops pacing about her office and looks around. There's nothing out of place but things feel touched, moved, picked up, put down. Not quite in their place. She closes her eyes, willing her nerves to stop vibrating. She's meant to be having dinner at Arden, to check in on Bella and get an update from Charlie, but Mark has soured her mood and she's so exhausted she wants to scream. Right now, she thinks, holding Leo's stone tightly, right now what she needs most is sleep.

* * *

Arriving at Arden a half-hour before dinner, Meredith takes a few minutes in the 'back garden' – Evelyn's name for her world-class heritage plant collection. It carpets a terraced slope with gravelled switchbacks, and benches placed at vantage points that each reveal a different view of the ocean.

This is where Meredith had come to escape the arguments that tore through her family's house when she was in her early teens – it was a comfort to be swallowed up by the vastness of the trees. The permanence of the natural world made her problems feel fleeting, and sitting under a canopy of leaves was a powerful antidote for two remote parents and a sister struggling with an undiagnosed illness.

'So, my dear,' a voice says quietly behind her, 'are you annihilating all that's made, to a green thought in a green shade?'

Meredith turns to see Evelyn smiling at her. 'Those words sound familiar. I should know them, shouldn't I?'

'You should,' Evelyn says, walking over and sitting next to Meredith. 'They're from one of Andrew Marvell's most famous poems.'

'I'm afraid I studied science, not poetry.'

'And you chose well,' Evelyn replies, wrapping her arm around Meredith's shoulders. 'But that's no excuse for not knowing poetry.' She gives her a squeeze. 'I knew I'd find you here. Dinner is ten minutes away and it's in the grey room tonight. I'll see you shortly.'

The 'grey room' is Evelyn's term for her smaller dining room that she reserves for family. While it enjoys its share of grandeur – soaring ceilings, elaborate cornicing and a lacey, intricate chandelier – it's muted, with light grey walls, and a washed grey dining table with delicately carved legs. The room is bookmarked by two large windows, the front one covered by layers of opaque sheer curtains that diffuse the light and give one a sense of being suspended in mist. The back window frames a grand westwards aspect, towards Scots Harbour and the vast blue of the sea. For all the room's delicacy – even the small fireplace, nestled in the corner, encased in white ceramic tiles, is understated – it remains intoxicating and, for Meredith, it typifies Evelyn.

When Josie tells her to sit, she sits, and when a glass of white burgundy is put in front of her, she drinks. She slowly closes her eyes, waiting for the headrush from the wine.

'Meredith,' Evelyn's voice chimes as she enters the room with Bella. 'It's been ages since you and Bella have been here together!' Charlie is right behind them with a fresh bottle of wine, followed by Josie with plates full of salad. As they all sit down to eat, the conversation whirls around Meredith, and she takes in the fact that Bella is not only following its back and forth, but often leading it.

As they pass the food around, Bella describes the game of draughts they played the weekend before. 'As we were playing, Charlie was researching how the rules of the game differed in various countries. So we got a commentary on the different interpretations you could run of any result, depending on where you were playing. Charlie, you're the only person I know who's a workaholic while they work but also while they play.'

Charlie smiles proudly. 'I'm a work hard, play hard kind of gal.'

'I'll say,' Evelyn says wryly. 'And not such a great loser. You were incredibly unsportsmanlike when Bella beat you for three out of five.'

'What can I say? If we were playing with Italian or Russian rules, I would have won!'

They all laugh. 'Spoken like a true advocate!' Bella says, raising her glass of water to Charlie. 'Remind me never to sue you. I don't want to play against you in any court other than tennis!'

Watching them all laugh reminds Meredith of how things were when they were teenagers, and it's a welcome relief from the thoughts of Mark Roth swirling through her brain.

'I expect nothing less from you, Charlotte, than a passionate defence,' Evelyn says. 'It's who you are – your first reflex is to fight for people. Just like Meredith's first reflex is to care for people. And Bella's first reflex—'

'Oh no you don't,' Bella says, interrupting Evelyn. 'You're next. What's your first reflex, Evelyn?'

Evelyn fixes her blue eyes on Bella and pauses. The sound of the sea comes through the back window and she takes a sip of wine. 'My first reflex,' she says, 'is to ensure each one of you fulfils your promise.' Her eyes stay on Bella and she repeats, 'Each one of you.'

All the women fall silent for a beat or two. But then, as if on cue, she changes the subject. 'Charlotte, help me in the kitchen with the tea and coffee, will you?'

They leave Meredith and Bella on their own.

'Trust Evelyn to do that,' Meredith says.

'Do what?'

'To always make her point.'

'True,' Bella says. 'And to do it in a way that leaves your dignity intact.'

There's a silence and Meredith feels Bella's eyes on her. She knows she's distracted – she's felt disconnected since she got here, with thoughts of crime scenes and bullies, and hospital administrators running interference against the investigation she knows must take place.

'Mere, you're doing it.'

'Doing what?'

She doesn't have to look down to know what Bella's talking about. She takes her hands off the table and puts them in her lap. But, within a minute, she's back at it – making sure the bottom curve of the knife, fork and spoon are in a perfect line, the wineglass is nestled at the top right corner of the placemat, with edges aligned, the water jug's sitting directly in front of her nose, above her placemat.

'Mere ...' her sister says.

Meredith takes a deep breath. 'I'm just lining everything up.'

'I know,' Bella says, smiling gently.

'I hate it when things don't line up.'

'I know, Mere. But don't fret – you always end up connecting the dots.'

Chapter 9

'The research supports my hypothesis: there are *families* of psychiatric disorders that affect genetically related groups,' Stuart is saying, as Meredith enters the large lecture theatre.

St Jude's new research wing has a lecture theatre designed for corporate funders, complete with mood lighting, plush seats and a million-dollar view over Scots Harbour. Stuart regularly holds his psychiatry seminars there, lighting up all three retractable screens with his latest research. Today, three of the most senior members of his staff sit behind him. Mark Roth's in the middle.

It's Meredith's rule that, given the number of presentations in Emergency that are linked to mental health issues, all acute trauma staff attend Stuart's lectures – which is why when she's late, she sneaks in sheepishly through the back door. But the auditorium room is so full, Meredith is forced to sit in the front row. The chair isn't comfortable, which vexes her, given the money it has cost the hospital.

Her mind is on the chart audit and Mark's gaslighting, but when Stuart gets a particular question from the audience, she resurfaces, concentrating hard on his response. 'The research is strongest in siblings – where a condition is turned on in one sibling via an external circumstance, and the resulting psychosis turns on a different condition in the second sibling. Usually the effect is pronounced when the second sibling is a carer.'

Stuart's eyes find Meredith in the front row and fix on her with benign curiosity. As he continues to talk, she can feel her blood pressure rise. She grips the water bottle in her lap to stop her hands from shaking, and the man beside her turns to glare when its loud crack slices the air.

'We've found correlations between schizophrenia and OCD/anxiety,' Stuart says, his words making her heart beat even faster. 'The research shows that the symptoms in one family member can trigger symptoms in another, without any previous indications.' He speaks directly to her, as if they are the only two people in the room, his fascination with her pinning Meredith to her chair.

'It's as if the genes are literally rewritten and family resemblances, in the form of mental disorders, are created right in front of our eyes. Once again, the disorders that correlate most strongly are OCD and schizophrenia.'

When Stuart's gaze moves away, it's as if she's come up for air, but she can sense the weight of her colleagues' presence, like a hard granite wall at her back. No one in that room is an idiot – many of them have known Meredith for years, and they know about her sister. Bella's been in and out of St Jude since she was a teen. Many of the older staff would be thinking that she and Bella are a real-life example of Stuart's research hypothesis. She doesn't have to turn around to see the looks on their faces – the mix of compassion and curiosity, their professional judgement.

Stuart must know about Bella, Meredith thinks. She's never been a patient in his clinic, but his talk seemed to be directed straight at her and her sister. Her skin prickles with discomfort.

* * *

As the small crowd files out of the lecture theatre she hangs back. When she dares to look up and sees pity on some of her colleagues' faces, a bitter anger trickles through her like an underground spring. She feels for Leo's stone in her pocket and squeezes it between her fingers until her eyes tear up from the pain.

Head down, pretending to be absorbed in the emails on her phone, she ducks into a side hallway and waits for the crowd to pass. Then she walks back to Emergency alone, well behind clumps of colleagues talking quietly among themselves.

Emergency is unusually quiet, as if even Meredith's own team don't want to associate with her. Back in the office, throwing things into her bag, she wishes she had given Stuart's talk a miss. She really didn't need to hear about a possible epigenetic connection between her slight OCD and her sister's schizophrenia. All it does is make her more tired.

Absent-mindedly she searches for her coat on the hook behind the door and finds it's not there. Shaken out of her funk, she looks around and sees it thrown over the chair opposite her desk. Paralysed for a moment, she stands in the middle of the office. She always hangs her coat on the back of the door. Why would she have thrown it on the chair, she thinks, trying to retrace her steps. But she's too tired to remember things – she can't even remember coming into the hospital that morning.

For heaven's sake, she thinks, go home.

She grabs her coat roughly and turns, flicking off the light and slamming the door, eager to put the hospital behind her.

She sees her old friend Jacob de Rhiz at the reception desk. 'Have a good evening, Jacob,' she says, giving him a wave.

'You too, Griff. Don't get into any trouble.'

She laughs lightly, grateful for his paternal attitude. Jacob has led the St Jude security operation for nearly twenty years and she's known him for thirteen of them. He's one of the saints of

St Jude, she thinks, as she walks through the parking lot – for the times he's seen her here with Bella, both of them stumbling through the front doors, him running for a wheelchair; for the times she's called on him to fetch the police, or help secure a patient, or escort a deceased person's family back to their car. Over the years, watching him get more and more frustrated with security roles, she coaxed him to lobby for a promotion. She'd even helped him with his application. Now, as well as running facilities security, he liaises with IT to keep St Jude's computer systems secure.

As she hears the click of her car door unlocking, it dawns on her: Jacob would know. He would know if anyone has been swiping into her office when she's not there. Jacob had programmed her a special pass that gave her access to certain areas of the hospital, including, when necessary, access to systems that allowed her to override drug counts in automatic drug cabinets.

She pulls out her phone and sends him a text: *Hey Jacob, Meredith here. I have a security question. Do you have a minute to chat?*

As always, he responds in an instant. *Call you in ten.*

Despite the brief lift the prospect of Jacob's help gave her, melancholy washes over Meredith. The idea behind Stuart's research, that she and Bella are linked by disturbed genetic traits, that they feed each other's mental health issues still feels too much to bear.

'I need to come to you tonight,' she says to Leo on hands free, as she drives under St Jude's stone arch and into the street. The thought of sleep makes her panic, she's so desperate for it. The early hours of the evening are a torment of anticipating the sleeplessness that will leave her strafed, her mind foggy and disoriented.

The streetlights reflect off the wet road like pools of broken glass. A heavy mist hangs in the air, submerging the street in an opaque sea. 'I'm still not sleeping,' she says, her words thick in her mouth.

'So come over. I'm making a comfort curry.' Leo's voice fills the car and wraps around her like soft wool. 'What do you think about that?'

'I can't think at all.'

'Well how do you feel?'

Her tyres slice through the deep water pooling on the side of the road. The streets are empty. There is only the sound of rain.

'I feel lonely.'

'Oh love,' Leo says gently, 'you're just tired.'

She stops at an intersection and breathes, waiting for the light to change, bathing in the sound of his voice.

'Come on now,' he coaxes, 'come stay with me, Red.'

Her route takes her through a street of elegant shops, and past a small restaurant – Le Brasserie, it's called. In the restaurant's front window a bistro table is set, where a young girl sits opposite a man who looks at least three times her age. As Meredith waits for the light to change she stares at the pair of them, convinced the man is the girl's father. There's a striking family resemblance but also a familiar look on the girl's face – one she knows she's worn in moments with her own father – a look of painful distraction, revealing she'd rather be anywhere than there with him.

She's reminded, with intense clarity, of the complex memory of her own father and realises it has three layers – yearning, when he was away for long and painful absences; confusion, when he was physically there but palpably remote; and delight, when he was actually present and wanting to be with her. She knows she used those few moments of connection to define their relationship and paper over his long absences and emotional remove, as if they made up for it all.

The light changes and she heads down to Leo's street, feeling strangely lighter. It's small and bittersweet but a triumph nonetheless: recognising the emotional separation required on her father's part, to have an entire family — an entire life — outside of theirs, and knowing what her young brain did to make that abandonment tolerable.

Her thoughts are interrupted by a call coming in. Seeing it's Jacob, she answers.

'Hey, Jacob. How's things?'

'Not bad, Meredith. What can I do for you?'

'This is going to sound strange but I'm getting an odd feeling that someone's been in my office. It could be nothing, but I'm wondering if you could search the system records to see if anyone's recently had access?'

'Sure I can, but can you tell me what's giving you the bad feeling?'

'It's hard to describe. Things just seem out of place.'

'I've had that complaint before. Could it be the cleaners?'

Meredith pauses, focusing on parking in front of Leo's house. 'No, they know not to move anything in my office. I've talked to them — they know everything has its place.'

'Right, okay, listen, I'll run a check and see what comes up. Can you give me until tomorrow?'

'Of course. Thanks a mill, Jacob.'

She locks the car and, as she heads up Leo's front path, hears paws running along the wooden corridor that leads to his front door, then Juno's short bark and Jezebel's excited whine. The door opens and Leo fills the doorway.

The sleeves of his T-shirt are cut off, revealing the length of his arms. Meredith tries not to be distracted by their architecture – the heady mix of bone, muscle and vein. Juno is standing beside him, whining, her tail wagging violently, but he nudges the dog back with his foot. 'She's my girlfriend, not yours, Juno,' he says, laughing. Then he leans against the doorframe and smiles. 'A nice surprise to get your call.'

She smiles back, and then looks at him imploringly. 'I hope you have wine.'

His eyebrows lift at her tone. 'But of course, madam.' He backs up and motions her in with aplomb, closing the door behind her. 'Have a seat – I'll get you a glass.'

Meredith stretches out on the old grey sofa in the lounge room. Reaching over to give Jez a tummy rub, she pulls a book out from the seat under her.

'Sherlock Holmes,' she says, as Leo comes into the room. 'Is that what inspired you to go into homicide?'

'Nah,' he says. He holds a full glass out to her and she takes it greedily. 'I was just an angry young man, who wanted to beat up bad guys,' he continues as he walks to the chair opposite her. His voice gets quiet. 'You know,' he says, taking a long drink of wine, 'the guys who think they're god.'

The room is still and the smell of curry floats from the kitchen. He sits down and Juno lays at his feet. Unless commanded to, Juno doesn't leave Leo's side. They both look at her and cock their heads. It's charming, and Meredith chuckles.

'What's on your mind, Red?'

She sighs and throws her head back. 'Work, Bella, colleagues, patients – particularly the patients we've lost.' She intersperses all this with pulls at her wine.

Then she stops, and sits up straight to empty her glass. 'You know,' she motions to him with it, 'you and I, we get them when they're already cut up. We never get a chance to intervene beforehand. It's bloody exhausting.'

A shadow crosses Leo's face. 'I know. We're highly trained janitors. We pick up the pieces.'

They both stay silent and the dogs sniff the air. Meredith takes a deep breath. 'The curry smells amazing,' she says. 'Do you have any beer?'

'Sorry, Red.'

'Leo,' she says, shaking her head, her eyes wide in shock. 'You can't serve Indian food without Indian beer ... where on earth is the Kingfisher?'

He looks at her sideways. 'Woman, for someone so *privileged*, I expect you to have a more open mind.'

'But *curry* isn't *curry* without *Kingfisher*.'

Leo stands up with a sigh of desperation. 'Meredith, you can be such a snob sometimes.'

'I'm not a snob.'

'Yes, you are. Particularly with food. You insist on purity and it completely limits your palette.'

'How can insisting on Indian beer with an Indian curry be snobbish? What were you planning to serve, French pinot?'

Leo shakes his head and goes to the kitchen, talking over his shoulder. 'Beer or no beer, Silver, my Peshawari chicken is going to knock your socks off.' He stops and turns to face her. 'Anyway, it's not Indian. Just what do you propose I serve with a Pakistani dish? By your standards, we shouldn't be drinking alcohol at all.'

She sighs and rolls her eyes in exasperation. 'Leo, don't be extreme.'

'My point exactly!' he says, leaving her to stew in the lounge.

When the food's ready, they eat at the coffee table, tucking into the curry like two ravens on a corpse.

'Oh my god, Leo,' Meredith mumbles between mouthfuls of curry and homemade naan. 'This is bloody good.'

He nods but doesn't say anything and they both keep on eating until she puts down her cutlery and studies Leo's profile.

'You know,' she says, 'I really am a snob about some things.'

'Oh yeah?' he says, eyeing her sceptically. 'What things are those?'

'Men.'

'Oh yeah?' he says.

'Yeah.'

Leo puts his fork down slowly and deliberately. One arm circles her waist and the other goes around the back of her neck. His thumb traces her lips. Dinner's over.

Chapter 10

A crack of lightning wakes her.

She forgets where she is and jumps as another crack cuts the air. The four corners of the room light up and she realises she's at Arden. She'd come back for another dinner and stayed the night.

Thunder rolls overhead like a steam train.

Fully awake, she can hear that behind the wall of sound there's something brittle and human. A glass breaks and a voice cries out.

She throws the covers off and runs towards the sounds. She can't make out the words but recognises Bella's voice. She flies across the upstairs gallery hallway, the lightning flashing on paintings on the walls. She runs down the stairs and heads to the back of the house.

'Get out! Stop!' the voice cries and more glass breaks.

'Bella! Please, you're hurting yourself!'

The storm above is raging and the rolling thunder is like a landslide, burying them under a mountain.

'Charlie?' Meredith yells. 'Charlie!' she screams again, running past the drawing room, searching for them.

'Back here!' she hears Charlie yell.

She finds them in the games room. The back wall of the room is constructed almost entirely of stained glass. In the centre is an arched glass door with floral designs. Surrounding it is another arch, filled with more glass, repeating the pattern. Outside, on the patio behind the stained glass, a strong light is flashing like a strobe, lighting the room with changing colour.

Against this backdrop, Charlie is struggling to restrain Bella, whose arms are covered in blood. Her sister gets away, starts to run awkwardly, but falls in the blood on the floor.

Charlie has blood on her face – Meredith isn't sure whose it is.

She runs to them, tripping on the dark leather settee in the centre of the room. She sprawls along the floor, falling next to her sister, and wraps her arms and legs around her. Bella's breathing heavily. Her tongue is moving from side to side, her limbs jerking involuntarily. Meredith can read the signs – she's in the middle of an auditory hallucination.

Meredith waves frantically to Charlie. 'Get my phone. Bring the earphones too. And Bella's meds,' she says, as quietly as possible. Managing to pin Bella down in a restraining hold, she whispers, 'I've got you, Belle, it's okay.' She imagines the cruel voices that have taken hold of Bella's mind. 'It's Mere. You're safe. I'm holding you. Listen to me. Only my voice. I'm here. We're at Arden. It's raining. You've cut yourself, but you'll be okay. There's a storm outside, but we're inside. It's dry here. You're inside. With me. Listen to me.'

As she's talking, Meredith can hear Charlie behind her. She whispers to her, 'Find the Bach Preludes.' She continues to speak softly and calmly in Bella's ear while holding her down.

Charlie holds the earbuds out.

'Put them in her ears. Can you bring me gauze – or even a torn sheet – I need some pressure bandages,' she whispers.

They lie on the floor, Bella squirming underneath her until Meredith feels her sister's legs relax. Bella's arms stop fighting and her torso goes limp. Outside, the only sound is rain, the thunder having moved on.

From where they're lying she can see the entire expanse of the stained-glass wall. Several panes in the central arch are shattered. Dark liquid runs down the shards of glass still sticking out from the wooden window frames like crystal daggers. It's as if a flock of birds had flown into the windows, except that the shards of glass are lying on the patio outside. The bird was Bella. She'd tried to throw herself through the stained glass.

Meredith sees Evelyn rounding the snooker table, phone in hand, Josie beside her, and Charlie returning with bandages. As she wraps them around Bella's cuts, they hear the ambulance.

Reluctantly, Meredith retreats to let the paramedics do their work. Charlie sits her down and puts a glass of whisky in her hand, but when Evelyn drapes a wool throw over her shoulders she shrugs it off.

'I have to get changed. I'm going with them,' she mumbles.

Evelyn's voice cuts through like a razor. 'No, Meredith. You're not.'

Meredith looks around and sees Charlie wearing a coat, blood still on her face, walking out through the front door beside Bella's stretcher.

'Wait! Wait!' she yells, running after them. Evelyn reaches out to pull her back, but Meredith evades her.

Charlie turns and puts both hands up in protest. 'Meredith. Let me take her to the hospital. You can see her tomorrow. Please just let me do this.'

'I can't leave her, Charlie,' she pleads, looking up at her friend. 'Look what happens when I leave her.'

'Babe. This happens whether you're with her or not. I'll take her to St Jude and you can see her in the morning.'

Meredith turns to walk back to the games room, but then freezes, circles back, and runs after Charlie, through the front door and out into the rain.

'Hold on!' The paramedics take no heed and slide Bella's stretcher into the back of the ambulance. 'I said wait!' she cries, grabbing the arm of the closest paramedic. For the first time since the lightning woke her, she's crystal clear – there's no way she's letting Bella be admitted to St Jude Psych.

Charlie's already in the ambulance and looks out at her.

'Not St Jude,' Meredith says, pushing wet hair out of her eyes.

Charlie gives her a confused look. 'But I'd have thought it's the best place—'

'No,' Meredith says, shaking her head at all of them. 'Not St Jude. New Westdale General. Take her to New West Gen.'

'New West Gen's closer,' the paramedic says quietly, carefully removing Meredith's hand from his arm and giving his partner a knowing look. 'You're right. It's probably best for the patient if we take her there.'

Meredith nods vigorously. She stands in the way of the ambulance door closing. 'Charlie!' she yells over the sheeting rain. 'Promise me: You'll take her to New West Gen.'

'Whatever you say. New West Gen it is,' Charlie replies, concern knitting her forehead. 'Now, go back inside.'

When Meredith returns to the games room Evelyn is sitting on the settee wrapped in a kimono, legs crossed and spine straight. She's sipping a glass of cognac, studying the slipper dangling on her foot.

Meredith sees another glass of whisky's been poured for her. She sits down in the brown leather chair beside the settee, and wraps her fingers around it, feeling the weight of the crystal in her hand, the burn of the liquor down her throat.

'I'm not surprised Bella threw herself into the glass,' Evelyn says, breaking the silence. 'The storm was enough to drive anyone around the bend. And then to come in here and see that horrible flashing.'

Meredith turns to face her. 'What caused the flashing light?'

'Charlie thinks a branch came down, off the Arbutus tree. It must have set off the motion detector and then, I don't know, perhaps there was a short in the system? There's damage on the patio.'

The women are quiet, sipping their drinks, listening to the rain. Josie is quietly sweeping up shards of glass. 'So, she's woken by the storm and comes downstairs,' Meredith says. 'She sees images of flowers and leaves – that would have been what set her off, the slightest feeling that nature's on the attack.'

She walks towards the wall of broken stained glass. It had been the toast of the town when Evelyn's grandmother commissioned it – a painting in glass, an homage to the local flora. The famous glazier Jean Luc Dejureaux had flown in from France to handcraft it. As Josie starts to tape old bits of cardboard across the larger holes, Meredith tries to calculate the damage.

Evelyn appears beside her with the whisky carafe, and pours her another drink. 'Were you the one who came down first?'

'Yes,' Evelyn says. 'When I came down she was throwing her fists through the glass. The storm, the flashing light, the colour – Meredith, the room was madness. I can only imagine what it must have been like for Bella.'

They stand there, watching Josie, and the older woman shakes her head. 'Bella struggled with the connections in her mind even when she was a very young girl. I remember her like it was yesterday, when she was no more than seven, at one of your mother's birthday parties we hosted here at Arden. Do you recall? She was in a bright orange sundress and we were all standing around the barbecue.'

An image appears in Meredith's mind, of her sister starting to scream. 'I do remember, she was yelling at the cook.'

'Exactly! She ran onto the patio as the chicken was grilling, waving her arms, yelling "Stop! Stop roasting the chicken—"'

'"—you're upsetting the birds!"' Meredith chimed in.

They both laugh, but it brings tears, and Meredith looks away, unable to bear the guilt coursing through her. When Charlie suggested that Bella stay at Arden, it was precisely this kind of episode she had feared.

'I'm so glad I was here,' Meredith says, almost to herself.

'Well, I wish you weren't.'

She turns to Evelyn. 'I'm so, so sorry,' she gushes, stumbling over a sob. 'I'll put this right, we'll hire the best artisans to restore the glass. Whatever it takes—'

'Oh, shush, dear,' Evelyn says, putting her arm around Meredith. 'What I meant was that I wish you hadn't been here for Bella's attack. Charlie and I could have handled this. The whole point of having Bella stay at Arden was to give you a break. You know as well as I do that, more often than not, she has psychotic episodes when any one of us three is around – we're the ones she trusts. In many ways, she knows her own mind – she knows she's safe with us.'

Evelyn takes her hand and pulls her back to the sofa, and when they sit down, keeps hold of it firmly. 'Meredith, how long have we known each other? Almost twenty-five years?' Her thin face is sculpted by the dim light, her high cheekbones prominent, large blue eyes heavily lidded. 'If you hadn't had a mother, I would have taken you in, like I did Charlie. God knows there were times I wanted to, regardless.'

Meredith looks at her with surprise, and Evelyn returns the look with an uncompromising stare. 'Absolutely I wanted to and I make no apology for it. You don't have to be mine for me to love you. Whenever Elizabeth fell into one of her depressive troughs, I wanted to take you away from that house and tuck you away here, where I could keep a proper eye on you.'

Evelyn turns to take another sip of cognac and Meredith can see her eyes glisten.

'And then you were alone. Dad leaves. Mom dies. Then Dad's plane crashes into the Bering Strait. All of a sudden, at nineteen, you're an orphan. With no one to help you take care of Bella.' Evelyn gives her hand a squeeze. 'It all happened very fast, didn't it?

'And how did you cope?' Without waiting for an answer, she continues, turning to face Meredith directly. 'You threw yourself into looking after Bella. You became her saviour.'

Meredith opens her mouth to protest but then thinks better of it. Evelyn holds her hand, keeping her on the sofa. 'Hold on, this needs to be said.'

Meredith sits in silence, listening to Josie still taping bits of cardboard over the broken windowpanes.

'You insist on carrying the entire load of Bella's schizophrenia. Why?'

When Meredith makes a point of looking away, Evelyn presses on. 'It's an intrusive question, I know, but it must be asked.'

She keeps her eyes fixed on Meredith. 'Why do you think you can single-handedly save your sister?'

Meredith breathes in heavily and then exhales her answer: 'I don't know – she's my sister, Evelyn.'

'Of course she is. But why do you insist on doing it alone?'

Meredith doesn't have an answer, so takes another pull at her whisky glass.

'Listen to me,' Evelyn says, squeezing Meredith's hand again. 'Be helpful to Bella. Use your intelligence for Bella. Go ahead and break the rules for her if you have to. I'm with you all the way.'

Then she stops before continuing. 'But you have to stop trying to save everyone, Meredith. No one will respect you for it. Martyrs don't end up saving the world. They just end up crucified.'

Chapter 11

The bodies are laid out on the stainless steel tables in the post-mortem room. Four naked men with crisp white sheets covering their lower halves. At least they're cleaned up, she thinks gratefully. Only one cadaver shows signs of the brain injuries that killed them all.

The pathologist walks into the room and gives Meredith a grim look. He talks in a quiet tone, sombre as a priest, noting how unfortunate the circumstances are. She can only nod in agreement.

A hydroplaning lorry on the Georgia Bridge jack-knifed. Three oncoming cars slid under the lorry's careening trailer, which sliced off the tops of two of them like a knife through cheese. Drivers and passengers alike suffered critical injuries but the ones lying in the morgue took the brunt of the impact. The man lying in front of Meredith is almost decapitated.

Emergency staff are still on high alert, handling the critically injured, and Ros is sitting with the lorry driver, who's unable to string a sentence together. Meredith's in the morgue to help the pathologist identify which body is which, before the families come in to claim their dead.

They do their work quietly: Meredith, the pathologist and the attending doctor. They work through the paramedic records and the hospital admission files, until they agree which name goes with which corpse.

When the job is done, she leaves the morgue in a dark cloud, a tight band of fatigue across her eyes. The recurring dream came back the night before. She still can't piece it together – she's crawling upwards, then the sandy ground slips beneath her. There's a feeling of free fall, and then she's awake and anxious for the rest of the night.

Hunger pulls at her belly. Its midafternoon and she's not had a moment to eat. Outside the morgue, she glances up and down the hallway, unable to decide the fastest way to the canteen, sleep deprivation making the simplest decision hard.

Then she catches something in her peripheral vision. It's a shadow – a figure. Then it's gone. It was a man – she's sure of it – of taller than average height, stepping quickly around the corner, dressed in dark clothes, wearing a dark hoodie.

Like a slide show on warp speed, the photos from Patrice's police file flash before her eyes. The CCTV screenshot of a taller than average figure standing at the door of Patrice's house in dark Gore-Tex running pants; the image of a figure in a crowd of people, wearing a dark hoodie and a crucifix.

Meredith runs after the figure, rounds the corner and sees it again. She yells, 'Wait! Stop!' but it's at the end of the corridor, going round another corner. She sprints, turns the next corner – it's gone. She keeps sprinting. Around another corner, she sees the emergency exit to parking lot D slam shut. She accelerates towards the door, the walls of the hallway compressing around her. She throws it open and stands there, breathless, scanning the parking lot, scouring the space for movement, searching the exits.

There's nothing. No one.

Her heart is going like a trip hammer.

Breathless, she leans against the cement wall, her eyes raking over the rows of parked cars. The lot is cavernous and silent.

She was sure she saw a dark figure dressed like the man at Patrice's door the night of her party.

But she's so tired, maybe she didn't?

She can barely remember her name these days.

Fatigue can so often play tricks on your mind.

* * *

Back in Emergency things have started to settle down. When Meredith knows her staff have all had a chance to rest and eat, she sees an opportunity to get some air.

The stone paths in the St Jude patient garden are slick from a recent shower. The rain has stopped, and she steps carefully towards a covered gazebo, chewing on a cheese sandwich, grateful for the solitude. The bench in the gazebo gives her a view of the entire garden. In a quiet corner stands another statue of St Jude, smaller than the one at the front of the hospital. He's holding a club to signify how he was supposedly martyred. The rectangular plinth on which he stands has engraved words by AL Gordon: *Two things stand like stone, kindness in another's troubles, courage in one's own.*

In the garden, cedar branches hang low and sloppy. The ferns at their feet are a deep luscious green, spread open, like long tongues licking in the moisture. Beyond that, the flower gardens are pulverised from the months of rain, but their greens and browns still pulse with the promise of vigour. The air is thick with the smell of mud and leaf mulch, and she breathes it in deeply, drinking in the scent of raw earth.

She slips her hand into the deep pocket of her lab coat, reaching for the cool, smooth surface of the serpentine stone.

She runs her thumb over its solid curves and feels the weight of it in her hand, anchoring her to the ground, clearing her head. She pulls it out and holds it on her palm, her arm stretched out in front of her, letting water drip from the gazebo's eaves onto its glossy surface.

'Meredith.' Her head snaps up at the sound of her name. She sees Stuart, Mark and Jacob standing by her, their hair wet with sweat and rain. She realises Stuart's looking at the stone.

'Is that your talisman?' he asks gently, head cocked to one side, looking intently at her face. She quickly drops the stone back into her pocket, not able to bear him studying it. The less he thinks he knows about her, the better, particularly after his talk the other day.

'Just something I picked up,' she says, painting on a confident grin. 'What are you all up to?'

'Just finished ten k,' Jacob says brightly. She remembers the running paths that circle Dorset Point and lead up the cliffs to the St Jude patient garden. The gates from those paths to the courtyard remain open during the day. That must be how they got in without her noticing, from the back.

'Sorry, no time to chat,' Mark says, looking at his watch. 'I've got to get back for a patient session.' He nods to Meredith and turns to leave.

'Wait, I'm coming,' Stuart responds. As he turns to follow Mark, he casts a long glance at Meredith, a searching look in his eyes. 'Ms Griffin,' he says, nodding a farewell and giving her a kind smile.

Jacob winks at her, turning to leave, then turns back. 'Shit!' he whispers. 'I owe you security information! I'm sorry, Meredith, that slipped off my plate.'

'It's okay, just whenever you can, Jacob,' she says quietly, not wanting Stuart or Mark to hear.

'I'll run the report today and call you as soon as I can,' he says. 'Promise.'

Meredith watches him jog away to join Stuart and Mark, who are well ahead, Mark gesturing and joking with Stuart. They're so different, she thinks – Mark so arrogant, Stuart so relaxed and inclusive – it's perplexing how they manage to work together. She sees Mark give Jacob a slap on the back and feels a jab of disappointment that Jacob and Mark are friendly. She's always been a bit like that – wanting the good guys all to herself. As they retreat into the distance, they're all silhouetted against the dim sky, dressed in the Gore-Tex pants and dark hoodies of the St Jude running club.

Her heart drops, and then starts to pound.

Fumbling for her phone, she takes a picture of the three of them as they walk away. All long legged, fit. All slightly taller than average. All dressed in dark hoodies.

She sends the photo to Leo with a text: *check photo of suspect at party – any insignia on clothes? st jude running club?*

Meredith's pulse races as she heads back to her office. Once there, she starts to run through the roster for the following week but can't concentrate. Her head is tight with exhaustion and she feels the beginning of a migraine. Distracted, she glances at her phone – hoping to hear from Bella, Leo, Charlie, anyone. Seeing no messages, she throws the phone on her desk, sits back in her chair and looks around.

It's not just the outfits they're wearing that gives her a growing sense of unease. It's her office. It's changed since she was last there, but she can't tell how.

The air is thick with another presence, like a lingering cologne.

Frustrated that Jacob hasn't come through with the report for her, she texts him a reminder. Then she types another to Charlie, asking after Bella.

* * *

The dream wakes her again – with no narrative, just the insecure feeling of her feet on shifting sands, leaving her awake all night. She drifts off fitfully as the sky breathes its first light.

Meredith wakes up a second time, with a thick head, having slept through her alarm. She rolls over and reaches for her handbag, fingers grasping for the Ritalin that will help her surface.

Late into work, she's forced underground to find a parking spot. The quickest way to Emergency is through the tunnels, so she sprints through the dark corridors, her nursing shoes springing silently off the concrete floor as she texts an apology to Ros.

As she passes the morgue, she swipes in, thinking she'll invite Ben to lunch, but overhears familiar voices coming from the post-mortem room. When she recognises Stuart's languid Californian accent, she backs up into the tiny alcove in the morgue's anteroom.

'Yes, I saw the email, and of course I'll respond, but we've had a psychiatrist on parental leave and another on vacation,' Stuart drawls.

'Yes, but even when we get Psych department files, Stuart, they're incomplete.' Camilla's faint Filipino accent is emerging, as it always does when she's close to anger. It's a way of speaking she's learned to mask – a cold, rough rhythm she learned growing up in the streets of Manila. 'We've taken a look recently. Mark Roth, for example – his counselling records from the Outpatient Clinic are *non-existent.*'

Stuart's tone becomes increasingly tense. 'Don't single out Mark, Camilla, he's just following protocol. His sessions with patients are recorded. The transcripts are then summarised for research. Mark hasn't done anything wrong.'

'Regardless of how your department runs its patient sessions, Stuart, the hospital policy is clear: your department must not keep a separate set of files hidden away from hospital management. Ghost files are utterly unacceptable. We've talked about this.'

Another pause and then Meredith hears Stuart's response – he speaks slowly and kindly, as if he's with a patient. 'Camilla, they're *outpatient* files, not hospital files. We're dealing with extremely sensitive medical information at the clinic. It's best for the patients that we keep it quarantined.'

An edge in his voice has started to surface and Meredith knows it will grate on Camilla. She's the deputy CEO and he's the key to a spectacular amount of private sector funds, most recently from Biophysica, a multinational pharmaceutical company. It doesn't sound like the first time they've crossed swords.

'Stuart, don't try and change the rules. Not with me.' Meredith can hear the anger as Camilla's accent gets heavier. 'The *core* focus of your research is the efficacy of medication and psychotherapy. You got your funding from this hospital on the basis that the research would be undertaken in *fully integrated* care. How can it be integrated if your colleagues can't see what you are doing?' Camilla's voice gets both softer and steelier. 'If you don't fulfil your side of the bargain, the hospital has no obligation to continue to fund you.'

Stuart's chuckle bounces off the tiled walls. 'We both know St Jude gives me a pittance, and if you pull your funding, Biophysica will pull theirs – not just from my project, but from the hospital too. St Jude would never survive it. Is that the legacy you want?'

There's a pause. Meredith strains to hear the quieter exchange that follows, when Stuart's voice becomes more conciliatory.

'No problem, Camilla. Give me a few weeks – I just need some time, space and a few more resources.'

'We'll help you with space,' Camilla says, her voice now calmer as well. 'And you'll have the full cooperation of Medical Records to consolidate your ghost files into hospital records.'

More words are exchanged and then a curt goodbye. Seeing Stuart approach the anteroom, Meredith bends down to tie her shoes. Looking up, she watches him stride out. She stays where she is until she sees Camilla leave too.

Both their faces are drawn tight and each has its own shade. Stuart's is red with outrage. Camilla's is as white as a spectre.

Chapter 12

The first nurse has arrived for the night shift and it's a welcome harbinger of the day's end. Meredith steps out of Emergency to stretch her legs and take some air, carrying a faint hope that, through sheer physical exhaustion, she may sleep through the night.

Dusk mutes the landscape as if a fine layer of charcoal has settled on the world. Above, between the tops of St Jude's pavilions, she can see the last feeble light at the sky's edges. Turning back inside, Meredith joins the sombre march of nurses at shift end, all of them moving like tired oxen as if the air has become viscous, their limbs lead. They silently pad around, each in their own monastic silence, contemplating what comes next – the bus ride home, domestic chores. Spouses, kids, happenstance lovers.

Out of nowhere, the sharp ring of the bat phone rips through the air. With a collective heave, they all bear down against the onslaught, as the faint wail of a siren grows, and then keens through the corridors.

The ambulance drives in at speed, braking loudly. Two paramedics hop out, and pull open the back door violently. They lunge into the ambulance and Meredith can hear shouting. The triage nurse on duty runs to help and then runs back in, shouting, 'Two injured. Heavy bleeding. Double gunshot wound. Skull fracture. Paras think they're using meth. They've identified one of the injured. It's a man – Mark Roth's patient.'

'Call Mark,' Meredith says quickly.

A paramedic is using his body to hold one of the men down while trying to restrain him to the gurney – Meredith runs to his side to help. Whatever drug is in his veins pumps furious power to the man's muscles – the paramedic's face is bleeding from his flailing, scratching hands. Finally restrained, the patient tries to sit up, pulling against the restraints, wheezing heavily, his neck ropey with tendons, and then falls back against the gurney, limp. She checks for a pulse.

'Ros!' she yells. 'I need you here!

'I can't find a pulse,' she says under her breath to Ros at her side. 'Start compressions. I'll relieve you in a minute.'

The other patient is wheeled through, eyes rolling in his head, right arm and leg jumping in random spasms. 'Severe bleeding from two wounds to the chest,' the paramedic says, as Meredith points him to the second trauma room. In the flurry of activity, she can see Mark towering above the busy nurses.

She waves him over and starts speaking in rapid-fire staccato: 'Two injured, the one shot is named Jerry Brixton.' Mark nods quickly. 'Paras picked him up at King and Jersey.' As she speaks, the restrained patient is being wheeled into the trauma room, Ros perched on the lower railing of the gurney, applying chest compressions.

'I know King and Jersey. Jerry goes there for drugs,' Mark says, his voice fast and clipped. 'What does he have on board?'

She shrugs. 'No idea. The paras think it's ice.' She points to his gurney. 'They're taking him to pre-op.'

Mark nods and turns to follow the gurney, Meredith close behind him – a second later, she hears Ros's voice yelling from the trauma room: 'Need help in here!'

Meredith runs in. Ros, still applying CPR, is flushed. 'Still no pulse,' she says. Meredith grabs the intercom phone: 'Code Blue – trauma one.'

When a third nurse – Judith – runs in with equipment, Meredith starts issuing orders. 'I'm running the code. I need the crash cart next to the patient, here.' She steps back and conducts traffic. 'No, we need it right here, next to the bed. Move it, please.'

Pointing to a fourth nurse, she spits out more orders, motioning with her arms. 'Val get the pads and move the defibrillator here, please. Ros, you're doing good, do you need a break?'

Ros shakes her head, focusing on pumping a clear rhythm, strands of hair hanging in front of her face.

Meredith motions to Val. 'Prepare to start the ventilations, please, right here.'

She glances at the ECG monitor and sees an organised heart rhythm. She shakes her head vehemently at the nurse with the defibrillator. 'No shocks – we have electrical activity,' she says, checking for a pulse. She squints at the monitor and frowns – the ECG says the heart is pumping but she can't find a pulse to go with it.

'Continue chest compressions,' she says to Ros, as she checks her watch. And to Judith, 'Bump up the IV and run the fluids wide open.'

As they work, she checks for a pulse again, the man's arm heavy in her hand. There's still nothing. 'No pulse, everyone; we have pulseless electrical activity and need to keep going. How's he bagging?' she asks Val leaning over the man's head.

'Okay – it's getting hard going,' she says.

'Check the secretions. We need more hands.' Meredith steps out of the trauma room and calls down the hallway: 'More help in here, please!'

She looks around. 'Who's running the paperwork?' To Clark, a nursing aide who's just run into the room, she yells, 'Get Sarah Sampson in here, please, we need her running the paper!'

A second later, Sarah runs in with Clark. 'Sampson, you're doing the code paper.' Meredith points in Ros's direction. 'Clark, take over the compressions.'

With her lead clinical nurse free, Meredith tells her, 'We need a doctor in here now; find Jackson and tell him we have PEA – fast!' Ros runs out of the room.

'Come off the chest each time, Clark,' she says, checking his handiwork, and feeling again for the patient's pulse. There's still nothing.

Meredith turns to Val. 'How's he ventilating?'

'It's getting harder.'

'Okay, keep going but yell when you need a break.' Meredith puts her head out the door and looks up and down the hallway, eyebrows knitted, searching for Ros and the code doctor. No sign of them, and she can see the bagging is getting more difficult. 'Judith, help Val with suction and get ready for intubation, please.'

Behind her she hears movement. Ros runs in with Dr Jackson. 'How long has he been PEA?' he asks.

'He arrived about three, four minutes ago.' Meredith replies. 'Patient went into cardiac arrest about a minute later. We've been doing CPR since.'

'Drop a mill of epinephrine,' he says to Ros, 'and forty units of vasopressin. I want the epinephrine every three minutes.'

Meredith feels again for the patient's pulse and shakes her head. 'Still in PEA,' she says quickly.

Dr Jackson runs his hands through his hair. 'Okay, people,' he says, 'help me out here – why is this patient still in PEA?!'

He leans over to listen to the patient's chest. 'I'm getting heart tones, Griffin – what does his rhythm look like?'

'Narrow, complexed, slightly tachycardic. Looks like his heart is compensating for something.'

'Sounds hypovolemic; are we running fluids high?'

'Yes, but maybe it's not enough? Do you want me to start an IO infusion?'

'Yup – can you set it up?'

'Yes,' she says, reaching for the crash cart.

Meredith takes the IO drill and injects it into the man's tibia, as Ros prepares another shot of epinephrine. They all watch Dr Jackson feel the man's wrist again, with Joe pumping, Val bagging, Judith suctioning, Ros waiting to administer the next shot, Meredith standing by, eyes on the ECG monitor.

Dr Jackson exhales slowly. 'Okay, guys – we got a pulse! His blood is officially pumping. Good work, Griffin and team,' he says, 'as usual.' He then turns to Meredith and says under his breath, 'I need your best in here to monitor this patient until we can get him a bed in the ICU. Let's go call Cardiology.'

* * *

The post-code bustle continues, but silence and order slowly descend with the steady beat of shift's end. Meredith makes her way through Emergency, ensuring things are put back in place after one of the hardest days they've ever had – that was the twelfth resuscitation. As she moves through the ward, watching the staff pack up, gratitude fills her chest, and she plans to speak to Camilla about doing something in recognition of how brilliant her team is. After arranging with Sarah to leave the code report on her desk to review before shift change, she makes her way back to her office.

When she gets there, she can barely grip the door knob. Her forearms and hands burn with fatigue after restraining Jerry Brixton. She remembers that feeling – the acute exhaustion after restraining Bella during her psychotic episodes as a teen. Her sister's fits were less intense now but her muscles had screamed with adrenalin then.

Thinking about Bella makes her nerves sing. After the attack she'd had at Arden, Charlie moved her to Glencoe – an assisted care facility for young people with mental disorders. That was over a week ago and Meredith still hasn't visited. Charlie's been handling it, just like she said she would, but guilt bubbles up in odd moments, distracting her from the present.

An image of a single-dose Ativan packet appears in her head. She shuts her eyes against it but the pull is too strong, and she grabs a strip of pills out of her desk drawer and swallows two down. She walks out to the drinking fountain and pours herself some water. Drinking deeply she feels the pills go down her throat, wondering at how even that small aspect of her Ativan ritual starts to relax her.

Ros and a few departing nurses are joking at the desk and Meredith walks up, putting an arm around her waist. 'So, Ros, tell me, would you still take a double gunshot victim over a few hours in Medical Records?' Ros starts laughing and the nurses join in. Meredith says her goodbyes and heads back into her office, grateful for having had a good laugh with the team.

In the corridor, Mark's talking with the paramedics. Walking past, she hears them exchange details of where Brixton was found, while Mark makes notes on the chart. The angle of light shows a small glimmering at his neck, and she sees it's a crucifix.

A minute later, she hears her surname being called and turns to see Mark walking briskly towards her.

He gives her a casual smile. 'A bit of excitement, hey, Griffin?'

'Not really,' she laughs, making it clear she's leaving and wants to keep the conversation short. 'Par for the course.'

'Right,' he says smugly, and as she turns away she can hear him mutter, 'Nothing that a few tablets won't cure.'

Feeling the last drops of patience drain out of her, she whips around and glares at him. 'What the *fuck* did you say?' she whispers.

He grabs her elbow and pulls her to the side of the hallway feigning a private conversation but making no effort to whisper. 'Meredith, I can tell an Ativan/Clonazepam addiction a mile away. Most of us can.'

When she feels the staff looking at them and then looking away, a lurid fury comes over her. 'Oh yeah?' she snarls in a whisper. 'Well, if you've got an issue, report it.'

'Maybe I should.'

The feel of his hand gripping her arm makes her want to retch, but she stares straight at the dark red mark on his forehead. The one she left on him that night, all those years ago. 'Go ahead.'

His voice becomes patronising and softer. 'Meredith, we both know you've had this dependence since university, but you're a senior manager now. You need to model the *best possible* behaviour.'

Having Mark Roth lecture her about good behaviour rips away every vestige of restraint. Her head feels like it's splitting. 'Don't you,' she says slowly, 'ever talk to me about good behaviour. Now, let go,' she growls, shaking his hand from her elbow and turning away, but not before whispering furiously, 'and if you ever touch me again, I'll report *you*.'

Back in her office, her hands can't stop shaking. A dark wave of anxiety surges through her as she thinks about Mark reporting her drug use to Camilla. She paces in a circle, trying to gain control of her breathing, trying not to vomit.

She doesn't just dislike Mark, she hates him and the strong taste it leaves in her mouth surprises her. He's a bully, she thinks. A predator.

'A murderous psychopath.'

She stops pacing. Did she just say that out loud? Her office door is closed and no one can hear but a big part of her wants to scream it down the corridors. Instead, she swallows it down, pushing the thought out of her mind. 'For goodness sake, Meredith,' she can hear Camilla say. 'Get a hold of yourself. He may be a prick but that's a long way from being a murderer.'

A brisk knock on the door makes her jump. She wipes mascara from under her eyes and tightens her topknot, willing her hands not to shake.

The door opens and she breathes a sigh of relief when she sees Ros.

'I'm off soon and just wanted to see how you're faring,' she says, her eyes scanning Meredith's face.

Meredith looks at her askance. 'What do you mean? I'm fine.'

'Meredith, you know I'll always be straight with you.' Ros's voice changes and Meredith recognises the tone – it's the firm, dour voice that Ros sometimes uses with her junior team members. 'The staff are starting to talk.'

As Meredith rolls her eyes, Ros puts up her hand. 'Listen. It's not just nurses' gossip. This tension between you and Mark – it's getting out of hand. It's not a good look for either of you.'

Meredith exhales, knowing Ros is right. She knows she can't afford to let the troops see this discord – and that they already have. She's felt them look at her strangely, seen them avoid eye contact. She hears sometimes, how their conversations go quiet, just as she approaches.

'It is not entirely clear what I can do, Ros. I don't try and provoke the attacks.'

'Well – he clearly has it in for you,' she replies. 'He's an asshole. Everyone knows it. But he's smart and Stuart Chester protects him – they both have powerful friends. I don't want you to end up like Valeska Stein, having to run away from here to save your career on account of him. Can you just stay out of his way?'

It's a little late for that, Ros, Meredith thinks as she looks at her young lieutenant. She takes in Ros's strong-boned, tall frame, her straight brown hair, pulled back in a band, her cheeks always rosy from running after patients, children, staff. Here's a woman who would stand with her against the world.

Meredith pushes Mark to the back of her mind and matches Ros's stare. 'You're right. As always. I'll do what I can. Now, go home. Time's a wasting and it's almost dinner.' She winks, making like everything is fine, and then turns her attention back to her desk. When she sees she's left a strip of Ativan on her desk, she whips her head around to Ros, who has clearly seen it too.

'If you end up having to do battle with management over Mark, those aren't going to help your case,' she says, nodding at the pills. 'They could compromise everything – your job, your relationship with Leo, everything.'

'Those are nothing to worry about.'

'You're a shit liar, Meredith,' Ros says gently, 'except when you're lying to yourself.'

Meredith sees the look on Ros's face. It's one she sees every day on the ward – it's fearless and loyal and righteous. And it's more than she deserves.

'You better get going,' Meredith says quietly, avoiding Ros's gaze. 'You've got to pick up your boys.'

Slowly, as if moving through tar, she hangs her lab coat on the back of the door and starts packing up, reaching automatically for her things: computer, budget files, coat, umbrella ... Her hand comes up empty. The umbrella is gone from its usual place by the door, where she always leaves it so it can drain. She looks around and sees it's sitting on the other side of the door. That's the wrong corner.

She stands there silently, looking around the office, trying to see if anything else is out of place. She breathes in deeply and walks out, closing the door, hearing the lock click securely behind her. She grabs the knob and pushes the door hard, trying to open it from the outside. The lock holds fast.

Meredith shakes her head, punching another text to Jacob: *How's that report coming?*

It's curt, but she's frustrated. It's not like him to keep her waiting.

His response is quick: *Yes! Sorry, I ran the report. Am in the chapel fixing the IT system on the lights. Can you come by?*

On her way to the elevators, she passes Mark behind the Emergency reception desk, talking to one of the nurses. There's a large mirror hanging over reception, allowing staff to keep an eye on the people in the waiting room. As she waits for the elevator, she sees Mark reflected in it, purposefully leaving his chart on the bench behind reception, even though she's told him, repeatedly, not to. She looks away, letting out a frustrated sigh, but not before she sees him looking back at her, with a smug grin.

* * *

The chapel is located at ground level and while Meredith prefers the patient garden, she can't deny feeling a sense of calm as she enters the quiet, dark space, lit by stained glass and soft amber light. Its location hasn't changed – it's still the same small chapel as when it was first built, although one wall has been removed, to allow for a breezeway between the old structure and the newer wings of the hospital. As she walks in, she sees the large wooden crucifix at the front of the altar, rich with gold inlay, and three tall, graceful candles on either side.

Hearing someone in the alcove next to the door, she turns to see Jacob fiddling with the controls of a lighting panel.

'Hey, how are you?' he asks.

'I'm good.'

'I'm really sorry that you had to chase me for this. I probably put it at the back of my mind because the report doesn't say anything interesting. There's no indication anyone has swiped into your office.'

Meredith doesn't say anything, she just nods.

'You know – how often is your door actually closed and locked? Could people come in during the day? Could it be someone on your staff?'

'No, they wouldn't do that. If a member of my staff needed something from my office they would ask first or tell me why after. And they're run off their feet – no one has time to poke around. So, no one's swiped into my office other than me?'

'No. Just you and the cleaners.'

'Well, how do you monitor them?'

'Very carefully,' he says, suddenly curt. 'But, you know, even that doesn't necessarily tell you the whole story. I mean, a cleaner could be in an office and another senior doctor could come in while they're there. Often, that doctor has a reason to be there. At least that's what a cleaner will assume.'

Meredith sees his point. She's often entered offices that have been open for cleaning. Many of the cleaning staff don't speak good English – it would be easy for someone with apparent authority to get access.

'There's always trade-offs in security,' he says, his voice getting quieter. 'You can build a system that's as solid as a German tank, and never have a breach or a gap or a breakdown. But with security like that, it won't take long for some people to start complaining that it's getting in the way of delivering care. You have to have some flex. And, as you know,' he says, with a pointed stare, 'there's always exceptions.'

'What do you mean? Other people have passes like mine?'

He sighs exasperatedly. 'I'm just saying there's lots of professionals in the building with special needs. You're not the only one.'

'Well, can you at least send me the report, so I can see which cleaners?'

'Meredith, you won't even know who they are. If it'll make you feel better, I will, but what do you plan to do? Interview them all?'

Meredith takes a deep breath. She knows he's right – she's not going to spend what little time she has speaking to every cleaner who's been in her office in the past few months. She'd just be putting them on the spot.

'Listen,' Jacob says, 'I don't have time right now to talk. They need the chapel for an eight pm memorial service and the lighting system has decided to play up. Here,' he adds, typing into his phone, clearly frustrated. 'I've just sent the report to your inbox.' He holds up his phone, just a little too close to her face. 'See? Sent. Just to show you I've got nothing to hide.'

Chapter 13

'You couldn't warn me?' Meredith says to Leo when she sees him at the entrance to the hospital, standing near the statue of St Jude.

'Good afternoon to you too,' Leo says, without a hint of an apology in his voice. He lifts his chin and tightens the tie around his neck. 'You're a bad actor, Red. And I needed you to be surprised.' He leans over to pick up his briefcase and then looks around. 'Now, which way is the boardroom?'

Two hours earlier, Camilla had walked into Meredith's office with a withering look. 'We received this late yesterday,' she said, handing her a piece of paper. 'Some decisions were made overnight.'

The document was a warrant demanding comprehensive files for selected patients – Tabitha Norsman, Katherine Richardson, Patrice Ladouceur and others, including 'all outpatient, psychiatric and psychotherapy session files created by Mark Roth, Stuart Chester and any other employee of the St Jude Outpatient Psychiatric Clinic.' The warrant was signed Leo Donnelly, Detective Chief Investigator, Central Crime Command – Homicide.

When Meredith looked up, Camilla was glaring at her. 'You're needed at four pm in the boardroom,' she said. Then she turned and walked off, leaving Meredith to stew.

* * *

An icy silence hangs in the air as Leo and Meredith ride the elevator up to corporate. The original floorplan of St Jude was designed as a Catholic cross, and the west end of that cross pointed to the coast, linking the hospital to the old chapel. When the elevator opens to Level 5 West, Meredith strides through the long corridor with Leo in tow, heading to the boardroom door that yawns open at the far end.

Before they reach the boardroom, she turns around abruptly and asks in a whisper, 'So you want Stuart's files too? Why?'

Leo speaks under his breath. 'Seems the practice in Psych is to record each patient session. The recordings get transcribed and collected for Stuart, who summarises them for research. I want everything. The whole shebang. But, for the record, Meredith, I'm not planning to explain my methodology to you.'

She stands aside at the boardroom door, and ushers him in coolly.

The table in the centre of the room is a thick oak slab, surrounded by twenty high-backed chairs standing at attention. Cardinals in full Roman Catholic regalia stare sombrely from portraits that run the length of one wall. Opposite them, the light from stained-glass windows sends slashes of red across the table.

Lachlan Murphy and Camilla are already there, sitting across from each other, waiting in silence. Lachlan scribbles in an open notebook, the dark fabric of his suit stretched taut over his beefy shoulders. Camilla's head is bent over budget spreadsheets laid out on the table in front of her. In the space that would normally have been filled with pleasantries, the air spikes with electricity.

Three years earlier Meredith sat in that room for the first time, after her promotion to management. Since then she's been summoned there repeatedly, to present case histories or defend hospital spend. She's accustomed to the room's heavy air: its dim lighting, its inertia. It strikes her as she walks in — how different this room is from Emergency, a space vibrating with energy, purpose and life. In comparison, the boardroom feels fetid, a neglected wound in the heart of that vast space of healing.

As Meredith sits down, Camilla gathers her documents and puts them in a file. Lachlan looks up and gives Meredith a cursory nod. His ruddy skin is thick with pockmarks, his nose laced with the fine filigree veins of a regular drinker. His eyes slide slowly between her and Camilla. They're a striking blue, but hidden deep in the rough terrain between his thick cheekbones and heavy brows.

John Cullen, the CEO of St Jude, arrives and Meredith gives him a faint smile. Stuart is the last to join them, walking in with a young, suited gentleman at his side. Stuart has a patrician air as he moves gracefully to a seat near Lachlan. He nods to Camilla and then looks over to Meredith, his eyes travelling over her face, before he breaks into a friendly smile.

With Stuart seated, John calls the meeting to order, and then turns it over to his general counsel.

'You all know why we're here,' Lachlan says. Meredith's been introduced to him before but has never needed to attend meetings with him. His voice is a deep bass — resonant and deliberate — and it roots her to the ground.

'For the record,' he continues, moving his head in the direction of the man beside Stuart, who Meredith surmises is a lawyer, 'I'm group general counsel, Sisters of Mercy Trust Holdings. I represent the hospital, and its owner, the New

Westdale Catholic Diocese.' He directs this last point clearly at Camilla.

A long pause follows, in which he puts his pen down and straightens his papers. 'This is obviously a very disturbing and sensitive matter – for the families, for staff, for the whole hospital. Of course, we'll support a proper formal investigation, but crafted carefully, to protect patient confidentiality.' He turns to Leo and assures him that the police will have open, unimpeded access to the Psych department's complete files – digital and print – whatever is needed.

Lachlan clears his throat as his gaze then turns to Stuart. 'The second issue we're here to address is personnel.' At this, he pauses and Stuart shifts in his seat. His eyes narrow but he retains his composure.

'With an investigation on foot there has to be a clear sign that the hospital is taking steps to secure patient safety.' Lachlan rubs his hands together, looking at John Cullen, Camilla and, finally, Stuart. 'For that reason, the hospital has decided to withdraw certain hospital privileges from Mark Roth.'

Meredith realises she's been holding her breath and exhales. Well, she thinks, at least that's something.

'The clinic's work and research will continue unimpeded. However, Mark Roth will be suspended as deputy head of psychiatry. We'll appoint an interim deputy until the investigation is over.' Lachlan gathers his papers together as if that concludes the meeting. 'Or until the investigation moves on, which I am sure will be soon.'

He looks back at John Cullen and, as if on cue, John cuts in with an apologetic tone, directing his comments at Stuart, 'Mark's suspension will be explained to staff as a voluntary and brief hiatus, due to personal family issues.'

Stuart says nothing, but nods sombrely, as if the decision was appropriate. The room becomes silent as his lawyer scratches notes on the legal pad in front of him.

After an uncomfortable pause, as if the whole room has tilted and no one knows how to right it, Lachlan describes the arrangements to give Leo access to hospital records. With a cursory nod to the table, Lachlan makes to leave.

'I'm sorry, but I must be missing something,' Leo says.

Lachlan turns his large frame to Leo, eyebrows raised.

'I just want to be crystal clear here. What about the Outpatient Clinic?'

The general counsel leans in. Like fog lifting, revealing the true mass of a mountain, Lachlan's weight fills the space. But, as if in counterpoint to his physicality, his voice remains melodious, transfixing.

'There will be no changes in that regard, Mr Donnelly.'

Leo's voice becomes gravelly. 'That's certainly the hospital's prerogative, Mr Murphy. But we're dealing with an ongoing police investigation, and the perception—'

'Mr Donnelly, if you had a case against any of our physicians, you'd charge them. Dr Roth was the supervising psychiatrist of the deceased patients. His contact with patients will cease until the investigation proves him innocent, but Stuart's outpatient clinic will continue serving patients until we think it prudent to do otherwise.' Lachlan turns to Stuart, who nods appreciatively, and then turns back to Leo. 'We're not going to do your work for you, Mr Donnelly – not at the expense of the patients who are receiving daily care through Stuart's Outpatient Clinic, or to the detriment of any of our senior physicians' reputations,' he says, putting heavy emphasis on this last phrase.

At that, Meredith can't contain herself. 'But if these women *were* victims of foul play and someone at this hospital *was* responsible, surely not doing enough poses just as high a risk to reputation.'

Lachlan stops moving and looks straight at her. 'Ms Griffin. If you're accusing—'

'She's not accusing anyone of anything,' Leo interjects loudly. 'Obviously, the progress of our current investigation is confidential—'

'Of course it is,' Lachlan interrupts, his voice even and reasonable. 'We're here to assist and we certainly don't want to interfere. But we're also comfortable we've struck the right balance – helping the investigation, maintaining patient safety, and ensuring valuable research and patient care can continue.' A mean smile crosses his face. 'And, of course, what we all have to do, Mr Donnelly,' he says, his eyes sliding between Meredith and Leo, 'is maintain our objectivity and professionalism throughout the investigation.'

John Cullen cuts loudly into their conversation. 'Stuart, we'll draft a statement for you and Mark to review. You'll need to ensure clinic staff cooperate with Mr Donnelly's team in handing over files and information. Other than that, the work at the clinic can proceed and the Biophysica research can continue uninterrupted.'

He pauses, thanks the room, and then scuttles out with a bent head, as if cowering from the cardinals' gaze.

* * *

It takes a few hours for Leo to make the necessary arrangements for file and computer transfers. When he's done, he picks Meredith up at Emergency and they make their way to Buzo, an Italian joint around the corner from the hospital. They're both silent on the walk through the rain, slouched under Leo's umbrella, his arm pulling her close. It's plaguing Meredith – knowing something of the investigation but not all. 'I'm still not happy you didn't warn me,' she says as they approach the restaurant. 'I've been wondering what you've been up to. I haven't heard from you since our curry night.'

'And what a night it was,' Leo says, grinning. 'I'm still recovering.'

'So am I,' she says, thinking back to it and feeling blood rush to her cheeks. 'But really, Leo, where have you been?'

'Red, it's not like you've been banging down my door to see me.'

'I know, but I'm relying on you to show some interest! You're a guy, isn't that what you're supposed to do?'

'Woman,' Leo says, stopping at Buzo's front door and turning her around to face him. 'I'm working day and night because I know this case is keeping us *both* up at night. And anyways,' he says matter-of-factly, opening the door for her, 'you're not police. You don't get to know everything,'

As they wait for a table, a familiar face catches Meredith's eye.

'Charlie!' she says, waving, and then turning to Leo with a half grin. They both can see Charlie sitting with a group of friends at one of the large communal tables at the centre of the restaurant. When she hears Meredith, she stands up and waves them to her.

Leo turns to face Meredith with a pleading look. 'Really? I'm *so* not in the mood.'

'Neither am I, but let's just say hello – it's time you met.'

'Do I have a choice?'

'No,' she says, grabbing his hand and leading him to Charlie, who is already waving down the waiter, arranging extra chairs, and planning for a party.

'Hello, friend,' she says to Meredith before training her eyes on Leo. 'You must be Leo.'

Meredith is standing between them, dwarfed by Charlie's lanky height and Leo's bulk. 'Charlie, Leo; Leo, Charlie,' she says. 'You both know about each other. Now you can see for yourselves.'

'Hey,' Leo says, smiling weakly.

'Well, well,' Charlie says, giving Leo the once-over. 'I can see why Meredith's been hiding you. You know, Leo,' she whispers conspiratorially, putting her arms around both of them, 'she may be smarter than me, but I'm better in bed.'

She clucks at the look on Leo's face and lets out a throaty laugh. 'Don't worry, Leo! I'm not into men,' Charlie says and then her voice drops back into a whisper, 'but if I were ...' she continues, cackling again. 'Please sit down. We have wine open.'

Leo pulls out a chair for Meredith at the end of the table. 'I was hoping for something stronger,' he says, his face softening into a smile.

Charlie's gang is friendly enough but too engrossed in dinner chatter to pay much attention to the new arrivals, so Leo and Meredith are left alone to ponder Mark's suspension, amid the noise and clatter of the restaurant. As they tuck into platefuls of fruit and cheese and sopressa, a double shot of Laphroaig appears at Leo's elbow, compliments of Charlie.

'We have full access to the Psych department files now, including all Mark's session notes and Stuart's summaries. It's a good result,' Leo says quietly between sips, stuffing a rolled-up piece of prosciutto into his mouth. He waves his whisky at Meredith. 'This is good.'

'I told her you like the peaty ones.'

Leo nods approvingly at her and continues, 'I've got the best computer forensic on the case. If there's any clue in the Psych department patient files, we'll find it.'

'I'm sure you will, but that's not what's eating at me.'

'Then what is it?'

Meredith reaches for the wine bottle and pours a glass for herself. She takes a long pull at it and then turns back to Leo, speaking quietly.

'It was just bizarre, don't you think?' She pauses. 'Why was Stuart so composed? His deputy's being investigated for three suspicious deaths and he's prancing around like it's nothing? And John and Lachlan, they just went on and on about "continuing the Biophysica research", as if that was more important than getting to the bottom of what happened to these women.' Her voice starts getting tighter. 'And Lachlan, acting like this was business as usual, Camilla sitting there like a *mouse*,' Meredith says derisively. 'It was just *bizarre*.'

Leo looks at her silently, mulling it over. He puts his hand on her back, pressing his fingers into the space between her shoulders, pushing into the tendons as if the answer to her questions were there. She closes her eyes, feeling her shoulder blades drop and her muscles soften. 'We'll dig into it, Red. Right now, every lead is precious. You're the one who brought us Mark – he seems to be a clear connecting factor. And now we have all the patient files – including the counselling records. It's a good lead.' When he takes his hand away, she opens her eyes and looks at him imploringly.

He grins at her, satisfied that she's satisfied. 'I need the bathroom,' he says, pushing his empty glass towards her and getting up. 'Order me another?'

When Leo comes back, he tugs at her sleeve. 'Hey. Hey, look. In the mirror – towards the back wall.'

A long, narrow mirror runs around all four walls of the restaurant, like a silver ribbon. Pitched at eye level, about a foot wide, it tilts slightly downwards, providing a clear view of all the patrons for the waitstaff: what they're eating, what they're drinking and whether they need a refill.

She follows Leo's gaze to a back corner table. In deep conversation, hands gesticulating, is Stuart, sitting across the table from Lachlan. The general counsel has taken off his glasses and is rubbing his eyes. He refills both their wineglasses and lays a hand on Stuart's shoulder, as if to soothe him.

'So,' Meredith whispers, 'looks like they're fast friends.'

Chapter 14

Lachlan and Leo agreed that the police would clone all the relevant hospital computers within twelve hours to ensure the Psych department and Stuart's Outpatient Clinic could continue uninterrupted. No uniformed officers were to search any office – all searches were to be done by Leo's delegates, in plain clothes.

'The plain-clothes bit was John Cullen's idea,' Leo says with a cynical smile as Meredith meets him in the parking lot, early in the morning after the boardroom meeting. 'Keeps up the ruse that Mark is leaving for family reasons.'

Meredith just raises her eyebrows. 'Everyone knows who you are. How will you do this discreetly?'

'It looks like Stuart Chester is at a conference this morning, so we're using his office to do all the cloning. It's all happening behind closed doors. I'm meeting Jacob de Rhiz this morning and we'll go to Stuart's office together. The announcement about Mark will come out next week, putting some time between us being here and him leaving. Jacob's a friend of yours, isn't he?'

'Yeah – he's a good guy. When do you think you'll be done?'

'Not sure – it'll take at least a few hours. Probably around noon?'

'Okay – text me when you're finished.' She heads to the staff canteen for a second coffee, before seeing if she can get a minute with Camilla.

* * *

Camilla's office is just large enough for a small desk and matching credenza. Jessica has told Meredith to wait for her inside.

Like Camilla's home, her office is spotless and free of personal effects, save for a framed photo on the credenza. It's of a much younger Camilla, wearing a modest black dress, smiling and standing proudly beside a very tall woman in full habit. They're both squinting in bright sunlight and laughing as if sharing a joke. The photo is amateurish and overexposed but captures a moment of pure joy. There's no clear indication of place but the women's surroundings seem shabby and poor. Wherever they are, it's definitely not New Westdale.

'I just had that photo framed,' Camilla says from behind her. When Meredith turns around, Camilla's putting on her glasses to see it better. 'I found it in a box of old things. That was Sister Marie Murphy – my mentor.'

'You both look happy.'

'We'd just opened up a women's reproductive health centre in the Philippines. We were *thrilled*,' Camilla says, walking around to sit behind her desk. 'The Church? Well,' she gives Meredith a mischievous grin, 'needless to say, the Church wasn't as thrilled. So,' she says, matter-of-factly, looking squarely at Meredith. 'Blindsided by the meeting, I assume?'

'You could say that.'

'Meredith, we got the warrant and acted quickly. I know you have concerns about Mark Roth, but a suspension was all that was appropriate. You can't take away someone's livelihood without evidence.'

'Of course,' Meredith says, gripping the back of her chair, trying her best not to blurt out how much she distrusts Mark. 'But after the meeting, Leo and I stopped at Buzo and saw Lachlan and Stuart there, having dinner. Together.'

She stops to measure Camilla's reaction. Getting nothing, she jumps right in. 'Did you know they were friends?'

Camilla's eyes narrow for a moment, then she laughs dismissively. 'I think they may have met at St Vincent's boys school, but even without that connection, it's hardly surprising. Lachlan's been on the executive of the hospital for almost two decades and Stuart's one of the best-funded research doctors we have.' She shrugs her shoulders. 'What do you expect?'

'Lachlan was protecting Stuart in that meeting.'

Camilla blinks slowly and pauses, as if trying to gather her patience. 'Meredith, you're boxing at shadows. Lachlan wasn't protecting Stuart. He was protecting the hospital. If Stuart's team is wrongly treated, it creates a huge reputational risk, for everyone. Just be patient – let the investigation run its course and stop jumping to conclusions.'

Meredith looks away and sighs audibly but Camilla just shrugs her shoulders. 'Lachlan's not the devil. He's a lawyer. He's simply protecting the Church.'

Meredith frowns at her and shakes her head in confusion. 'What does the Church have to do with it?'

Camilla frowns back and then laughs bitterly. 'Who do you think owns this hospital, the land it sits on and all the damn land up the coast?' She catches herself and sighs. In a more clipped tone, she continues, 'Look, Stuart and Mark are senior professionals here. Stuart's research has elevated this hospital and brought in national funding. Stuart brought Mark with him because Mark is a rising star. In defending Stuart's team, Lachlan defends the hospital. The Church owns the hospital. That's all I mean when I say he's protecting the Church.'

Subtlety has never been Meredith's strong suit and she can't contain a reckless urge to break through her boss's pragmatism. 'You and Lachlan clearly don't get along,' she says, her accusatory tone surprising even herself.

Camilla inhales audibly and stands up from her desk. She walks to the window and Meredith waits for the withering comment that is sure to come her way. Slowly, Camilla turns back, her voice quiet and cool.

'You're a professional, Meredith, with a job to do. Just get on with it. Don't get distracted. What you do at St Jude is really important. We need you to just focus on that. Let the police do what they're best at.' And then she adds, slowly, icily, a hint of the Manila street child seeping into her tone, 'and don't worry about Lachlan and me.'

Meredith looks down, knowing to leave the conversation there. She stands up in silence.

'One more thing before you go.' Camilla pauses. 'Mark came to me last week and mentioned some activity in Emergency that concerned him. I told him I would talk to you about it.'

Meredith inhales, waiting for the bomb to go off. Fuck, she thinks. This is it. It's happening. Mark's told Camilla about the drugs. Her blood pressure starts to rise. She opens her mouth to say something, but she's not sure what to do. Come clean? Deny it? Weak in the knees, she sits back down, the cumulative exhaustion of five weeks of insomnia falling on her shoulders like a pack of stones. This is it. This is what it feels like to be reported to the hospital disciplinary board for drug use at work.

'He said you all had a really difficult presentation – two patients, one high on street drugs and the other with a double gunshot wound. Mark was called down to Emergency because the double GSW victim was one of his patients.'

Meredith nods. 'That's right. We had twelve resuscitations that shift — twelve, Camilla. It was hell. But we got through it, like always. The team did incredible work, and I wanted to talk to you about it. We need to recognise how much the Emergency team do. They're world class.'

'I agree. But Mark said there was laughing at the nurses' station, and the patients could hear it. You were joking about gunshot victims.'

Meredith's forehead creases as the words tick over in her brain. 'What did he say?' she whispers, her face twisting. 'What did he say?' she says again, this time louder, as she stands up and approaches Camilla.

Her boss puts up both hands, as if to calm her down. 'In *his* words, the joke was indiscreet, he felt you were making fun at the patients' expense and—'

'You've got to be *kidding* me!' Meredith says, the words hurtling up her throat. '*Every day* in Emergency we face violent offenders.' She jabs her finger on Camilla's desk in time with her words. 'Some days it's just threats; other days, we're actually physically abused, by every manner of human who comes in off the street. And every day, we deliver the highest standard of emergency care on the west coast. You know it. And Mark knows it. And with all that, what's our biggest threat?'

Camilla just stands there, looking at Meredith.

'It isn't physical injury, Camilla. It's burnout, PTSD, mental exhaustion. I could go on and on.'

Meredith breathes deeply and walks in a circle, hands on hips, shaking her head at the floor. 'If once in a while we joke around, you can tell Mark Roth it's a small price to pay for having the best Emergency department on the coast.'

She stops pacing and stares at her boss. 'If we can't share the odd joke, this hospital won't have an Emergency ward.'

Camilla continues to stand there, silently listening, eyes wide.

Meredith keeps staring her down. 'Mark should know better. He's a *rising star*, isn't he?'

At the sarcasm in Meredith's voice, Camilla's face breaks into a grin and a look of mischief flashes in her eyes. She lifts her hands in surrender. 'Heard and understood. We'll speak of it no more.'

Meredith continues to look at her, making sure the words have landed. Finally satisfied, she nods at Camilla and then heads out the door, her heart banging like a jackhammer against her chest.

Walking back to Emergency, anger and frustration stew in her. Feeling the pull of desire for drugs, she breathes deeply, changing her mind. Instead, she reaches into her lab coat pocket, searching for the cool surface of her serpentine stone.

But her fingers don't find it.

Her hand moves up and down the inside seams of the pocket. Then she tries the chest pocket. And then the other side. It's gone. Back in her office, she checks her desk, moving the papers and files, looking through the drawers, scanning the floor, checking her pockets again. Where is it, she thinks, retracing her steps. It's her lucky stone. She's sure the last time she had it was in her office, in her lab coat. She throws open her handbag, gets on her knees, checks under her desk. It's 10.40 am, she has a staff meeting in twenty minutes, but she runs to the Emergency reception desk.

'Just looking for a file,' Meredith says, as if searching for something important and confidential. She knows it's pointless – the stone is never out of her pocket. It must have fallen out.

And then she remembers the meeting in the boardroom. She had leaned down from her chair to rub a bunion on her foot. Maybe it had fallen out?

There's only ten minutes before the staff meeting but she sprints through the tunnels, takes the elevator to Level 5 West and runs down the long corridor to the boardroom. Knocking on the door and getting no response, she pushes it open and runs to where she was sitting. On her knees, she scans the floor. There's nothing there.

* * *

After the staff meeting, Meredith gets a text from Leo: *Done*.

Coming, she responds.

She heads up to Stuart's office, where she expects Leo and his team will be, and sees Allie, Stuart's assistant. She doesn't look at Meredith and pretends to fiddle with the photocopier. When Meredith says hello brightly, the woman shoots her a dark look and turns away.

The door to Stuart's office is closed, so Meredith knocks lightly and then pushes the door open to see Leo in the far corner, lifting books from the shelves and checking behind them.

'Looking for secret hiding places?' she asks, only half joking.

'Hey, Red,' Leo says, rushing towards her, 'I should have locked the door and told you to meet me outside. You shouldn't be in here.' He puts his hand on her arm and moves her towards the door.

She looks at him, confused. 'Well, can I help with anything?'

'No – almost done. My team did a lot of what they needed to do last night, after hours. But it's better for you to not be seen in this office.'

At the look on Meredith's face, Leo goes on to say, 'It's just protocol, Red.'

She stops. 'Okay, I get it, but I just wanted to ask you something – it's about the police files you let me read.'

'Oh, right. Yeah. What is it?' he says, still distracted by the fact she's in Stuart's office.

She pauses and looks around. She'd always known the seriousness of the investigation, but it hits her at that moment. Stuart's office is the biggest on Level 5 – it's a corner one, with loads of light, and a consulting area with sofa and chairs. Now it looks like it's been assaulted – picture frames are hanging crookedly, loose sheets of paper strewn on the desk, the furniture is misaligned. The space looks diminished, and Meredith, thinking of Allie's aggressive look, can't help the fear that rises in her gut. Ros's words echo in her head ... *he's smart and Stuart Chester protects him – they both have powerful friends.*

'I've been thinking about the CCTV records at Patrice's house. The fact that there was one man in particular, who went in and didn't come out. He must have been there, at the party, blending in. And the photograph that you got from Patrice's friends – the one that matches the description of the man who never came out of the house, the one with the crucifix around his neck.'

'Yeah ...' Leo says, nodding slowly, his expression circumspect.

'Patrice was in her late teens and most of the people at that party were her age. How could someone Mark's or Stuart's age blend in?'

'I never said that the man at the party was Mark or Stuart.'

'Well then, what's the point of Mark's suspension? What's the point of all this?' she says, gesturing to Stuart's upturned office.

'This,' Leo says, making the same gesture, 'is an investigation of a lead in a case, Meredith. That's all.'

Her voice goes quiet. 'So you don't think Mark did it?'

'He's a person of interest, Meredith. No more. No less. I'm not making any assumptions.' He gives her an apologetic look and adds, 'And I really can't talk about it.'

'But he knew each of these girls, intimately,' she says in a whisper.

'Exactly,' Leo whispers back, grabbing his suit jacket off a chair by the door and pulling it on, 'but that doesn't mean he killed them.' He puts his hands on her shoulders. 'Stay focused, Red. It's the Psych records we want. That's what matters right now.'

She looks away, not able to hide the doubt rumbling in her gut. She shakes her hair, as if to get rid of the feeling, and changes the subject. 'So, I see you're not taking computers. Did the cloning go okay? Was Jacob helpful?'

Leo rubs his face. 'He was pretty stiff, actually, and took his time with every one of our requests. So no, "helpful" isn't a word I would use.'

That news doesn't square with what she knows of Jacob, but if she were honest, she'd say he'd been that way with her in the chapel – reserved, even aggressive, and so very different from how he normally was.

'Hmm – something must be up with him.'

'Don't worry, I'm used to it. People get defensive when we move into their territory – and the scope of our search is very IT focused,' Leo says, looking at the two boxes he'll be taking. 'I'm sure he feels very much in the spotlight. And you – you really need to leave. Come on.'

As he turns to deal with the boxes, her eyes wander to Stuart's desk. It's a mess, with papers strewn on top of it. But there's something else.

Disregarding Leo, she walks over to take a closer look.

'Red, I have to lock up and you can't be in—' she hears Leo say as he comes up behind her. Then he stops talking.

It's there on the desk, sitting by itself, next to the phone and the leather pen holder, staring up at her with an accusing eye. Her serpentine stone.

In Persona Christi

24 December 1990
Level 5 West – St Jude Catholic Hospital

After Lachlan put the phone down, he ran through the numbers. If they could arrange the sale right away, the two eastern lots would fetch well over twenty million each. A handsome sum. Father Bart would be safe, the bishop would be pleased – it would be enough to cover the settlements for all the abuse complaints in the New Westdale Diocese. And there would even be a little something left over at the end – for services rendered. He smiled to himself.

A rustle in the hallway distracted him and he looked up to see her standing there, framed by the doorway, clothed in black, her blue eyes rimmed with pink. She was a tall, muscular woman, but age was winning and her flesh hung heavy from her frame, like meat on a butcher's hook.

'I didn't see you there,' he said, trying to be casual. But his eyes were tethered to her, watching her every move, wondering how long she'd been standing there and what she'd heard. 'I thought you'd be down in the chapel helping Father Collins prepare for Mass.'

'Father Collins can manage,' she said quietly, coming into the room with large strides, her nun's skirt rustling as she walked. She sat in the chair opposite his desk as if she owned it, her eyes scanning the papers under his hands. 'There are more pressing matters.'

Closing his notebook against her roving eyes, he began to organise his files. 'What matters do you mean?'

'You know what matters I mean, Lachlan.'

He looked up sharply and then closed his eyes, sighing heavily. 'You aren't going to start that again. I mean really, how many times—'

'Just stop. Right there.' Her eyes were wide and intense, their rims made redder by the light over his desk. He saw the muscles in her face, how they were set like concrete. He wanted to tell her to relax, that she was getting too worked up. But when had that ever worked with his mother? Since his father died and she grew closer to the Church, he'd never managed to calm her down. With every passing year, life had grown more rigid, until he left home and she became a nun.

'You simply cannot continue in this way,' she snapped. 'I need to know about the finances. It's utterly unacceptable that you haven't provided the hospital board with an audited financial statement in two years.'

'We've spoken about this.'

She leapt out of her chair and stood, towering over his desk. 'I know we've spoken about this!' she cried. 'I also know the eastern lots at Leyton were just sold. Everyone knows – it's in the newspaper, for heaven's sake! That's St Jude's land, Lachlan. Where's the money? Where have you put it this time?'

She started to pace in front of his desk, her legs moving heavily through the thick fabric of her skirt. She turned her head to look at him, eyes blazing. 'Is it going to pay off compensation claims again? Are you paying off the sex abuse victims? Buying their silence?'

He shook his head at her. 'How dare you?' he whispered.

She rounded back and faced him again, leaning over with her hands on his desk, her large breasts swinging. They reminded him of udders, large and misshapen. 'Where is it going?' she demanded. 'Is it going to you?'

He threw his pen across the desk and stood up, the chair rolling back on its castors. 'What gives you the right to come in here and accuse me of—'

'Of what? Of lining your pockets? Of paying off your friends? Who gets it this time? Father Bart? Your friend Joe Bradley?'

'Those were legal political donations. How dare you come in here and accuse—'

'Why not? Why shouldn't I accuse you? There are no records to prove otherwise. I'm left with my observations. And what do I see? A young man, not yet twenty-eight, a *junior* lawyer, buying a house in Boniface Heights. Boniface Heights!'

He shook his head and began thrusting files into his bag, refusing to look at her.

But he could hear her heavy steps coming round the desk. He could feel her dry, cold hand on his. She stood beside him – over him, like she always did – her breath hot on his face. Lachlan was a big man, but he had never grown as tall as her. The shame of being made to feel small was as old as the sea in him and it churned like a king tide.

He ripped his hand out from under hers and pushed her away, then closed his bag and pulled a set of keys from his suit pocket.

Lachlan's hands shook as he put a key in the padlock on the desk but his voice was steady. His choral training always served him well in moments like this – his words came out in a clear, strong baritone. 'This is a complex institution and managing the land is too. You needn't worry about money. There will always be enough,' he said, putting the keys back in his pocket and turning to face her. 'Even for your dirty little women's clinics.'

Her eyes narrowed, and when she stepped away, he felt a spurt of triumph.

'That's right. I know all about them. You come in here, implying I'm a fraud, and yet you put everything at risk, including me. I'm the one who has to sign the expense approvals for contraception and abortion counselling,' he spat. 'That's my signature on the approvals. That's me on the line, carrying the can. Every day! What would the bishop do if he knew the rules you were breaking?'

At the sound of a vacuum in the hallway, they both looked towards the open door.

When he turned back to his mother, her face looked cracked, her eyes watery.

'Even you, Mother,' he said quietly, standing straight, controlling his diaphragm and breathing, remembering his training as a choir boy at St Vincent's. 'Even you break the rules. You stray from the path of righteousness. And yet, you come in here, to judge me.'

'Oh please, Lachlan. I'm not judging—'

He grimaced and shook his head. 'As I said before,' he continued, turning to walk around his desk, past her, out of his office, 'you needn't worry about money. It's all in hand.'

'Okay,' she said quietly, following him.

The chilly tone in her voice made him stop and turn, and they stood still, daring each other to move.

'Okay,' she said again, 'if you want to continue to manage things this way, I'll need something from you.' Her voice was soft now and he knew what that meant. It meant she was winning.

'What exactly do you need?' he asked, biting his bottom lip to stop it from twitching.

'I'll need your signature on this,' she said, pulling a folded piece of paper from her skirt pocket. 'It's an approval for the termination of a pregnancy.'

He put his briefcase down and grabbed the paper. He scanned it quickly and then peered at her. 'Is the mother's life at risk?'

'No,' she said.

The calm in her voice made an old, familiar petulance bubble up. 'Then I'm not signing anything,' he said, throwing the document at her, letting it sink slowly to the ground. 'We don't do abortions here! You should know better.'

'I do know better, Lachlan. But you will sign it,' she said, still very quietly, 'or I'll report you to the corporate regulator and Department of Health for two years of lapsed reporting.'

He looked at her sideways, afraid of facing her, afraid of what he might do. He could control his voice, but wasn't sure he could control anything else.

'How do you think the bishop will feel about that, Lachlan? What will Father Bart say?' she said, keeping her voice neutral. Then she looked at her watch. 'Government offices are open until two pm today. I still have time.'

He continued to look at her. The king tide surged in him and left him speechless.

She put her hands in her pockets and stared at him. 'Now, be good, son,' she said, nodding to the paper on the floor. 'Pick it up and sign it.'

AUGUST 2015

Chapter 15

'Meredith, bloody hell. You're a grown woman,' Charlie says, her silk kimono flying open as she thunders past, a cloud of cologne following her. 'When are you going to learn to tend a fire?' She drops to her knees at the fireplace and throws on another log, sending sparks flying.

In response, Meredith just lifts an eyebrow. She's stretched on the sofa, flipping idly through the documents on her lap. They're not sisters, but Meredith has mastered the cool disregard of an older sibling and it works a treat on Charlie.

Floor-to-ceiling curtains in Arden's second-floor study shut out the drizzly Saturday afternoon weather because Charlie can't abide daylight today. Being a successful litigator hasn't killed her taste for the smoke and the drink and the night before had been a big one. That morning, she'd declared in a text to Meredith that she would spend the next forty-eight hours in her bathrobe and asked if she'd like to come over to Arden, watch films and catch up on work.

Weekend campouts in Arden's study had been a ritual since they were ten – Charlie, sitting at her late great-uncle's desk, acting important; Meredith, stretched out on the sofa, cutting her down to size; Josie, calling them for dinner or scolding them to bed.

During their teenage years, when all the girls at school were sleeping with boys and going to parties, Meredith was confronting her sister's psychosis, her mother's depression, her father's affair — a series of disasters that layered up like a mountain inside her. The bright, shiny friendships with the girls at school couldn't bear the weight of it.

But Charlie never scared. The more Meredith's world collapsed, the closer Charlie drew. The shock of being sent across the 'big pond' to another country as a small girl, without parents or siblings, left Charlie grasping in the dark and Meredith was the one she reached for. The study at Arden was where the two of them always bunkered down. Between the sofa and the desk, there were twenty-five years of friendship.

'Fire making is your domain,' Meredith responds idly, too absorbed by the transcripts from Mark's counselling sessions to even look at Charlie. Leo's been complaining about the lack of physical evidence in all the women's cases, but the transcripts are a treasure trove. Meredith's insomnia has finally lifted and she's deep into the detail of them — until she notices the smell of cologne trailing behind Charlie.

'Is that *men's* cologne?' she says, sniffing the air and grimacing.

'Perhaps,' Charlie replies, stabbing at the fire with a poker.

'Since when do you wear men's cologne?'

'It's called Fierce,' Charlie says, with a conspiratorial smile, 'the young women love it.'

'How young is young?'

Charlie stays quiet, pretending to study the fire implements.

'Charlie ...'

'What?' she says, looking innocently back at Meredith. Then she turns again to look at the fire. 'Mind your own business. A woman's allowed her dirty little secrets.'

That's enough for Meredith to put her papers down. 'How dirty?'

Charlie's face goes pink. 'Twenty-three years dirty?'

'Holy shit, Charlie,' Meredith says, sitting up. 'That's twelve years your junior!' She sighs, looking up at the ceiling in despair. 'You know, my friend, sometimes I really do worry about your moral centre.'

Charlie looks sharply over her shoulder, an earnest look on her face. 'Meredith, *you're* my moral centre.'

'Oh god,' Meredith groans, rolling her eyes, 'now we're really in trouble.' She furrows her brow. 'Does she still live with her parents?'

'No,' Charlie says, swivelling on her knees and facing Meredith. 'She's a modern dancer. Really gifted. She lives in a share house with other dancers from New West Dance.' Charlie's blue eyes are wide pools in her face, fringed by long black eyelashes that flutter and blink. 'Oh my god, she makes me swoon!'

'Does she have a name?'

Charlie nods vigorously. 'Annabelle,' she says breathlessly, 'the delightful, captivating Annabelle.'

'When were you planning to tell me?' Meredith asks, her tone teetering between delight and indignation.

'The dough's still rising on this one,' Charlie says, her eyes trained back on the fire as she moves a log and teases the flames. 'I'll tell you when it's baked.' She shifts her eyes sideways again to Meredith. 'Have you spoken to Bella?'

'Every day. Either a text or a call. She seems good. She loves Glencoe. They have a piano in the main building, and she's got the whole staff coming for Thursday evening recitals. She calls it her *salon*.'

Charlie cackles. 'She belongs on the Left Bank. When are you going to see her?'

'In a few days. It's been too long. I miss her.'

Charlie nods, then slides her eyes to the wad of papers in Meredith's hands. 'You haven't put those patient files down all day. They must be riveting.'

Meredith gives her a look of searing disapproval and then sits back, holding the papers up in front of her face.

Charlie has no idea what's going on at St Jude. She knows nothing about the patient deaths, the investigation, the fact that Mark has sussed Meredith's drug issues. She hates hiding things from her friend, but she has to. What Charlie's doing – taking the lead on Bella's care – that's enough.

Charlie gets up in a huff for being ignored. She makes her way back to her uncle's desk and pulls the chair under it with a loud scrape. Meredith's used to her friend's post-party surliness, so sinks back into the sofa unperturbed, letting the transcripts pull her beyond the reach of her friend's hangover.

When she compares Mark's recorded transcripts with the research summaries Stuart has converted them into, her focus intensifies. Stuart has turned the raw material of the transcripts into intricate narratives of each woman's life: her habits, her distress, when she's most likely to be alone, where she seeks comfort. He describes each woman's character vividly – her fears, her pressure points, her weak spots, her blinkers. Meredith's never read anything like it.

The fire cracks and sparks fly, making her jump. 'I need to make a call,' she says to Charlie, walking out to the gallery hallway that overlooks Arden's main foyer, closing the study door behind her. She digs her heels into the heavy carpet as she taps Leo's number on her phone.

'Mark's transcribed patient sessions are *how-to* books for murder, Leo!' she whispers urgently, not wanting Charlie to overhear.

Getting no response, she shakes the thick transcript in her hand as if Leo is standing in the hallway with her. 'Katherine explains to Mark that she always went to Victor Allen Park on Sunday evenings to pick up speed. Tabitha describes precisely where the shooting gallery was; how she always went there on a Wednesday night, when the dealer prepared his packages. Patrice says she was planning a big party. She even explains she can turn off the CCTV when she wants, to frustrate her parents. It's right here in the transcript,' Meredith says, holding the pages in front of her: '"*the control panel is in the kitchen pantry – I can turn the cameras off any time I like. I do it all the time – it makes them so annoyed.*"'

Leo remains silent.

'Need I say more?' she says a bit louder into the phone, but quietly enough not to let Charlie hear.

When there's still no response, she continues. 'Okay, I will. Another example – the way they cut themselves. It's all in the files. Anyone reading these would know that Katherine used a scalpel, Tabitha a razor, Patrice a straight razor. All someone needed to do was read this transcript, Leo, to know what weapon to use to make it look like suicide. It's all in here.'

'I know, Red. It's the best lead we have.'

'So,' Meredith says, starting to pace, trying to keep the urgency out of her voice, 'why do you say the case is going cold?'

There's a long pause on the other end of the phone. Finally, Leo says, 'It's the only lead we have.'

She waits. And waits. 'And?'

'They don't really incriminate Mark.'

'Why the hell not?'

'I can't get into the detail, Red.'

Leo's voice is starting to sound businesslike and it vexes her. 'Your only lead points directly to a bullying physician, who happens to be intimately connected to every single victim, and the case is going cold?'

Leo sighs. 'He's got alibis.'

Of course, she thinks. Of course he has. 'Are they any good?'

'Listen, I said I'm not going into the details. They're not perfect but they're very strong. His wife attests to him being home each night. We've interviewed her.'

Meredith thinks back to the time she met Mark's wife. Alice was her name. A thin blonde in a red dress, with an arid laugh and disinterested eyes. She remembers Mark steering Alice through the crowd at the St Jude Christmas party, introducing her to his colleagues, long fingers gripping her elbow.

'So? That doesn't let him off. All the murders happened late at night. She would have been asleep.'

'For the last time, I'm not going into the details.' Leo's voice is strained. 'You need to trust me on this, Red. Other than the transcripts, there's nothing that points to Mark Roth.'

She breathes deeply, trying to rein in her suspicions about Mark. 'I'm sorry, Leo.' She looks at her pale face in a mirror on the hallway wall and then turns away. 'I'm just having a hard time believing … I just … he's just such an asshole.' She shakes her head. 'I know I'm biased. But he's always been … He's got a bad side.'

Her throat tightens. 'And then it's the patients. They're always on my mind, Leo. Three women gone and no one at St Jude seems to care. Only you and I, struggling to find out what happened.'

'I know. You're right in the middle of it,' he says and then his voice goes quiet. 'But what is it about Mark? What bad side? What happened between you two?'

She inhales and exhales slowly. 'Nothing,' she says. 'I mean, we dated a few times, back when we were both in pre-med.'

Meredith walks along the hallway, her fingers brushing the wooden railing. 'We ended up in a room. At the pre-med Christmas party. We had a fight.'

'Did he—'

'He got the wrong impression,' she says, cutting him off. 'He thought I liked him more than I did.'

There is a tense silence on the other end of the phone. 'What happened, Red?'

Words catch in her throat. She remembers that night in moments of brightness, like seeing the countryside in a flash of lightning, then a cascading series of senses: whisky burning a hole in her belly, hot breath on her cheek, a hand on her throat, words in her ear: *you like it rough.*

'Did he force himself on you?' she hears Leo ask.

The next memory is like a kinetic surge: her hand uncoiling, her fingernails tearing at skin, her body pushing against a door, running through a crowd of carousing classmates. That final feeling – of her body released and running through space – unlocks her voice.

'Yes,' she says, swallowing. 'We were both really drunk and I don't remember all the details. Someone knocked on the door, just at the right time and I was able to get away. I know he ripped my clothes and left bruises. I know I left scratches on his forehead. That was the only visible evidence by the end of it. I know his ego was sore, because after that he turned into a complete asshole and things haven't changed between us since.'

'Did you report—?'

'No.'

'What—'

'I thought about it, believe me. I went to Charlie and she wanted me to go to the police – she begged me – but I was too wrecked. I just couldn't do it.'

'You couldn't do it? Why the hell not, Red? If he attacked you, he probably attacked—'

'Leo!' she yells, wanting to jump through the phone and throttle him and then feeling like a shit for it, because this man, this gorgeous man, is not why she's angry. 'Seriously? Are you seriously going to try to make me feel bad about how I handled it?'

'You're just not the type who'd shy away from calling out that kind of behaviour and—'

'Well, you're right – I'm not the type who would shy away from that.' She starts to pace along the hallway again. 'Frankly, I wish I had reported him! But I was blind drunk, the details were blurry and all I wanted to do was forget it. You know, I was a bit busy that Christmas – organising my father's funeral, surviving pre-med, dealing with Bella. Jesus, Leo, don't make me feel bad about it—'

'I'm sorry,' he cuts in. 'But the guy is a criminal and I hate that there's no record of what he did to you that night.'

Meredith stops pacing. 'I didn't say there was no record, Leo. No record? Are you kidding? Charlie was studying law at the time. She made me write down everything I could remember, and the names of every one of my classmates who might have seen me run out of the bedroom. She made me date and sign it. She took pictures of my bruises. She made me save the ripped clothes. Don't you worry. There's a complete, contemporaneous record of what happened that night. It's in a box at home and it hasn't been touched in years.'

'Good,' Leo says coldly, 'very good.' She can almost hear him thinking. 'But do you ever plan to use it? File an official report?'

She wants to say something but can't. The weight of revisiting that period of her life is too heavy.

Meredith hears a low whistle through the phone as Leo exhales slowly. 'Is he ... is Mark the reason you dropped out of pre-med?' he asks quietly.

'Absolutely not,' she says, her voice suddenly crystalline. 'What happened with Mark scared me, no question. But if it'd been the only thing I was dealing with I could have handled it. There were just so many curveballs flying around. My dad.' She swallows. 'And Bella. Bella was completely out of control.'

She turns to look at herself in the hallway mirror again. Her words, sharp as arrows, are aimed at herself as much as Leo. 'Mark Roth is not the reason I quit pre-med. I would never have quit something I wanted that badly on account of a prick like him. The truth is: I quit for Bella. And I never regretted it.'

He's silent but she presses on, needing to put the topic to bed. 'Do me a favour, Leo. What happened between me and Mark was ages ago. I'll admit it, I hate him. Because he *was* a bully and *is* a bully. And not just to me, to everyone. Okay?'

Leo's voice is soft. 'Okay.'

'Okay then,' she says. 'Are you going to tell the hospital that Mark's been eliminated as a suspect?'

He clears his throat, as if to buy time. 'I'm not sure we're there yet.' There's a pause. 'But I'm getting pressure to pursue other leads.'

'What kind of pressure?' Her voice shakes.

'It's par for the course, Red. When a lead goes cold you have to change tack.'

'I ... You ... So, the police are—'

'It's complicated.' She can hear that he's choosing his words carefully. 'The report you gave me and Camilla, must have been passed by her to Lachlan Murphy, who sent it to the commissioner, Joe Bradley. Joe was going to transfer the case from me to one of his more favoured detectives, but I had your report well over a week before he caught wind of anything and I was too far down the track. He couldn't justify the transfer.'

Meredith remembers how she was so worried about Camilla and Lachlan not doing the right thing that it took her over a week to send her boss a copy of the report she'd handed to Leo back in July. 'Why would they transfer the case?' she asks.

'A lot of different reasons. They want to keep tight control over it.' He pauses. 'Do you know if Lachlan has ties to the police?'

Meredith thinks. 'I'm not sure; why?'

Leo doesn't answer immediately – she knows he's still selecting his words carefully. 'Hard to explain. There's been a lot of ... oversight recently.' He pauses again. 'The case is full of media dynamite – multiple suspicious deaths, vulnerable populations. Famous doctors and an established Catholic institution at the centre of it all. There are lots of eyes on it. Lots of eyes on me.'

Meredith's not heard Leo sound this way before, like he's picking his way through the dark, not wanting to wake a sleeping tiger.

'Is that normal?'

'None of this is normal, Red. It's a big case. Lots at stake.'

The line goes quiet.

'Are you still there?' she asks.

'Yeah,' he says, and changes the subject. 'So, you're camping out with Charlie all weekend?'

'I'm afraid so,' she says, realising how much she misses him. 'Charlie isn't well and it's the least I can do. Especially given everything she's doing for Bella.'

'Fair enough,' he says, clearly trying to sound upbeat. 'So, what are you both up to?'

'Charlie's nursing a vicious hangover and I'm going through Mark's transcripts and Stuart's summaries.' She pauses. 'Which reminds me, have you compared the two?'

'No. Why?'

'I'm not sure – but it's strange, Stuart's summaries read like fine prose. He's obviously put a lot of work into them. They read as if he was right there in the counselling session with Mark and his patients.'

'Are you sure you want to spend your weekend poring over patient files, Red?'

'Yeah, I do. There's something about Stuart's summaries that doesn't line up for me.'

'Well, I don't want you to lose more sleep – don't obsess about them.'

His choice of words makes her ropable. 'I'm not *obsessing*, Leo. The truth is in the files – in the words, in the cracks between things. The places where the details don't line up.'

'Okay, okay. I'm sorry,' Leo says. She hears him let out a big sigh, and then, as if he's decided something, blurts out, 'Listen, how are you fixed on Monday?'

She pauses to think about her schedule.

'We're bringing Stuart in for questioning at four pm.'

Meredith stays quiet.

'After the interview, we'll be discussing the case with our forensic psychologist. It may be useful having you there.'

'Okay, thanks. I'll try to get away,' she says softly.

They say their goodbyes and Meredith walks back to the study, a stew of anxiety in her guts as she thinks about the pressure Leo's under. She's almost at the study door when it swings wide open.

Charlie stands in the doorway, hands high on either side of the frame, arms forming a 'V' for victory, the sleeves of her kimono hanging in bright loops at her side. She has a look of achievement on her face. 'I think my stomach can finally handle food.'

'Well done, sweetheart,' Meredith says, not trying to hide her sarcasm. 'Things are looking up. Do you want to order in?'

'How about we go to Buzo?'

Meredith raises her eyebrows. 'So, you're ready to change out of your dressing-gown?' That would be a first for a detox weekend.

'What do you mean?' Charlie says, looking mortified.

Meredith rolls her eyes. 'For god's sake, Charlie. You're not wearing a dressing-gown to Buzo. I won't allow it.' She stands back, jutting out a hip, arms crossed over her chest. 'Can I get back into the study, please?'

Charlie drops her arms and lets her pass. Meredith hears her plead at her back, 'I've done it before. They love me there.'

'Well, I'm not going with you if you don't put on real clothes.'

'Fine,' Charlie says, piqued, walking to the desk with purpose. 'We'll have them deliver.'

'Since when does Buzo deliver?'

'Since I became a regular,' she replies, picking up her phone with a flourish. 'I have the chef on speed dial, darling.'

Meredith raises her eyebrows again. Then she smells the air around Charlie and grimaces. 'Your cologne reeks.' She lies back on the couch, satisfied with the huffy look on Charlie's face. 'If *Annabelle* doesn't have the balls to tell you, I seriously question her suitability.'

Chapter 16

Late afternoon the following Monday, Meredith's being led down a maze of hallways by a short, stern policewoman in full uniform. The tight bun at the back of the woman's head reminds her how much her own head aches, her long mane pulled tightly into a topknot. As she walks she pulls it out, shaking her hair and rubbing her temples.

Suddenly, the policewoman stops, opens a door and ushers her through to a small room containing a computer screen, motioning for her to sit. 'Leo Donnelly will be right with you,' she says.

When Leo arrives, he's moving fast. 'Hey, Red,' he says, and then turns the computer on, punches in passwords and opens a video file. 'The interview's done but we're debriefing with the forensic psychologist shortly. It should take you about thirty minutes to watch the recording, and then I'll bring you into the debrief room. Got it?' He pushes play, opens the door and is gone.

Leo was talking so fast, she'd not had a moment to ask him why he's put her in a room, alone, watching an interview with Stuart Chester. But before she knows it, Stuart's face pops up on the screen, so she puts that aside and starts to watch.

He's chatting with a young man Meredith recognises as the lawyer who attended the meeting in the St Jude boardroom.

Stuart's laughing with him, one long leg crossed over the other, his navy blue suede shoe bouncing casually up and down.

Seconds later, Leo enters the room with a man who looks like he hasn't cracked thirty.

'Thanks for agreeing to come in, Dr Chester,' Leo says and gestures to the man at his side. 'This is my deputy, Tom Scanlon. I want to emphasise again that we're here just to ask some routine questions. You can leave at any time. We're speaking to a lot of different people who had knowledge of the patients, so you're just one of many. We're videotaping the interview and you're welcome to get a copy.'

At different points in the interview, Stuart leans over to listen to something his lawyer's telling him, but otherwise his attention is trained on the two detectives. The conversation starts with Leo asking Stuart to recount how he came to St Jude, what he was hired to do and who his team is.

Meredith watches Stuart pick lint off his bright blue cashmere sweater and recalls her first encounter with him. It was at his welcome cocktails two years earlier, on the terrace of St Jude's new research wing. He towered above the crowd, wearing a button-down shirt in the same robin egg blue, moving lithely between the execs and senior doctors, bending his lean frame to look directly into residents' eager faces, sharing jokes with one and all.

Stuart had been highly sought after. He had an unusual double specialty – psychiatry and internal medicine – and after five gruelling years as an internal specialist, had moved to St Jude to follow his primary interest in psychiatric disorders.

Meredith remembers how the CEO at the time had introduced Stuart, calling him a doctor's doctor, highly trained in disorders that were riddled with diagnostic complexity. He praised Stuart's recently published paper on high-functioning erotomania, a delusional disorder in which the afflicted patient believes a prominent person desires and needs them. 'While their delusions can drive them to obsessive extremes, erotomaniacs lead functional lives, making them extremely hard to identify and treat,' the CEO said. 'This is just one of the baffling corners of psychiatry that Stuart Chester is helping us understand. With him and his team on board, it's our aim to propel St Jude into a leadership position in psychiatry – a longstanding speciality that St Jude has built since it opened in 1932.'

St Jude had coaxed Stuart away from the Misericordia, a UK research hospital specialising in the treatment of personality disorders, and given him the lead role in Psych, as well as sole management of an Outpatient Clinic for those with acute and chronic mental health issues. But everyone knew that Stuart wrote his own job description; his research was funded by one of the largest pharmaceutical companies in the world.

When Meredith introduced herself at the reception, Stuart seemed friendly enough. But she remembers the deliberate way he moved, his dark eyes, the way he quoted from her CV. 'Congratulations on the recent Henry Salter Award, Meredith. Quite the honour, that is.' She had just won St Jude's biennial award for patient advocacy. The decision was unanimous – her reputation as a 'patient soldier' was widely lauded and commanded great loyalty from her colleagues. But part of her shrank when he mentioned it. She knew that her obsession with protocol had driven some people to tears, particularly junior staff. Sometimes, it even drove them out the door, to other jobs at other hospitals.

He shook her hand hard, as if to make sure she'd heard him, and studied her closely. Meredith remembers looking up at him, wishing she'd worn higher heels, craving more wine, wanting him to stop shaking her hand. She recalls looking into his eyes as he leaned over her, and finding nothing there.

'I'm curious about your process.' Leo's voice takes her back to the present. 'I mean, your approach to recording counselling sessions – can you explain that?'

'Sure,' Stuart says. 'It's an approach required for the kind of holistic care we provide in the clinic and for the research we're undertaking. We don't operate in silos, and the patients fully consent to us, as a team, sharing expertise to deliver the right kinds of treatment. So, yes, records are shared, but there's a therapeutic framework for that, and all written consents are received beforehand.'

Throughout the interview, Stuart is poised and attentive, unfazed by the fact that he's in a police interrogation room, with a lawyer at his side.

When questioned further about his process and research, he continues to be relaxed and articulate. 'There's a real problem with split treatment of mental health issues, where patients need to see a psychologist or counsellor for psychotherapy, and a psychiatrist for diagnosis and pharmaceutical regimes. Our clinic and our research bring that all together – this delivers a better outcome for the patient and progresses our understanding of disorders.'

'And when you heard about each woman's death, what crossed your mind?'

'How do you mean?'

'Well, in each case, suicide was a possibility. But did anything else cross your mind?'

At this question, Stuart's shoulders slouch a bit. 'Everything crossed my mind. As physicians, we're fundamentally scientists. We don't rule things out, until the facts do it for us.' His voice goes quiet and he looks at Leo, his lips pressed together in a thin line. 'When I heard about the circumstances of how these patients died, by deep cuts to the skin, and knowing they were self-harmers, obviously my thoughts turned to suicide. And that's deeply distressing, because so much of what we do is geared towards suicide prevention.

'But then the similarity of the fatal cut takes you in a different direction, doesn't it? Particularly given, as far as we know, these women didn't know each other. That certainly suggests foul play – unless they were part of some unknown tribe of self-harmers, engaging in ritualistic cutting and telling each other about it. That isn't unheard of, but there was no indication of that in our counselling sessions. It's a tragedy and a mystery, Mr Donnelly. I'll do everything I can to help you get to the bottom of it.'

At this, Leo leans back and stretches his legs out, crossing one foot over the other, like they're having a fireside chat. 'Just on that, how do you know the girls didn't talk to one another?'

'Well, I don't know. Not for certain. But, given the depth and regularity of our counselling, we'd likely know if our patients were friends, or shared information. I suppose you'd be the expert on that, given you've likely scoured their devices.'

'What about through social media? They could have formed their own groups?'

Stuart frowns and his voice gets emphatic. 'We don't encourage or sponsor any social media groups in the clinic. They aren't controlled environments, and there's too much potential for negative dynamics – bullying, exposure to really over-the-top ideas or practices. That said, people find each other on the internet all the time. That's not new with social media – it's been around since the chat rooms of the early internet.'

Leo nods, but presses further. 'If your staff heard about these kinds of things – chat rooms, platforms, Facebook groups –

would they join them to find out what's going on? To see if any of their patients are at risk of these negative dynamics?'

'If we heard about them, we might join, but our time is limited. We'd only do that if we felt there was a useful therapeutic basis for doing so – to understand the patient, or to monitor exposure to risk. It's often hard to know who your patients are on the internet – many of the more alternative platforms don't require a real identity. People use aliases, alternative devices. As I said, you probably know more about it than I do.'

The interview ended with a request that Stuart bring to the police's attention any other self-harmers he had on his patient roster.

As Meredith sat quietly, waiting for Leo, she couldn't deny it. Everything about Stuart – the look on his face, his gestures, his answers – exuded the deep, anxious concern of an earnest professional, wanting to understand how three patients from his clinic could have ended up brutally slain.

* * *

'He seemed so polished,' Meredith says, a bit out of breath as she struggles to keep pace with Leo. They're heading to a debriefing room.

'Maybe,' he says, his voice even.

'He didn't fidget. He maintained eye contact. He was Mr Calm. He even looked like he enjoyed it.'

'I know.' Leo opens a door and motions her into a room with no windows and a boardroom table with chairs around it. No one else is there. As the door closes behind him, he shrugs his shoulders. 'That means he wasn't nervous but it doesn't mean he was telling the truth,' he says. He turns to Meredith and puts his hand on the door so no one can come in. 'Listen, just so you know – only Rachel, the forensic psychologist, knows you've seen the interview with Stuart. The debrief in this room won't be about that. It's to hear Rachel's early theories of the case.'

'Am I allowed to be here?'

Leo runs his free hand through his hair. 'Well, listen, given your connection with the hospital, your being here is ... non-routine. But as I've said, you've graduated from an informant to an adviser. Do you know how many advisers I have to talk to, to get to the truth?' he asks. Then he shrugs his shoulders. 'Anyways, it's my case. So take a seat and don't worry about it.'

'Okay,' she says, putting her bag down on the table. 'Leo, you mentioned social media in the interview, but I thought ritualistic cutting, social media influences – all that stuff – was ruled out. The files you showed me didn't indicate any patterns between the victims.'

'Yeah, well, sometimes people cover their tracks. Just like Stuart said – they use aliases, they use devices you don't know about.'

'But the chloroform suggests it couldn't have been suicide.'

'For Patrice, perhaps,' Leo says. 'But it could have been assisted suicide. We have to keep all lines of inquiry open.'

'But there's no evidence in support of it,' she says.

'There's no evidence against it either,' Leo says, the look on his face darkening. 'Listen, there may be people on this case who'd prefer to believe it's an internet stalker who's responsible. Leo pauses but then continues. 'Even if I think that theory's garbage,' he says, then shakes his head, as if he's already said too much. 'As I've said, we have to keep all lines of inquiry open.'

Meredith takes a deep breath. 'Okay, I'm heading to the ladies. I'll be back in a flash.'

Five minutes later, she returns to see the door closed and when she turns the knob, she realises it's locked. She knocks and Leo opens it, waving her in. Two men in suits are sitting along one side of the table, with a dark-haired woman – also in a suit. She's sitting ramrod straight and her hair hangs long, with a black fringe framing her face. She's wearing heavy black glasses and looks severe but for the wide, warm smile she aims in Meredith's direction.

Before Meredith can introduce herself, Leo motions to her. 'This is Meredith Griffin, one of our confidential advisers on hospital procedure, who, as you all know, is internal to St Jude. Meredith,' he says, and then motions to the woman, 'this is Rachel Gelfand MD, one of our expert forensic psychologists.' Meredith recognises the name from the police files.

Leo gestures to the officers on the other side of the table. 'DS Ferris and DS Dalgliesh,' he says, as they nod coolly at Meredith.

The woman looks over her glasses at Meredith and nods, then looks back to Leo. 'Rachel, please continue,' he urges.

'Right,' she says, launching back in. 'You know how this works, Leo. To find out the *who*, you quite often have to find out the *why*. And a helpful way to understand the why is to look at the victimology.'

Rachel now addresses everyone around the table, speaking quickly, as if she's telling them something they all already know.

'For the purposes of this meeting we'll assume that each woman was a victim of foul play, perpetrated by the same person. I think that's a safe assumption for a number of reasons. First, the location of the deaths: all of them were killed in places that presented forensic challenges. A public washroom, a house numerous people had recently attended, a shooting gallery for heroin addicts. Each attack occurred when there was little chance of eyewitnesses or CCTV recordings. Second, if the women were murdered,' she shakes her head emphatically at one of the men opposite, who looks like he wants to interrupt, 'And no, I am not yet ruling out ritualistic suicide, although the presence of chloroform on Patrice's face does raise a strong inference that there was a perpetrator and this was not suicide.' Rachel then turns to the other man, as if to head him off at the pass, 'And yes, I know that the presence of chloroform could still mean there was some form of cooperative ritualistic behaviour.' She leans forward and says firmly, 'But putting all those theories aside for the moment, if the women were murdered, it was clearly premeditated. The lack of physical evidence of assault rules out the theory that these were crimes of passion, and the locations of the attacks were, in my view, purposefully chosen. The person, or people, who did this, planned it. Circumstances like this don't just happen – not three times in a row.'

Still staring down the officers, she continues. 'So, let's play out the theory that the women were victims of a premeditated attack. What supports the theory that we have only one perpetrator? Three things. First – the injury, of course. It's unique and the same across all the victims, each time delivered surgically, in precisely the same manner. Three people in Emergency saw Tabitha's injury and all of them have been spoken to by the police – they told no one about it. Her injury was not publicly known – it's highly unlikely that Katherine and Patrice were copycat killings. We also know from computer forensics that of the three women, only one spent time on internet sites relevant to cutting, scarification or self-harm, and there's no indication the girls knew each other, or communicated any plan to cut themselves in this way to a third party.' Rachel puts her hand up to stop an imminent interruption by one of the suits. 'I know, Roy, they could have used other devices, but there's no evidence of that. It's pure speculation at this point.' She pauses to make sure her words have landed. 'Second – the manner in which the bodies were treated after death. Each woman was treated the same way: reverentially. This person is not angry or frustrated or vengeful. This tells us a lot about the perpetrator and supports the theory that we're only looking for one person. Third – the degree of planning. Each murder was planned, done with deliberate care and attention to detail, leaving no marks on the bodies and virtually nothing in the way of forensic traces.'

Rachel stops to take a long drink of coffee, then resumes, as if lecturing a class. 'Now, what does the victimology tell us about the perpetrator? Apologies to all, but for ease, I'll use the male pronoun. First, he very likely has medical training. The incisions were precise but deep – only a medically trained person would know precisely where to cut into the femoral. Second, he's methodical. He takes great pains to plan his attack and leave no trace. Third, he's done his research. In each case, the instrument used to make the incision was the same one each young woman used to cut or scar herself. This underscores the degree to which the individual knows intimate details about each woman, and has taken the time to construct a murder scene that could lead the authorities to suspect suicide.'

'What about the fact the injury's in the shape of a cross?' Meredith pipes up. 'What does that say about the perpetrator?'

Rachel trains her gaze on Meredith.

'I'm told the injury is what originally piqued your interest, Ms Griffin. Without it, you wouldn't have identified the pattern,' she says. 'The shape of the cut? I do believe it's relevant. It's a Latin cross. One long vertical incision, a second, shorter one, perpendicular to the first, the crossing incision made about one third down the length of the first incision. I think it's relevant but there's no evidence supporting religious fervour as the motive. Yes, I know,' she holds her palms up against Meredith's protestations, in the same way she fended off the suits opposite, 'yes, I've seen the photographs of the man at the party, wearing a crucifix around his neck. But in my view, it's not enough to support the conclusion that this is a crime driven by religious fanaticism.'

She takes another sip of her coffee. 'The crucifix worn by the person at the party could suggest a connection to Christianity, and, perhaps, a commitment to a religious institution – for example, a Catholic hospital, like St Jude. So it may provide clues about the identity of the perpetrator, but I don't think it goes to motive.' She looks pointedly around the table, pausing.

'On the other hand, the shape of the cut could have served an entirely different purpose. It may not be a crucifix at all. Perhaps it's simply a cut that's known to be effective and final – a cut designed to kill?'

After a few more questions, Leo declares the meeting closed and everyone gets up to leave. Meredith walks around the table and waits until Rachel finishes speaking to one of the officers.

When the psychologist turns to her, Meredith puts out her hand.

Rachel grasps it in a hearty shake and smiles broadly. 'I've been wanting to meet you. I understand you're our confidential source.'

Meredith smiles self-consciously. 'Hmmm,' she says, hesitating, 'source, whistleblower, adviser, random helper.' She shrugs her shoulders and lets out an embarrassed laugh. 'Frankly, I'm not sure how to describe me but, definitely, I'm a concerned party. I don't want to lose another patient this way.'

'Indeed,' Rachel says softly, giving Meredith a grim look as she starts to pack up.

Seeing the two other officers talking to Leo, Meredith stands silently, unsure how far to push things. Then she says,

'Rachel, tell me if you can't answer this right now, but you saw the interview with Stuart. Knowing what you know about the victimology, do you think he's a suspect?'

As Rachel closes her computer down, she shakes her head. 'Stuart could be an expert liar, so I don't base much on the session we've just watched. But from what I've seen so far, my answer would be a definite no.'

She takes another look at Meredith and continues, 'Leo's mentioned that you suspect people in the Psych department, but in my view, all of them – Stuart, Mark, all the psychiatrists – have way too much to lose. Let me ask you this – if Stuart were driven to this kind of crime, why would he choose victims this close to him?' She continues to pack up and looks apologetic. 'I don't mean to be rude, but I have to run. Mondays are my day for the after-school pick-up.'

'Of course,' Meredith says, standing back to give Rachel some space. She wants to like this woman – she's smart, all business, straightforward – but she's not ready to let her off the hook as far as Stuart's concerned. She can't get it out of her mind that the serpentine stone found its way on to his desk, or ignore her instinct that someone has been accessing her office.

Just as Rachel heaves her bag over her shoulder, Meredith leans in for one more question. 'What if the fact that Stuart has so much to lose makes it all the more appealing? Since when did high stakes stop psychopathic tendencies?'

Rachel looks at her sideways but there's a smile on her face that makes it clear she doesn't hold Meredith's stubbornness against her. 'Look, you saw him for yourself. Sure, he might exhibit some abnormal psychology. His behaviour might verge on the grandiose. He may be dogged, even obsessive about his research, but that's hardly unusual in his line of work – he's a scientific researcher. It's a viciously competitive field and many of his character defects were probably honed by it. They're probably the reason he's so successful!' She cackles loudly and there's a glint in her eye.

'Dogged, indeed. Particularly about the research.'

'Absolutely. That was crystal clear in the interview today. I doubt there's anything that Stuart cares about more than his research.' Rachel starts to walk towards the door. 'I've really gotta run or my kid will disown me.' As Meredith laughs, she looks at her with incredulity, her large brown eyes wide. 'Honestly! My son threatens to disown me when I'm late for after-school pick-up! Like, where does a six year old learn that kind of brinksmanship?'

She holds out her hand and Meredith shakes it again. 'Glad to have you on the team, Meredith.' Rachel gives her another wide smile and runs to the door where Leo's standing, waiting to take her downstairs and out of the building.

Meredith watches them leave. She didn't know she was 'on the team', but that must be how Leo described her. She smiles and turns to pack up her things.

Chapter 17

Leaning close to her hallway mirror, she puts on deep red lipstick and then stands back and puts her hands on her hips. Will the green dress pass muster or is the collar line too low? It's fine. She took the time to blow-dry her hair for once and it hangs straight past her shoulders, her long bangs framing her face. Evelyn will approve.

Meredith's phone vibrates to announce the car is out front and she takes a deep breath – they're off to see Bella at Glencoe. She's arranged for the afternoon away from work so she can get in a good visit with her sister and interview the staff. But before that, Evelyn is taking Meredith out for lunch. She's not sure which will be more testing – a formal lunch with Evelyn McCrae is a serious affair.

Meredith runs through the rain and hops into the back seat of the black sedan. Evelyn's perched there, in a neat black pant suit and black suede flats, a bright orange Hermès scarf around her neck. She's clearly just come from the salon. Her five foot eight frame may have shrunk a little over the last decade, but she remains expertly tailored and looks well south of seventy-five.

'I love your shoes,' Meredith says after the two women exchange kisses on the cheek.

'Thanks, dear,' Evelyn says and then whispers, 'my podiatrist has created an orthopaedic that can fit into a flat. It fools everyone and gives me back the inch I've lost over the years!' Flashing Meredith a devilish grin, she continues, 'Charlie's been busy with her new love affair and I've had no news of you. I'm hoping that with Bella at Glencoe you're getting on with your life? I need the details, Meredith. All the details.'

After they've ordered their meals, Evelyn peppers her with questions. At first, Meredith is cagey – she doesn't want Charlie to be burdened with what's going on with her at work – but she knows Evelyn's a steel trap, and after a glass of wine and assurances that the conversation is strictly between them, she holds forth about St Jude. Out it comes – the backbiting from Mark, the competition between them, the fact that he has friends in high places, her fear that she's losing Camilla's support.

'Mark's toxic, Evelyn.'

'Indeed, he sounds like a law unto himself.' She looks at Meredith squarely. 'Listen, not everyone collaborates. In fact, most people don't. And in those cases, you have to rule by fear.'

Meredith looks at her with surprise, and Evelyn keeps staring her down from across the table, her jaw set. 'What? You don't think I've been sitting around in my lounge, entertaining all my life, do you?'

She's right. The neighbourhood gossip in Shaughnessy Heights was that Evelyn's husband, William McCrae, only made business decisions that his wife endorsed. Evelyn's grandmother, Eliza Ritchie, received her doctor of letters from New Westdale University and was the first woman to sit on its board of governors. When her only child, Alice, died giving birth to Evelyn, Eliza brought her granddaughter up as her own. Evelyn's sole female role model was a heavyweight. It's no wonder she's a force of nature herself.

The combined effect of the pinot noir and Evelyn's sympathetic ear loosens Meredith's tongue. 'Mark's run into some trouble and he's on a brief hiatus. But I think he's got me in his crosshairs. He's threatened to report me to management.'

Evelyn puts her wine glass down and gazes directly at Meredith from under her heavily lidded eyes. 'Whatever for?' she asks quietly.

Meredith's throat dries and she swallows hard. She takes a long drink of water. 'I've had some problems with Ativan recently. It's an anti-anxiety pill. It's nothing serious,' she says quickly, 'nothing I can't handle.'

Evelyn's face remains motionless, like a stone effigy of a woman at lunch.

'It's complicated. He clearly knows about it. As far as I know, he hasn't reported me – yet.' She lets out a long sigh, thinking of what will happen if Mark is reinstated, 'but it's probably only a matter of time.'

Evelyn still just listens, her face inscrutable.

'It's really not a problem,' Meredith says, conscious she's rambling and unable to look Evelyn in the eye for long. 'Honestly.'

Evelyn's eyes are unblinking, but her face softens and Meredith can see her allegiance is unchanged. 'How long have you had the problem?'

'It started with a prescription a long time ago, back when Dad died. It's not an addiction. It comes and goes. It's quite low grade.'

'Are you getting help?'

Meredith's eyes lift to meet Evelyn's, but then slide away. 'I think I'm on top of it.'

Evelyn sits back in her chair, looking thoughtful. 'I knew you and Charlie played around with drugs when you were teens.

I let you do it. And don't think I didn't notice things taking a turn for the worse when you lost your parents.' She taps the table with a long, crooked finger. 'Drugs are great pain relief. Full stop. But you can never get enough of something that *almost* works. You must fix the problem, Meredith. Whatever it takes, whatever you need. You know I'll do everything I can to help you.'

As their meals arrive, Evelyn reaches across the table to put her hand over Meredith's. 'You have to realise what territory you're in with this man.'

She tips her head back haughtily and looks down her aquiline nose, eyelids heavy. 'What about him? Surely he isn't a saint. If he plays the drug card, can you play something in return?' Then her blue eyes flash steel. 'Some professional rivalries are downright dirty, Meredith – they're a fight to the death and you need to grab as much leverage as you can. By threatening to report you, he's let loose the dogs of war. Now you must go where they lead.'

* * *

The tall wrought-iron gates of Glencoe are fixed with giant steel hinges on stone walls that surround the entire facility. Once through them, the driveway leads to a central hall and, beyond that, wide open manicured lawns, dotted with individual cabins.

It looks expensive, Meredith thinks, as they drive through the grounds, but also very suitable. 'How did you know Glencoe would work for Bella?'

'It was quite simple, really. Charlie asked her what she wanted, Bella told her, and then all three of us set about trying to find it.' Evelyn gives Meredith's hand a squeeze. 'You know as well as I do that when it comes right down to it, Bella knows her own mind.'

The car drives into the circular driveway in front of the main building. 'So, you'll find your own way home?' Evelyn says to her.

'Yes ma'am,' she replies, gathering her bag and coat, stopping for a moment to take in the surroundings. 'Evelyn, I have no idea how to thank you for this.'

'Oh, shush, Meredith. You're family. And Charlie did most of the hard work. She's much more than a pretty face, that one.'

'Don't I know it. She's saved my butt more times than I can count.'

Evelyn's eyebrows raise and she laughs. 'Mine too!' she says, then reaches over and wraps her arm around Meredith, offering a cheek to be kissed. 'Now, go. Give Bella my love.'

The middle-aged attendant at reception smiles warmly when Meredith introduces herself. 'Oh, you're Isobel's sister! She talks about you all the time,' she says and gives her directions to Bella's cabin.

For the moment, the rain has stopped and puddles of sunlight dot the green. The air is full of the pungent smell of cut grass. This was just the right amount of nature for Bella – anything more would have been dangerous. Charlie chose well, she thinks.

Bella's place is small, separated from the rest for peace and privacy. A grey slate pathway, with thin flat stones interlocking in a herringbone pattern, leads up to the cabin. The path then snakes around to the side and hugs the outer wall. Four long vertical windows, each running from floor to ceiling, cut through the white stucco wall, inviting the sun inside.

Internal blinds are pulled down over three of them but the fourth is open. Meredith peeks through it and can see the unit is self-catering. Squinting further, she can see a door that leads to a small bedroom. An upright piano sits against the far wall of the lounge. Meredith breathes a sigh of gratitude to Charlie – for thinking of everything.

She rounds the corner and realises that there is only one door to the cabin and that the one she thought was the back door is actually the front. There's a front porch with a table and chair looking out over a small rise to a pond with a water feature and a Douglas fir standing proud beside it.

Just over the hillock, under the Douglas fir, she comes upon Bella sitting on a bench, knitting intently and wearing earphones, her head bobbing. She's in the zone, thoroughly preoccupied, so Meredith stops, not wanting to interrupt her too abruptly. She walks around and approaches from a point in front, and when Bella sees her, she breaks into a wide smile.

'I've missed you,' Meredith says as they hug.

'Same here,' Bella says, giving her sister a tight squeeze. 'Come on, let me show you around.'

As Bella takes her into the cabin and shows her around the grounds, the conversation is straightforward and Meredith almost relaxes. But she can't ignore the deep chord of guilt vibrating through her. After the incident at Arden, she took Evelyn's advice and left everything up to Charlie. She relinquished control entirely, letting Charlie make all the necessary decisions about Bella's welfare. It was a godsend, freeing her to deal with Mark and the investigation. But her conscience still rattles.

They take a walk past the neighbourhood shops, art galleries and florists that have sprung up along Queen West, the busy street that borders the grounds of Glencoe. Bella seems like herself – or like she was when she was young – friendly with the shopkeepers, enthusiastic and spirited. Since her teenage years, the drugs had dampened this, but moving to Glencoe has brightened her personality. No matter how deeply Meredith searches her sister's eyes, she can't find a shadow of sadness or glimmer of an accusation. Bella's made friends, she's playing piano, she's still in therapy.

'I'm glad things are working for you here, Belle,' Meredith says, as they wait for the pedestrian light to cross Queen West and get back to Glencoe. 'I haven't seen you this way since before Mom and Dad split.'

'Yeah, I know, I haven't felt this way for a long time,' Bella says, looking thoughtful. 'I guess it's a combination of things – Glencoe's a predictable place and they give me lots of independence. I can engage when I want. I can leave when I want. Hey, I've joined the gardening club!'

'Oh, Evelyn will love that!'

'I know – come to think of it, she's probably the reason I joined.'

As they turn the corner towards Glencoe, Bella says, 'I think the meds are also part of it. They've stayed the same, so that's been good – just a constant, you know? And,' she continues, pausing, 'I've finally realised I can't manage without them.'

Meredith looks cautiously at her sister, who avoids eye contact. She knows what a significant thing that is for Bella to say. For so many years, she struggled against medication. Surrendering to the idea that it might be the surest way to manage her illness was a huge act of acceptance.

'Also, life has gotten easier now that I've let go of some of my anger at Dad.'

Their eyes meet and Meredith smiles tightly. 'I know you blamed Dad for the break-up, Belle. But he was in an unhappy marriage. We all know Mom married him for his money,' Meredith says.

'Yeah, but Dad married Mom for her respectability,' Bella shoots back.

It's an old fight and they each have their allegiance – Meredith to their father and Bella to their mother. Bella's was so strong that she changed her surname to her mother's maiden name, as if to break every possible tie to her father. Meredith doesn't want to go down that rabbit hole, so they walk together quietly until Bella breaks the silence.

'God, I really don't want to fight about our parents – not ever again,' she says. 'Let's face it, Mere, they were both flawed. He married into an establishment family that was asset rich and cash poor. She married a man with a big bank balance. They may have been in love at the start, but it never took root.'

'True,' Meredith says. 'So, are you going to change your name back to Griffin?' she asks, smiling at her sister.

'Are you kidding?' Bella says, laughing. 'Hell no. Too much paperwork.'

As they make their way through the Glencoe grounds, she thinks back to Bella's decision to change her surname to Cavendish. After their father, Geoffrey Griffin, exited stage left from their upper crust marriage, Meredith's and Bella's mother diminished. But it wasn't the cancer, eating its way from breast to lung, that ultimately killed Elizabeth Cavendish. In the end it was short and sharp: ten months to the day after her husband left, her heart just stopped. After a long, dark coda, the curtain just fell.

From the day Isobel and Meredith Griffin buried their mother, her sister insisted on using their mother's maiden name, and once she was able to, she changed her surname legally. Perhaps it was an act of veneration – a way of wresting her mother from the depths, and honouring that part of them both that was scarred by illness and ill circumstances.

Saying goodbye, Meredith gives Bella a long, warm hug and walks to the admin building. Before she leaves, she takes one last look at Glencoe. With her medical hat on, she thinks about her sister. Bella's gained weight. Colour's back in her cheeks. She's on a course of meds that's working.

At the gates, Meredith waits for her ride back. Reaching into her bag for her phone, she feels the packets of Ativan – a long strip of foil circles, coiled like a snake. When her ride pulls up, she spots a garbage bin on the side of the road and throws the coil away.

Chapter 18

Sunlight sprinkles the beaten clay path. Up the hill, where the path leads her, a circle of blue sky floats in a tunnel of trees. Juno's sitting where the path crests, silhouetted against the sky, looking westwards, over the ocean towards the horizon. Meredith can see the dark outline of her black coat, her long snout sniffing the air for the late afternoon sea breezes.

They've climbed Dowager's Run – ten square kilometres of nature reserve covered with a maze of walking paths and dog trails, on the lower face of Baker Mountain, one of the coastal peaks. The path is quilted with layers of needles from the fir trees that intersperse the large cedars. At that altitude, the woodland is sparse, each tree claiming its own space. There's no underbrush, just tall trees in all directions, standing dead straight and soaring up to the sky – it hurts Meredith's neck to look up at the canopy. Everywhere is the smell of cedar, free-running water, and, sometimes, when the thin strands of the west breeze thread through the trees, the saltiness of the sea.

In her earliest memory of the Dowager, she's five and running off-piste, twisting and turning between the thick cedar trunks. Bella's three and sits on her dad's shoulders, the whole way up to the top. This time, it's Jezebel who's being carried. Leo has jerry-rigged a BabyBjörn for the three-legged dog, so she can join their walks and be carried over rough terrain. When they get to the top, he hoists Jezebel out and sits her down by Juno. The two dogs sit with their snouts pointing west, quivering at the strange scents of the sea.

At the lookout Leo sits down heavily and they both watch the swell.

'The case is struggling right now, Red,' he says. 'There's just no new leads.'

She looks at him quickly and then shifts her gaze north – towards the archipelago of islands up the coast – scanning the surface of the sea, watching its colour shift as the currents flow and eddy around the crinkled coastline.

'Have you checked all the doctors at St Jude? Are there any who had access to all these women?'

Leo shakes his head slowly. 'Not a one.'

The sun has burned its way through a metal sky, turning the sea silver, and Meredith's eyes move across its surface, searching for an answer.

'What about the injury? Other than the Psych department, it's the only connecting factor.'

Leo shakes his head, rubbing his scar, as if it's acting up. 'That's where we started and we had no luck. We've been to the coroner's; we investigated all girls and young women who have died from suspicious suicides. Nothing turns up.'

'What about other hospitals?'

He shakes his head again. 'No records of similar injuries.' He stands up and puts his hands on his hips, whistling at the dogs to come. 'We should head back or we'll be hiking in the dark.' His eyes scan Meredith's face. 'Don't worry, Red – this happens. Cases move in fits and starts. The hospital files are a huge help and we're still analysing the data. I just might need to go broader. Get some other leads.'

She squints out to the horizon, seeing a purple storm front growing in the distance; it matches the gloom forming in her mind. If they don't find the person who did this, another woman will end up dead in her Emergency room. The thought sparks a deep urge for the drugs she threw out at Glencoe. Sweat breaks out on her forehead.

As they make their way to lower ground, cool air follows them down. The cedar roots web the ground, locking around the contours of the terrain like a neural network, sending nutrients from tree to tree. 'Trees need each other,' she remembers her dad saying. 'Above ground, they look solitary and self-sufficient. But underneath the soil, they're social. They feed each other.' With the canopy overhead, the gnarled net of roots at her feet, the poker-straight trees around her like soldiers at attention, Meredith feels the living embrace of the forest. She draws a breath as if her whole body is a lung, trying to fill every pore with it – feeling it wash away her gloom.

Out of the blue, she remembers something Leo once said to her – he had heard it in a Sherlock Holmes episode: *Intuitions are not to be ignored*, he said, *they represent data processed too fast for the conscious mind to comprehend.*

She stops and turns to face Leo, who's several steps back, carrying Jezebel. 'Stuart's and Mark's files are still the best lead to the perpetrator,' she says as he gets close. 'Stuart had a system for his research. He organised it and set up the protocols. Maybe retrace his steps?' She takes a long drink from her water bottle, eyes not leaving his. 'Stuart's only been at St Jude for two years. Before that, he was at the Misericordia. Where was he before that?'

As he gets closer, he gives her a wide smile, cups her face in his hands and kisses her deeply. 'A large part of me wants to recruit you into homicide,' he says softly, 'but that would mean

I can't do this.' He kisses her again, his lips soft and insistent. 'Where do you get your brainwaves?'

Meredith looks up at the trees. 'From these ancient things,' she says. 'My best ideas come when I'm walking the coast.' She looks at him and then looks away. 'I know it's corny.'

'No it isn't,' he says, pulling her back close to him. 'I want you to show me all your secret places by the sea,' he whispers into her ear.

* * *

Baker Mountain watches over a community officially called Baker Valley but known derisively as 'Bankers' Alley' – an enclave of investment bankers, CEOs and doctors.

Leo pulls his jeep into the parking lot of an upmarket sports bar, next to a rack packed with high-end sports bikes. While he gives the dogs water and settles them to sleep in the back, Meredith grabs two seats at the bar and orders their usual fare. The bar is spirited in the late afternoon and the first beer goes down fast.

When Leo's in the bathroom and she's tucking into a plate of spicy wings and her second pint, Meredith hears a voice behind her.

'Well, well, well, what do you know?'

Meredith realises it's Mark and a rush of adrenalin courses through her. Turning, she sees him dressed in cycling garb, with a tall glass of beer in his hand. His usually handsome face is drawn – the thin skin around his eyes stretched taut over dark purple rings. 'I heard you and the detective were an item,' he says, taking a large swallow.

'Hey, Mark,' she says as cold fear settles in her gut. 'How are you keeping?'

'What do you care, Meredith?' he says, glaring at her with eyes as fierce as an alley cat's.

'Of course I care.' It's a fatuous thing to say and she knows it, but she's terrified and buying time until Leo gets back.

Mark puts his beer down and leans over, one hand on the counter and the other on the back of her chair, cornering Meredith against the bar. She can see the vein in his temple pulsate and feels the eyes in the room start to look their way.

'Don't play games with me,' he says, breathing heavily. 'I know the suspension was your idea.'

Meredith sees a blond woman put her napkin on the table and get up. As she approaches, Meredith recognises Alice's long, thin figure and feathered hair. Mark's voice is restrained but hostile. He brings his finger up to her face and points. 'If you want to play dirty, Meredith, the game is on.'

She needs a moment to breathe but he doesn't let her. His voice gets darker and he leans in further, like he did over Katherine's body in the morgue, like he leaned over Meredith, all those years back. 'Are you scared?' he asks, through gritted teeth. 'Because you should be: I'll report your drug problem in a heartbeat.'

The threat plucks the same chord that made her want to scratch his eyes out all those years back at the pre-med Christmas party. She snaps.

'How about you, Mark?' she spits back at him under her breath. 'Are you scared?' Evelyn's stone-faced stare is in her mind as she keeps going – if he's threatening war, she'll answer it. 'You report me for drugs and I'll report you for sexual harassment. It'll be a great party and you can kiss your career goodbye.'

She hears the loud scrape of a chair against the floor, and Leo is beside her with his arm around her shoulders. She knows it's meant to calm her, but she now feels sandwiched between the two of them. The air pulsates with male aggression.

A second later, Alice is by Mark's side. She's saying his name, putting her hand on his arm. Meredith can tell it isn't the first time she's had to intervene this way. Her movements are graceful, but quick. Her voice is gentle, but her worried eyes study Mark's face intensely, alert for signs of an explosion.

Mark steps back, looking at his wife. Saying nothing, he takes her hand in his and leads them back to their table.

The noise around Meredith resumes, although she's not quite sure when, or if, it had stopped. From the moment she heard Mark's voice to the time he retreated, time stood still. The world around her had blurred, the only thing in focus was Mark, on the attack, hanging over her, ready to devour.

Her heart hammers and she knows it's a craving for an opioid, but she focuses on the food, as if to bury the yearning to alter her mental state and dull her throbbing nerves. She can still feel him there in the restaurant, close by. She can feel his quiet, cold anger. Hate has more than one pitch and Mark's is low. It creeps, like the damp. She can feel it down to her marrow. And the fact that he came at her here — oblivious to the whole bar watching and despite Leo being in close proximity — makes her nerves quiver. What would he do if he happened upon her when she was alone?

Stop it, she thinks, shaking the thought out of her mind. And when Leo tells her she should press charges against Mark for uttering threats against her, she waves his suggestions away. She won't play that card until she has to, just like Evelyn suggested. Granted, his knowledge of her drug habit means he's a credible threat to her, but the little box of horrors she has sitting in her closet makes her a credible threat to him. They're like two nuclear warheads aimed at each other, each threatening mutually assured destruction.

Her anxiety pummels her insides and Meredith aches for the coil of pills she threw away. But there's another part of her that is just plain mad, and the rage fuels an untapped pool of willpower that she realises is bottomless. Her eyes lock onto Leo. He kicked a drug habit. If he did it, so could she. In her mind, she sees Bella, strong and healthy, and Evelyn, sitting on the other side of the lunch table, staring at her like an iron warrior.

And the last thing – the very last thing – that just might convince her to never take another Ativan is the fact that it will eliminate Mark's leverage. If she can kick this, he's got no case against her and she can go for his jugular. So there it is, she thinks: Bella, Leo, Evelyn and, ironically, Mark – the four pillars holding her up over the sweet river of craving that's raging in her belly.

Still feeling Mark's presence in the restaurant, she focuses on her food. Just chew, she thinks. Drink. Save your voice. Don't talk. Be calm.

He has a side. A dangerous side. One she can feel but not see. He's smart, he has friends. But none of that means – it really doesn't mean – that she can't bring him down.

Chapter 19

Two staff have called in sick, there's a heap of files on her desk, her inputs for next year's budget are a week late and Meredith can't remember a time she didn't feel choked with work.

The thought of Ativan creeps into her mind. The smooth foil wrapping around the pill, the feel when she rips it open, the release of a perfect circle of pleasure. The craving is almost imperceptible, just a mild hunger, but then it grows, minute by minute, until it explodes like a pipe bomb in her head. She squeezes Leo's serpentine stone in her lab coat pocket and moves on to another task, breathing until the next distraction propels her forward.

She's deep into a costing spreadsheet and the end of the day is close, but the promise of rest evaporates when the sirens start to peal. She hears the intercom: Code Blue, South Door.

A nurse runs past, yelling.

Meredith wants to cry. But instead, she jumps up and runs around her desk, out the door, towards the noise; automatically, like a compass needle to magnetic north. She's organising the triage, rounding up hands.

* * *

Two hours later, she trudges back to her office to see Sarah Sampson loitering in the hallway outside the door, holding something, trying to look inconspicuous.

'Why are you still here, Sarah? Shift's over. Go home and rest your legs.' Meredith's about to walk into her office when the nurse holds out a folded note.

'I was in the staffroom, getting ready to go, and a young woman from corporate came in and gave me this,' Sarah says. 'She said it was for you.'

'From corporate?'

'Yeah, she said she was from legal.'

Meredith takes the note gingerly, laughing off the formality of it. 'A handwritten note! A bit old school, isn't it?' Sarah laughs too, but it's short and polite. Meredith nods to the door. 'Go home, Sarah. Thanks for your help today.'

Meredith watches her go and turns into her office, opening the note.

The paper is thick and the scrawl is spidery.

Come see me when you can. Here until 7 pm. LM

LM – Lachlan Murphy. Like the notes Camilla gets.

Instantly she feels heavy and sick.

She's never been summoned before.

* * *

It's almost 7 pm and she can't avoid it any longer.

She takes another look at her phone. Still no response from Leo. The last time they talked was the day they walked the Dowager, when they ran into Mark at the pub. She's been texting him for days and she's heard nothing. Bella has sent her a photo of the herbaceous borders in late summer bloom at Glencoe – a background of Goatsbeard, showcasing Lewisia, blanket flowers and Pacific bleeding hearts – according to Bella's description in the text.

She takes the elevator up to Level 5 West and walks down the carpeted hallway, looking side to side. The corporate staff are gone – the offices are empty and the computers are off. She smiles at the janitor scrubbing down the coffee bay, grateful for another presence on the empty floor.

Lachlan's office is at the far western end of Level 5 – a large square of light at the end of a long hallway, right next to the boardroom. She walks towards it slowly, checking the names on the other office doors as she walks past. She can hear him talk as she approaches. He must be on the phone – his is the only voice she hears.

'Of course. I completely agree.' His sonorous voice travels outside the office door.

Meredith's not sure if she should interrupt, but to hell with it, she thinks. He's the one who's called me up here after a damn long day. She walks through into a small anteroom with a leather sofa. It looks antique but she realises it's new – made to look old, it's clubby and expensive. She can still hear Lachlan's disembodied voice in the air.

'I've spoken with His Grace. I suggested that we consider an option in the agreement, so that property ownership is retained. The church retains full control.'

Meredith's discomfort grows as she stands there, listening.

'I am handling that. I've had several conversations with Bishop Fisher. No need to worry.'

She's too tired to wait until he gets off the phone, so she knocks on the door frame and pokes her head in at the same time. Lachlan is leaning back in his chair, his large, thick legs stretched out, feet on the desk.

He looks over and motions for her to come in. He straightens up, puts his feet down and pulls his chair under the desk.

'James, can I call you back next week? I have someone here and I think we've covered the key points.'

After a pause, Lachlan lets out a large belly laugh. 'Always, absolutely, my friend … You can rely on that … Thanks a mill … And to you.'

Lachlan puts the phone down. He comes round the desk and smiles at her. 'I'm sorry to keep you waiting, Meredith.'

'Not at all.'

'Thank you for coming.' His voice is deep and musical. She's sure it's meant to soothe, but it sends a nervous surge through her gut instead. 'I wanted to chat and thought, better sooner than later.'

Lachlan leads her to a cluster of leather chairs at the centre of the room. When he motions for her to sit, she sinks down into the chair, her small frame swallowed by the soft leather. Lachlan sits beside her and leans in, resting his chin on his hand. His smile makes her want to run from the room.

'How are things going in Emergency? You're our frontline and I rarely get a chance to find out how you're managing.'

The question makes the hair on the back of her neck stand up. Really? We're here to talk about her job? She smiles obligingly. 'Thanks for asking. It's,' she pauses, trying to find the words, thinking of Camilla's diplomacy lessons, 'challenged, as most departments are – the same issues are everywhere. We're lean – we do the best we can.'

Lachlan nods his head, looking sympathetic. 'Indeed. I hear you run a tight ship. St Jude has the best-run Emergency in the region. I've never had a chance to congratulate you on the Henry Salter Award. Well deserved, Meredith.'

'Thanks, Lachlan,' she says. It strains her neck to look at

him, so she shifts in her seat. The chair is low and soft and steals precious inches off her height.

'I just want you to know how much we value your service. You've been here over a decade and have done so much for the hospital. Your name has even been sent to Rome.' Lachlan nods, seeing the surprise on her face. 'Oh yes. We take our high performers seriously – we earmark them for future opportunities in the Catholic hospital system.' He pauses and his voice gets quieter and slower. 'Particularly those who are really committed to the institution.'

'Thank you, Lachlan. That means a lot,' she says. 'St Jude has been home for a long time.'

He nods again, eyes studying his Rolex, fingers playing with its buttons. 'Of course.' He looks up at her, his face serious. 'Of course it has.' He pauses. 'The investigation into the female patients has put a lot of strain on St Jude. It's really unpleasant stuff.'

Meredith chooses her words carefully. 'We deal with unpleasant stuff in Emergency every day.'

'Yes, of course you do,' he says, looking at her with a raised eyebrow, measuring her. 'You're highly trained for trauma.' Then he leans in further and lowers his voice. His words come out gently, with the timbre of a bass oboe playing the darker parts. 'But this case is really police work, isn't it, Meredith? You're trained for injury and death. But you're not really trained for murder, are you?'

She can feel his eyes bearing down on her, closely monitoring her reaction. Sweat breaks out on her palms.

'I'm sure the investigation is interesting. And, of course, being involved with Leo, you can't help but be somewhat involved in what he does. You get to meet all kinds of specialists. I know Rachel Gelfand – she's the best of the best. She'd be my first choice as an expert witness – hands down.'

At the mention of Leo and Rachel, Meredith's belly twists and a flash of heat rises in her chest. 'I'm not that familiar with Rachel Gel—'

Lachlan doesn't let her finish. 'I understand you want to help, Meredith. That's your strongest quality, and it makes you fearless. Your courage comes from the heart. Have you studied Latin? The root of the word courage is "cor" – the heart. It's precisely your kind of fearless empathy that we need at St Jude. But the investigation,' he pauses, 'the investigation is really for the police, isn't it?'

Meredith licks her lips and swallows, focusing on the point where the carpet meets the wall.

'I'm really not sure what you mean, Lachlan,' she says, her voice clear. 'Of course it's for the police. I assume the investigation started when Camilla sent you my report? Presumably, you sent it on to the police and got the ball rolling?'

Lachlan chuckles and sits back. He takes off his glasses and starts to clean them. 'Well, I think we both know your involvement with the investigation started well before that, Meredith.'

His fingers grasp the silk cloth and rub his glasses back and forth between it, the thin wire frames looking breakable in his large hands. Sweat starts to trickle down her back. The room seems to dim and when she looks up, his mouth is a straight line.

'I don't want you to get into trouble.' The words come out at a slightly different pitch, as if an implacable edge has formed around Lachlan's baritone. 'Leave the police to do their work, Meredith. You have your own issues to manage. With Bella, for example.'

'My sister is fine,' she says, the words feeling pointy in her mouth.

'Yes, I know. She's at Glencoe,' he says, in a matter-of-fact way, like he's reporting the temperature outside.

A swell of incredulity rises inside her but she says nothing, her lips pressed together, keeping the subject of her sister sealed shut. When Lachlan chuckles at her silence, it's not clear whether he's intending to comfort or mock her. Anger rises like vapour in her mind.

'Don't worry, Meredith, there's nothing sinister here. The Church owns Glencoe's land and we invest in the associated clinic. I get a list of new purchases every month. Your friend Charlotte Ainsworth purchased a unit for your sister.'

Meredith doesn't trust herself to say anything. Even she didn't know Bella's cabin was purchased by Charlie as freehold property.

'Wipe the frown off your face, Meredith, I'm just giving you some friendly advice. Your skills and your care are needed here, at St Jude, and for your sister. Focus on that.'

When her eyes meet Lachlan's, it takes everything she has not to spit at him for waving information about her sister at her, like he knows more than she does.

'I completely agree with you, Lachlan,' she says. Her voice sounds hard and desperate. She can't help it, she can't control her voice. She's not like him; she's never sung in a choir. 'It's been quite stressful these past few months. I'll take what you've said on board.'

She puts her hands on her knees and makes to get up from the chair. 'I really should be heading off. Is that all you wanted?'

'Yes, yes. Are you going down to the main floor? I might come with you – I have to discuss something with Security.'

Meredith follows Lachlan out of his office and down the hallway. She watches his hulking back, and wants to jump on top of it and claw away at him – for his arrogance, his presumption, thinking he can tell her what to do, waving his knowledge of her sister in her face.

The elevator comes quickly and she hops in first, pushing G for ground and willing it to move fast. As it starts to make its way down, Lachlan says, 'Actually, I might need to just stop at Level 1 to visit the logistics offices.' His arm shoots out, but instead of pushing Level 1, he hits Stop.

The elevator screeches to a halt, bouncing inside the elevator well.

'I must have pushed the wrong button,' Lachlan says, turning towards her. He hulks over her, using up the air.

Meredith remains silent, backed into the corner of the elevator, hands stuck to the wall on either side of her, trying to catch her breath. She peeks around him, motioning to the controls. 'It … it should get going again, if … if you just push another floor. Perhaps try?' Her voice sounds faint.

Lachlan looks down at her very intently, as if studying a specimen through a lens, the elevator light glinting off the rim of his eyeglasses. 'See, Meredith?' he asks calmly. 'You're so jumpy.' He doesn't expect a response, he just lets the words pour over her. 'You really need to stop making life so hard for yourself.'

He then turns his back to her, pushes Level 1, and the elevator heaves back into motion.

When the doors open, he walks out. Barely looking at her, he says, 'Goodnight to you,' and is gone.

When the doors close again, Meredith collapses against the corner of the elevator and slides down the wall.

Freeze. They always talk about fight or flight, but they never tell you about freeze. Freeze is the third F. It's what happens when you can't run and you know better than to fight back.

She pulls her phone out. *Where are you?* she texts Leo.

Then she leans forward and rests her head between her knees. She has to, or she'll be sick all over.

Chapter 20

A yellow clump of flour and fat lands in the middle of the cookbook. Before she can stop it, the page folds over, pressing the blob into a greasy circle.

'Shit!' she whispers. It's Julia Child's *Mastering the Art of French Cooking* and it was pristine when Camilla lent it to her.

Just as she adds more hot milk to the roux, her mobile rings. 'Damn,' she whispers, leaving the whisk in the pan, which has a heavy handle and flips over, spraying the cookbook with more floury clumps. 'Oh, for fuck's sake!' she says into the phone, as she reaches to get the pan off the stove.

'Well, hello,' Leo says, his voice relaxed.

'Jesus!' she yells as she drops the pan, the hot handle burning her hand.

'What's happening, Red?' he asks, clearly trying to contain a chuckle.

'I'm trying to make a bechamel!' she shouts over the sound of the running water she's holding her hand under.

'Fancied a challenge?'

'It's just a damn sauce – is it supposed to be this hard?'

'I need you to put all of that down, and come and join me. I'm at the Carlton. I have news.'

'I've been trying to talk to you for the last week, Leo – where the hell have you been?' She's yelling louder now, seeing in him the perfect target for her rage.

'Red, slow down. I've been out of town. Come on. Get in your car and drive down here. If you tell me you're leaving now, I'll put in an order for their beer-battered fish and chips. It's on special and it rocks.'

Meredith takes a look at the carnage in her kitchen and rolls her eyes. 'Okay. I'm coming. But I'm right pissed off, Leo. Why haven't you called me? There's shit going on.'

'Tell me about it,' he says, and hangs up.

The Carlton is a cave of a pub. It's dark wood-panelled walls are dotted with faux streetlights that illuminate green leather booths and a long bar, where Leo's sitting, his tall frame bent over a whisky glass.

'Hi,' she says coldly, sidling up next to him.

He turns and smiles, refusing to be drawn, and holds up his hands in a peace gesture. 'Okay, first things first, Red.' There's a bit of a slur in his voice. 'Why a bechamel?'

'I bought some fish,' she says, shrugging her shoulders, motioning at the bartender to bring her a glass of what Leo's drinking. 'Isn't bechamel a thing you're supposed to make for fish?'

Leo starts to laugh. 'I think you meant to make a bearnaise.'

She closes her eyes and sighs, gripping the glass of whisky the bartender's put in front of her. 'Don't laugh at me. I never claimed to be a cook. In fact, you're the cook and you've been incommunicado for days. I blame you.'

When she sees he's still smiling, she decides to shift the spotlight. 'I thought this was a business meeting?'

'It is.' He looks over his shoulder to an empty booth in the corner. 'Let's move over there.'

There's no one else at the bar and the place is almost empty but Meredith follows him to the booth. When they sit down, she looks at him with a raised eyebrow. 'Why the secret squirrel stuff?'

He looks around and lowers his voice. 'I thought you should be the first to know. Stuart and Mark have been eliminated.'

'What do you mean?'

'I mean, it's not them.'

Meredith just puts her hands on the table and shakes her head. 'And what crystal ball has shown you this?'

Leo pulls a thick envelope out of the inner pocket of his jacket and pushes it to her side of the table. It's a report of a suspicious suicide in July 2011, and copies of patient files from St Therese, the Catholic hospital for the southern coast. The victim was a Kelly Kosovic, eighteen, who lived in Sunderland, a small town three hundred kilometres south of New Westdale. She died of blood loss from a cut to her femoral artery, in the shape of a cross. She was also a self-harmer, and a frequent flyer at St Therese's Emergency. The file has a full hospital report, including psychiatric notes, signed by the attending psychiatric resident. Meredith knows the signature. It's Stuart's.

She pores over the information, stopping only when her dinner comes. She continues to read as she eats.

'When did you find this?' she asks, her mouth full.

'When nothing turned up in New Westdale for similar injuries on victims, I widened the circle to all metro centres along the coast within a hundred-mile radius. We still didn't find anything. But then I took your advice and retraced Stuart's steps. He was a visiting psychiatric teaching resident at St Therese four years ago, just before he went to the Misericordia in the UK.'

Meredith's stomach drops and her head starts to pound. 'Leo, what am I missing here? How does this clear Stuart?'

'Look at the last page.'

It's a press release announcing Stuart Chester's appointment to the Misericordia hospital in Surrey.

'Take a look at the date, Red. Take a look at when Stuart started in the UK.'

She reads the press release – Stuart's start date was 16 July 2011.

Meredith immediately looks back at the date of death of Kelly Kosovic: 30 July 2011.

'Well, could he have come back?'

'There's no record of him flying back. By mid-July, Stuart was full-throttle with the clinic in the UK. On the date of Kelly's murder, he was running a three-day retreat for the resident physicians in the UK. They were in session ten hours a day. A complete alibi.'

Meredith lets this sink in. Then she picks up the press release and scans it. 'What about Mark? Was he ever at St Therese?'

Leo looks at her, his face changing at the mention of Mark. He shakes his head slowly. 'Mark was nowhere near St Therese. He was employed at the Misericordia – that's where he and Stuart met. When Stuart got the role of head of Psych at St Jude, he brought Mark with him.'

She reads the dates again and nods, closing her eyes and thinking back to when she found out Stuart Chester was bringing his deputy – a psychiatrist named Mark Roth – to St Jude with him. That was a really bad day.

She shakes her head slowly. 'So, you're saying I'm wrong about Mark. And I'm wrong to suspect Stuart.'

'Both Mark and Stuart were nowhere near Kelly Kosovic when she died.' He takes a long drink of his whisky, keeping his eyes on her the whole time. 'We know Mark has alibis for the night Tabitha, Katherine and Patrice were killed. And Stuart's alibis are even more solid. It's just not them, Meredith.'

It takes a while for her to muster speech. 'I don't know, none of this feels right,' she says, avoiding Leo's gaze. She's embarrassed at getting it wrong, but can't shake her doubts. 'So much for wanting to recruit me to your homicide team.'

He waves her comment away. 'Whatever. Do you know how many times you have to get it wrong before you get it right in my line of work?'

She shakes her head as doubt rumbles through her. 'I don't know, Leo. Reading Stuart's patient summaries, his research into OCD, seeing my stone in his office – it's made me think he must have been in *my* office, you know, looking through my things, watching me.'

They sit in silence for a while, listening to the bartender clean glasses.

'I still think the key to this lies somewhere in St Jude Psych, Leo. I know you doubt my theories but—'

'Meredith,' Leo says, clearly trying to sound patient. 'You have to admit it. Stuart and Mark were a long shot. You can't deny that the whole time you've been suspecting them, you haven't been at your best.'

When she fires an angry look at him, he keeps going. 'I mean it, Red,' he says, his voice getting softer and quieter. 'You have to admit it – with the drugs, with Bella's episodes. You weren't able to sleep for most of July. It wouldn't be a surprise if you weren't thinking clearly.'

When these words land, she crosses her arms tightly over her chest, refusing to admit defeat. 'Well, you may think we're back at square one regarding the perpetrator, but I don't. And you're a complete fool if you let up on the psychiatric files. They're the best evidence we've got,' she says slowly.

'Okay – maybe so – to a point. But the case has just become a whole bunch harder,' he says, raising another glass of Jameson's. 'Cheers to that.'

'Is this new information the reason you're so drunk?'

That makes Leo chuckle. 'No, darling, having cases wobble in front of you is part of the job.'

'Then what is it?'

'It's nothing.'

Meredith knows better than to push it, but can tell Leo is ruminating hard on something.

'Do you want to come to my place?'

He stays silent, lost in thought, almost like he isn't hearing her.

'I really don't want to stay here, Leo. Come on, let's go to my place.' She organises the papers and pushes the envelope back to him. 'If not to mine, let's go to your place.'

Leo just looks around the bar, not saying anything.

'Am I having a conversation with myself here?' she asks.

He takes another long sip of his whisky and rolls an ice cube around his mouth. 'I don't want to go back to my place, Red.'

As Meredith looks at him, a nervous prickling starts along her arms, and then she remembers why she's been trying to reach him. 'Leo, Lachlan came at me yesterday.'

His head shoots up, his face stone. In the dark, his eyes look like obsidian stones. 'What do you mean *he came at you*?'

'He summoned me to his office and then basically told me to stop involving myself in the investigation. It's one of the reasons I was trying to get hold of you.'

Leo's eyes narrow but his face is still. 'Did he touch you?'

Meredith doesn't recognise his voice. It's so cold, it scares her. 'No! Not in the least. I mean,' she struggles to find the right words, 'he was menacing and threatening, but it was nothing like that.' She reaches across the table and puts her hand on his forearm. 'It was nothing like that, Leo.'

He throws the last of the whisky down this throat and swallows hard. 'The investigation is none of Lachlan's business. And, anyway, I haven't told anyone about your involvement – except for Rachel and …'

'… and the two other guys who were in the meeting with Rachel?'

'Yeah. Them too.'

'What were their names? Ferris and Dalgliesh. Who are they?'

'It doesn't matter.'

Meredith waits for him to say more, and when he doesn't, she presses on. 'Well, Lachlan clearly knows I gave you the original hospital file – well before I sent it to Camilla. And he knows Rachel Gelfand is involved in the investigation.'

That makes Leo grimace. 'What?'

'Yeah, he even mentioned her to me. He said he knew her, said she was "the best of the best". He clearly knows that I met with Rachel and am involved in the investigation.' Meredith searches Leo's face. 'Could she be telling Lachlan about what's going on with the investigation?'

'No,' he says, shaking his head quickly. 'Rach is a steel trap. She'd never tell Lachlan anything, or anyone else, for that matter. She's Jewish too – no connection to Lachlan and Joe Bradley's little Catholic club.' Leo runs his hands through his hair and a wry smile starts to form on his face. 'This is brilliant.'

'How so?'

'I had a feeling the top brass put someone on my team to watch over things.'

'Do they normally do that?'

'Nope,' Leo says. 'Only when something is really sensitive. Or *someone* is really sensitive.' He pauses and stares at a point in the distance behind Meredith. 'The report you gave Camilla went to Lachlan, and then he must have sent it to the top of the police food chain to Joe Bradley. By the time Joe got it, I was well down the path of investigating Patrice and Tabitha.'

He waves at the bartender and motions for the bill. 'I told you they tried to transfer the case off me. When that didn't work, I was told Rob Ferris was assigned to the team. And after our meeting in the St Jude boardroom? Lo and behold, I got a second new member, Roy Dalgliesh.'

Leo smiles, as if things are slotting into place in his mind. 'So. Now we know who's "supervising" the investigation on the part of senior management. And we now know that Lachlan's getting updates. And, given Lachlan and Stuart are best buddies, that's probably why Lachlan's flexing his muscle with you.'

He studies Meredith from across the table. The morose expression he had when she arrived has changed to a look of hardened determination.

'So, why don't you want to go back to your place?' she asks slowly.

Leo reaches into his front pocket when the waiter comes back and hands him a credit card. He watches him walk away and keeps quiet until he's out of earshot.

'I don't know how far the supervision goes,' he says under his breath.

Meredith just sits there, staring at him. 'What, you mean your house is bugged?' Her eyebrows shoot up and her mind races. 'What about me? Could my place be bugged? Could my office—'

'Red,' Leo says, holding up his hands, 'chill.' He looks at her intently. 'It's really, really unlikely that they would have any surveillance on you. Yeah, I've shared some things with you. Things that I want your advice on. But not everything. It's like I said before – you're not police.'

'Yeah, but I've been feeling watched. Someone's been in my office. And finding my stone, on Stuart's desk – that didn't just happen, Leo. Someone rifled through my office and found it.'

He nods. 'Yup, Stuart may very well have been in your office, wondering what you're up to. We know he's friends with Lachlan, so he knows you're involved in the investigation. Maybe he was in your office looking for things to hold against you?'

An image of the single-dose Ativans that she used to keep in her desk drawer flashes into her mind; and Mark's accusations, his threats to report her to management for drug use. She avoids Leo's eyes, not wanting him to see the shame written all over her face, not wanting him to know that, despite that shame, her head still aches every day for just one more pill.

'But Red,' he says, putting his hands over hers, 'like I said, I really don't think you have to worry about police surveillance. It would be me they'd focus on.'

As he manoeuvres himself out of the booth and stands, she looks up at Leo, watching him pull his leather coat on, seeing he looks relaxed, as if he's already moved on. 'Is that supposed to make me feel better?' she asks.

He smiles and nods. 'Yup. So,' he continues, offering her his hand, 'is the invite to your place still open?'

Chapter 21

'So, you're telling us the spotlight has shifted?' Camilla's voice is tight and she's leaning over the boardroom table, hackles up. She's looking straight at Leo and completely ignoring Meredith.

All four of them are back in the hospital boardroom but this time Camilla and Lachlan are sitting on the same side of the table, shoulder to shoulder, poised to tear Leo to pieces. Meredith can see budget spreadsheets laid out in front of the two of them, covered in red ink.

'Basically, yes,' Leo says, 'Mark Roth was close to the patients and we may have further questions for him, but our focus has shifted away from Psych.' His expression is composed and he's all business, clearly used to telling people half the story, keeping to the upper reaches.

'Are you saying we can reinstate Mark Roth?' Camilla asks.

'I think that would be premature, but obviously that's entirely up to you.'

'Oh, for god's sake,' Lachlan growls, throwing his pen down on the oak table.

Before the general counsel can start in on him, Leo tries to keep the pressure in the room down. 'Life doesn't happen in watertight compartments, Lachlan. Police investigations are no different. We've explained to Mark that he's no longer under investigation. But, for now, I think it would be wise to keep things as they are.'

A look passes between Lachlan and Camilla. 'That could mean he's suspended indefinitely,' Camilla says to Lachlan, her voice giving nothing away.

Leo shifts in his seat. 'Listen,' he says, 'up to this point, we've been able to keep the media away from this investigation. If the press heard about it, how do you think it would look if you reinstated Mark now?'

Lachlan puts his hand up. 'This hospital will make its own decisions – not the police, thank you very much, Mr Donnelly. I assume it's safe to say that St Jude is no longer under investigation?'

'It's too early to tell, I'm afraid.'

'So, should we expect more warrants?'

'Again, anything's possible, but I think it's unlikely.'

Meredith checks again to see if her boss will look at her. Camilla's mouth is pursed as she studies the spreadsheets in front of her.

Lachlan asks, 'Anything else?'

'No,' Leo says, pushing his chair back, and thanking them for the meeting.

'Did you want me to stay?' Meredith asks Camilla. It's the first thing she's said since the meeting started.

'No,' Camilla replies, her voice distant, looking at Meredith for the first time. 'Just give us the room, please.' Meredith feels the floor crack open and a wide gulf spread between them.

She swallows and turns to leave, following Leo out, glancing back into the room, where Camilla and Lachlan sit in stony silence.

She and Leo had talked about how to play this meeting. Despite his doubts that Stuart was still in the frame, Leo couldn't argue that the strongest connecting factor between the victims was St Jude's Psychiatry department or that Mark's and Stuart's files remained the best repository of evidence they had. But it was becoming clear that neither the police nor the hospital wanted this to come to light.

So they needed everyone to think the investigation had shifted away from St Jude. It would take the heat off Meredith and perhaps Leo too. He had to quarantine the investigation, regain some control and keep information from running up the chain of command.

They had agreed: the best thing to do was to go to ground.

* * *

Back at her place, Meredith crumples into a love seat in the lounge, letting her head sink back into the soft arm rest. Leo's lying on her sofa, firmly ensconced at her place – along with his dogs. Jezebel is lying on her feet, sniffing her socks as usual, and Meredith closes her eyes and breathes.

When she opens her eyes, Leo is still on the sofa, with his computer on his lap.

'How long was I out for?' she asks, mid-yawn.

'About an hour,' he says, sitting up, motioning for her to join him on the sofa. She goes over and he pulls her onto his lap. 'Diego, my computer genius, has created a database on all of Stuart's patients: the ones on record at St Jude, as well as every other hospital Stuart's worked at, including St Therese.

'We started with the four women – Kelly, Tabitha, Katherine and Patrice – and inserted any key information we could find about them into the database. We're now doing that across all the patients, looking for patterns.'

'Is Diego trustworthy?'

Leo nods. 'It's just me, Rach, Diego and Tom in the tent now.'

'Who's Tom?'

'Tom Scanlon. The guy that was with me at Stuart's interview. I know he's loyal because I trained him,' Leo says, looking away, the lack of trust in the force not something he wants to dwell on. 'Everyone else thinks I've put the case on the shelf for a while.'

The thought infuriates Meredith – four vulnerable women have died under suspicious circumstances and, due to police politics and strange machinations at St Jude, they have to pretend the case is going cold. 'Is there anything I can do to help?' she asks, keeping her rage under wraps.

'Well, glad you asked.' He opens one file and hides a few columns from it. 'This database now contains files that go beyond St Jude or Stuart's Outpatient Clinic, so I'm just going to show you data without the patient names. Hospitals aren't the only ones concerned with confidentiality.'

The document is a short table called Victim Profiles – V5. 'You see, the women could not be more different. Each of them has a completely different family history, they circulate in different crowds, they don't know each other. The similarities that we've identified are the ones you know about: one, they're self-harmers; two, they're all patients in Stuart's research; and three, they're taking some form of antidepressant or antipsychotic, and participating in psychotherapy.'

After examining the V5 table, she turns to look at him. 'So, no real progress yet, right?'

'Well, get this: after going through Stuart's ghost files, and trolling through the session notes, we found one more similarity: they've all had abortions.'

Meredith frowns. It doesn't feel that compelling. Terminations are not uncommon. 'Even Kelly Kosovic? The earliest victim?'

Leo nods.

She remains sceptical. 'Are you really telling me that none of Stuart's other patients have terminated a pregnancy?'

'We'll see. We haven't found any other patients with that constellation of factors. Just the four victims. Kelly had an abortion at seventeen, three months before she was found dead; Katherine at twenty-two; Tabitha at nineteen; Patrice at sixteen, around six months before her house party.'

Meredith recalls the crucifix around the man's neck at Patrice's party. 'So, are we back in the territory of a religious fanatic or cult?'

Leo keeps staring at the computer, his face impassive. 'Could be. All theories stay open, until they're closed. But what connects these women is their vulnerability.'

She shakes her head slowly. 'All psych patients are vulnerable.'

'Yes, but if you go by Stuart's summaries, these ones are in a peculiar state of pain.'

Ad Clerum

28 August 2015
Buzo private dining room
New Westdale

Lachlan swallows the Barolo, and a gentle wave of leather, raisin and pepper rises through his nose. He laughs with the pleasure of it all – the soft booth cocooning him, the sharp smells of arrabbiata and romano in the air. 'That's magnificent,' he says, his mouth watering. It's moments like these that make it all worthwhile.

His friend laughs and slaps his thigh. 'Didn't I tell you it was a great vintage?' he says. 'Unbelievable.'

Lachlan takes another sip of wine and closes his eyes, resting his head on the velvet booth behind him, savouring the taste. He's the one who called the meeting, they can all just wait.

When he opens his eyes, the art on the opposite wall comes into focus. It's a dark seascape and he squints at it in the low light. It reminds him of the view from St Vincent's seminary, where his mother sent him when he was seven, just after his father died. It was where he met Cardinal Bart and learned how to sing in the boys choir. Where he became a man.

'That's a fantastic portrait,' he says, gesturing to it with his wineglass. 'It looks like the view from the window of St Vincent's dining room. Don't you think?'

The two others turn towards it and start nodding. There are exclamations of agreement. 'I never noticed that before, but you're right.' They start to reminisce about their youth.

Their immediate sycophantic agreement annoys him. It's shallow and insulting. All of them will do anything to stay in favour, to make sure the property keeps on getting sold and the money keeps on flowing.

Lachlan listens to their conversation, swirling the wine in his glass. Both of the men he's invited to dinner are sitting opposite him. As they talk, they face one another, an elbow on the table, glass of wine in hand, turned to the portrait, laughing as they recall their old schoolmates at the seminary. Then he can't take it anymore.

'Joe,' he says. 'Hey, Joseph,' he says more loudly, as if he's hailing a taxi from across the room.

When the man on the right turns to look at Lachlan, he continues, 'What's the guy's first name again? The Donnelly guy? The one who started the investigation, without you even knowing about it?'

The man casts a nervous glance at Lachlan's other guest and swivels back to the table, his jaw set. He starts to massage his forearm, like he's nursing an injury.

'Leo. Leo Donnelly.'

Lachlan runs his fingers down the stem of his glass, not looking at his friend across the table. The glass is thin between his fingers. There is silence now, as the other two men take cautious sips of wine, their eyes downcast.

He enjoys this: turning the mood in a room. He likes making them stop what they're doing and think twice. 'What do you know about Leo Donnelly?' he asks Joe.

'He started in narcotics and moved to homicide eight years ago. He's a senior investigator.'

Lachlan stays silent, watching the light play on the deep red wine in his glass. When he looks up at his old friend, he can see a light sheen of sweat on his upper lip.

'You've got this covered, right, Joey?' he asks, pursing his thick lips, pointing at the man opposite him. 'Can I tell Cardinal Bart you've got this investigation covered?'

Joe starts to nod, slowly and then faster.

'Of course,' he says. In the light, Joe's whole forehead shines with sweat. 'Of course you can, Lachie.'

THREE DAYS BEFORE

Tuesday 1 September
6.20 am
Meredith's place

Her phone rattles against the bedside table. She grabs it and tries to focus on the screen. It's a text from Charlie.

Evelyn's gone

Meredith squints at the screen and reads it again, trying to compute.

??? she sends back.

Died 4.20 am

The text nails her to the bed. She can barely lift the phone to call Charlie back. When she does, it rings through to voicemail. She repeats the exercise five times, and struggles to sit upright but she's too dizzy. Winded. When she finally gets up and walks to the kitchen, she can't feel the floor under her feet.

The only thought her mind allows is an image of Evelyn, as Meredith last saw her, the day she dropped her at Glencoe to see Bella. All she can see is Evelyn's face, her graceful gestures, and those hooded, uncompromising eyes. The eagle eye. The one she gave Meredith over lunch. The one Evelyn had given Meredith since she was ten.

Died 4.20 am

As she waits for the moka pot to boil, she looks at her phone again, as if that could change things. She tries to call – again.

Finally, Charlie picks up.

The voice coming through the phone is barely a whisper. 'She never told me she had a heart condition,' Charlie rasps. 'The only person who knew was Dr Carrington. It was a heart attack in her sleep.'

'Who found her?'

'Josie. She heard sounds coming from her room. The paramedics came but they were too late.'

'Charlie—'

'The funeral is Friday.'

Meredith knows better than to question the timing. She also knows she can't ask where Charlie was last night. She would have been where she always is these days – with Annabelle – and Meredith knows Charlie will be blaming herself for not being at Arden.

Her heart squeezes at not being with Charlie right at that moment. But her friend needs her to stay calm, the way she always is for Meredith.

'What do you need, babe?'

'Just be at Marsden House on Friday. The funeral's at one pm.'

Meredith's unable to speak.

'Just be there.'

Marsden is the McCrae family farm, an hour up the coast, with a small graveyard plot. Evelyn always called it her final resting place.

'Of course I'll be there.'

'I'll call you during the week. I'll check in.'

Meredith inhales deeply, realising she's been holding her breath. 'No way. I'm coming over right now.'

'No, you're not,' Charlie says. 'I'm at the office. I came straight here from the hospital morgue. I'm in court all day today.'

'Can't you get compassionate leave?'

'I haven't asked for it, Mere.'

'Why the hell not?'

Charlie breathes heavily into the phone. 'Evelyn wouldn't have wanted me to.'

'She just died, Charlie!'

'Yeah – and you know what she would have said: *Chin up, Charlotte. You've got your whole life to grieve.*'

Meredith chokes back a sob. 'I'm coming to Arden after my shift today. I'm staying with you this week.'

'That's what I hoped you'd say. Can you tell Bella?'

'Of course,' she says and Charlie ends the call.

Call me when you get this, Meredith texts Bella.

She flings herself onto her bed, turns her head to her pillow and moans like an animal. A craving for drugs begins in a slow pulse, then the ache crawls into her bones.

On the day Meredith's father's plane crashed into the Bering Strait, Evelyn and Charlie came to her apartment. Evelyn said it was to pay her respects, but really it was to wrap Meredith up in a blanket, speak softly to her and make her tea. She remembers Charlie on the phone, making arrangements, and Evelyn sitting on the sofa with an arm around her, whispering in her ear, *In the end, we're all orphans, Meredith. Every single one of us.*

On that day, sixteen years ago, Meredith technically became an orphan.

But only today did she feel like one.

It's all she can do to text Camilla and Ros: *Evelyn died – taking some leave*. Ros calls her and they make arrangements for the week's roster. Ros can take charge today but her little one's ill – they're short-staffed and they need to bring in backup.

Camilla texts back: *Please take all the time you need.*

Meredith lies spread-eagled on the bed, every cell struggling under a dull heaviness, like she's floating beneath the ocean. Her skin feels thin. The rain outside feels like it's inside her, her tears like a river in spate, her sobs like the heaving swells of the sea.

Her phone rings and she puts it on speaker.

'I just saw your text. All okay?'

'Bella ... It's Evelyn. She had heart problems. None of us knew – not even Charlie. She died last night.'

There's a long silence, which both women share. Then Bella breaks it. 'Are you okay?'

'I don't know. It ... she ...'

'She was the kind of woman who made the world work,' Bella says, her voice shaking.

'Yeah.'

'When is the funeral?'

'Friday.'

'I'm coming. You're going to need me.'

'I know.'

Two hours later, Meredith can't take it anymore. Staying at home isn't an answer and neither is going to Arden – if Charlie's working, so will she. She pulls herself off the bed and into the shower as if moving through tar. Then, not knowing what to do with herself, she drives over the Georgia Bridge and into the St Jude parking lot. She goes down into the tunnels, past the morgue, past Medical Records, down a separate set of stairs to the lower basement, to the archives. She starts to wander through the shelves, struggling to think of what she's looking for.

Abortions, terminations, procedures. Names of other girls. It's going to be pointless, she tells herself. St Jude's patient files aren't organised according to procedure, and the electronic database doesn't go back that far. Plus, it's a Catholic hospital – they don't even *do* terminations.

But she doesn't care – she's just passing time until she can see Charlie. Between then and now, she just needs to survive. If abortion played a part in the death of each woman, she can do some of her own research and find out if there were other patients transferred to hospitals for terminations.

Meredith's alone and thankful for the solitude. She wouldn't know how to explain to anyone why she's there and she can barely talk anyway. She knows she shouldn't be riffling through patient files, but she may find something useful to the case. Her thoughts keep turning round and round, as she walks up and down between the tall shelves, wandering in circles like a lost child, unsure where to start, reaching out for files, the labels making no sense to her. Finally, she ends up in a corner at a table where a computer terminal is gathering dust. She sits down and starts punching in words. She goes deep into the past, as far as the database will let her, as if she wants to find the beginning of it all.

Tuesday 1 September
7 pm
Camilla's office

'What ... on earth?' Camilla asks, her hands gripping the piece of paper so tightly it's quivering, threatening to rip in two.

'It just popped up,' Meredith mutters quickly.

When she surfaced from the archives, Meredith ran straight to Level 5 West. Seeing the light on in Camilla's office, she steamrolled ahead, convinced she needed to share what she'd found. But the flinty look on her boss's face is melting her resolve.

'*My file?*' Camilla says, spitting the words. '*My* patient file just *popped* up?'

Meredith swallows hard, her mind racing to explain why she's spent the day rooting through archives to find abortion records. *She's* not even sure – it was to help Leo, to help with the investigation. But she can barely think.

Leo says she's a terrible liar, but she knows the best lies are based in truth. 'One of our patients said a relative had received an abortion here. I said it couldn't be true – I told her about the Catholic health directives and their prohibition on abortion. But she insisted, so I decided to take a deeper look.' A patient had once told her this and, at the time, she challenged it. Now she knew better.

Camilla juts out her chin and throws the paper down. It floats down to rest sideways in front of Meredith. 'How *dare* you?' she whispers, and then her brow furrows. 'And why on earth would you be here, researching procedures, when you've just lost Evelyn—'

'I needed a distraction.'

Camilla looks back down at the document and straightens her skirt over her knees. Putting both elbows on the desk, she leans in, mustering for battle.

'Well, you don't know the whole story.'

'No,' Meredith says, shaking her head. 'That's right, I don't. I just know that you received an abortion here, at St Jude, on the twenty-fourth of December 1990. Twenty-five years ago.'

Camilla's eyes slide to her office door. It's wide open.

Meredith looks over to the door as well, then leans forward to whisper. 'There were others, Camilla – I found the files. From 1990 to 2000, St Jude gave young women abortions, countless ones, all in violation of the Catholic health directive.'

Camilla doesn't acknowledge Meredith's words – she's refusing to look at her.

When the silence becomes too much to bear, Meredith grabs the document and stands. 'Camilla, I'm sorry,' she says, her voice shaking. 'This is private and you don't need to talk to me about it. Forget I even mentioned it.'

Camilla's head snaps up and her lip curls. 'Damn right, it's private, Meredith.' Her Filipino accent uncoiling under the words. She nods to the hallway. 'Shut the door on your way out.'

Meredith walks to the door and then pauses. Instead of walking out, she closes it softly, and turns back to the desk, where Camilla's sitting, her back straight and her shoulders set. She sits back down.

'I am very, very sorry that I breached your privacy, Camilla. It was inappropriate. But since when did St Jude do abortions?' She gets up from her chair again and starts to pace. 'You know my politics; I don't agree with the Catholic health directive. Women need access to the procedure, with counselling and support. But at St Jude? The shining jewel in the crown of the Catholic healthcare system? Since when? I transfer young pregnant patients away from St Jude all the time, so they can get objective advice about their options. Am I wrong to do that? Can I give those women the care and advice they need, right here at St Jude?'

'No. You're right to transfer them.'

'But like I said, I've found records showing that St Jude terminated pregnancies. Not once. Not twice. But over and over—'

'That was a long time ago. Not anymore.'

Meredith throws up her hands. 'Well, when did things change?' she asks. 'When did the hospital start following its own rules?'

Camilla looks at her with a cynical smile. 'Are you really going to start lecturing me about rules, Meredith?'

She looks away, feeling dirty, and needs to sit back down. Camilla doesn't know half the rules she's broken. Images of stolen drugs whiz around her mind, like stones hurled through the air.

Her boss's businesslike voice breaks through her thoughts. 'The abortions stopped when Sister Marie Murphy retired.'

Meredith looks back at her, confused, and then motions to the photo on Camilla's credenza. 'That Sister Marie? Your mentor?'

Camilla nods at the surprised look on her face. 'She was on the board of the hospital – until fifteen years ago. She had,' she pauses, choosing her words carefully, 'a *liberal* approach to women's health issues.' Then Camilla's expression grows firm. 'Or perhaps I should say a *rational* approach. As far as Marie was concerned, until the Church allowed women access to birth control, she would pull out all the stops to help them deal with unwanted pregnancies.

'It started with me.' Camilla is as still as marble and the words come out heavily, as if heaved into the air by sheer force of will. 'Marie ordered the doctors to give me a termination here, at St Jude's – *against* the rules.' She takes a large sip of water from a glass beside her and then points her chin forward as if daring Meredith to challenge her.

'I was working with two nuns in a clinic in El Salvador. We were attacked by a gang of Contra paramilitaries. We were raped. I fell pregnant.'

Camilla pauses and stares into the distance. There is no sound in the room until she shifts in her seat. She pulls a package of tissues from her handbag and wipes her forehead. 'The priest assigned to counsel me about my unwanted pregnancy told me something beautiful had grown from something ugly.' Camilla laughs sarcastically. 'It was astonishing how he shaped my reality to reflect a doctrine.' Her neck turns a bright red. 'Staggering.'

When she looks at Meredith, her eyes are hard and unrepentant. 'The fact is, I did not want to be a single mother at thirty-eight, nor did I want to be pregnant. When I called Sister Marie, she told me to come back here, to St Jude.' She looks over to the photo of her old friend. 'Marie had mentored me in the Philippines. By that time – being a widow, with no dependent children – she had become a nun. She'd joined the Daughters of Mercy, to help build women's health clinics in various countries. She was the closest thing I had to family.'

Meredith chews her bottom lip, hoping Camilla won't jump down her throat at her next question. 'Lachlan Murphy's name is in the file. He approved the termination.'

Camilla's eyes bore into Meredith and her voice is frosty. 'I know.'

'Our Lachlan Murphy?'

'Lachlan ran the legal department of St Jude at the time. Marie Murphy was his mother.'

Meredith looks at Camilla with wide eyes. 'Your mentor, Sister Marie, was Lachlan's mom?'

Camilla nods. 'She came into her calling after her husband died and Lachlan left home. Marie was the one who told me I should go and help in the El Salvador mission. She felt responsible for what happened to me there, so she made Lachlan help me. He signed a document that provided for an exception to the Catholic health directive in this particular case, where the pregnancy was a result of rape.'

'But there isn't an exception for that.' Meredith knows the rules – she and Camilla gripe about them all the time.

'Nope, there isn't. Lachlan lied for me, I got the termination and the hospital file was buried. Until now,' Camilla nods at the document in Meredith's hand, 'thanks to you,' she adds, her voice thick with acid.

'Did you ever talk about it with Lachlan?'

Camilla starts to laugh again, but the sound is empty and bitter. 'Are you kidding?' She shakes her head. 'Lachlan is a different beast from you and me. He's Opus Dei. He has friends in the Curia. This,' she stretches her arms wide, 'is his life's work. Do you remember that nun who helped a young woman terminate her pregnancy? Lachlan made sure she was excommunicated. And all the young women who come seeking advice for unwanted pregnancies? Lachlan ensures they're transferred. Whenever he can, he makes a point of interpreting the directives as strictly as possible, to the best effect, in front of the widest audience. Like he's diverting attention from what's going on behind closed doors.'

Meredith's confused but listens, not wanting to interrupt.

Her boss's eyes are distant, as if she's remembering a vague dream, but then she looks sharply at Meredith. 'You have to see things for what they are. Lachlan is of the Church.' Camilla stands, as if to stretch her legs, then leans over, her voice becomes a bitter whisper. 'This is how it works, Meredith. All these rules – the rules of celibacy, the rule against abortion, the rule against homosexuality. Catholics break them. *All the time.* And then we spend the rest of our days feeling guilty.' She hunches her shoulders, pretending to cower from someone. 'Always looking over our shoulders, worried about who's going to find out, making corrupt deals to keep our secrets hidden.' She sighs. 'Sister Marie always said, *Rules that don't acknowledge our humanity do nothing but corrode our hearts and minds.* That was her philosophy – it was what she lived by. And, yes, it meant she broke rules. But I believe she led a just life.'

Both women are quiet for a time. Then Camilla sits back down, picking up the document and folding it, putting it in her desk.

As she watches Camilla, Meredith shakes her head. 'I can't see how Marie convinced Lachlan to approve abortions. Maybe once. But not repeatedly. Not over and over. What do you mean he's diverting attention from what's going on behind closed doors?'

'Oh, I don't know,' Camilla says, shaking her head vigorously. 'I don't know how Marie got Lachlan to do things. She probably had something on him. That's the only way you get to a man like Lachlan. You need leverage,' she says quietly, as if her mind is miles away.

They can hear the cleaning staff in the hallway and Camilla starts to fiddle with the papers on her desk, putting things into careful piles.

Feeling an obligation to share the real reason why she found Camilla's file, Meredith overrides caution and blurts out, 'Leo's found another connecting factor between the victims. They've each had an abortion.'

Camilla keeps packing up, but her motions get more deliberate. She slowly looks at Meredith and holds her gaze. 'I thought you weren't helping with the investigation. I thought that had stopped.'

'I'm not helping,' she lies. 'I just found out this fact and that's the real reason I went into the archives.' Feeling desperate, her voice starts to break. 'I just want to make sure we don't lose another woman, Camilla. I want to be aware of any other patients who've had abortions. Or anyone else exposed to the same risk factors as these women. I just want to keep our patients safe.'

Camilla swallows. 'So, in doing your research, you found my file?'

Meredith nods.

'And each of the victims has had an abortion?'

'Yes, but ...' Meredith looks at her imploringly, 'that's confidential – I'm not really supposed to know.'

Camilla breathes in heavily and rubs her face with her hands. 'God, Meredith, seriously?' She slaps the desk hard. 'Are you seriously cautioning me about confidentiality?' She waves her hands as if to dismiss the subject and hits the glass of water, spilling it over her desk. 'Damn!' she yells, pushing her chair away.

Meredith springs out of her seat. 'I'll grab some paper towels,' she says, sprinting out of the office, down the hallway to the coffee bay. Her phone vibrates in her pocket as she's running back.

She races into the room just as Camilla is putting down her mobile. Her boss grabs some paper towel, and both women mop up the mess, focusing on the table rather than each other.

Camilla stands and grabs her bag again, signalling the meeting is over. 'I have another round of budget and forecast meetings with the Department of Health to prepare for.

'Meredith, you have no idea how complicated this place is,' she continues, as she clips her bag closed. 'You dig and you find things and you judge, but you have no idea about the complexities; how many compromises are required, just to keep the doors open.'

Meredith is still trying to catch her breath. Without knowing why, her eyes start to well up. 'All I want to do is get to the truth. I just don't want to see another woman die by the same hand.'

Camilla walks around the desk. Taking a look at Meredith, she stops. 'You look pale,' she says, gently placing her hands on her shoulders. 'You shouldn't even be here. Go to your friend Charlie. Take as much time as you need. I know Evelyn was like a mother to you.'

For that moment, Camilla is the person Meredith knows her to be. She takes Meredith's head in her hands and pulls their foreheads together gently. *'Requiem aeternam dona eis, Domine, et lux perpetua luceat eis; Requiescant in pace. Amen,'* she whispers, her eyes closed. Then she picks up her things, throws her handbag over her shoulder and walks out of the room, shoes clicking with steely professionalism down the hallway.

Meredith turns to leave, throwing wet wads of paper towel in the garbage on her way out.

Remembering her phone vibrating earlier, she reaches for it to find out who texted her, but has to read the message three times to understand it.

She knows about the abortions – I don't know what else she knows.

It's from Camilla.

But Camilla was in the room. Why would she have texted Meredith?

She must have meant to send it to someone else.

A wave of fear crashes through her. Then rage.

Pity, Camilla, she thinks. Pity that with everything you can do with a smartphone, you can't 'undo' a text.

Wednesday 2 September
12 pm
Lab C

Leo's text arrives at 10 am: *Cambden and jeffries – can you come at noon? Urgent.*

Then it's rush, rush, rush, and Meredith dives into a cab at noon. She's late but she's not sure it matters. She has no idea where she's going or why. Once again, Leo is not returning her calls.

The corner of Cambden and Jeffries sits in the middle of a suburban business park. Her cab pulls up to a squat block of grey concrete, sheathed in smoked glass. There's no sign on the door and no street number.

She stands on the sidewalk as her taxi pulls away, and then spots Leo hopping out of a black car on the opposite side of the street. With a quick hello and a wink, he whisks her inside, where she's searched, scanned and swiped into a small elevator. After being spat out on Level 4, she follows him through a winding warren of hallways to a door labelled Lab C.

Leo pushes the bell by the door knob and waits.

Meredith looks at him with her eyebrows raised. 'Are you going to give me a hint of what this is about? I had to lie to leave the ward—'

Just then, the door opens and a short, dark-haired man, dishevelled and harried, ushers them into a room with a long table and several chairs. One wall of the room has a large glass window that overlooks another room with two rows of computers, battery-hen style. The seats are empty.

'Diego, this is Meredith Griffin, Lead Operations Manager at St Jude Emergency. She's our main contact at the hospital,' Leo says.

Diego's hand shoots out and Meredith's trapped in a furious handshake, her shoulder joint rattling. The man is talking with a heavy Spanish accent at the speed of a rushing rapid. 'Diego Santander, Computer Forensics. I run Lab C. Great you could come. We have several questions – it didn't make sense to use Leo as a conduit. Best to just get the hospital expert in, do it direct, you know. Please, please, sit down.'

Mercifully released, Meredith sits down at the table where Diego has pulled out a chair for her. While he's busy opening his computer and arranging his things, she shoots Leo a slightly horrified look. 'Hospital expert?' she mouths.

Diego's hands never stop moving – they run through his hair, pick up and play with his pen, go in and out of his pockets. His frenetic energy fills the room and rattles Meredith's nerves. After the meeting with Camilla, she spent the night awake at Arden with Charlie, planning Evelyn's funeral. It's been a hard morning in Emergency, it's lunchtime and she hasn't eaten a thing since yesterday. She raced to get here by the time in Leo's cryptic text and she's not been told why she's needed. Tonight she's working the ten to eight because Ros has a sick kid at home, and the relief staff have relieved themselves by failing to show up. There's still nineteen hours of shiftwork left on the clock and she's already sick with exhaustion. What she really needs is a quiet moment in the St Jude patient courtyard, with a cheese sandwich and her meditation podcast, not a meeting in a windowless safe house with a hyperactive computer scientist.

The sound of Diego clicking his pen up and down, over and over, grinds her thoughts back to the present moment. 'I'm Leo's forensic analyst,' he says. 'My world is computers – network analysis, code analysis. We track people's use of their computer and phone, the systems they've linked to, their internet search behaviour, you name it. I've taken clones of Mark Roth's and Stuart Chester's computers.'

Diego hops up from his chair and bounds over to the whiteboard. 'Mark's computer was pretty boring. But Stuart's,' he smiles, picking up a marker and waving it around, 'Stuart's was interesting.'

Diego turns back to the whiteboard and starts drawing diagrams as he talks. 'Stuart uses three computers – a desktop in his office, a desktop in his study, and a small laptop that he uses with patients and while travelling. They're all linked to the hospital network, through Citrix – a completely standard architecture for remote working. This is a set-up that allows him access to hospital systems, patient files and directories, from any computer. Nothing unusual there.'

'Right. I have a similar system.'

'Yes. Well, Stuart keeps a special cache on his local drive. This is where he has his summaries of the recorded patient sessions – the files he kept out of the hospital filing system.'

'Yup,' Meredith says. 'St Jude prohibits doctors keeping separate, secret, files. We call them ghost files.'

'Well, it's the ghost files where we spent the most time. And they turned up a few anomalies.'

At this point, Diego runs back to the table and turns his small laptop around so Meredith can see the screen.

'This shows you the metadata of Stuart's laptop. It's an access log.' He leans across the table and points to the screen. 'These dates and times show you when this file was accessed.' Diego traces the code down the screen with his index finger. 'There,' he says, his finger stopping at a particular line of code, 'do you see this line in the log, here?'

Meredith nods and then looks at him with a small furrow in her brow. 'I do, but I'm sorry, to me it looks like all the rest.'

'Indeed. It does look the same. Except for one thing. Do you see this suffix here?' He points to a short line of code.

'Yes.'

'This is a signature of technology that erases spyware. It's an indication that someone has viewed Stuart's computer and then tried to erase their steps. They've used spyware to infiltrate his computer, and the spyware contained deletion code to remove any trace – except for this fingerprint, which we've detected.'

He beams at Meredith with pride. 'We think someone's been accessing Stuart Chester's files. And it's been happening for at least a year.'

'Would Stuart have known he was being watched?'

Diego shakes his head furiously. 'It's very possible for someone to use spyware without you knowing it, they just need to find a way to load it onto your hard drive. To make it all work, they just need access.'

Meredith's pulse quickens. If Stuart was being watched, who else was? Was she being monitored? Images of her umbrella being moved, her coat not on its hook, her serpentine stone vanishing and then appearing on Stuart's desk – they flash through her mind in quick staccato. She can see Lachlan standing over her in the elevator, saliva shining on his lips. She puts her face in her hands and starts to rub her tired eyes, trying to push the image of an Ativan packet out of her mind's eye. 'Well, can you track it somehow? Can you track the computer that sent the spyware?'

'Not precisely. But we know generally where it comes from.' Diego pauses and gives her another big smile. 'That's where you come in.'

'What do you mean?'

'The spyware was dropped by someone "in network".'

Meredith looks over to Leo. His face is blank. 'Meaning?'

'The spyware was sent via email from a computer within the hospital.'

Her tongue runs along the inside of her bottom lip where she's been chewing it. The flesh is ragged. 'So, someone within the hospital has been spying on Stuart? All this time?'

'Yup.'

The usual prickling in her skin starts and her head begins to ache for chemical relief. Then it dawns on her. 'Wait, you've just taken a clone. If there's spyware on the clone, there's still spyware on Stuart's computer. And Stuart's still seeing patients at his clinic, which means he's still being spied upon.'

'Indeed.'

Meredith looks at Diego and then at Leo. A sound comes from her throat but she seems to have lost the power of speech.

'Yup,' Diego says, as if to encourage her, 'but that's not all. As soon as we discovered the spyware, we recalled Stuart's computer on the false pretence that the original clone had been faulty. We then planted our own spyware and returned the computer to Stuart.'

'So, you're spying on Stuart too.'

'Not really—'

'You're spying on the spy?'

'Yes! Exactly!' Diego flashes her an enthusiastic grin and bounces back to his seat, laughing in the direction of Leo. His exuberance produces an intense craving for Ativan, which she tries to ignore by reaching for a glass of water on the table and drinking it down in one go. Leo is sitting opposite, leaning back in his chair, hands behind his head, watching his colleague in action. 'We see every time the spy gets access to Stuart's computer and we see every file he opens.'

Meredith plays with a strand of hair that's escaped her topknot. 'What sort of stuff does he open?'

'Most of his time is spent on Stuart's patient summaries. He spends hours and hours on them.'

'Has he made copies of—'

'Yes,' Leo says, in a fierce voice. 'He's made copies of the summaries for Katherine, Tabitha and Patrice. But not just those. He's made copies of others too.'

Meredith's blood starts to surge in her head. 'Leo, Stuart needs to stop seeing patients immediately. He's like a gateway for the perpetrator to access fresh victims!'

At this, Diego jumps in, leaning across the table with an expression of earnest self-righteousness. 'Meredith, if we tell Stuart to stop – to fully stop seeing his patients – we can't monitor the perpetrator's access and identify who it is.'

'Then we're using the patients as bait!'

She looks at Leo, speechless. She can't believe he's agreeing to this. She can't believe she's a part of this.

Leo just looks back at her, neutrally, offering no apology and no explanation.

She gets up and makes for the door. 'Well, I can't be part of it,' she states emphatically. Turning back, she looks at Leo as if he has two heads. 'Why on earth are you telling me this, Leo? Why am I here?'

He stands and puts his hands up to try to calm her. 'Slow down, Meredith.'

She sighs and steps back from him, crossing her arms over her chest and looking away.

He moves closer. 'This is a controlled operation. We're managing the risks. And we can't give up this lead.'

She's fuming, but holds fire, waiting to hear what else Leo has to say for himself.

'Listen, you can turn around and walk out of this investigation any time you want Meredith, you know that. You owe us nothing. You brought us a lead, and I'm grateful for it. But now that we've narrowed this down to St Jude employees, I need a St Jude employee list covering the period that Stuart's worked there.'

Meredith just looks back at him with a dumbfounded stare as he keeps talking. 'If the perpetrator is an employee of St Jude, it's likely he was also an employee of St Therese when Kelly Kosovic died. I've got the employee files for St Therese. Now I need St Jude's, to crosscheck. You can get access to these records, on your own and quickly, without alerting St Jude management.'

Leo keeps looking at her intently, holding her gaze, then speaks more quietly: 'It'll take the push of a button, Red – you know it and so do I. I need these files now, and if I ask for a search warrant—' he stops, and rubs his hands over his face and through his hair, shaking his head. 'If I do this via search warrant, Joe Bradley will circle the wagons around the hospital, Lachlan and Stuart. It's happened to me before, Meredith.'

She remembers him telling her, the night he showed her the photos of Patrice, how easily cases can derail.

Meredith pulls him aside, further out of Diego's earshot. 'I can't keep on doing this, Leo,' she whispers, trying to keep the desperation out of her voice. Fear and shame are pummelling her insides – but overriding everything is panic. If she doesn't help Leo, if she waits for due process, what if it all gets gummed up? What if Lachlan stonewalls to stop the investigation into his beloved hospital? And, in the meantime, what if another woman turns up in Emergency, bleeding from a cut femoral?

'I know it's a hard time for you, Red – with Evelyn and all. But, as I said, this is a controlled operation. We're monitoring the perpetrator. We're narrowing in on employees. And we have to do it without alerting anyone. As soon as Bradley knows, Lachlan will know, and then Stuart will know, and then ...' Leo shrugs his shoulders, going quiet for a moment, and with a quick glance at Diego, continues in a whisper. 'For some reason, no one likes this investigation. No one at State Crime Command and no one at your hospital. I don't know why, all I know is that we have to keep our methodology quiet. And I know, I know, I'm asking you to break rules here. But you shared a bit of information with me once. All I'm asking you to do is share a bit more.'

Leo slurs his last words and Meredith looks up at him sharply. His eyelids are swollen and his skin drawn. It's clear he hasn't slept for days. She knows he's following the lead on Stuart's files on the down-low, with the few police resources he absolutely trusts. During the day, he's working on other cases, making it clear he's busy, filing case reports and all the time he's trying to find other leads for this case. He's doing a double shift – and he's been doing it since they told everyone the case was going cold.

In the silence, Meredith wonders when she started down this road. When did she begin breaking all the rules? Was it the night at the police station when she gave Leo her report on the three female patients they'd lost, or was it way back when she pocketed her first Ativan, inadvertently left at the bedside of a discharged patient?

When Leo tries to speak, she puts her hand up and closes her eyes, nodding quickly. 'Okay, okay,' she whispers.

Leo's wrong. Her access rights don't entitle her to go rooting through employee records.

But he's right about everything else.

She's broken the rules before. If she can break them to get high, she can break them to stop a murderer.

Thursday 3 September
5 am
St Jude Emergency

Meredith's at the triage station, reviewing the files of the night's work. It's finally quiet, and an image of the steaming-hot bath she'll run when she gets home floats past her eyes.

There are two young women in the diagnostic treatment unit who the physicians may admit to hospital. Tests on one of them have confirmed she has Type 2 diabetes, missed taking her insulin and is recovering from taking too much ecstasy at a rave. The other has an acute urinary tract infection. She's getting penicillin and fluids before possible discharge. If neither improves by shift change, Meredith suspects the physicians will admit them to hospital. She has two patients on fast track: one at the end of a quick IV, the other getting a few stitches to a head wound.

The case she's really worried about is a six-year-old boy in the recovery room with what looks like a fractured arm, sitting next to his mother, who's covered in bruises. The father is nowhere to be seen, and when Meredith asks the mother for his name she looks away, bottom lip quivering.

Sarah Sampson is with the little boy, trying to dress what appears to be a carpet burn on his face. She hears Sarah's voice over his sobs: 'What colour bandaid would you like, Michael? We have blue and orange. And, look, here's a Winnie-the-Pooh bandaid – would you like that one?' Meredith turns away, making a mental note to call Social Services and confirm if the police received a domestic violence report on him and his mother.

When she hears quick footsteps behind her in the hallway, her spirits sink. She needs a break and the Emergency team does too. Steeling herself, she turns around to see Leo. His hair is messy and he's wearing the same suit he wore the day before at Cambden and Jeffriès. He's also out of breath.

'Hey,' he says, 'happy to see me?'

'Thrilled, actually,' she says with as much of a smile as she can muster. 'If you'd been a trauma case, I would have run the other way.'

He has something in his hand – a USB. 'You've done the compare already?' she asks, eyebrows raised.

Leo had been right, after all. Once she had found her way to the correct database, it had taken her all of a couple of minutes to download a complete list of St Jude employees. Not trusting email or any other police employee, Leo had picked up the list from her around midnight.

She looks at the colour of his face and feels worried. 'Babe, have you had any sleep?'

'Some,' he says, looking around and giving her hand a squeeze. 'Diego has cots in Lab C.' He waves the USB at her. 'Is there somewhere we can go to look at this in private?'

Meredith glances around. Leo's visit has brought her energy back and she's on high alert. It isn't unusual for detectives to be roaming around Emergency at all hours and no one's fazed to see Meredith with him, so she motions that he follow her to her office and shuts the door. They both pull up chairs and open the file on her computer screen. It's a list of ten surnames.

'These people all worked at St Therese when Kelly died. Now they're employees of St Jude. Their employment period covers the dates of each woman's death. I need their employment files.'

Her brain is whirring now, trying to piece together how she'll get access to specific employment files. 'I have to think about how I can arrange this …'

He leans over and takes her hand. 'Are you going to be all right? When does your shift end?'

'Soon,' she says, hitting print on her computer. The clock above the door says 5.20 am. 'Give me a few hours. I'll see what I can do. I'll text you when I'm done.'

They both stand up at the same time. Leo turns to her, his face drawn, but his eyes clear and hungry. He wraps her in his arms and pulls her close. 'You look like the walking dead, Leo,' she says into his shoulder.

'I feel like it,' he says back. She squeezes him tight until he releases her.

'I'll be back around nine am,' he says, 'Oh – and be sure to include their rosters. I need to know if they're working today or tomorrow, so I know how to contact them for an interview.'

As Leo makes to leave, she grabs the list off the printer and looks through the surnames and first initials. Then she does a double take. The last name is J de Rhiz – Jacob de Rhiz, her old friend from security.

'It can't be,' she says. 'It can't be Jacob.'

Leo turns, with a grim look on his face. 'Oh, really, Meredith? It can't be Jacob? The head of IT and Facilities? The main liaison between St Jude's technology department and the hospital's security systems? The guy with access to every room, computer and electronic record St Jude has?'

The thought immobilises her. A sore hollow starts to form in her middle, like someone's cut out her entrails – it's the knowledge that she may discover something horrific about someone she's spent thirteen years befriending. She's frozen with fear, but every cell in her wants to run, past Leo, down the corridor and out the door, away from the investigation and the hospital, away from her patients.

With his hand on the door knob, Leo turns back to her again. 'Almost forgot. I need something else: the dates of each woman's visit to the hospital and whether these six were on shift at the time.'

She looks blankly at him, still trying to compute the fact that Jacob's name is on the list. 'Meredith,' he says, 'I know this is hard, but I need to know if these employees were rostered on the same days the women were admitted to the hospital. If they were, there's a greater chance the people on this list would have known about them.' He walks out of the office, careful to look down the hall both ways before he leaves. He's clearly as concerned as she is about running into Lachlan or Camilla.

'Wait!' she whispers, waving him back into her office. 'Have you crosschecked these against the list of running-club members that I gave you?'

He approaches her nodding his head. 'Yes,' he says, keeping his voice down. 'But just so you know, our computers didn't detect any insignia on the clothes of the man at Patrice's party.' He looks at her with an earnest smile and starts to head off again.

'Where are you going?'

He musters a wider grin. 'Home to shower and feed my girls,' he says over his shoulder, winking at her. 'Thanks, Red.'

She looks at the clock again. She only has a few hours.

As seven am draws near, Meredith finds time to down some coffee and take a quick shower in the staff locker room. When the day shift comes in, she's ready for changeover and moves through it at speed. Her heart rate rises as she runs down the hallway, thinking of how she's going to pull each employee's entire file, gripping her laptop against her chest like a piece of body armour.

When the elevator opens at Level 3, Meredith finds Vicky, the HR director's executive assistant.

'Hey, Vick,' she says, turning on the charm. 'I was meaning to ask you. Do you remember the Emergency training program we rolled out last spring? Well, there are about ten employees who missed the training entirely.' She shrugs her shoulders, 'I don't know how it happened – it just did.

'Anyways – sorry, I'm in a bit of a rush – I was thinking, given we're almost at year end, it might be good to get them all in for a short session. *But,*' she says, with a smile, and an apologetic look for being disorganised, 'it would help if I can just check their files to confirm, so I'm not wasting anyone's time, you know?'

'Sure, Meredith,' Vicky says, and starts leading the way to her office. She's been in HR for a good fifteen years, and known Meredith for thirteen of them. 'You can work off my computer – I'll head down for a coffee.'

She lets Meredith sit on her chair. 'Do you want one?'

'Oh, that would be great, Vick – thanks a mill,' she says, flashing her a stellar smile.

Once Meredith hears the elevator doors close, she pulls out the USB and gets to work.

Fifteen minutes later, Vicky is back with her coffee and someone else. It's Margaret Lawson, the director of HR. After an exchange of pleasantries, Meredith takes the USB and her coffee, and heads out of the office.

'Meredith,' she hears a tense voice say behind her. When she turns around, she sees Margaret holding a document in her hand. 'Did you leave this?'

Meredith looks down. It's the list of names she printed. In her sleep-deprived state, she left it on the desk. 'Oh dear, yes! Of course I did.'

She takes it from Margaret, giving her a rueful look. 'It must be fatigue. It's been quite a long night.'

Margaret just smiles thinly in response, her eyes drilling holes into Meredith.

Leo's right, Meredith thinks, she can't lie to save her life. Particularly when she hasn't slept for thirty-six hours.

She turns around, feeling Margaret's furious look, checking her watch as she jabs at the elevator button to take her down to Medical Records.

Thursday 3 September
7.30 am
St Jude Medical Records

The elevator crawls down to the tunnels, stopping on every floor. When the door opens to the basement she charges out, heading towards Medical Records at a fierce clip.

There's not a soul in the tunnels, so Meredith's walk turns into a jog as she thinks through how she's going to manually pull dates for each woman's visit to the hospital. She grips her laptop as she rushes past the supply rooms, past the morgue, past the corridor to Surgery.

At the door to Medical Records, she swipes in. Her security card doesn't work and the door stays locked. She does it again, listening for the familiar click. No luck. 'Fuck!' she whispers, trying again, her hands shaking. When she hears the welcoming click, she pulls the door open with such force, her shoulder is almost knocked out of its socket. As she bolts through the door, she runs straight into a young man on his way out, knocking several files out of his arms onto the floor.

'Oh my god – I'm so sorry!' she cries. Sweat breaks out on her back, there isn't time for this. She curses to herself as she helps him pick up files, continuing to apologise and making small talk. He's soft spoken and shy, and assures her it's no problem.

Crouched down within close range, she sees his toned forearms and his fine, pale skin. He's the young man from the records reception desk who helped her the first time she came down to check Tabitha's file, back in June. The same one Stuart and Mark were chatting to.

'God, you work hard,' she says, still feeling bad. 'The last time I saw you here was on a Sunday and now you're here at the crack of dawn on a Thursday? Don't you ever take a break?'

He turns to face her with an earnest look. 'I only take vacations when I'm not needed by the lead physicians.'

Meredith wants to laugh, thinking he's being facetious, but the look on his face tells her it's a grave matter for him. She glances at his badge, not remembering his name. 'Everyone needs a break, Daniel.'

'Yeah. Maybe. But I like what I do. I don't need that kind of physical release.' A thoughtful smile passes over his face as she hands him the last file, and he nods towards the door. 'Thanks. I have to take these files to Cardiology. Melissa can assist you – she's watching the desk. Can you help me with the door?'

With another look at her watch, she realises she has a little over an hour. She runs up to the desk and bangs on the bell, hoping Melissa isn't the girl who prefers looking at her newsfeed to doing her job.

'Coming,' a voice whines from behind some shelving. A few seconds later, a girl walks towards the counter, engrossed in her phone.

Meredith swallows her frustration and paints a sweet smile on her face.

Thursday 3 September
8.45 am
St Jude Emergency

Back in her office, she sends a text to Leo: *Done – at my office now.*

Meredith can feel the last drops of energy seep out of her as she looks again at the list of surnames and roles Leo's given her. None of these people seem like the right person. Her eyes run over Jacob's surname again. It seems he moonlighted for a period of two years – working the night shift at St Therese – a period that overlaps with Kelly Kosovic's death.

She shakes her head with disbelief. Jacob's a forty-year-old man with a family – she can't imagine him stalking young girls and killing them. But then her mind clicks back to the conversation they had when she asked how easy it would be for him to program an access card for her to override dispensing records in an automatic drug cabinet. How he winked at her when he handed it to her, how excited he was to get the promotion to head of IT and Facilities.

She shudders, and studies the other surnames on the list to try to put Jacob out of her mind. The other individuals are various aides, clerks, nurses and porters – people with limited access to records or patients or sensitive areas of the hospital. Somehow it feels like another dead end, and she's broken all the road rules to end up at it. She remembers Margaret Lawson's suspicious look and her shoulders slump, thinking about what it will feel like to be fired.

As she starts to throw things in her file bag, the image of a steamy bath resurfaces in her mind. That's what she'll do first, she thinks, as she pulls on her raincoat. Hot bath, then sleep, then to Arden, to be with Charlie.

A heavy knock on the door shakes her back into the present. Before she's had a chance to respond, the door opens and Lachlan Murphy's large body fills the frame.

'Meredith,' he says, his baritone voice rolling through the room.

'Lachlan,' she responds, feeling her brain catch on fire and her pulse quicken. 'How's things?'

'All good, thank you,' he says, walking in, slamming the door shut behind him. 'Margaret Lawson tells me you're having a particularly busy day,' he continues, sitting down in the chair across from her desk, ignoring the fact that she's got her coat on, ready to leave.

'Yeah, there's … there's some unfinished business to do with training—'

'Meredith,' he says curtly, holding his hand up. 'The director of HR told me you've pulled employee files. Here, at the hospital, this morning.'

She looks away, scanning the room, trying not to look at the USB sitting beside her handbag on the desk, trying not to think of Leo bursting through the door of her office to pick it up.

'I was just leaving – can we talk on my way out?' she says hopefully, picking up her bag and putting her hand over the USB.

Lachlan shifts his weight and the spindly chair creaks underneath him. 'Surely you can spare me a few minutes,' he says calmly.

She puts her bag down heavily on the desk, making sure to put it on top of the list of names, picturing her phone deep inside it, resisting the urge to reach in and type a quick text to Leo – telling him to stay away from her office.

Lachlan crosses his hands in his lap and looks across at her with his fleshy lips pressed together. 'The last time we spoke, I thought we had an understanding.'

She faces him, exhaustion reducing her care factor to zero. She leans against the edge of her desk and crosses her arms over her chest. 'Did we? How so?'

'We talked about how important it was for you to focus on your strengths. To focus on your *job*,' he says, glaring over his glasses at her.

She breathes in deeply and looks at the clock above her door. She hopes Leo's stuck in traffic.

'Have there been any complaints about my performance?'

Lachlan starts to laugh, but it's indulgent and sarcastic. 'Meredith, police requests for information come to my office. You know that.'

'Well, that's not quite right, Lachlan. I deal with police requests all the time.'

'Leo Donnelly has been in and out of here several times in the past twenty-four hours. I know that.'

'Leo Donnelly is in and out of here all the time. This is an Emergency ward. He's a homicide detective.'

Lachlan's face turns a darker shade of crimson. 'He's also in and out of here all the time because of you, Meredith. You have to know how bad it looks for you to be dating the detective who's investigating the hospital. And for you to be involved. Where are your professional boundaries? Do they even exist?'

Her stomach starts to turn, but as she starts to defend herself, he speaks again. 'It's time you told me what you know about the investigation, Meredith. I'm being serious now.'

She's about to ask him flippantly what investigation he's talking about, but catches herself, feeling the vibration of his anger. Instead, she opens her arms to show him she has nothing to hide.

'I don't know any more about the investigation than what Leo told us the last time we all met in the boardroom. You know the broad themes. The suspicious deaths involve patients from this hospital. Stuart's Psych department was the main connecting factor between all three girls – they were all self-harmers, had problems with depression or anxiety or post-traumatic stress, they were all involved in his research. All I know is what Leo's told you – the Psych department is no longer of interest to the police.'

Lachlan studies his nails as she's speaking. 'So,' he says, looking up at her. 'The Psych department, depression, self-harmers, suspicious suicides – what else?'

'I really am not—' she pauses, searching for words. She has a tension headache and the temperature in the room has gone up. 'I'm not that close to the investigation.'

Lachlan brushes lint off his shoulder. His cufflink glints in the light. 'But you've been digging into private medical files that do not concern you.' Seeing the surprise on her face, his mouth twists into a cruel smile.

'Don't deny it, Meredith. Camilla's told me you've even been going through the archives.' At the mention of Camilla and the archives, Meredith feels like a dead weight sinking to the bottom of the sea. Camilla's told him – about her involvement in the investigation and her search through the archives. She's told him that Meredith knows about the abortions performed at St Jude. It was Lachlan who Camilla had tried to text last night. She must have been so angry that she texted Meredith by mistake.

Her breathing gets shallow and a righteous anger rises inside her. 'Young women are showing up dead in my Emergency room, Lachlan, and there's been a startling lack of interest on the part of the hospital—'

'Be careful, Meredith,' Lachlan says slowly, 'before you start making accusations. Caution is hardly the same thing as a lack of interest. St Jude delivers care, the police investigate murder.'

'Okay, call it caution. Be cautious – fine. But lack of cooperation is an outrage. This has all been happening here,' Meredith says, pointing to the ground with her index finger, 'right here, at St Jude, on our watch.'

At this, Lachlan's face twists into a grimace. 'How dare you? I know what's happening. I know everything that goes on in this hospital. I have done for twenty-seven years. It's a complicated place, with a complicated history. You may poke around, play sleuth, conduct your amateur investigations into personnel files and archives, but you don't understand what's going on and you have no context.'

'I understand enough to know that there's a pattern going on, which no one has cared to pay any attention to.'

Lachlan looks at her, shaking his head, eyebrows drawn together in a furrow. 'What on earth are you talking about?'

'I am talking about the abortions,' she says.

'Well, so am I.'

'Well, it's relevant.'

'Relevant to what, precisely?' he asks, a shadow of confusion falling over his face.

'Relevant to this hospital! Relevant to our reputation! Relevant to the fact that there could be a murderer on our staff, right now, today!' Meredith's saying this at the top of her voice, but it's as if the words aren't landing. Lachlan's face just registers more confusion.

'What on earth do you mean?' he asks again.

'I'm talking about the abortions. The one that each of the victims had!'

Lachlan breathes out heavily, the penny clearly dropping. 'Oh god, you mean the women, the patients who died ...'

'What else would I be talking about—' she says, stopping, realising how crossed their wires are. She looks up at the ceiling and lets out an ironic laugh. 'No, Lachlan, I'm not talking about the abortions that happened at St Jude. I'm not talking about whatever you and your mother got up to all those years ago. Right now, that is not my concern. Hard as it is to believe, I'm actually thinking about the victims, the current investigation, not the range of different rules you may have broken in the past.'

Lachlan looks at her sharply, and his thick lips curl into a smile. 'Rules, Meredith?' He throws his head back and laughs. 'Really? You want to get self-righteous, with me, about the rules?'

Her eyes move up to the clock. Please, Leo – please don't come yet, she thinks.

'Fine,' Lachlan says, smiling confidently. 'You want me to show interest in the investigation? Then let's talk. Let's see who's being the uncooperative one,' he continues, motioning to Meredith as if to invite her to start. 'Tell me, do the police think this is all about some madman who kills women for getting abortions?' He looks at her with a penetrating stare. 'Do you think the perpetrator is some sort of fanatic?'

Meredith swallows hard. Her mind feels like it's cleaved in two and she's trying to put it back together. She sees that playing dumb is futile and exhales audibly. 'I really couldn't say, Lachlan.'

When she sees he's not going to let her off the hook, she holds on to her analytical side, like a rock in a storm. 'I really have no idea if abortion contributed to motive here. It could be entirely coincidental that each victim had an abortion.'

'That would be a pretty significant coincidence.'

'I disagree.' When he looks at her with his eyebrows raised in surprise, she continues. 'Lachlan, abortion may be anathema to you. But the statistics are clear. The number of girls who self-harm, deal with unwanted pregnancies, suffer from depression? We're not talking about statistically small numbers. And it's no surprise when these conditions overlap.'

'I see.' Lachlan's gaze drops to Meredith's desk. Her serpentine stone is sitting there and he reaches over to touch it. When it disappears into his large paws, she looks away. The thought of anything of hers in Lachlan's hands riles.

'So, what will the police do next?'

'Lachlan,' she says sighing, too exhausted to keep the exasperation out of her voice, and picturing Leo bursting through the door at any moment. 'The police really aren't sharing that much with me. I don't know what happens next.'

The serpentine stone pops out of Lachlan's grasp and drops onto the hard wood of her desk, with a loud crack. She winces at the sound.

'I think you do know, Meredith. I think you're participating in a police investigation into the hospital without consultation with your manager, or your legal counsel. That's a very serious breach of hospital protocol.'

She holds her ground, refusing to be drawn, her face stone. 'You're going to have to be more specific with your accusations. What's the charge, exactly? How exactly have I participated in the investigation?'

'Meredith, the fact that you even know abortion is a factor shared by all the victims is an obvious indication—'

'Abortion is a medical procedure,' she says sharply, failing to keep the ice out of her tone, 'that can sometimes lead to feelings of *profound* relief for the patient. *Other times*, it can lead to grief, and extreme feelings of loss, failure and self-persecution, which can in turn lead to depression and then to self-harm. Especially for a young woman who hasn't received proper support. Indeed,' she pauses, looking straight at Lachlan with the same accusatory glare she has seen him cast Camilla's way innumerable times, 'those feelings of grief and loss would apply to any woman, of any age, who has to terminate an unwanted pregnancy without proper support and care.'

Lachlan meets her stare and then looks away, shrugging his shoulders dismissively. While his eyes are facing in the opposite direction, she takes the chance to slip the USB into her coat pocket.

When he looks back at her, she meets his gaze. This man needed to understand how many young women his religious beliefs had cast adrift. 'Church doctrine might not recognise the number of unwanted pregnancies in this world, Lachlan, but the statistics are clear. The possibility that many of the self-harmers we see may have had an abortion is not a revelation. So, it's another characteristic that these young women share? So what? It's hardly a newsflash. And the fact that I know it features in the investigation is hardly proof of any misdemeanour on my part.'

She keeps holding his gaze. It takes only a moment, but the look passing from her to Lachlan says it all: *You've broken the rules of this place too. Now, get the hell out of my office, motherfucker.*

Lachlan holds her gaze too but says nothing. Then he stands up. 'There'll be consequences, Meredith.'

'Consequences for what, exactly?'

'For any breaches of hospital policy.'

'I'm sure there will be, Lachlan,' she replies, and then watches him turn and walk out her door.

When the door closes, she exhales. 'Fuck,' she says, putting her head in her hands.

A minute later, the door slams open. It's Leo.

'Jesus Christ, I thought he would never leave,' he says. I've been waiting around the corner for ten minutes!' Then he stops, seeing Meredith's hands shake. He comes straight over and takes both her hands in his. 'Red, are you okay?'

'I'm fucked, Leo,' she whispers, shaking her head. 'Royally fucked. I have to get out of here. They're going to fire me.'

Leo starts to say something, but she puts her hand up to silence him as she looks at her phone, reaching into her coat pocket with her other hand for the USB.

The text is from Camilla: *Call me right now.*

Thursday 3 September
9.05 am
Georgia Bridge

She puts the phone on hands free as she drives through the rain. Her eyes are starting to tear up with exhaustion. When Camilla answers, she doesn't get a chance to say hello to her.

'What the hell is going on?' Her boss's voice cracks like a whip through the interior of Meredith's car.

The traffic is thick for that time of the morning. Lorries, backed up all the way to Georgia Drive, suggest an accident on the bridge.

'I'm just gathering some information,' Meredith says, trying to weave her way through the traffic to get to the lane that appears to be moving.

'Employment records? For the police? Are you shitting me?'

'I am allowed to provide information on—'

'On *routine* Emergency patient queries, Meredith. Since when is pulling hospital employee files routine? Margaret Lawson told me you were at her assistant's desk, pulling files. She could barely get the words out, she was so angry. How could you be so stupid?'

Meredith's mind races. She squints through the rain to see the traffic, trying to focus on the voice yelling at her through the phone. 'I can't keep on protecting you, Meredith,' Camilla says in a tone that's tight and shrill, almost hysterical. 'I want a full report of what you know about this investigation. I want it in my office asap.'

It feels as though something bursts behind Meredith's right eye, and a searing pain rips through her head, tearing away any last vestige of restraint. 'Well, I'll tell you what I want, Camilla. I want to know why you aren't supporting this investigation. I want to know what the hospital is trying to hide.'

She starts seeing lights at the edge of her vision. She can hear Camilla breathing.

'Camilla?' she asks.

There is only silence. And then the line clicks dead.

'Fuck!' she yells as rain sheets down onto the roof of her car. The traffic ahead stops abruptly and she has to slam the brakes to stop from driving into the car in front of her. 'Fuck, Camilla,' she whispers, laying her forehead on the steering wheel, 'what the fuck is going on?'

Thursday 3 September
6.30 pm
Arden

She awakens to her phone vibrating on the bedside table, her head full of fog. It's always like this, the sleep after a night shift – never restful, feeling like your body is made of wet concrete, your head full of gravel.

'I'm packing my bags now. I'll be right over,' she mumbles in response to Charlie's pleading voice at the other end of the phone.

An hour later, she's punching the code into the security pad at the front gates of Arden and driving through, a packed bag beside her. When Josie lets her in the front door, she can hear talking from the sitting room, so makes her way down the main hallway towards it.

Charlie's walking around the room in her kimono, a crystal whisky decanter in her right hand, her phone in her left. She waves the decanter at Meredith and motions at her to sit next to Annabelle, who is curled up on the sofa, her long, balletic legs wrapped in a blanket, her skin pale, black circles around her eyes. Charlie swings the decanter around for emphasis, arguing with the funeral home about how to get the flowers from Arden to Marsden House.

'I told her I would arrange things,' Annabelle says under her breath, 'but she just won't let me.' Meredith puts her arm around the young woman's shoulders and Annabelle curls up against her. 'You know what Charlie's like, she wants to do it all.' Annabelle's voice gets even quieter. 'And she won't sleep.'

Charlie turns around to face them both, holds the phone away from her, and rolls her eyes at the person on the other end of the line. In the dim light, she looks skeletal – her eyes cavernous, and the hollows under her cheekbones deep. It strikes Meredith like a hammer blow how much Charlie looks like Evelyn in that light – her large blue eyes, her prominent, symmetrical bones, her aquiline nose. Charlie comes up to Meredith and leans over, giving Meredith a cheek to kiss. Then she's back at it, hurling instructions and insults at the person on the phone.

Meredith and Annabelle keep on watching Charlie waving the decanter in the air. 'She's going to drop that thing,' Annabelle whispers.

'No she won't,' Meredith whispers back. 'It's got single malt whisky in it.'

Annabelle lets out a soft laugh and curls deeper into Meredith's arms. 'What are your plans for tomorrow morning?' she asks. 'Will you drive up with us?'

'No, I'll meet you there,' Meredith says, noticing Charlie looking at her and quickly telling the funeral director to hold for a minute.

'What did you say?' Charlie asks, striding across the room. She sits on the other side of Meredith and grabs her hand. 'I need you to drive up with us.'

They can all hear the man on the other end of the phone: 'Hello? Hello?'

'I said, hold on!' Charlie yells into the phone.

Meredith's made arrangements to stop at Cambden and Jeffries to pick up a file from Diego Santander with material about the case. She also knows that Charlie will want to stay at Marsden for the weekend – along with a host of others. Meredith is aware the weekend could stretch into a week. She needs to have her own wheels, to get back to the city to help Leo.

Charlie, not really making sense, makes needy pleas for Meredith to ride in their car, then yells into the phone, 'I need another two minutes! No! Do not hang up! We need to settle this now!'

'Charlie,' Meredith says, looking at her friend with a kind smile, putting a hand on her thigh. 'You don't need to settle anything with the funeral director.'

'I do need to settle this,' Charlie says, 'the flowers need to be moved tonight and,' she starts shaking her phone, 'this prick is being impossible.'

'Come on,' Meredith says, squeezing her thigh, speaking softly. 'Let Annabelle deal with the flowers.' Charlie's about to put the phone back to her ear when Meredith stops her. 'Babe, you're obsessing. I know. I do it myself. You need to let Annabelle and me help.'

Charlie looks at her intently, her breathing rapid, chest moving in and out. 'Give the phone to Annabelle,' Meredith says.

Slowly, Charlie does what she says and passes the phone to Annabelle. The young dancer gets out from under the blanket and walks into the hallway to continue the conversation with the funeral director.

Meredith puts her arm around Charlie. 'Babe, I'm here for you tonight, I'll be here in the morning. And I absolutely promise I'll be at Marsden early – let's meet at Robert's Point at ten am. I really do need to just run into the office for a second before I leave the city.'

'What about Bella?'

'I've arranged it with Josie. A driver will pick Bella up and bring her here tomorrow morning. She'll drive up with you and Annabelle, and Josie will bring her back to Glencoe when the funeral's over.'

Josie's there with cups of tea when Meredith's phone starts ringing. With the housekeeper doting on Charlie, and giving her something to drink that's not alcoholic, Meredith grabs her phone and walks out of the room, past Annabelle.

It's Leo. He tries to keep the disappointment out of his voice as he explains he's had a chance to speak to everyone – except for two of the men, who aren't on shift and who he's tracking down. The first was an employee in the security department. Nothing worthy of comment came from him. He was a retiree – from the force, who Leo had been able to get a full write-up on. He had excellent references, and alibis for the nights when all three girls – Katherine, Patrice and Tabitha – had been killed. Three were nurses – one in Palliative and two in the Burn Unit. There was an administrative clerk they were still trying to find.

'One thing you should know, Meredith,' Leo says, his voice serious. 'We're still trying to track down Jacob. He's off today and, for some reason, doesn't want to answer his phone.'

As she hangs up and walks back to the lounge, despair trickles through her like tar. Josie goes past her through the hallway with a look of disapproval, and when Meredith gets back to the lounge, she can see why. Charlie's pouring whisky into her cup of tea and motioning to Meredith, asking if she wants the same.

An image of her friend Jacob de Rhiz flashes into her mind – how tall he is, how pale and fair, how young he looks, despite his forty years. And of course, she thinks, as she nods at Charlie's offer of a generous pour, how damned talented he is with computers.

Friday 4 September
8.30 am
Marsden House

The road to Marsden House runs like a ribbon up the crumpled coast. It hugs the jagged rock, winding its way around the peninsulas, carving deep into the inlets. What the road takes with a heavy death toll, it pays back with dizzying views of the crashing surf below, and then across the Pacific Ocean, to the west. Meredith remembers herself and Charlie, as teens, hanging their heads out the back-seat window, as Evelyn's zippy Alfa Romeo careened around the corners – each girl daring the other to lean further over the edge, both screaming with terrified glee, Evelyn barking at them to be careful, but unable to keep a wide grin off her face.

Around the tip of each point, Meredith feels suspended in air, surrounded on three sides by sea, light-headed with the memory of those long weekends and summer holidays she spent with Charlie up north at Marsden. Surrounding the house was a modest garden and wide lawns, which dropped off suddenly, with cliffs on the north, south and west. Beyond the cliffs were the rough beaches of the Pacific northwest coast, covered with grey granite pebbles, miles of seaweed and driftwood, where Evelyn had her favourite spot for bonfires, and the best outcrops to sit and watch autumn storms.

The weather had lifted for Evelyn's funeral. Searching the sky as she drives, Meredith knows the view from Marsden will be spectacular in all directions. After the exit to Robert's Point, she turns onto the private road that heads due west towards the sea.

The road forks and Meredith avoids going right, which leads up to the house. Instead, she continues to the left, to the promontory that looks southwest. After a few hundred metres, she pulls over to the side of the road and walks up the path to an old bench built by the McCraes, offering a long view back down the coast from where she had come. Her watch says 8.45, giving her some time before Bella, Charlie and Annabelle would arrive.

Sitting on the old wooden bench, she looks out to sea, thinking back over her life with Evelyn – how much the old dame demanded and how much she gave back. Evelyn wasn't just a mentor – she was a comrade. It was Evelyn, Charlie and Meredith against the world. She was an absolute loyalist.

As Meredith scans the surface of the sea, she realises it was more than that. Evelyn saved her. At nineteen, Meredith was alone in the world with a deeply troubled sister to watch over. She was the same age as Tabitha Norsman, and several years younger than Katherine Richardson. Without Evelyn, she could have been one of those girls, running blades through her skin, shooting dirty heroin into her veins.

The thought makes her look down at the large yellow envelope peeking out of her handbag. Diego had brought it down to the lobby for her at Cambden and Jeffries before she left the city. It had everything – the hospital files on all four girls, Stuart's summaries of Mark's counselling sessions, the police files, the victim profiles.

As she starts flipping through it, the story of each woman unfurls off the page. In background and circumstance, each was different. But in Meredith's mind, they mingle together, like thin wisps of sea mist, each curling around the other, before disappearing with the shifting breeze. She sees in each of their stories the same vine of vulnerability that creeps up and bursts in a final, brutal release.

Release. Strangely, the word doesn't appear in Mark's transcribed counselling sessions – only in Stuart's carefully worded summaries. Each of Stuart's treatment plans speak of it. It's not a medical term, yet he prescribes it over and over for each woman – they were each to seek 'physical release'. The phrase keeps repeating and it's a strange reference – suggesting some sort of physical relaxation. Perhaps exercise, Meredith thinks.

The sound of Bella, Charlie and Annabelle walking up the path interrupts Meredith's ruminations. She stuffs the papers back into her handbag and rises to meet them. She does a double take when she sees her sister. In a narrow, long-sleeved black dress, tights and shoes, with her hair tightly pulled back and her eyes heavily made up, she looks strikingly like their mother. Annabelle's wearing a black shift dress with ballet flats. Her long brown hair is braided down her back. Charlie's in a black pant suit with large sunglasses, her short hair combed back and glistening with gel. They hug and kiss, not exchanging a word, and then sit on the bench together, all eyes trained on the western horizon.

But as they sit there, a thought keeps intruding into Meredith's meditations – the words 'physical release' clang around in her head and their strangeness unsettles her. On the way back to the car, she sends a quick text to Leo: *Victims' treatment plans prescribe 'physical release' – check – another similarity to add to the victim profile database?*

At the sound of a car, she looks up. The hearse has arrived, along with a series of other cars, moving slowly up the road to the house. Then she turns her phone off, drops it into her handbag and locks everything in her trunk.

The rest of the day is for Evelyn.

Friday 4 September
10.25 pm
Darley's Beach

It was just meant to be a short walk by the sea.

The reception after Evelyn's funeral promised to carry on until late, but at seven pm she said her farewells and Charlie saw her to her car. Meredith was going to go straight home but the turn-off to Darley's Beach beckoned – it was the signpost to a twenty-five-year-old ritual. Walking past the abandoned lookout with its broken picnic tables, and going down the wooden stairs to the shoreline, she took her time, recalling how she, Charlie and Evelyn would often stop there for one final look at the western horizon on the drive home from long weekends spent at Marsden.

But the dark has started to bother her and the tide is coming in. Turning on her phone, she sees Leo's texts and the last one shoots adrenalin through her.

What did he say? He said they were monitoring the predator, that it was a controlled operation. But her doubts about using patients as bait explode in her head. Now she knows who the next victim is. It's there, in Leo's last text:

She's next.

Her thighs burn as she runs through the deep sand, her breath like sandpaper on her throat. She trips on driftwood, stumbles and falls, a bloody cross driven into flesh flashing before her eyes as her face hits the sand.

She gets to the base of the wooden steps and takes them two at a time, her feet slamming on the planks. Driving rain slices across her face and the wind bites through her coat. The top step is loose and her foot catches on it, sending her flying forward over the pavement, soaring in midair, arms splayed in front, coat trailing behind. When she hits the ground, it's face first again, the gravel road grating her cheek, shredding the palms of her hands, ripping the delicate skin on the insides of her wrists.

She makes it to her car, wet with sweat and her cheek bloody. Her hands, bleeding and burning hot with road rash, push against the cool steering wheel and her back presses against the seat. She floors it and spins the car around, sending a rooster tail of gravel flying over the broken picnic tables, her tyres squealing as they make contact with the asphalt of Darley's Beach Road.

She swings into the opposite lane to overtake holiday traffic, zipping back just in time to avoid an oncoming car. An angry horn blasts through her window as she speeds up the ramp to the highway, passing three other cars. She crests the next hill and rounds the first peninsula corner, her tyres almost leaving the road. Her car scrapes the guardrail and sparks fly.

Meredith knows the timings – twenty minutes from Darley's Road to North Head, thirty minutes on the ring road after that. She grips the steering wheel and presses the pedal to the floor.

It's the fatigue, she thinks. Fuck! That's why she didn't see it sooner. Her heart's going so hard, she thinks it will seize. As she careens around corners, a series of images flash through her mind like a strobe. The access he had to the patient records; the crucifix, the fair hair and fair skin. And the words. The words that now lie in her throat like dry stones. *Physical release*. The words he spoke to her. Only yesterday, when they were both crouched on the floor, picking up the mess of files lying near the door of Medical Records. The words that spell murder.

The traffic thickens as she reaches the suburbs. Streetlights pulse past her. She weaves and threads through cars that appear motionless. Blood. She can see it now – the slash on white skin, a red river gushing from an artery, bleeding into a bathroom drain in Victor Allen Park, a mattress in a shooting gallery, the clear water of a white porcelain bathtub in a chic bathroom on Church Point.

The timings, the timings – how much time does she have? When did the text come in? She reaches for her phone, trying to keep her eyes on the road, and attempts to punch in her password. It fails. She tries again. The phone slips from her bloody hands and falls to her feet. She bends down, reaches between her legs, tries to steer as her fingers grasp at the floor, then veers onto the wrong side of the road and swings back. She finds the phone and punches in her password a second time. She scrolls through to the last text. It came in at 9.45, almost forty-five minutes ago. She's still twenty minutes away. She floors it.

She phones Leo again – it keeps going straight through to voicemail.

Ten minutes away, and stuck behind a slowcoach. Meredith swings onto the footpath. They only do this in the movies. She's doing it. She's doing what they do in movies. It's three roundabouts away. She speeds straight through all of them. There are pedestrians. She throws her weight on her horn and they jump out of her way, swearing and smashing her trunk with their fists as she speeds past.

She flies through the open front gates of Glencoe and brakes right behind Leo's parked car – she wants to breathe, but can't. Something's not right.

She runs up to the cabin, her mind empty, her body propelled by terror, feet springing up from the grey slate. She looks down at the herringbone pattern of stone, feels its hardness as she plants each step, grateful that it's stone and not sand under her feet.

She runs the footpath up to the cabin and it feels a mile long, then turns around to the side, past the first of the four tall windows. All the blinds are up but no lights are on. Flashes of violent movement and muffled sounds come through the glass; the walls seem to heave, containing a monstrous, murderous force behind them. The capricious moonlight gives her a glimpse of a face, then an arm, then a hand. Body parts appear and then disappear, as if on flashcards.

She rounds the corner and sees the front door wide open. There's a crash of furniture, the grunt of grown men, the sick sound of bone against skin, the thumping of hard bodies against soft surfaces. There's swearing, shoes against floors, more furniture breaking, the sound of running, the sound of falling, more cursing. Then silence.

'Leo!' she screams. A roar like a jet engine surges through her head – a combustible wave of terror and panic and fury. A man is sitting on Leo, strangling him, but when he hears her scream, he turns his head towards her, a crucifix dangling from his neck, swinging back and forth. There he is, looking the way he did when she first noticed him, standing there behind the desk, smiling sweetly at her as she asked for Tabitha Norsman's files; then the second time, when he turned to look at her as he crouched over his dropped files. The hardworking young Catholic from Medical Records. Daniel. The protector angel.

There's a gun on the floor in front of her. She picks it up – she's never used one before. It's heavy, and when she grips it tightly in her hand, it feels like part of her. An extension of her arm. The jet engine in her head is still going and she just starts shooting.

Three shots. At the sound of the last shot, the jet engine stops. She sees blood and her stomach turns. She lurches to the side, getting out of the way of something or someone, and vomits. Behind her, she hears sirens, people shouting, confusion. She thinks it's Leo's voice but can't make it out – she feels like she's losing consciousness. The gun in her hand is hot. She drops it and propels herself forward, out of the grasp of someone, she's not sure who.

She stumbles through a doorway, grabbing the door frame for support. Her eyes focus on a body, spread-eagled on a bed. Her vision is blurred, she's seeing things in threes. It takes a second to register and then she falls to her knees.

AFTER

Saturday 5 September
12.01 am

As they speed towards the hospital, Meredith keeps her fingertips on Bella's wrist, concentrating on her pulse, eyes glued to her sister's face.

The patient, Cavendish ILL, had entered Diego's database a few days earlier with the most recent data dump. But he and Leo didn't know it was Bella, and neither Diego or Leo showed Meredith the patients' names in the database.

She leans over and drops her head onto Bella's stretcher. Cavendish, the voice in her head wails, she's Isobel Cavendish. Griffin isn't her surname, Cavendish is. She looks up at Bella's face, eyes tracing her sister's delicate profile. *I never knew how close you were to danger and I nearly lost you.*

She looks down at her phone.

Tears fall onto the screen.

3.20 pm: *Do you know an employee named daniel shelling?*
3.22 pm: *He's a records manager*
3.23 pm: *Recommended by stuart*
8.20 pm: *Call me*

8.45 pm: *Need to talk*
9.05 pm: *Is bella isobel?*
9.10 pm: *Where the fuck are you?*
9.15 pm: *Is bella cavendish ill ???*
9.25 pm: *Need to know bella's address*
9.45 pm: *She's next*

Meredith and Leo rock back and forth in the ambulance on either side of Bella. As they speed through New Westdale, streetlights glide across the windows, showing the blood and bruises on Leo's face. His right eye is a swollen, pulpy mess. Now he'll have two scars, she thinks, as the light swoops past and his face falls back into shadow.

When they arrive at New Westdale General, Meredith's in a daze. Her legs are numb as she gets out of the ambulance. She half walks, half stumbles towards the roster nurses huddling at the assessment zone, wanting to issue an order. But words fail her; she stammers and then stops. She stands in the middle of the pavement, watching the paramedics lower Bella from the ambulance. She wants to go to her but is held back by the triage nurse, who has a hand on her shoulder, saying something.

Sounds are muffled – like everyone is underwater. The dark shapes of police officers move past her slowly as if pushed along by a murky current. The paramedics wheel her sister towards the double doors of Emergency. The nurses stop them, gather around the gurney, check the IV and cannula in her arm – one of them grabs Bella's wrist, checks her pulse, then puts the arm down. She's distracted and Bella's arm rolls off the gurney. It hangs there, swinging back and forth, over the edge. Meredith steps back, out of the way, and presses her back against the wall as Bella's gurney rushes past her, an oxygen mask strapped across her pale face. As she watches her sister rushed down the corridor, Meredith bends forward and retches, like someone's slugged her in the gut. For a split second, she's back at St Jude, the morning that Katherine Richardson bled to death.

A surge of heat rises up her legs, to her chest, then her head. The corridor starts to spin and she gulps down air. Her knees buckle. Leo grabs her. *She's going to be fine*, he keeps on saying, *We got there in time*. With his hand on her arm, he leads her through to a chair at the admitting desk, where he speaks to the nurse. The fact that Leo ran into the apartment and tackled Daniel before he got a chance to cut Bella, feels strangely irrelevant. The fact that her sister's lack of consciousness is due to a heavy dose of chloroform and not cardiac arrest, doesn't make it better. The thought of how close Meredith was to losing her, how close Bella came to the abyss, is turning her guts to liquid.

She hears a nurse behind her whisper, 'It's Meredith Griffin, from St Jude Emergency,' and then another responding, 'Take her to the private room.' A young nurse gently takes her arm, and shepherds her and Leo through an unmarked door, into a suite with a bed, armchair and settee, off reception. She sits down on the settee, too exhausted to crawl onto the bed. The nurse brings her some water, puts a cool towel on the back of her neck and then holds it there. She shuts her eyes against more tears, humbled by the deep comfort delivered by this stranger, with his kind, trained touch.

As she leans over with her chest to her knees, she can hear Leo walk around the room. He starts to pace as he issues orders into his phone. He's instructing someone to lay a charge. She can make out that Daniel's been taken into custody by the State Crime Command. There's mention of a temporary facility, legal representation, a bail hearing the following Monday. He's saying something about an objective psychiatric assessment. She hears Leo say Rachel Gelfand's name.

It's not clear how long Meredith stays like that, with her chest on her knees. When she brings her head back up, her vision is clear. As she looks across the small room at Leo, leaning against the opposite wall, still speaking on the phone in a low voice, words come into her head. They're soothing, like a deep drink of clean air, like the smell of a forest. *She's okay.*

The nurse with the cloth returns with more water. She drinks it in three gulps and then holds the cup out to him for more, smiling weakly. When he comes back with another cup, Leo is off the phone.

'A new dump of data came in from Stuart's computer on Wednesday, and his summaries of Bella were in it. The guys got straight to work feeding the new information into the victim profile database.' He pauses and gives her a crooked grin, his swollen, bloody face brimming with pride. She can't help but laugh. The wide smile on his face makes him look like a gentle hoodlum. 'It was the words in your last text that clinched it, Red.'

'Physical release?'

Leo nods, coming to sit beside her, putting his arm around her, kissing her hair. 'That phrase was like a code word, peppered all over Bella's file. And when we checked the other four victims, it was all over their summaries too. By eight-thirty pm, we suspected that a patient with the name Cavendish ILL was the next target.'

She curls into the space under Leo's arm. *She's okay.* The words cocoon her.

He keeps talking. 'I had no idea the patient Cavendish ILL was Bella. Not until I crosschecked that name with the St Jude patient file. The last address recorded was yours. That's what gave it away.'

A doctor comes to tell them Bella has stabilised and leads them to her room. They sit in silence for a while by the side of the bed. Meredith watches her sister's chest rise and fall, unable to take her eyes off her.

'Did I shoot someone?' she asks Leo, her brain in a muddle. 'I remember holding a gun and shots were fired. Was that me? Did I hurt anyone?'

Leo smiles. 'You have terrible aim, Red,' he says. 'You may have to buy Bella a new sofa. You left three bullet holes in it.'

She smiles faintly and closes her eyes as Leo takes another call and starts to pace the room again, talking quietly on his phone. As she turns his words over in her mind, a question starts knocking against the walls of her brain. Quietly at first, but then harder and harder, clattering through the calm. Why Bella?

When Leo gets off the phone, Meredith looks up at him. 'Bella was a target. Does that mean she's had an abortion?' she asks, her voice sounding harsh against the quiet whirring of the instruments.

Leo leans against the wall, hands in his coat pocket, and shakes his head. 'If she had one, she didn't tell Stuart about it — or at least he didn't write it down. That's why we didn't identify her before this morning. She didn't share any of the victim profile characteristics. She also wasn't a self-harmer.'

At the mention of Stuart's name, Meredith frowns deeply. It takes a moment for her brain to click over. 'Wait — Stuart? What did Stuart have to do with Bella? He counselled her?'

Leo looks at Meredith sideways, as if afraid to broach the subject head on. He nods.

The room seems to tilt as she tries to compute what he's just indicated. When was the last time she chose Bella's counsellor? Her head starts to hurt as she puts it together. The last time was way back, back when Bella had been stripping. Since then, the only person involved in Bella's care was Charlie.

'How on earth did Bella become Stuart's patient? She was never admitted to his Outpatient Clinic,' she says, baffled that something so important could have escaped her attention.

'It looks like Stuart is the main consulting physician at Glencoe. When she moved there, she became his patient. She moved to Glencoe, what ... a few weeks ago? Her summaries came in with the latest data dump.'

Meredith gets up and starts to pace the room, shaking her head.

'But it still doesn't make sense, Leo. Why was Bella a target? The words "physical release" may have been in her treatment plan, but she didn't share any other similarity.' The whirring of the instruments starts up again but it feels like it's no longer happening in the room. It's in her brain, derailing her train of thought, upsetting her logic.

'How did you know it was Daniel?' she hears herself ask. It's another question coming out of the blue, sounding like a cross-examination. Or an accusation. Her insides feel like a coiled bullwhip, ready to unwind and lash out at anyone within range.

If Leo hears her anger, he pretends not to notice. 'We found Jacob early this morning and eliminated him pretty quickly,' he says, looking calmly at Meredith's surprised face. 'Daniel was the only man we couldn't find to interview. We hunted him down all day Thursday. He wasn't at the hospital. His manager said he was on leave.' He opens the satchel slung around his shoulders and reaches into it.

'So I decided to pay Daniel a visit at home.' He opens the bag, and pulls out something wrapped in plastic and labelled with an evidence tag. 'Turns out he lives with his mom.'

Leo starts unwrapping the plastic. 'Lovely lady. She invites me in and tells me Daniel took a few days off. When I ask to use the bathroom, I pass a bedroom. The door's open and there's this photo, sitting on a chest of drawers. I take a photo of it on my phone and come back two hours later with a warrant to search Daniel's room. Take a look at this.'

He holds it up for Meredith. It's a photo of Daniel and Stuart, working behind a kitchen griddle, smiling for the camera. They're both wearing chef's hats. Stuart's standing tall, arms crossed over his wide chest. Daniel has his arm around him. They're shoulder to shoulder – their heights and builds are identical. Stuart's eyebrows are arched and he's wearing a wide, proud grin. The frame has a small plaque at the bottom: *St Therese – Annual Sick Kids Pancake Breakfast – 2011.*

Bella's eyes flutter open and Meredith leans down, whispering her sister back to sleep. She turns back to the photo. 'How did you know to go to Bella's tonight?'

'As soon as we saw the words "physical release" in the treatment plan, we identified her as the next possible victim. That's why I was frantic to get hold of you. I wanted her new address, so we could set up surveillance. Catching Daniel there? On the attack? That was just sheer luck.'

Saturday 5 September
8.45 am

When she wakes up, Meredith's neck has seized, and pins and needles shoot up the back of her head. Sleeping on the chair by Bella's bed has turned her body to concrete.

Her phone is already ringing. The first call is a reporter from the *New Westdale Herald*, then one from National Radio. Her answer is short and sharp: 'No comment.' The ringing rouses Bella, but only for a moment, until the sedation pulls her back into the deep.

After several more rings from unknown callers, Meredith goes to turn her phone off but stops when she sees Camilla's name appear on the screen, calling from St Jude. Exhausted, she's about to let the call go to voicemail, but then she changes her mind.

'Meredith Griffin,' she says walking out of the room. Best to keep it formal. The call could be from Camilla alone, or she could be on speaker, with others listening in. She inhales deeply, preparing herself for the verdict: that she'll be reported to the College of Nurses, that she'll be fired.

'Meredith, it's Camilla. How are you?' Camilla pauses, apparently waiting for an answer. When there isn't one, she keeps going. 'How's Bella? Are you both okay?'

Her voice is soft. She's not on speaker.

'Is it just you on the phone?' Meredith asks, unable to mask the aggression in her voice.

There's another pause. 'As far as I know, yes.' Her tone turns cautious. 'Meredith, are you at home and are you okay?'

Meredith holds her tongue. She's sitting in the corridor of a hospital, having rescued her sister from a murderer. Is she okay?

'Meredith. You're my employee, it's my business to know that you're okay—'

'Am I still an employee of St Jude?' Her voice sounds accusatory again.

'Of course you are. Why wouldn't you be?'

Meredith can hear the concern in Camilla's voice. She wants to believe it's genuine but can't coax her guard down, so she sticks to the facts. She explains Bella's situation and current condition.

'You need to be with Bella,' Camilla says. 'Take as much time as you need.'

'You mean you want me back?'

'Of course I want you back,' she answers, a hint of shock in her voice. She pauses. 'But I want you to take some *personal* leave. Take care of Bella, and yourself. You've both been through a huge ordeal.'

Meredith thanks Camilla and tells her she'll take a couple of days.

'No. I mean it,' her boss says, sounding more insistent. 'Take *as much time* as you need.'

'I can be back in on Tuesday or Wednesday, once I know Bella has—'

'Meredith,' Camilla starts talking over her. 'St Jude will be a difficult place for the next few weeks.' The softness is gone. It's replaced by a warning tone, and Meredith's not sure whether it's intended to protect or scare her. 'The last thing I want you to have to deal with,' Camilla pauses again, 'is the press.'

Two months ago, the ambiguity of Camilla's words would have sent Meredith into a spiral of questions, but she feels nothing. Her insides feel like her body – hardened into granite.

'Why would I have to deal with the press?'

'Meredith, you're tired and probably haven't seen the reports. Daniel's arrest is breaking news. Biophysica has cut our funding, which means we're ... we're left with Church money, because the state's funding has shrunk.'

Meredith is silent. Camilla continues, 'It ... I'm ... it's just not clear what's going to happen in the next few weeks. The government reduced funding to Catholic hospitals a few months ago. With Biophysica out too ... and the Diocese broke, well, it's just going to be an interesting time and—'

'The Diocese? Broke?' Meredith starts to laugh. 'You've got to be kidding me.'

'The Diocese has been selling off property since the nineties, Meredith. They've been paying out claims from child sex abuse victims for decades, and the money's had to come from somewhere. There isn't much land to sell anymore. The coffers have run dry.' Camilla's voice gets quieter, as if she's talking to herself. 'So Lachlan says.'

She clears her throat. 'Anyways, never mind. We'll manage the load in Emergency. Like I said, I want you to take a few weeks off. Stay away from the press, give yourself a break from the ward. Spend time with Bella. And then come back. We need you at St Jude.'

Meredith goes silent again. She remembers how absent Camilla was for weeks, earlier on, when she wanted to talk to her about her early investigations into St Jude's patient files. She always thought Camilla was avoiding her, but recalls being told that she was at a senate inquiry on state funding for Catholic hospitals.

The gears in her head click. Camilla wasn't avoiding Meredith, she was trying to secure St Jude's funding. She wasn't shying away from a fight with Stuart and Lachlan, she was just deeply concerned about how the hospital could survive the investigation, and which funders would stick by St Jude in the shadow of a scandal. And now all those problems were here, on their doorstep.

'We stopped him, Camilla,' she says, her voice clear.

Camilla breathes heavily into the phone. 'Of course you did. You did the right thing, Meredith. You did what you had to do. You found your rock bottom.'

'My what?'

'What you stand for. What you'll fight for. The place from where you can't fall.'

Rock bottom. So that's what it felt like to hit it. She thinks about what it will be like – to go back to work at St Jude, to work with Mark and Stuart, to run into Lachlan, to report to Camilla, to keep their secrets, to pretend that the Catholic health directive is ethical and defendable, to know how much they have to compromise to keep the institution alive, to hold herself back from digging back into the files, to find out why on earth Lachlan was approving abortions at the hospital. She can't fathom stepping foot in the place. Whatever she stands for now – she knows it isn't St Jude.

As her mind starts to play out the fantasy of resigning, she hears herself saying, 'You're right, Camilla. You're exactly right. On all fronts. I'll take my time.'

There is silence on the other end of the phone, but Meredith says nothing. There is nothing else to say.

'Okay,' Camilla says cautiously. 'So, just let me know when you're ready to come back.'

Meredith's mouth stays shut, like a solid steel door has rolled down and locked her words away.

'Goodbye, Meredith,' Camilla says softly and hangs up.

Meredith stands, holding the phone against her ear, the silence drilling the moment into her mind. At times like these, she would normally pop a pill, but something's changed. It's like the sand underneath her has shifted one last time. She leans her head against the wall behind her and closes her eyes. Then she turns her ringer to silent and does a quick Google search for St Jude.

HOSPITAL HOUSES A KILLER is the first result, posted on the *New Westdale Herald* website an hour earlier.

She scrolls down. Three other publications have picked up the story of Daniel's arrest. The *Financial Post* is running a story about Biophysica's decision to cut funding to St Jude based on concerns about record keeping and patient confidentiality.

None of the stories mention Bella or Meredith. She glances up and down the corridor, and pulls her coat collar up around her neck. Two nurses are deep in quiet discussion. A doctor is talking to a colleague further down the hallway. Nothing looks unusual. Just the slow pulse of a hospital ward on a Saturday morning. No one's looking at her.

She texts Leo: *Are you at home? Can I stay with you?*

The reply comes back in seconds: *Yes please.*

She closes her eyes and breathes. Then she shoves her phone in her pocket, walks back into Bella's hospital room and rings for the attending physician for a consult.

Sunday 6 September
2 pm

'Leo's told me about you,' Rachel Gelfand says, looking hard at Meredith, her appraising eyes narrowed. 'You have serious psychiatric training.'

Meredith laughs thinly and closes her eyes, leaning her head against the wall of the hospital corridor. 'A lot of help my training's been to me.' Then she tilts her head in the direction of Bella's hospital room. 'A lot of help it's been to my sister.'

The corridors of New Westdale General are quiet. The nurses are helping Bella shower, so Meredith's sitting in the hallway on a wooden bench, trying to convince herself that the muddy liquid from the hospital canteen is coffee.

Leo must have sent Rachel. Until that moment, Meredith assumed she was mostly invisible to the psychologist. Just a source, wheeled in by Leo to assist with a case. Meredith barely knows Rachel but her presence is strangely comforting. She's sitting next to her, not saying much, but the silence is comfortable.

Rachel's words are professional but her voice is kind. 'I don't know Bella and I can't say for sure, but I suspect your sister will be fine. She was drugged. She won't recall the violence.' She moves to the edge of the bench and turns towards Meredith. 'You, on the other hand, you had quite a scare ...' she says, pulling her smart black handbag over her shoulder and getting up. She's got a motherly look on her face, which Meredith doesn't resent her for.

She's standing in front of her now, with her hands in her pockets and Meredith smiles, amused. Rachel's wearing a tailored black dress and fishnet stockings. Her high, black patent leather pumps have pointy toes and a sexy little zipper on the back of each heel. She's dressed for a cocktail party, not a Sunday afternoon trip to the hospital to see the girlfriend of a friend. The more Meredith sees of Rachel, the less she can fit her into the picture of domesticity Leo's provided, of a straight, overachieving Jewish academic. She can't seem to pair Rachel's streetwise attitude and current dominatrix wardrobe with her having a classics scholar for a husband and two kids in elementary school.

Rachel starts to play with something in her pocket. When Meredith looks directly at her, she sees she's being studied, but the psychologist's eyes are soft and kind.

'You'd be right to think I'd be traumatised,' Meredith says, putting the coffee on a side table beside the bench and folding her hands on her lap. 'But, strangely, I feel the complete opposite.'

Rachel keeps quiet and just nods. There's a faint smile on her face, but Meredith feels it's directed at herself. Like she knows she's underestimated Meredith and won't make that mistake again.

'Here,' Rachel says, pulling a USB out of her pocket and offering it to Meredith. 'I interviewed Daniel Shelling today. This is the first part of the session. Leo said I could show it to you. If you feel so inclined, there's an email address on the memory stick – I have my theories about Daniel and a preliminary diagnosis, but I'd be interested to know your views.'

Meredith looks at the USB warily, and cautiously picks it up. Rachel reaches out to put her hand on Meredith's shoulder, and gives it a firm, gentle squeeze.

No more words. Just a brief, warm touch and Rachel's away, her heels clicking along the floor, the zippers on the back of her shoes swinging in time with her strides.

The whole way home from New Westdale General, Meredith sits in the back of a cab watching the city roll past, playing with the USB in her pocket. She gets the driver to drop her off on an adjacent street and enters her place from the back alley to avoid any media, just like Leo told her to. She pours herself a large glass of wine, inserts the USB and pushes play.

Daniel's face fills the screen. He's striking, with clear skin and blue eyes. His strawberry blond hair is cut very short.

… *I met Stuart at the St Therese Pancake Breakfast for Sick Kids. He and I worked the grill together …*

He said his research was going to be his magnum opus. I didn't know what that meant at the time but I looked it up. His research was going to be his 'great work' …

He was always inviting me to play squash and go running. Dropping by Medical Records to say hello. His feelings were clear …

Daniel speaks with earnest intensity, like he has a message to deliver, like he needs to make sure he is not misunderstood.

… *He told me that there were many, many people involved in making his research a success. Experts and laypeople alike. It was going to be completely revolutionary. We were going to set people free. He wanted me to be on his team, he said I was essential to him …*

He said that if it weren't for people like me, he'd never be able to do what he needed to do. The hospital always hounded him about his record keeping. He said he needed my help to stay on top of it …

He wanted to give me open access to his system, so I could take care of his diary and remind him to file his paperwork. He said that would be ideal, but hospital protocol just wouldn't allow it ...

Daniel starts to rub the back of his neck as he talks, his voice becoming clipped, his face tensing. He begins to rock back and forth on his chair, as if to emphasise to himself the importance of his task.

... I sent him software to remind him to file his paperwork. He told me to go ahead and install it remotely. I knew he wouldn't have the time to use it properly. So I dropped in some other software, so I could monitor him myself ...

... I was doing him a favour. I could keep track of his files, and I set the system to ping him when he needed to file a discharge summary ...

I saw on the internet that he had joined St Jude, and when a job opening came up, I jumped at the chance ...

Intense concern changes the look on his face when he speaks about the women he's killed.

... I had to review the files, and when I did, it was clear what needed to happen. The girls were in such pain. He told me so. That's why they cut themselves ...

... I was always very careful with them. I didn't want to hurt them. No hitting. No anger. A gentle release from their pain ... a short, quick physical release. That's what Stuart wanted.

Meredith plays the interview over and over, late into the night, refilling her wineglass regularly. It's on her fourth viewing that she realises how important Daniel's method has been. How it brought the girls to her. How the placement of Katherine's left leg, on top of the right one, meant the damaged artery was held firm by the weight of her upper leg. How her body, curled around the toilet base, worked to slow the speed of the bleeding. How it kept her alive long enough to get her to St Jude's Emergency, rather than the city morgue.

It was Daniel's gentle placement of Katherine's body that led Meredith to see the connection between Katherine's and Tabitha's injuries, made her insist that Leo involve her in the investigation into Patrice, and led them to connect the dots between all three women, and then Kelly. That image of young Katherine Richardson, her hands pressed together in prayer and placed under her head, lying on her side, her body curled around the ceramic stalk of a toilet, was printed indelibly onto Meredith's mind.

Before turning the computer off at 1 am, she emails one word to Rachel's email address pasted on the USB – *erotomania*.

But as Meredith staggers to bed, stopping in the kitchen for Tylenol and a large bottle of water, a shadow falls over her. Her drunken thoughts loop round and round, and as the night deepens, certain facts keep popping into her mind, piercing through the fog of alcohol, like red flags blowing in the breeze. Stuart's research into erotomania. His beautifully written patient summaries. Her stone in his office. The obsessive looks he gave Meredith when he presented his research findings on OCD and schizophrenia, like she herself was the subject of his research. The look on his face in the photo of him and Daniel at the St Therese pancake breakfast – his arms crossed proudly across his chest, his wide stance and Cheshire smile, like a predator with his prize.

She knows it's too late to call Leo, but she does so anyway. He's groggy and not happy when he answers.

'Stuart played a part in this, Leo,' she says, not even saying hello.

Leo grunts – she can hear him moving around in bed, as if trying to get his bearings.

'Red, hi. What? What did you say?'

'Stuart is a master of live experiment. That's what he does professionally. His entire research project is a live experiment. How do you know he wasn't experimenting with Daniel? You heard his interview, how much credit Stuart gave him for helping with his research. How he built Daniel up – made him feel part of the team.'

'Red,' Leo says, in the voice he uses to calm people, 'slow down. We have the perpetrator. Yes, he might be convinced that Stuart directed him to do this – that he was following doctor's orders or whatever – but that was just in his mind. Rachel's made a diagnosis – he had erotomania. He was delusional.'

'Leo. It's Stuart. He's behind this. I'm convinced of it. I agree that Daniel suffers from erotomania. But Stuart's the world expert in erotomania – no one would know how to manipulate a person with that disorder better than Stuart.'

A low whistle comes from the other end of the phone. 'Meredith, you need to get a hold of yourself. You were wrong about Mark, remember?'

'What do you mean "You were wrong about Mark"? You suspected him too – you named him as a person of interest. The hospital even suspended him, for god's sake! What do you mean *I* was wrong about Mark? We were *all* wrong about Mark.'

'Red.' Leo's voice is firm. 'Listen to me. You're right. Forget about Mark. Now you need to let go of Stuart.'

She exhales and just hangs up. There's nothing more to say.

In that moment, all she can think about is Bella. This is how she must feel every day. Her veracity questioned. Her instincts fighting through the fog. Two months ago, it would have thrown Meredith to have Leo challenge her like that. But now? She's unfazed. She's already been thrown, and now she's landed. At rock bottom.

Monday 7 September
8 pm

'So you agree with me,' Meredith says, looking over her glass of pinot noir at Rachel, who's perched on a stool beside her. She's dressed in a body-hugging black dress with thigh-high black boots, her back ballerina straight. They're both sitting at Meredith's breakfast bar – Rachel had swung by to pick up the USB and Meredith had invited her in.

'Totally,' Rachel says, giving her a deep nod. 'Daniel has erotomania. He believes Stuart needs him, trusts him and is desperate for his help.' Rachel's long fingers grip a round glass of chardonnay. Her hair is parted in the middle and hanging thickly on either side of her face, a rich black curtain framing her dark, pencilled eyes.

She seems open to talking, so Meredith reaches into her bag for a black notebook and pen. 'Is he fully functional? At work? Does he have friends?' Meredith asks, keen to understand Daniel's psychology, and how he could have done what he did right under their noses.

Rachel nods again, eyebrows lifted thoughtfully. 'I didn't see any indications of other psych issues. Granted, I've only had the one interview, but outside of his delusion, he seems normal.'

On a roll, she takes a large gulp of wine and continues. 'His deep belief that Stuart needs his help seems to stem from their initial meeting at the St Therese pancake breakfast. Stuart called Daniel a "Good Samaritan" because of the interest he showed in Stuart's work with the mentally ill. Then it seems Daniel's erotomania was fuelled by Stuart's need for assistance with his filing when Daniel worked in St Therese's records department. After that, some early confiding by Stuart about his patients' conditions fed Daniel's persistent belief that he needed his help to heal his patients.'

'You only gave me part of the interview,' Meredith says.

'I gave you the cogent part for diagnostic purposes. That's what I wanted your view on.'

'Do you mind if I ask a few other questions?'

'Shoot,' Rachel says, taking another sip.

'Do you think Stuart breached doctor–patient confidentiality?'

Rachel shakes her head. 'No. Daniel insists Stuart was extremely strict about confidentiality. According to him, Stuart wanted to relieve these particular women of pain, but he insists he was always professional. Daniel holds Stuart in very high regard, like there's a kind of code of honour between them.'

'So, why did he feel entitled to look into Stuart's files? What was honourable about that?'

Rachel places her hands on the bar and nods as if agreeing with Meredith's scepticism. 'Daniel's erotomania contains a heightened sense of self-reverence. Stuart's initial request for his help with filing? Daniel viewed this with symbolic import – as if he was *meant* to assist Stuart to fulfil his destiny as a great research scientist. He believes he and Stuart have a special relationship of trust. I think this belief arises from a conversation they had while playing squash. Stuart was visibly upset about the vulnerability and guilt of a patient who had terminated her pregnancy. This was Kelly Kosovic, the first victim. Daniel said Stuart was desperate to release Kelly from a state of perpetual pain – and didn't know how.'

Meredith shakes her head slowly in disbelief. 'It's a pretty powerful delusional system – to drive him deep into Stuart's files and then to murder.'

Rachel reaches into her bag and pulls out a transcript of her interview with Daniel. 'Meredith, you heard this yourself in

Daniel's interview. He was convinced Stuart wanted him to read the patient files.' The psychologist thumbs through the transcript, finds the page and starts reading out loud, pointing at words as she goes. *'You should see these girls, Daniel, you should hear their stories. They suffer so much. I really don't know how to help them.'* This is what Stuart told Daniel. Daniel's memory of this conversation is extremely precise. I believe this is where he gets his primary motivation to kill. Daniel believes that Stuart has asked him to read his patient files and release these women from their pain, through death.'

Meredith just raises an eyebrow and shakes her head.

'Daniel's delusion may be based on incorrect premises, but it's also *steeped* in facts that reinforce it. When the position at St Jude's Medical Records department opened up, Stuart gave him a reference. When Daniel joined the St Jude squash team, Stuart became his regular partner. It was Stuart who invited him to join the St Jude running club. His close contact with Stuart has enabled him to interweave imaginary beliefs with real events. He has an airtight delusional structure that fits into his reality perfectly, like a jigsaw puzzle.' Rachel's bony fingers interlock for emphasis. 'That's why his delusion is so strong.'

'Does his history indicate he would develop erotomania?'

Rachel smiles. 'He's had abnormal attachments to older men and role models in positions of authority. He attended the New Westdale Cadet Academy as a teenager and was discharged from cadet duties in 2004. The reason for discharge? Obsessive connection to his commanding officer. He also trained to provide medical support to navy seals but was discharged for aberrant behaviour towards a superior officer in 2010, just before he started at St Therese and met Stuart.'

'Well,' Meredith says, 'that certainly explains the cuts to the femoral. He knew what he was doing.'

Rachel looks grimly back at her and nods. 'Indeed he did.'

'Is he a strong Catholic? A fanatic?'

'He and his mother definitely have strong beliefs,' she nods slowly at Meredith, seeming to know where her question is going. 'The abortions may have contributed to Daniel's delusion that the women were mired in guilt. But ...'

She pauses, looks down at her glass and then reaches for the bottle to pour another glass.

'But?' Meredith says.

Rachel turns and looks at her directly. 'But that doesn't really explain why your sister was a target.'

Meredith looks back at her and then down at her notebook. She draws circles on the page and starts to fill them in, feeling her breath get shallow.

'Did you ask him why he went after Bella?' she asks quietly.

'Meredith,' Rachel says and then waits until she looks up from her notebook. 'I held some of the interview back for a reason. I didn't give you the part about Bella.'

'Right,' Meredith says, her throat dry. 'What can you share with me?'

'I asked him why he thought those particular women were hard for Stuart to help. He said they stood out. Then I asked him if it was because they had abortions. He said yes. But when I challenged him about Bella, who didn't have an abortion and didn't share the other women's characteristics, he was less specific.'

Rachel opens up the transcript again and finds the passage she's looking for.

'He said Bella jumped off the page in the same way the others did, as if Stuart was speaking to him and calling him to action.'

Meredith slowly puts the pen down. It rolls off the kitchen bar and drops onto the tiled floor.

'So Bella was a complete anomaly,' she says. 'She didn't match the pattern at all. For some reason, Stuart's notes motivated Daniel to target my sister, despite the fact that she,' Meredith raises a finger to make each point, 'has not had an abortion, is not clinically depressed and does not self-harm.'

Rachel takes a sip of wine, then sets the glass down, nodding. 'Bella didn't fit the pattern. And while I hate admitting it, Meredith, I can't explain it.'

Meredith's insides churn with conflicting emotions – gratitude for what Rachel's found out, frustration at the lingering gaps in their understanding of Daniel's motives, fear about what the gaps mean for her ability to put this case behind her. But the positive sheen over everything is her genuine respect for the woman sitting beside her.

'Leo said you were driven, Rachel. You're proving him right. I want to thank you for being so driven to find the answers in this case. And also, of course, for your incredible sense of style! For that, you have my most enduring thanks,' Meredith says, laughing and raising her glass. 'Here's to the most stylish forensic psychologist I've ever laid eyes on!'

Rachel raises her glass in response. 'Well, it's been my pleasure to be of service – in all ways, including the style department. But driven? Really? Leo said that? That's interesting.'

'Why "interesting"?'

'Because Leo never ceases to amaze me. As usual, he's right – I was born driven. In fact, I was driven before I was born!'

'That sounds like something a mother would say.'

'My mother did say it. Although not in so many words.'

'What words did your mother use?'

Rachel eyes Meredith, as if to suss out whether she can handle something. 'After my sister was born, my mother terminated two pregnancies, and then decided enough was enough and got her tubes tied. A year later, I was born. So she told me I was a medical mistake.'

'Your mother used those words?'

Rachel takes another sip of wine, eyeing Meredith over her glass. 'No sympathy is necessary. Knowing I survived the early odds against me gave me purpose.'

'Still, it's a pretty strong thing for a mother to say. Did she drape it in any kind words?'

She shrugs. 'Words always got screwed up in my mother's mouth — a compliment was always wrapped up in an insult, or the other way around. You could never tell if she was calculating or just confused. It was a mixed blessing — a hard thing to recover from, but probably the main thing that drove me into psychology.'

Rachel pauses. 'Sometimes I think we live our lives in a circle. We spend our youth looking straight ahead, hungry for the future. And then we spend our adult lives looking back, reliving things, reinterpreting, trying to understand what drove us to where we are.'

'So your mother drove you into being an expert on deviant personalities and criminal minds?'

Rachel nods. 'Yeah. I think I have her to thank for much of what I do. And for what it's worth, I think your sister drove you. To being a nurse, so you could take care of people.'

Tuesday 8 September
7.05 pm

Buzo's buzzing but Charlie's not holding court at her usual table. Instead, she and Meredith are in a corner booth, alone, huddled over a plate of antipasto. Meredith's low in her seat, hunched down and keeping an eye on the wall mirror, scanning the room for reporters.

Across from her, Charlie's face is drawn. Deep purple circles ring her eyes and her short hair is a tousled mess. After Evelyn's funeral she had flown to the Caribbean, but just as the plane was taxiing into the St Barths airport, she got Meredith's text about Bella.

'I got the first possible flight home,' she says. Her hands shake as she pours more wine. She knocks back half the glass and then looks at Meredith with wide eyes. 'Why on earth didn't you tell me about what was going on in the St Jude Psych department?' she asks, her voice croaky.

Meredith tries to comfort her. 'With everything you were doing for Bella, I didn't want to tell you about the investigation into St Jude.'

Charlie throws her hands up. 'And *I* didn't want to tell *you* about *Bella* moving into *Stuart's* care, because the whole point of me taking over her care was to give you a break. He's one of the best in his field, if not *the* best. That was one of the reasons I thought moving Bella to Glencoe was a masterstroke!'

Her voice rises in intensity. 'Fuck!' she says, rubbing her hair, making it stand up even more. 'Unbelievable,' she adds, taking another huge gulp of wine. 'So, while you and I were keeping each other in the dark, thinking it was in each other's best interests, a serial killer is preying on Stuart's patients and stalking Bella? Bloody hell!'

The waiter comes with their second course. After he retreats, Charlie launches back in, speaking in an urgent whisper. 'But things are okay now, right? Bella's fine, and they've made an arrest. That's what the papers are saying.'

Meredith chews and takes a long pull of wine. 'Yeah, they've made an arrest.' She's speaking slowly now.

'And Bella's okay?' Charlie asks again.

'Yes, she's at New West Gen. Under police protection.'

'Police protection?' she says quietly, putting her cutlery down. 'Who arranged that?'

'Yours truly,' Meredith says. 'I insisted.'

Charlie keeps on looking at her, a crease starting to form in her forehead. 'What? Why?'

'At first,' Meredith says, hesitating, 'at first it was because I was hysterical.' She takes another gulp of wine and looks seriously at Charlie, trying to decide whether to tell her. 'But now …'

Charlie's eyes narrow as it dawns on her. 'You don't think they have the right guy?'

'No,' Meredith says, sighing. 'They definitely have the right guy.'

Then she pauses to look hard at her best friend's face. If anyone deserves to know what she really thinks, it's the woman sitting across the table from her.

'I just don't think he did it alone.'

Wednesday 9 September
5 pm

The dog park is boggy where the ground's refused to soak up the rain. Meredith heads to Leo's favourite meeting place, trying to dodge the puddles, failing to keep her shoes dry. Wherever she goes these days, the smell of the sea hangs in the air. With the reprieve from the rain, the sun is fighting back, and the beaches, ravaged by storms, are strewn with drying piles of seaweed and driftwood.

Her eyes play along the surface of the flowered border that runs along the path beside her. A low bush catches her eye, thick with hundreds of thin green stems, each with a small white flower balanced on its end, an open bloom trained to the sky, hoping for sun. The breeze moves the stems in unison, like a thick green wave topped with a lick of white caps.

Leo's sitting on the bench, supervising Juno, with Jez leaning against his leg. His arms are outstretched resting on the back of the bench, as if to capture the whole park in their embrace. As Meredith approaches, Juno runs out of the bushes to bark a greeting and Leo turns to see her.

'Hey, Red.'

'Room for me?'

'Always,' he says, moving to make space.

'Good day?' she asks.

'Not bad,' he says, smiling at her. 'Better now.'

She notices another dog sniffing the bushes near Juno. It looks like a border terrier and has an anxious way about it. When Meredith sits down near Leo, it looks up at her and starts wagging its tail

'Whose is that?' she asks suspiciously.

'Well …' he says, a bashful grin breaking out on his face.

'Leo—'

He puts his hands up in surrender. 'Hold on, Red, before you start judging, hear me out.'

She clicks her tongue, shakes her head and crosses her arms over her chest. 'You have no boundaries, Leo. Honestly, I think you need help.'

Leo starts in again, as if stating the facts of a case. 'One of the EAs at work, she's not very good with dogs. She got this one from her boyfriend. The poor thing has anxiety issues, Red, and this girl can't handle him. So …' he finishes with a shrug, opening his palms to the sky, as if the conclusion is self-evident.

'Leo—'

'Listen, the dog's super nervous. He needs an experienced owner. And being around Jezebel will help him.'

'What's his name?'

'Well, you see, that sealed it for me,' Leo says, smiling ruefully and avoiding Meredith's look. 'His name's Jasper.' The dog skips towards them at the sound of his name and Leo starts to laugh. 'Can you believe it? Juno, Jezebel, Jasper. It was a sign!' He rubs him between the ears, and watches him and Jez sniff each other. 'It'll do him a world of good to hang out with my girls. And Jez always needs company. Juno is just focused on me, you know. Jez gets lonely—'

Meredith holds up her hands and rolls her eyes. 'Stop it – please. Just stop there – you're killing me.'

Leo starts to laugh but tries to change the subject when Meredith joins in only half-heartedly. 'The case is really shaping up. Hard evidence is coming in thick and fast. Diego's checked Daniel's phone. Seems the spyware was set up to send a text every time Stuart logged into his personal computer so Daniel could hop on and get a data dump. It means that, at any one time, he was just a step behind Stuart.'

Meredith merely nods. 'Right,' she says, looking away, squinting into the distance.

'Red?' Leo's hand is on her shoulder, massaging her neck. 'What's up? This is good news, love.'

He keeps on touching her but she shrugs him off.

'Red? What's going on?'

She moves away from him and rests her elbows on her knees, watching the dogs. She can hear the faint sounds of dog walkers calling for their pets.

'Meredith Griffin? Hello?' Leo says, leaning over so his face is next to hers. 'Come on, Red – what's up?'

Finally, she sits up and faces him.

'You know what's up, Leo?' she says, failing to keep an accusatory tone out of her voice, 'What's up is: you've only done half the job.'

He just looks at her for a moment. Then he slowly shakes his head. 'Really, Red? Are we doing this again?'

'Leo. Have you actually sat down and read all of Stuart's summaries? I mean, all of them? You haven't, have you? You got your man, and now it's case closed, isn't it?'

He doesn't say anything. He inhales audibly and exhales, then runs his hands through his hair, and looks away.

'Leo,' she says, snapping her fingers in his face. 'Leo, look at me. I've kept you on the right trail throughout this entire investigation. Have the decency to focus.' When he turns to look at her, she launches in. 'Now, I want you to go home and compare the way Stuart has written his summaries for each of the five women – including Bella. Compare these summaries with the ones he's written for other patients. You'll see – they all follow the same pattern: he paints a picture of intense pain and then he instructs each woman to seek *physical release*. Stuart was building a case with these summaries: a case for Daniel to release them from pain. He was testing the resilience of his delusion. It was an experiment,' she says insistently, banging her fist on the park bench.

Leo looks at her, his face angry. 'You've got to be kidding me.' He lowers his voice as a few dog walkers go past.

Meredith watches them leave. She recognises his anger but can't stop going. 'Stuart knew exactly where this would lead, Leo. My theory is that Kelly Kosovic was the first. And when Daniel followed him to St Jude, Stuart tried it again with Tabitha, and then with Katherine and Patrice. He painted a particular picture of these young women – and the picture was for Daniel. He was egging him on, Leo. Manipulating him to commit murder.'

'Oh god, Red, please! Can you please stop? Why the hell would Stuart do this?'

'The research, Leo!' she yells, oblivious to the others in the dog park. 'Why else? All he cares about is his fucking research!'

'For god's sake,' Leo whispers, 'you're being ridiculous. I'm sorry, Red, but I'm done. I can't jump on this train. Even if just one cell of my police brain followed your logic, what would I do with that hunch? How could I possibly prove that Stuart was an accomplice?'

Meredith can't answer that.

She feels Leo's hand move over hers. He intertwines their fingers and grasps her hand tight. 'Red, you need to let this guy go. I know he's the main reason why a bully like Mark Roth can do such damage. I know he protects Mark and pulls the strings at St Jude. But you need to let up. You need it for yourself, more than anything.'

They sit there in silence, watching Juno sniff through the trees and roll in the grass. Meredith can feel the warm length of Leo's thigh against hers on the bench, and the rough skin of his palm. She's falling in love with him, and part of her wants to do whatever he says – let it go, move on, just be with him. But something stops her – it's like a stone deep inside her that she can't dislodge.

The wind shifts and the smell of cedar floats in the air. Juno senses the change in direction and turns towards them, putting her long snout in the air. Her eyes lock onto Meredith, who takes a deep breath of the cedar-laced air. Then Juno trots up to Meredith and sits at her feet, leaning against her leg, pressing her body against her.

Meredith wraps her hand around the dog's neck, sinking her fingers into the thick coat, feeling the warm, solid curve of

Juno's shoulder. 'You know, Leo,' she says, looking at him with a smile. 'Work in my job for long enough and you develop something. Call it what you want – intuition, gut instinct, whatever.' She puts her head on top of Juno's, kisses it, and moves the dog over so she can stand up. 'You don't know whether the guy with the chest pain is having an acute MI, suffering a thoracic aneurysm, or just needs a blanket and a cup of tea. You don't know if the babbling woman in the waiting room is suffering from delirium or a massive subdural bleed. You just move. Quickly. Your feet and hands lead the way, taking their instructions from somewhere deep inside your subconscious mind. And with every move of your body, your instincts get sharper, and then, before you know it, you've cracked it. The diagnosis is clear and you're telling the doctor what it is.'

By now, she's standing in front of Leo. He's squinting up at her, chewing on a piece of grass. 'So, you think you've cracked this one, Red?'

'Damned right I do,' she says. She bends over, takes his head in her hands and kisses his forehead. Then she walks away.

As she does, Juno follows her for a few metres, whining. Meredith looks back at the dog and sees that she's stopped but hasn't let Meredith out of her sight. She sits, eyes bright, ears alert, watching over her as she goes.

Thursday 10 September
5.05 pm

From the chair Meredith's sitting in, she can see Bella's chest gently rise and fall. It's well past visiting hours and there are few sounds to break the silence in the room. Her sister has been here for five days. The effects of the chloroform have long worn off but the doctor has insisted on keeping her under observation. Meredith puts her head back against the chair, focusing on the moment of calm. Several days of sedation and care have regulated Bella. She'll be released the next day.

She looks around the private room Bella has been allocated. The staff at New West Gen have been impeccable. *I wonder if they have any openings for a slightly OCD nursing manager who's recovering from a prescription drug addiction,* she thinks with a cynical smile.

Distracted by a sound, she looks up and hears Bella whispering her name, a faint smile on her face. 'You came to Glencoe,' her sister says. 'The other night, you came to my place.'

Meredith had gone over all of this with Bella when the effects of the chloroform had first worn off, but knows it's worth repeating. 'Yes, yes, we did,' she says in a soothing voice. 'Leo and I thought you were in trouble, so we came to your place. We kept you safe.'

She remembers the night in Bella's unit like a series of snapshots. Daniel and Leo attacking each other. The gun heavy in her hand, firing, as if by itself. Bella on the bed, unconscious.

'How did you know to come to my place?' Bella asks.

She has asked this question before too. 'We read the files. Your psychiatrist, Stuart Chester. He kept files. There were things he had written in the files that gave us clues.'

'I thought Stuart was trying to help me.'

'The man who was going to hurt you that night was named Daniel. He was a friend of Stuart. He'd found Stuart's files and read them, so he knew a lot about you.'

'So, you looked at files?'

'Yeah – I did,' Meredith says, smiling at her. 'Pretty boring, isn't it? Solving a mystery by looking at files.' She rolls her eyes in self-mockery. 'I wish it had been more dramatic.'

Bella laughs softly at her. 'You're never boring, Mere,' she says. Meredith looks at her again and sees she is smiling, her eyes clear.

Bella turns her head to stare at the ceiling and says, as if to herself, 'So, you found the Jesus file.'

'Um, no,' Meredith says, stumbling over the words. Confused, she stands up and comes closer to the bed. 'The Jesus file?' She starts to feel the conversation's derailing into the territory of Bella's imagination.

Bella's eyes open wide and she looks straight at Meredith. 'Yes, Mere, the Jesus file.' Her hand finds Meredith's and grips it hard. 'You found his iPad.' She squeezes Meredith's hand even harder for emphasis. 'The one with Jesus on it. The one he hides.' Her voice gets more insistent. 'Leo told me that Stuart's files saved me. I thought it was the Jesus file.'

Meredith's heartbeat speeds up, but she tries to slow it down with her breathing. She looks at Bella, attempting to keep her face calm while her mind races to find the thread of sense. Is this real or not?

One long look at her sister makes it clear. She sits on the edge of the mattress and leans in. 'Tell me what you mean, Bella.'

Bella's voice is low and clear. 'He locks an iPad in the top of his desk. I saw it one night when I was waiting for my session – he was tapping away on it. I was early, so I was sitting outside his office, but the door was open. Just a crack. The iPad has a sticker of Jesus on it. It's bizarre; he's not religious, but he has this iPad with Jesus on the cover.'

Meredith just listens, her hand in Bella's, holding it tight. 'His office? You mean Stuart keeps an office at Glencoe? Is that the desk you mean?'

'Yes,' she says emphatically. 'Stuart has a temporary office there. He uses it twice a week. The iPad is locked in his desk.'

Meredith stares at her sister as nausea turns her stomach inside out. Then she swallows hard and stands up.

'I'll be right back,' she says, walking out of the room and calling Leo.

It takes a few hours for Leo to come to Bella's hospital bed, record her evidence and call it through, then get an officer to type up an affidavit for the search warrant. It takes another hour for Leo and Diego to contact the Glencoe director and escort him to Stuart's office, where he unlocks Stuart's desk.

Inside, they find an iPad with an image of Jesus on its cover. It's a close-up of his face, bearded and handsome, looking up to the sky and bleeding from a crown of thorns.

It only takes two hours for Diego to access the iPad and recover Stuart's detailed notes on the entire history of his relationship with Daniel, both at St Therese and St Jude. Each page has a table with five columns, like a medical chart. The first column has dates, the second has details of conversations between Daniel and Stuart. The third has another set of dates, and the fourth contains selections from Stuart's summaries of *Kosovic K, Norsman T, Richardson KE, Ladouceur PM* and, finally, *Cavendish ILL*. The file contains a running tally of everything Stuart has said and done to reinforce the delusions that led Daniel to murder.

The fifth column has the date that each woman was pronounced dead. *Kosovic K* – 30 July 2011, *Norsman T* – 21 February 2015, *Richardson KE* – 1 June 2015, *Ladouceur PM* – 13 June 2015.

Beside the name *Cavendish ILL*, the fifth column is empty.

Friday 11 September
8 am

'I can't believe it,' Meredith says from the passenger seat, shaking her head at her phone.

'What's up?' Leo asks, as he turns the corner and drives towards St Jude.

'I just got a text from Camilla, listen to this,' she says: *'Meredith, Mark Roth has just resigned. We need to recruit into Psych. I want you to lead the selection committee. When are you coming back?'*

Leo lets out a loud guffaw. 'No kidding,' he says, shaking his head too. 'With Stuart gone, Mark's lost his protection – of course he's going to scurry away. It takes a sociopath or two in senior management to keep a bully in the ranks. Once you get rid of the person at the top, they all run for cover.' He smiles at her and winks. 'I know something about these things, Red. I'm police.'

Meredith looks at him wryly. 'I was thinking about that this morning. Stuart definitely protected Mark, but he got something in return. Mark drew antipathy towards himself, which gave Stuart the air cover he needed,' she says, scrolling through her emails. 'The announcement of Mark's resignation says he's going to St Therese,' she says quietly. Then she looks intently at Leo. 'Maybe now's the time to share my little box of memories of Dr Roth?'

Leo nods slowly and reaches for her hand. 'No time like the present.'

When they get closer to St Jude, they can see the front entrance is swarming.

As soon as Meredith's out of the vehicle, the crowd surges. When she sees the pack of reporters rush towards her, she stands her ground, keeping her back against the steel door of the police van. Leo rushes around from the driver's side to stop them, to no avail.

A man thrusts a microphone in her face. He's standing so close, she can see his nose hairs. Straining to get away, she looks around for an escape route, but by then the microphones are everywhere. Faces crowd her on either side, yelling questions. The voices blend into white noise, the words seeming foreign, like the crowd is speaking in tongues.

Meredith can't formulate a sentence. All she can feel is the hole where her privacy has been ripped away from her. But in her refusal to speak, she finds resolve, and her fear swiftly turns to repulsion. How close they've all come, in their clumsy stampede, their greedy imposition of brutal intimacy. A dark part of her flares up. In the place of words, she wants to snarl. She's just about to fling a curse at a woman who's trodden on her foot, when the whole crowd peels away in the opposite direction, like a school of fish.

Meredith sees Stuart Chester being led out of St Jude by the police and she watches the press encircle him.

Nearby, a TV reporter is talking into a camera. 'New Westdale police have today charged a man with being an accomplice in the murder of four women and the attempted murder of a fifth. The man has been identified as Stuart Chester, former head of the Psychiatry department of St Jude Hospital …'

The gaggle of reporters follow Stuart, as he is led to Leo's police van. As the police move him forward and bat away the reporters, he is pushed against Meredith.

He looks at her with probing eyes, and then leans over, his voice no more than a quiet hiss. 'I sensed how much you wanted to save your sister. I was curious about how you'd fare if you failed her.'

His words pierce Meredith but her face doesn't register it and she stays stone still. She was right all along. Stuart was obsessed with his research. He was studying and manipulating Daniel. But he was also studying and manipulating her.

'I didn't fail her,' she says.

He remains silent and just cocks his head, his dark eyes fixed on hers. A vein under the skin of his cheek swells, then relaxes.

The scrape of metal on metal slices the air as the police throw open the van's sliding door. She keeps looking at him and nods in its direction, letting the words she's just spoken take seed inside her. She'll keep them there and let them flourish. They'll remind her that, this time, she didn't fail Bella. This time, she saved her.

The police press his head down and push him into the back of the van. One uniformed officer follows him into the cage and the other walks around to the driver's seat. The door scrapes closed and the deep rumble of an engine fills the air.

When the van disappears around the far corner, she feels Leo's hand on her shoulder. It's warm and reassuring but she just stands still, her feet solid, her body one with the ground.

Looking up, she smells a hint of rain in the air. But for now, the sky holds a fragile hope. And a cool sea breeze from the west.

Acknowledgements

There were many people who helped write this book. My thanks go to all of them and in particular to:

Sue Melnychuk, for being my original collaborator. Thank you, Sue, for the initial kernel of the idea, priceless help with plotting and a river of insight into psychiatry, nursing and hospital practices. This book would not be what it is, and I would not be who I am, if it weren't for you.

Jane Novak for being a true believer, from the very start. You are simply the best.

The entire team at Pantera Press, including Katherine Hassett, Lex Hirst, Alison Green, Katy McEwen, Léa Antigny, Kajal Narayan, Taliesyn Gottlieb, Lucy Bell and Kirsty van der Veer for their commitment, belief and support, and freelancers Sarina Rowell and Rochelle Fernandez.

The Faber Academy's Writing a Novel course, which helped me lay the pipes for *The Scarlet Cross*.

The members of the 2019 jury of the Crime Writers of Canada's Awards of Excellence and Toronto's Dundurn Press for their sponsorship of the Unpublished Manuscript Award.

Richard Smart for his unwavering support and insights into the publishing world.

Kathryn Heyman for her inspiration, humour and gentle insistence to write every day.

My little community of fellow writers – Lisa Emanuel, Diane Jenkins and Sean Baron Levi – for supportive conversation and insights during the writing journey.

The professionals at the New South Wales and Victoria police, for their patient willingness to answer questions about policing practices from a budding writer.

The writings of Esmé Weijun Wang and Elyn Saks, whose moving first-person accounts of the experience of schizophrenia informed this book.

St. Vincent, PJ Harvey, Taylor Swift, Dirty Three, Elbow and Nick Cave, for their musical company over the years of writing and editing this book.

The writings of Gabor Maté, the Canadian doctor and social activist, whose expertise on addiction, and commitment to the vulnerable populations of Vancouver's downtown east side, deepened my understanding of addiction and mental health.

The nurses in our Australian and Canadian communities, who are my quiet heroes.

Sarah Wells for her invaluable insight into nursing practices, but more importantly for her friendship and intelligence, which I am blessed to have in my life.

Sandra Melnychuk for her honest, heart-felt feedback at various points in the journey and her rock solid support at critical points in my life. I'm so lucky to have you by my side.

Laurie Lawson for being a constant source of ideas, perspectives and inspiration. Sisters are a big theme in this book and I am lucky to count you as one of mine.

Barb Fraser, Louise Hird and numerous other Canadian and Australian medical professionals who provided medical and therapeutic insights.

My parents for everything they have given me and for showing me a mental and physical toughness that I aspire to every day.

The members of the Gough, Samoil and Melnychuk clans who have provided such a supportive community for my writing endeavours.

Richard Gough for his love, intelligence, grit and belief. Without him this book, and so much else, would not exist.

About the author

Lyn McFarlane is a Canadian-Australian author who splits her time between Sydney and Vancouver Island. She's a former freelance journalist and holds degrees in commerce, journalism and law.

Lyn is a member of the Australian Society of Authors and the Crime Writers of Canada, a graduate of The Faber Academy and a mentee with the Australian Writers' Mentorship Program. *The Scarlet Cross* is her debut novel and won the 2019 Crime Writers of Canada Award of Excellence for best unpublished manuscript.

'Lisa Emanuel writes of family, of love, of anger and desire with lyricism and authority.'
- KATHRYN HEYMAN

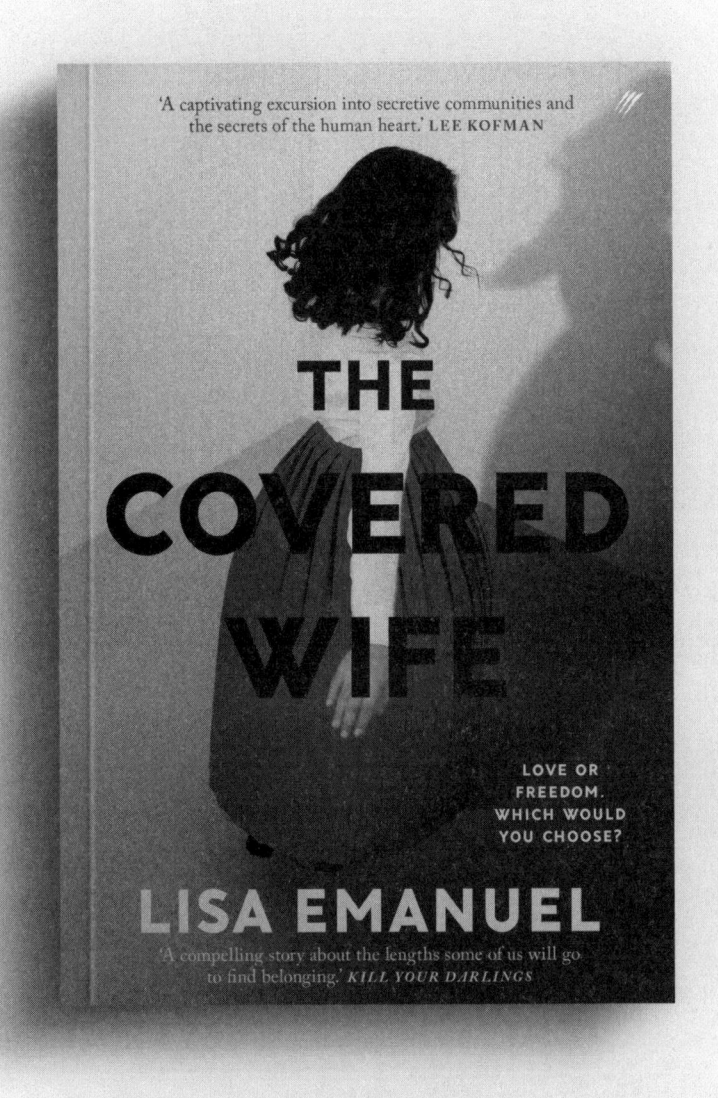

THE COVERED WIFE

'A captivating excursion into secretive communities and the secrets of the human heart.' LEE KOFMAN

LOVE OR FREEDOM. WHICH WOULD YOU CHOOSE?

LISA EMANUEL

'A compelling story about the lengths some of us will go to find belonging.' KILL YOUR DARLINGS

PANTERA PRESS | SPARKING IMAGINATION, CONVERSATION & CHANGE

True villains are the ones we never see

THE DEVIL INSIDE

D.L. HICKS

'laser sharp'
—JACK HEATH, *HANGMAN*

'darkly compelling'
CHRISTIAN WHITE, *THE NOWHERE CHILD*

true villains are the ones we never see

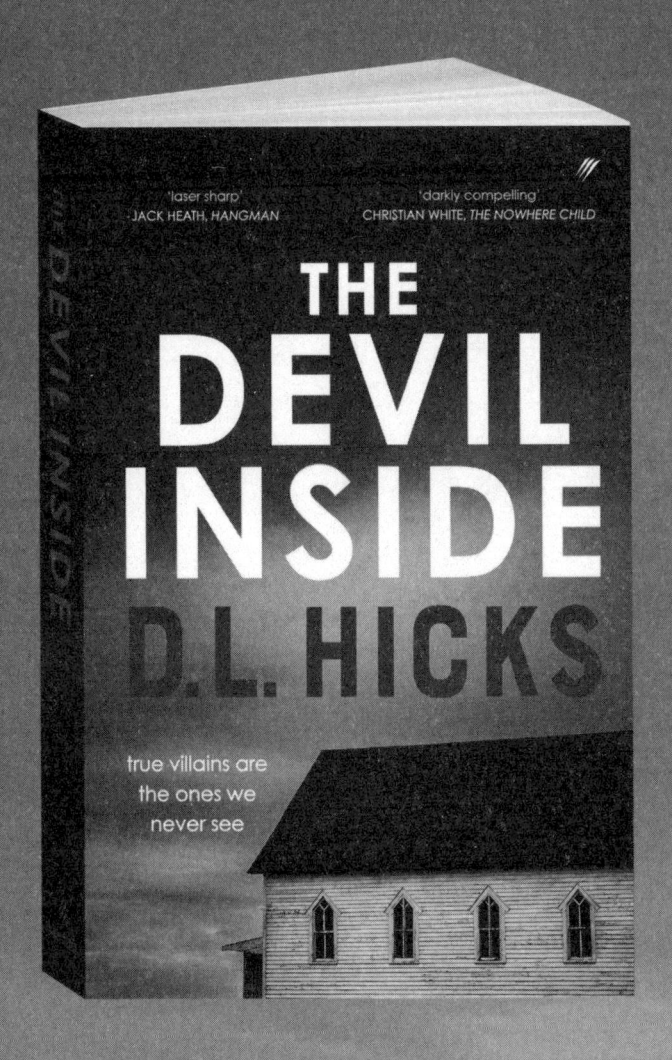

PANTERA PRESS

SPARKING IMAGINATION, CONVERSATION & CHANGE